SINS OF CHAOS

A Novel of the Breedline Series

by SHANA CONGROVE

Original artwork by: Silvia Mauloabook/Mauloabook.com

Published by: Shana Congrove

To order signed copies of this book, contact:

shanacongrove@yahoo.com

Novels of the Breedline Series by Shana Congrove

Sweet Chaos

Total Chaos

Unleashed Chaos

Sins of Chaos

The Immortal

The Curse... *coming soon!*

Available wherever books are sold online

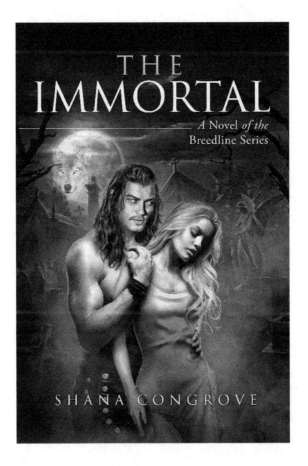

Author's Acknowledgments

In memory of my Sissy girl. Saying goodbye is hard to do. You weren't just a fur baby, but a best friend, a comforting companion, and my partner in crime. I will miss you, my Sweet Babboo.

With love, Mommy, XOXO

Dedicated to all my talented friends on FanStory.com. Without your helpful advice and continuing support, none of this would exist. Good friends are hard to find. Thank you for being mine.

As always, immense gratitude to God's loving grace. Thank you for giving me guidance and courage with everything I do.

To all the readers, family, and friends: Thank you for stepping into my fantasy world of the Breedline. I appreciate your support!

A special thanks to Jason Momoa for inspiring my new character Apollyon. It was a pleasure meeting you! I hope you enjoy your book. Thanks for signing my author's copy!

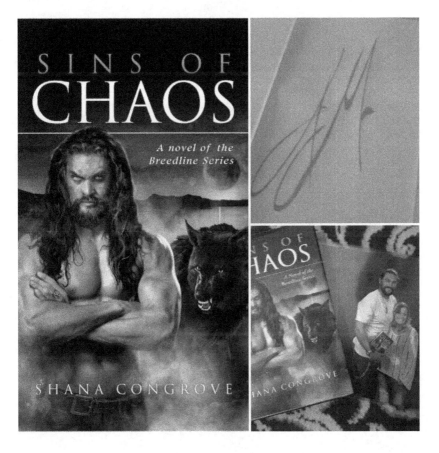

6

The Legend of the Breedline

Imagine all the myths, legends, and folktales that both captivated and terrified you as a child—*the monsters under your bed, the boogeyman in the closet, werewolves, vampires, witches, demons, ghosts, and so on*—really existed.

The story I'm about to tell you goes beyond unbelievable.

This is the legend of the Breedline.

The story goes that a secret species of humans born with an identical twin had the power to shift into wolves. Some say it is an old tall tale, ancient lore derived from Native American legends, known mainly as stories of shapeshifting creatures.

For the Navajo and other tribes of the Southwest, each has their own version of supernatural creatures called skinwalkers, but each boils down to the same thing: a majestic being capable of transforming itself into a wolf, coyote, bear, bird, or any other animal. When the transformation is complete, the human inherits the speed, strength, and cunning of the animal whose shape it has taken.

So the question remains...

Do supernatural beings really exist among our mundane, humdrum existence? The thing about myths, legends, and folktales is sometimes they're true.

How do I know, you ask? Because I'm their queen, and this is our story.

Prologue

A prison laboratory in Munich, Germany, ten years ago

Steven woke with Abbey next to him, her head resting against his chest. Even her legs entwined with his as if she were anchoring herself to the only solid thing in her life. Her body molded to his like a glove. A perfect fit.

He was tempted to roll over, slide between her legs and make love to her. Instead, he watched her sleep peacefully. It felt good just being able to hold Abbey.

While snuggled against her, he listened to the sounds of her soft breathing as it lightly brushed over his skin. As the strands of her long auburn hair closest to his mouth fluttered with his breath, he gently smoothed them away. Then the past suddenly assailed him. He would never forget the day Dr. Hans Autenburg—a ruthless German scientist backed by an underground group of military officials and wealthy prospects—locked him and Abbey together in a cell. They were just five years old. She was like a feral animal trapped in a cage.

The unethical scientist had a mission when he found out Abbey had inherited her mother's genetics. He wanted to create a new breed, combining Steven's and Abbey's DNA.

Born in Dr. Autenburg's lab, Steven had no knowledge of his birth parents and no official identification. After discovering his true identity, born half Breedline and half Adalwolf—a human-wolf-like creature with healing abilities—Steven had endured years of painful experiments.

The day Dr. Autenburg's men forced Abbey's parents, Jonah and Mary Winthrop, into captivity, they kept them caged in the same compound for research.

At first, Jonah and Mary refused to reveal any information about their species. But when Dr. Autenburg found out Mary was pregnant, they surrendered the truth after he systematically tormented them with threats against their unborn child. With similar abilities as Steven, Jonah inherited the genetics of an Adalwolf. Mary, on the other hand, was something entirely different. Her ancestors had descended from the old legend of the lycanthrope, although the moon had no power over them, and it couldn't be passed on to others like a virus. Only the female offspring, also known as a Lupa—*a she-wolf*—inherited the genetics. Mary could shapeshift into a therianthropic, hybrid wolf-like creature. Her species was dangerous... *cursed.* It was the reason why Jonah and Mary had secluded themselves deep in the rainforest, far away from humans, until *now.*

In 1975, the group of scientists funded a project interested in psychic and telepathic powers. They wanted a way into the heads of foreign governments to gain their top-secret weapons. It all changed when they discovered the Breedline species. It marked a complete turn for other possibilities. The scientists tested them extensively until some of their experiments transformed into a monstrosity. They created a new breed of hybrid Breedlines, far more dangerous and capable of surviving silver. After their transformation, they remained hybrids, no longer possessing the ability to shift back to their human forms.

Five years later, Dr. Autenburg inducted Dr. Hubert Crane into his team of colleagues. With an odd resemblance and similar trademarks of the evil leader of the German Nazi Party, Dr. Crane searched out individuals with unique abilities. Forcing them into captivity, he studied every case of unexplainable gifts. Some proved to be useless, although there were others who clearly displayed resourceful talents and rare genetics.

Focusing back on reality, Steven wrapped his arm around Abbey and pulled her close. As her eyelids fluttered and opened, she lifted her head, and sleepy blue eyes gazed into his emerald-green ones.

Steven's face softened as the memories of the past slipped from his mind. "Good morning," he murmured, brushing his lips against her forehead.

"Good morning," Abbey muttered around a yawn.

As he looked into her eyes, everything else seemed a world away, and they seemed removed from reality. Even though the bitter truth was waiting outside their cell, it was nice, just for a while, to get a sense that the only thing that mattered was right here in his arms.

Abbey, short for Mary Abigail, had been Steven's reason to live. It was his life mission to do everything in his control to keep her safe. Even if it took the power to move heaven and hell, Steven had promised her father—the only family member she had left since her mother died in childbirth—he'd find a way to escape and get Abbey far away from an eternity of torment and endless painful experiments.

He shook the thought off just as she whispered in a sleepy voice, "I've never had a better dream."

At that, glee entered his eyes. Steven smiled and lifted his brows. "Was it about me?"

She nodded and let out a sigh. "I've had so many nightmares." Her voice trembled, causing Steven's brows to tighten. "It's the first time..." She paused as tears clouded her vision. "...I've dreamed *good*. You make me feel safe, Steven."

He closed his eyes and held her more firmly against his body. He inhaled deeply, wanting to savor this one moment in time. Even though she felt safe with him, he was overwhelmed with helplessness. So much regret surged through his body, wondering how he was going to keep her out of harm's way. For once, her sleep wasn't consumed by torture and death. Then revenge gripped Steven by the throat. The pain in her voice made him want to kill Dr. Autenburg and every person who put their hands on her. He hadn't seen anyone in several days, except the guards who brought their meals.

Steven opened his eyes, and his scrambled mind could only come up with one promise. "No matter what happens..." He let out a deep breath. "...I'll always be with you. I love you, Abbey."

She wiped her eyes. "I love you too, Steven."

Her soft voice settled over him, soothing some of the tension. As she moved closer to him, the blanket fell away, exposing her bare breasts. As she hovered above him, a spark of desire resonated from his eyes, but they also flashed with uncertainty. It was gone almost before she registered it happening, but his eyes never lied. They were the doors to his soul.

"Kiss me," she whispered.

At the same time he reached for her, she leaned forward and pressed her lips to his, just once. Heat licked from the brief contact, warming him to the bone. When she stared back at him with contentment, there was a hint of something else. Was it fear?

He smoothed his thumb over her cheek to reassure her.

Abbey felt a wall crumble inside her, falling away like the blanket covering her naked body. She fell back against the pillows as he positioned himself above her, resting his weight atop her soft curves. Their skin brushed together in a tantalizing caress. Her fingers stroked the masculine contours of Steven's back and trailed further to his firm hips.

They made love, gasping and panting as their intertwined bodies came together again and again. He was hers, and she was his, she thought as they ascended the heights of passion. Right now, she didn't want to consider their fate, or all the pain they'd suffered and would suffer again. She only thought of this blissful moment, lying in the arms of her beloved.

An hour later, after their lovemaking and drifting into a deep slumber, Abbey suddenly came awake in a panic. Lifting her head, she looked at the clock by the bed. Next, she reached out to Steven and nudged his arm. "Steven, wake up. It's almost noon."

Before he got a word out, the lock on the door clicked. A chill slithered up his spine, realizing they'd let the morning slip by. He quickly reached for the blanket and drew it over her.

His eyes widened in quick alarm as the door swung open. As armed men barged into the room, he sprang to his feet and stood beside the bed, shielding her.

When one of the guards aimed a tranquilizer gun and shot Steven, pain suddenly seared into his shoulder, leaving him dazed. His arm went numb as he tried to get to Abbey, the drug already taking effect. As he fell forward, he heard Abbey scream, and then everything around him blurred.

He had failed Abbey's father. He'd failed himself, but most of all, he'd failed the one thing that mattered to him. As the room around him began to fade, a single tear slipped from the corner of his eye. "I'm sorry," he gasped, his voice barely audible. "I'm so sorry, Abbey."

Hours later, Abbey awoke from heavy sedation and looked wildly around her, trying to perceive her surroundings. But what she found brought back all the memories of the endless lab tests she'd suffered as a child. Treating her as less than human, Dr. Autenburg's men had shackled her wrists and ankles like a dangerous animal, bound to the wall by thick chains. Even though someone had clothed her, Abbey's state of mind was physically exposed and vulnerable.

Her breathing came out erratically as she glanced around the enclosed, dark space she found herself trapped in. Gritting her teeth, she pulled and tugged against the tight restraints until they cut into her skin.

A noise filtered through the walls, coming from the next room, and she froze. It was the disturbing sound of a blunt object hitting flesh. Sudden terror tore through her body at the sound of a high-pitched shriek, the sound of someone in unspeakable agony. As the screams persisted, she recognized the voice.

She scooted against the wall, lifted her head toward the ceiling, and closed her eyes, squeezing them tight. "Oh, God, no," she gasped. "*Father...*"

She tucked her knees against her chest and rocked herself back and forth, weeping, not just from fear, but from the horror her father was enduring. Both Dr. Autenburg and Dr. Crane had tried to break her until she no longer cared whether she lived or died. When their tireless efforts to force Abbey to shift into her Lupa failed, they became frustrated. Her ability to withstand pain was proving difficult. It was hard to hurt someone who just didn't care. But what she did care for were her father and Steven.

When the door opened, the flash of light blinded Abbey. With her eyes squinted, she could barely make out the images that entered the room.

"You have proved *ein* disappointment," Dr. Autenburg said in a thick German accent. "Now your father vill pay zee price for your continuous defiance, Fräulein Abigail."

She scrambled to her feet as they shoved her father to the floor. "Father!" she cried out.

The door slammed shut behind him, plunging the cell into temporary darkness once more.

She dropped to her knees and tried to wrap her arms around him, but the short chains that bound her wrists and ankles wouldn't reach far enough.

"Oh, my God." Her voice trembled. "Daddy, are you okay?"

His breaths came in low, pain-filled rasps as he reached out to her. "I'm okay, sweetheart," Jonah said in a whispered voice.

"I'm so sorry," she pleaded with her sobs. "It's my fault. They're punishing you because of me."

She could feel his battle as he struggled to move. Then slowly he maneuvered himself closer and grasped hold of her hand. "No, Abbey. Don't blame yourself for this. You didn't do anything."

She never felt so helpless in her life. She didn't know what to do—she wanted to offer him comfort if nothing else. Lightly squeezing his hand, she whispered, "What did they do?"

"Ah, honey, don't worry about me. I'll be okay," Jonah gritted out. "Nothing's broken. Besides, you know I will heal in no time."

She knew her father was an Adalwolf, but she couldn't stand the thought of him suffering because she refused to turn. Rage built in her veins until her blood simmered and boiled. She could feel the she-wolf from inside itching to be released. She hated Dr. Autenburg and all his bastard colleagues as much as she imagined ever hating anyone, but here and now, her anger was dangerous.

"Those bastards," she spat, her voice ending in a growl. "I'll make them pay for what they did to you."

Jonah squeezed her hand to offer her comfort and tensed in pain. "Please, sweetheart. You must stay calm. Don't let your anger get out of control."

She could feel his gaze burning into her even though the darkness prevented her from seeing much more than the outline of her father's face. Slipping his hand from hers, he reached up and caressed her cheek. She knew what he was telling her. He'd always warned her as she grew up. *Don't let the anger take control, Abbey, even if it came to the worst. Never reveal your Lupa to them.*

"You're a survivor, Abbey. Don't worry about me. What they've done to me is nothing I can't heal from, honey. Have faith that I can endure, and don't react to anything they do to me."

Tears slipped down her cheeks. It was telling that even now, when her father appeared so beaten, that his strength held them both up. If he could suffer so much, then so could she.

"What do we do, now?" she asked, infusing strength into her voice.

"They'll probably leave us here with no food or water. Try to wear us down. If that doesn't work, they'll take another shot at me."

Despite her restraint not to become angry, she couldn't control the shiver that racked her body.

"Maybe if I turn... I can, somehow, get away."

"No, Abbey," he demanded. "You do nothing, and I mean *nothing*. You do whatever it is you have to do to keep from turning. Trust me, honey. I've tried using my Adalwolf against them. They will only sedate you. I'll get us out of this Abbey, I swear."

The door suddenly burst open, bringing with it a blinding flood of light. Jonah lifted himself upright on his knees, and Abbey didn't know how he'd managed after what had been done to him only moments ago. She knew it had been excruciating, as he got to his feet, his hands fisted at his sides.

A stream of German erupted from the doorway, and two men came into the room and took Jonah by the arms.

Stay calm, she silently said told herself. *Don't lose control.* She wouldn't give in to the anger. Her father wanted her to stay strong, like him. She wouldn't fail him, especially when he was sacrificing so much for her.

Moments later, her mental focus snapped to full attention as she fell back against the wall to steady herself when a distant explosion rocked the compound. And then the door flew open, but this time she heard a familiar voice call out to her.

"Abbey."

"Steven?"

"Yes, baby. It's me," he said, rushing toward her.

She opened her arms and swallowed back a sob. The shackles attached to her wrists rattled as he gathered her close. "Abbey," he said reassuringly. "It's okay now."

Her knees buckled as realization set in. Steven tightened his arms around her before she fell. She anchored herself to him, holding on for dear life.

He pulled back and ran his hand over her face, wiping the tears away. "Abbey, we need to get out of here *now*."

Her brow wrinkled in question. "What happened?"

"I'm not sure." He shook his head. "I barely made it out of my cell. The walls completely collapsed. We've got to go before the whole compound crumbles."

She lifted her bound hands and extended them. "How are we going to get these off?"

When he reached for the chains attached to her ankles and wrists, she shuddered as she looked into his eyes. Steven's green irises shifted into a shimmering white glow. They reminded her of two brilliant, sparkling diamonds.

She watched as his body transformed into the most beautiful creature. Steven's skin took on a luminous sheen, expanding until his frame grew twice the size. Powerful muscles bulged atop his bare chest, and claws jutted from his hands and feet.

Without any effort, he snapped the chains like twigs, freeing her ankles and wrists. "Abbey, let's go," he said, his voice sounding deeper and distorted.

As he reached for her hand, another blast hit the compound, shaking the walls. Steven quickly grasped hold of Abbey to steady her.

With his hand gripping hers, he tugged her forward. "Come on. Let's get out of here."

When they got to the center of the facility, she stopped when she heard screams in the near distance. "Wait. What about my father? We need to find him."

"We don't have time, Abbey," he said, pulling at her arm. "If we wait any longer, we'll get trapped inside."

Her expression became desperate. "But we can't just leave him behind. What about the other prisoners held captive?" she pleaded with him. "We can't let them all die."

Steven shook his head. "I promised your father I would get you to safety."

When she opened her mouth to disagree, windows exploded everywhere, sending slivers slicing her small frame. Then she hit the floor as he threw her down and covered her with his body. A portion of the ceiling came crashing down, nearly hitting them, and electric lights shattered in an explosion of glass and sparks. Only the glow of a few fluorescent tubes lit their surroundings, casting flickering shadows over them.

"Cover your ears!" he yelled.

Abbey barely had time to cover her ears before a tremendous impact shook the compound, as though a bomb had gone off. The palms of her hands did little to stop the concussion from the blast.

Before she could collect herself, Steven was dragging her to a small opening in the wall a short distance away.

Panic flooded her as she grasped at the fate of her father. "No!" she screamed, a growl forming at the back of her throat. And then unbridled fury took control, awakening the she-wolf inside her.

As she embraced the change, bristling dark fur erupted from her skin, and her teeth tugged painfully at the roots. She no longer looked human as she rose to her feet. Her eyes were pools of molten blackness. When her petite frame swelled to massive proportions, shredding her constricting clothes, Steven shouted, "Please, Abbey! No!"

Although it was too late. Her transformation was almost complete. A canine snout protruded from her face, and sharp teeth filled her gaping jaws as she threw her head back and howled, echoing across the facility and beyond.

With a driving force to rescue her father, Abbey dropped onto all fours and bolted toward a long passageway in the building, putting as much distance as possible between them.

Out of the corner of his eye, Steven caught sight of dust and debris raining down from above. *Shit!* He ducked into a narrow hallway as the ceiling came crashing down into the center of the compound with a thunderous roar. Chunks of concrete slammed into the floor like meteors. Steven threw a hand up against the wall to steady himself. When tremors shook the floor, he began to fear that she would be buried alive.

Is this an earthquake? he wondered, momentarily pausing in his attempts to break free and search for Abbey. It was more like an explosion taking place somewhere within the facility. He had no doubt someone or something was attacking.

More rubble fell from the ceiling as the battered structure settled in the wake of the eruption. Steven's glowing eyes tracked the falling debris, and at last, the deafening roar of the desolation died down enough that he could hear himself think. Did Abbey survive?

He glared up through a massive opening in the ceiling when the sound of a helicopter hovered in close. Then, without warning, it opened fire on him with its heavy artillery, and Steven took a hit mere inches from his heart. He immediately grabbed his chest, covering his bloody wound, and roared furiously. He quickly ducked for cover as more bullets blasted from above.

When the firing ceased, an eerie silence descended over the compound. As he peered up through the dusty debris, the chopper had mysteriously disappeared. Suddenly, he spotted the only exit that hadn't been completely buried beneath all the destruction and rubble.

He wandered out of the opening into all the devastation, and stared blankly ahead. He couldn't comprehend what he was looking at. It was a young woman... *kind of*. She was more of a luminous, ghostly figure standing before him. She was beautiful—beautiful in the ethereal way of angels, with an unearthly glow emanating from her. Was she an angel? The white orbs of her eyes glowed, and her feet hovered above the ground as if she were floating in midair.

He frowned. "Who... are you?"

"My name is *Lilith*," she said, her voice casting an echo. "Are you a prisoner here?"

His eyes scanned the translucent apparition, but he wasn't sure what to say. He stared at her in silence and nodded.

"You're injured." Lilith brought her glowing hand forward. "I can heal you."

Steven flinched in response and put his hand up, rejecting her touch. "I'm an Adalwolf. I can heal myself."

As she lowered her hand, she seemed surprised at his declaration.

With dread, he looked to the long passageway of the facility, to the place he'd last seen Abbey. In the relative silence, the destruction of their surroundings sank into him, the hollow sound of the wind blowing amplifying the emptiness.

Oh, God. Did Abbey make it out alive?

As he struggled under the weight of his thoughts, his instinct was to search every inch of the compound until he found her. Instead, he turned toward Lilith and spoke through what was clearly a tight throat. "Can you help me find my beloved?"

"I'm sorry." There was a stretch of silence. "They took her and all the others that survived."

Steven glanced nervously over his shoulder at all the destruction. As he refocused his gaze toward Lilith, he raised a speculative eyebrow. "Did you do this?"

"Yes," she quickly replied. "You need to leave now. I'm going to turn what's left of this place to ash."

Before Steven turned to leave, he said, "Wait. Do you have any idea where they took them?"

"The place where it all started," Lilith said as she looked back at Steven, "to an underground research facility in Berkeley, California."

He nodded. "Thank you."

Lilith's chest ached at the pain in his voice. She hated sending him out to search for his loved one alone, but she had a personal mission, and this was something she had to do on her own.

Funny, though, as Steven walked away from the wreckage, he had the oddest sense that he was going to see Lilith again.

Chapter One

Even after time had passed, his mother's death still haunted Steven. Giving her life over to save Sebastian's had taken away a part of Steven's soul. Unable to heal her fatal wound, he felt cheated. From the moment he was born, his life had become derailed. The story of his life was "*what might have been.*" No relationship with a family, just a life caged in a cell, enduring endless torture, the happy memories expected of a normal childhood switched out at birth for years of lab tests. He'd felt like years of his life had been taken away.

All this time, the woman Steven had crossed paths with years ago—who called herself *Lilith*—was his mother. Indeed, their indifferent paths did not change how he felt. It layered his emotions with a cloak of bittersweet longing to have a family. But sometimes your destiny led you down a winding road of endless pain.

The loss of his mother was a horrible reminder of the disappearance of his beloved Abbey. Steven hadn't seen her in ten years, though he maintained that he could sense she was still alive. Maybe in some future era Abbey would come back to him. He'd rely on hope, no matter how long it took, because love in its many forms always endured.

Steven had ambition for a future after he'd found his twin sister, Tessa, and his father, Kenneth, especially since Sebastian had lost his mind and was institutionalized. Living the remainder of his life in a white, padded cell was enough gratification for all the evil Sebastian had done in this world. Death would be too easy.

After Steven's father revealed he'd inherited the genetics of his Adalwolf from his grandfather, his fraternal twin sister's special gift still remained a mystery. There had been no documented knowledge of any Breedline born without an identical twin that could shift into their wolf, although his sister Tessa possessed the rare ability.

* * *

Now that peace had finally settled into the Breedline Covenant, Jace and Tessa were married barefoot just before sunset as a golden glow from the west settled on the beach and the cliffs behind it. The soothing sounds of the waves rolling onto the beach and fading away created a peaceful ambiance for the occasion.

It was a simple, romantic ceremony. Tessa was breathtaking, her age frozen in time. After Dr. Helen Carrington had approved the cure she'd discovered—which stopped the natural aging process for the Breedline—Tessa was eager to take it. Already ten years older than Jace, and the fact that he would stop aging when he reached thirty, she wanted to stay young and youthful along with her beloved.

Tessa's hair was elegantly pulled up into a bun with a single lavender rose tucked in. The soft, cream, strapless gown she wore accentuated her slim, petite figure and flowed slightly above her knees.

Jace wore beige slacks and a white linen long-sleeve dress shirt rolled up just below his elbows. His blond hair was pulled back, the long strands stirring in the light breeze.

As the happy couple stood facing one another, fingers entwined, their family and close friends assembled in a half circle, anxiously waiting to witness two bonded mates promising each other a lifetime of love and devotion. Jem was standing next to Jace, representing as his best man, and Mia was alongside Tessa as her bridesmaid.

With only the soft sounds of the ocean breeze, Reverend Mike's voice broke the silence. "Family and friends, we are gathered here in this beautiful place, in the presence of God, to celebrate the very special love between Tessa and Jace. They have each prepared their vows to share with one another."

At that moment, after the Reverend said his part, Jace dropped to one knee and looked up into Tessa's emerald-green eyes. "My beloved, you have already given me the three greatest gifts of my life: your love and our two precious sons. Today I pledge to you what has already been yours all this time—my eternal love. As we have always done, I promise to walk hand in hand with you through life's journeys. No matter what lies in our path, it will be our path, together. In the joys and troubles that lie ahead of us, I will be faithful and loving to you. I vow to love and cherish you for all the days of my life."

When Jace got to his feet, he gently slid the beautiful ruby ring that belonged to his great-grandmother onto Tessa's finger. As tears fell from the corners of her eyes, he wiped them away and whispered, "I love you, Tessa."

She smiled as more tears slipped freely down her cheeks. "Jace, I love you. You are my best friend and the love of my life. Today I give myself to you in marriage. I promise to encourage and inspire you, to laugh with you, and to comfort you in times of sorrow and struggle. I promise to cherish you and always to hold you close to my heart. These things I give to you today, and all the days of our life."

After Tessa had placed a white-gold band on Jace's finger, he leaned down and pressed his lips to hers. In their passionate embrace, Reverend Mike spoke out, "I present to you... Mr. and Mrs. Chamberlain."

All at once, the sound of clapping erupted as Jace and Tessa turned to face their guests. Jem smiled, his eyes glistening as he turned to Jace with his hand out. "Congratulations, Brother. It does me good to see you both so happy."

When Jace took his hand, he pulled him into a tight embrace. "Thanks, bro. Thanks for always having my back."

As Jem pulled away, he patted Jace on the shoulder. "I'll always have your back. I love you, Brother."

"I love you too, bro."

Mia was the first to congratulate Tessa with a hug. "You look gorgeous, Tessa. I'm so happy for you and Jace."

"Thank you, Mia."

As Tessa pulled from Mia's embrace, she looked up to see Jem with his arms held out. "How about a hug for your new brother-in-law?" he asked, smiling ear to ear.

"How could I possibly refuse?" Tessa giggled, wrapping her arms around him. "Thank you for everything, Jem."

"You're welcome, Tessa. I'm the one that should be thanking you."

Tessa lifted her chin, looking up at him with a puzzled expression. "For what?"

"For saving my brother. Just when I thought there was no hope for Jace, you came into his life and turned everything around."

She smiled. "Jace saved me too."

"Okay, Brother..." Jace came up behind Jem and placed his hand on Jem's shoulder. "No hogging the bride."

Jem stepped back. "She's all yours."

With his arm around Tessa's waist, Jace led her toward the guests. As her eyes roamed through family and friends, Tessa's attention shifted to her twin boys, who were tucked securely in loving arms. Her father, Kenneth, held little Jem, and Alexander had Jax anchored to his hip. Both boys were identical and were already starting to crawl. They had Jace's blond hair and his gorgeous blue eyes. Everyone she loved was here except for her mother. Deep down in her heart, she knew her mother was here in spirit, a beautiful angel finally set free.

"You look stunning, Tessa," Steven murmured, his eyes glowing in approval. He wrapped his arms around her. "Congratulations, sis. I'm so happy for you."

"Thank you, Steven."

Embraced with hugs by all their family and friends, the wedding party was in full swing. John and Sarah Chamberlain had arranged a large tent beautifully decorated in lavender and ivory with an opening facing the breathtaking view of the ocean. Now that peace had finally settled with the Breedline, John and Sarah moved back home but visited the Covenant frequently to see their grandbabies.

Everyone enjoyed the food, champagne, and dancing. As the end of the night drew near, Jace put his mouth close to Tessa's ear and whispered, "Let's get out of here."

She shivered as his breath tingled her skin. "Where are we going?"

He winked at her. "It's a secret."

"A secret?" She arched a brow. "You mean like a secret honeymoon?"

He shrugged. "Maybe."

"What about the boys?"

"Everything's already been arranged." Jace grasped her hand and pulled her close. "Mom and Dad are taking care of them."

"Don't we need to pack?"

"It's already taken care of," he murmured, pressing a kiss to her forehead. "Mia and Cassie prepared everything you'll need. The car is packed and ready to go."

"Well... it sounds like you've been busy," she said with a coy smile. "How long have you been planning this... *secret?*"

"Um, a few weeks." His lips curled up like a bow. "Ready?" She smiled. "Yes."

* * *

In a dark padded cell, Sebastian lay with his arms bound inside a straitjacket and his ears tensed for the slightest noise. The buzzing coming from the fluorescent lights outside the door and the rhythm of his beating heart were the only sounds to be heard. Since Sebastian lost his ability to use a portal, this was the first time in his life he felt utterly helpless. When he'd told the Breedline of hearing Thomas's voice—his dead twin brother—they thought him insane, including Eve, and committed him to a Breedline psychiatric institution... *a lunatic asylum.* It was like a punch to the gut. Even though he was guilty of many things, death would be more merciful than eternal insanity.

He hadn't heard Thomas's voice for hours. Forcing himself to think of something else, he wondered how his sons were faring and thought of what Eve had said in the note she left him. Maybe she was right. Perhaps they were better off without him.

Although the sedative he was given made him doze off a couple of times, he concentrated on staying awake. As much as he fought to keep his eyes open, he lost the battle and sleep finally overtook him.

Out of nowhere, he sensed an eerie presence looming over him. He kept his lids closed and pretended to be asleep. He shivered when the temperature in the room dropped. Steam exhaled as he parted his lips.

Something prodded his leg with sharp fingers and whispered, "Wake up, *Sebastian*."

When an unknown presence leaned over Sebastian, a rank breath crept into his nostrils. Then strong hands grabbed a fistful of his hair and wrenched his head back and said, "I know you're awake, you worthless piece of crap."

He recognized his brother's angry voice and opened his eyes. Although, it was impossible. Thomas was dead. The monster taunting his sanity was something entirely different. But who was it? And what did it want?

Sebastian felt enraged but remained calm. In his current condition, he was helpless against whatever this *thing* was. If only he could manage to free himself of the restricting constraint.

"Where are you?" he called out as his eyes darted over the poorly lit room. "Show yourself."

He flinched at the sound of a chair scuffling along the floor. When it slid into his field of vision, he came face-to-face with his twin brother. His features appeared haunted and his eyes were black... *soulless*.

Thomas reached inside his jacket and pulled out a dagger. As he reached forward with it, Sebastian clenched his eyes shut and stiffened, preparing to feel the burn of the blade. Oddly, he found exquisite relief instead. His arms were now free.

"Why did you free me?" Sebastian asked. "You're not really Thomas, are you?"

"So many questions," his look-alike said in a smug tone. "The answer to your first question... who am I?" He arrogantly grinned, his fangs shining like ivory pins. "I was once God's favorite angel, and *now*..." he paused, drawing his lips tight. "I am the darkness of night."

"Lucifer," Sebastian muttered, narrowing his stare.

"Yesss..." he answered with the S lingering. "I have been called by that name for centuries now, along with many others. The devil... *Satan*. But if you prefer Lucifer, it's your choice."

"Why?" Sebastian said, swallowing the knot in his throat. "Why are you taking Thomas's form?"

"Why not?" Lucifer asked, leaning closer. "Does this body make you feel guilty?"

Sebastian gripped the bare mattress and pulled himself upright. "Why would I feel guilty? Thomas caused his own death."

Lucifer threw his head back and laughed. The short, sharp bark sent shivers up Sebastian's spine. "You hated your brother. You wanted Thomas to die."

"No!" Sebastian fired back. "That's not true!"

Lucifer crossed his arms. "Isn't it?"

"What the hell do you want with me?" Sebastian urged. "And why can't I use my powers?"

Lucifer rose to his feet, straightened his black, tailored suit, and leaned against the padded wall of Sebastian's cell. "I want something that belongs to you, but I cannot take it freely. You must convince your beloved Eve to give it to me of her free will. Give me what I want, and I will release you from this misery. I will then restore your power to create a portal."

Sebastian went quiet for a minute. He wondered what Lucifer wanted that was so precious. Then he realized it was his son. Lucifer wanted Arius for his powers.

Another surge of rage swept over Sebastian. He stood up on shaking legs, preparing to lunge at Lucifer, but found himself strangely confined in his straitjacket again. "Stay away from my son..." Sebastian snarled his upper lip. "I swear I'll—"

"You'll what?" Lucifer smirked. "Kill me?"

Sebastian looked at Lucifer, his yellow eyes shooting daggers.

"You know..." Lucifer cocked a brow. "...we're not that different."

"I'm nothing like you!"

"Aren't we?" Lucifer said, pursing his mouth in a self-satisfied grin. "I have to say, what you did to Tessa is an all-time low. Raping your half brother's mate is a detestable sin."

"I didn't rape her!"

"Same difference," Lucifer said. "You used your succubus skills and put those images in her head, leading her to believe it." He slowly shook his head. "Only to piss off Jace. By my book, that's shady as hell."

Sebastian glared at Lucifer. "Go to hell!"

"That," Lucifer said in a tone laced with promise, "can be arranged."

Before Sebastian knew what hit him, Lucifer shot over with incredible speed, so fast he was nearly a blur, and gripped him around the throat. "Give me what I want." He bared his sharp pointed teeth. "Or suffer your fate."

Sebastian choked and thrashed against Lucifer's hold.

Eve gasped as she peered through the tiny glass window of Sebastian's cell.

"Guards!" Eve yelled. "Open this door!"

Lucifer curled back his upper lip. "You will suffer my wrath with eternal sleep, reliving the horrors of your child-hood past."

Panic seized Sebastian. "No," he gasped. "Please... no."

Sebastian braced himself as Lucifer bit into his throat.

As the door sprang open, Lucifer instantly vanished. Eve caught her breath when she saw Sebastian drop to the floor. Blood trickled down his throat as though he'd been bitten.

Eve hesitated, but only for a moment, and rushed over to Sebastian. When she knelt beside him, she gently placed her hand on the side of his face. "Sebastian, talk to me, please," she helplessly cried out. "Sebastian..." She wiped at the blood on his neck. "Can you hear me?" When there was no response, she glanced up at the guard. "Get this damn thing off him. He needs medical attention, now!"

After the guard had called for backup, he quickly removed Sebastian's straitjacket.

When Bruce Carmichael, Eve's guard who escorted her each time she visited Sebastian at the mental institution, stepped into the room, he froze in his tracks, taken aback by the bizarre spectacle before him.

Eve looked down when she heard a light moan. Sebastian had his eyes slightly cracked. He strained to keep them open.

"Oh, thank God, Sebastian," Eve sobbed.

"Eve..." he said hoarsely. "Please... listen to me."

"You're going to be fine, Sebastian," Eve said in a tear-laced voice. "You just need my blood."

He shook his head as she held her wrist close to his lips. "No, Eve."

"Sebastian, please," Eve persisted. "I can fix this. Take my blood."

"You must save Arius... from Lucifer." He started to weep while struggling to keep his focus. "I love... you." Then he closed his eyes and went limp, falling deeper into a state of unconsciousness. The fault of his son's destiny was his. To keep Arius from the hands of evil, Sebastian was willing to suffer a thousandfold. Now his fate had come, the thing he had dreaded and feared long ago. His punishment was now a reality. Sebastian would be lost in the horrors of his childhood past, reliving each day he'd fought so hard to forget.

"No," Eve cried. "Please, Sebastian. Don't leave me. I believe you. Did you hear me?" She shook his shoulders, desperate for him to open his eyes. "You're not crazy. I saw him. I believe you, Sebastian."

The succubus side in her confirmed what her brain had been denying. Sebastian wasn't crazy. Someone had attacked him. She saw it with her own eyes. Eve had no idea how she was going to do it, but she had to fight to bring Sebastian back and protect her son from... *Lucifer*.

Chapter Two

Abbey cut the engine as the small, inflatable boat neared the sandy beach of Lake Anza in Berkeley, located in the hills of Tilden Regional Park. The moon shimmered as she looked up at the dark sky, and only one or two stars poked through the cloud cover. Surrounded by darkness, she focused on her destination to move quickly to shore without getting caught.

She swallowed her fear and glanced nervously over her shoulder before she stepped out of the boat. Abbey knew she was taking a risk, but she was out of options. A group of underground scientists hired by billionaire clients—who hunted men and women gifted with supernatural rarities—were closing in on her. She could sense them in every part of her body. The mere thought of them brought back haunted memories of the past.

The ruthless scientist known as Dr. Hans Autenburg sold her father Jonah for his healing abilities to a wealthy man on a mission to cure a woman he loved, who was dying of cancer. Valkin Steele wasn't a good man. He was the type of monster that would sell anything to achieve what he wanted. Valkin was cold... evil... the very devil....

Jonah was an Adalwolf, although his gift wasn't powerful enough to heal a fatal wound or illness. He died painfully after Valkin forced him to use his abilities in hope of healing Natasha. With enough power and wealth at his disposal, Valkin had Natasha seen by the best physicians in the world. But there was nothing they could do. She couldn't be healed.

Now, running out of time, Valkin was desperate to locate an Adalwolf that possessed the ability to cure his dying beloved. When Abbey overheard Dr. Autenburg's plans to capture and sell Steven to Mr. Valkin Steele, she wanted to kill him. Desperate to warn Steven, she planned her escape and the death of Dr. Hans Autenburg. Valkin Steele would be her next target. One way or the other, she would make damn sure he didn't get away unpunished. She remembered as though it had been only days since she looked into the mad physician's cold and calculating glare.

It was early in the morning when Abbey planned her escape. She managed to slip past the female nurse that always administered a heavy dose of sedatives. They used drugs to keep her sedated to control her she-wolf. Without a single glance back, she hurried down a long hallway. She'd spent months memorizing the passageway that led her to Dr. Autenburg's laboratory. She knew every turn by heart.

Before she reached to open the door, she heard voices nearby. She recognized the German accent of at least two guards, each willing to give their life for the man who hired them. Today she was more than happy to accommodate their sacrifice.

As she quickly pushed her way through the door, Dr. Autenburg stared unflinchingly at her.

"What is zee meaning of zis?" he retorted, his voice laced with his thick German accent.

She wasn't going waste her time talking to the bastard. She had only seconds to shift into her she-wolf and end his pathetic life before she made her getaway. *Even if it takes every bit of strength I have left*, she vowed, *I'm putting an end to this nightmare.*

The physician shrank back in fear, watching helplessly as her transformation accelerated at a phenomenal rate. She tore at her clothing, stripping herself, as her petite frame swelled to massive proportions. As she shifted, a human scream devolved into an anguished howl. Standing erect on two legs, her towering she-wolf was over seven feet tall. Coarse black fur covered her naked body. Little of humanity remained in her monstrous features. Abbey's she-wolf was larger and less human-looking than any other creature Dr. Autenburg had ever encountered. Coal-black eyes peered out from beneath a sloping brow. Tufted ears tapered to a point atop her bristled, dark head. Then her fleshy black muzzle formed into a sinister, wolfish grin.

In the blink of an eye, Abbey's she-wolf tackled Dr. Autenburg, knocking him to the cold concrete floor. He landed hard, with her weight on top of him. The impact drove the breath from his lungs. Before he could scream for help, a gaping maw closed on his face, crushing it between two powerful jaws. Bone crunched, and a geyser of crimson exploded over the creature's snout and fur. Only a death rattle escaped his throat.

When the two guards rushed inside, they came to an abrupt halt, taken aback by the nightmarish spectacle before them. They found Abbey's she-wolf hunched over Dr. Autenburg's mangled body. Gore dripped from her mammoth jaws as she ripped out the physician's heart with her teeth.

The she-wolf sniffed the air, catching the guards' scent. Abandoning her prey, she reared back on her haunches and unleashed an unearthly roar.

A guard opened fire on her, followed by the other gunman. She staggered back in surprise. The impact of the bullets caused her to gyrate upon her heels. As pools of blood spouted from the bullet holes, a righteous fury rose up inside her like a gathering storm. Fueled by anger, her heart pumped the bloodline of her Lupa ancestors through her body, infusing her with strength and purpose. With an unexpected burst of power, she moved with supernatural speed and struck the guards like a battering ram, knocking them to the ground. The she-wolf's hot breath blasted their faces, and her bloodthirsty roar thundered in their ears. As she bared her razor-sharp teeth and opened her jaws wide, saliva foamed from her gaping mouth in anticipation of their human flesh. Within seconds, their existence ended as the she-wolf tore them into pieces.

Abbey fled the compound, never once looking back. There was nothing for her there but memories of endless pain. Although she wasn't the only one that managed to break free. Something far more dangerous had escaped the confinements of the facility. A trio of unearthly creatures, created by the ruthless physician, broke free from their own confinement.

As she put miles between her and Dr. Autenburg's compound, she finally let herself relax, shifting back to her human form. Had she dared to hope for the impossible? After all these years, she yearned to reunite with her beloved, Steven.

Unbeknown to her, years ago, Dr. Autenburg had played God, creating what he called, the Fury. He used his own DNA and mixed it with three other species: a Breedline, an Adalwolf, and a powerful Wiccan. He'd placed three embryos inside the womb of a full-blooded succubus named Sonya Hothburn. She'd been taken against her will and forced by the mad physician into surrogacy. Dr. Autenburg forbade Sonya to see her own children after they were born and continued to keep her prisoner.

Even though children had never been his goal, Dr. Autenburg felt transformed after the birth of his son and two daughters. He named his firstborn Apollyon. It was also the name of the angel-prince of the infernal regions, the minister of death and author of havoc on earth.

When Autenburg laid eyes on his daughter, she was tiny and delicate as a porcelain doll. As he held her in his arms, the name Callisto came to mind, meaning "most beautiful." When the last child was born, her eyes glowed like two shimmering diamonds. He named her Electra, meaning "the shining one."

Dr. Autenburg created them for the sole purpose to destroy the Breedline species. The new breed would kill off their race until there was nothing left. His offspring were not like other children, hadn't been since birth, growing at a phenomenal rate. Inheriting their species' instinct and extraordinary power, their thirst to kill became uncontrollable. They were no more content to obey Autenburg's rules than a lion was satisfied confined in a small cage. As time went by, the Fury became more and more unstable and unruly. With an insatiable hunger for human flesh and unmanageable powers, they became a hindrance to the physician as they aged. Dr. Autenburg had no choice but to drug and imprison his grown children for all time, each one placed inside a sarcophagus in a state of deep slumber. To be forgotten forever. Now, Apollyon, Callisto, and Electra had been set free.

Abbey put the past behind her and snapped back to reality. For now, she refocused on her surroundings. Realizing time was of the essence, she had to find a way to locate Steven before Steele's men got to him first. As she eased the boat further onto the shore, a noise ahead alerted her. Then a loud pop blasted, the sound echoing from a short distance away. She immediately grabbed her arm as pain exploded inside her skin. Someone had shot her with a tranquilizer. She fought to keep her panic at bay as terror hit her hard.

She quickly averted her eyes from a bright light shining on her face.

"Don't move, Abbey," a slightly accented voice said.

She turned toward the voice and stared up at a man looming over her with a flashlight. She glanced around but couldn't see anyone else.

When he lowered the light, the ground became illuminated, and a sudden flash of fear nearly paralyzed her. Abbey's eyes widened when she recognized the icy expression in the face of Valkin Steele's hired bodyguard. Roman Kincaid was big and menacing. His skin was tanned like he'd spent hours in the sun. His dark hair was pulled back, and his eyes were as dark as night. Trained in military tactics, Roman was a special breed of hired warriors from Brazil and Valkin's right-hand man when it came to security.

"Where is the Adalwolf?"

Her brows wrinkled, and she tried to process her surroundings. Abbey was afraid she'd be right back in the hands of monsters, forced to endure more horrific experiments. And there was no way she was going to help them find Steven. The mere thought sent agony tearing through her body. It took everything she had to gather strength before the drugs kicked in. But it was too late. The effects of the tranquilizer blurred her vision. Abbey tumbled to the ground, landing in the soft, wet sand.

Roman cursed and immediately knelt beside her.

"Damn it, Abbey. I'm not here to hurt you."

Her lips parted, and her breath rushed out. She gasped, barely getting the words out, "I won't tell you... anything."

"Abbey, I want you to listen to me." His voice was calm and oddly soothing. "I had no other choice but to sedate you. I couldn't take the risk of you shifting into your she-wolf."

Her pulse leaped, and her throat tightened as she struggled to stay conscious. She stared up at Roman, knowing she didn't possess the strength to escape. She'd managed to maintain her freedom for years, keeping herself off the grid, desperately searching for Steven. Tears spilled from the corners of her eyes at the dreadful thought of having to go back to her old life.

"I'm also an Adalwolf," he confessed, wiping at the moisture on her cheeks.

His declaration surprised her. Was this a trap?

"Trust me, Abbey. I'm going to help you. We need to get you out of here and to a secure location. Steele's men are not far from here."

She nodded in silence, trying to focus on his face.

Roman turned away and motioned someone over.

She tensed when a big burly man came into her blurred field of vision and hovered over her. His arms and legs were as thick as tree trunks, bulging with muscles. Her pulse exploded as she tried to move, but Roman put his hand on her shoulder. "It's all right, Abbey," he said, looking up at the huge man towering above them. "This is a trusted friend of mine and a Breedline council member of the New Jersey Covenant. He's also a trained medic. His name is Lawrence Colbert."

"It's a pleasure, Ms. Abbey," Lawrence said in a deep baritone. "I'm here to help Roman get you to safety. Then I'm going to hunt the bastards down who hurt you and castrate every last one of them."

The gentleness in the voice of the giant man baffled her, and she seemed comforted by his savage vow. Abbey glanced nervously between the two men, wondering if they were real or a hallucination.

As Roman looked into her eyes, he saw the helplessness and fear resonating from them. God, he'd felt responsible. All this time employed by Valkin Steele, hired as his personal bodyguard, Roman had no idea the cold-hearted bastard was paying an underground organization to experiment on innocent people just for their supernatural rarities. He felt like a traitor to his own kind. With the help of the Breedline Covenants, he was going to expose everyone involved. The image of Valkin Steele made his gut churn. Roman had a mission. It involved Steele's head on a stake and his corpse blazing with fire.

Swallowing the knot in his throat, Roman gently smoothed a strand of her hair away from her face. "Take deep breaths,

Abbey. I promise. We'll reunite you with Steven, and we're not going to let anything happen to you."

This time Lawrence knelt by her side, his voice quiet and gentle, "All right, Ms. Abbey. I'm going to pick you up. Don't worry. You're in good hands."

She nodded her acceptance, and as soon as she did, Lawrence slid his arm underneath her legs. He hooked his other arm behind her and slowly lifted her into his massive arms.

"Ready, Abbey?" Roman said, standing next to Lawrence.

She nodded again. She had no idea why they professed to want to help her, but she decided to put herself in their hands. Besides, what other choice did she have?

Chapter Three

Eve ignored the male nurse when he came into Sebastian's room.

"Sebastian?" she said, desperate to wake him. "Sebastian..."

"Ma'am," the male nurse said, "we need to check his vitals."

At the sound of his voice, Eve snapped her head around and hissed.

Bruce Carmichael intervened. "Please, Eve," he said, his voice laced in a Scottish accent. "You've got to let him do his job."

Slowly, she got to her feet and stepped back.

When the nurse went to check Sebastian, a female wearing a white physician's coat rushed inside the room.

Bruce, who had witnessed Sebastian's mysterious incident, reached out to her and said, "It's okay. Please, let's step out and give them room."

When he ushered her through the door, she turned and watched through the opening as the female physician examined Sebastian's neck. "How did this happen?" the doctor asked the nurse. "It looks like he's been bitten."

The nurse shrugged. "After I gave him a sedative, I left him alone."

As the doctor refocused on Sebastian, his eyes blinked open and looked up at her. She flinched. *What the...* His eyes were as dark as night. With their locked stares, she was stunned into immobility as if he was looking into her very soul. She could sense another presence inside his body. It was something dark, and evil.

The physician finally said, "Call for an ambulance."

Moments later, two paramedics appeared down the hall. Eve stepped aside as they came into the constricted, padded cell at slingshot speed.

She sagged against the wall for what seemed like forever as she watched them strap Sebastian onto a gurney. Tears gathered in her eyes at the thought of her betrayal. She was

36

ashamed for not believing him when he'd told her of the visits of his dead brother.

The murmur of voices caught Eve's attention. She tensed when the paramedics quickly wheeled Sebastian out of the room and down the hall. She covered her mouth to stifle the sob that swelled in her throat.

When the paramedics and a guard disappeared into an elevator with Sebastian, she broke away and ran toward them.

"Eve," Bruce called out.

She rushed over as the elevator doors closed. Overwhelmed with grief, she sagged against the wall and sobbed into her hands.

Bruce offered her a handkerchief. "I'm sorry, Eve. I have to take you back to the Breedline Covenant."

"Okay..."

After she had wiped her eyes, she held up the small delicate material in a gesture to return his kindness. With a soft expression, he shook his head. "Please. Keep it."

She smiled a little. "Do you know what hospital they're taking him too?"

His expression immediately softened as he stared warmly down at her. He held up his hand and motioned Eve forward. "We should go," he said. Uncertainty flashed in his eyes, giving his large stature a vulnerable look. "I'm sure the Covenant will give the information to you."

Something in Bruce's tone soothed the tension that had knotted her insides. There was an odd note in his heavily accented voice. Eve noticed vulnerability creep into his gaze, giving her a glimpse of this hulking man's raw emotion shimmering back at her.

She nodded and said, "Will you tell the Covenant what you saw?"

"Aye," his reply was instantaneous.

She immediately relaxed, and some of the anxiety eased from her brows.

* * *

Later that night, after Roman and Lawrence got Abbey to a safe house, she was out for the night, heavily sedated. Roman spent the entire night tirelessly setting into motion plans for her protection. He'd hired a dedicated team of three Breedline Special Forces, who stood guard outside her room. They would have direct access to Abbey and be in charge of her transportation and safety. Lawrence had contacted the California Breedline Covenant to arrange a meeting with Tim Ross to have her transported there tomorrow morning. Roman was determined to take down Valkin Steele and all the unethical physicians he'd hired to do his evil bidding. Now, he relied on the Covenant's help to put an end to the innocent people who suffered, freeing them from a life filled with endless torture.

Before Roman had Abbey taken to the Breedline Covenant, he planned on meeting with the council head first. After discovering Steven was under the protection of the Covenant, he thought best to tell her tomorrow when his team brought her to the meeting. There was simply no need to wake her. She'd already experienced enough shock. He wanted her as stress free as possible, given the circumstances. With Abbey teetering on edge, he didn't want to push her further, in fear of her shifting.

Abbey would sleep tonight, but Roman and the others wouldn't. There was too much to sort through and decisions regarding her protection from Valkin Steele and his men.

Deep into a sedated slumber, Abbey saw her mother for the first time. On some level, she knew it had to be a dream. Her mother died when she was born.

And yet, as she came to her out of the darkness, she was alive, moving with ease, smiling at her. Mary's smile was as peaceful as an angel's.

"Mother?" Abbey said with wonder.

"Abigail."

At the sound of her mother's voice, Abbey sat upright. Mary was right beside the bed, her arms reaching out for her.

"Mother... is that really you?"

"Yes, my precious Abigail."

God, her voice was so tender, just as she'd thought it would be—and she vowed to memorize the sound. When

Abbey reached out and took hold of her mother's hand, she said, "Oh, how I've longed to see you, Mother."

Mary lightly squeezed her hand and said, "I never got to hold you." Then she pulled Abbey into a gentle embrace, and so the two of them hugged for the very first time. Abbey wanted to hold on to her mother forever and never let go.

When Mary pulled back, tears slipped down her cheeks. "I will always be right here," she said, pointing to the center of Abbey's chest... to her heart. "I love you so very, very much—"

When her mother's image finally faded, Abbey was alone again.

"I love you too," Abbey whispered.

When she awoke, two men stood by the door at the far end of the room. They looked like soldiers, all dressed in camouflage, muscled and disciplined.

No one noticed she was awake as she watched the two men quietly engaging in conversation with a female who was at least six-foot tall, broad shouldered, and oddly resembled the 1990s television fictional character Xena the Warrior Princess. When she turned to the side, her profile was surprisingly feminine looking. She had her long, dark hair pulled back in a thick braid, and she too was dressed in a black T-shirt, camo fatigues, and combat boots. She wore a shoulder holster with a pistol tucked inside. As Abbey stared at the woman, who apparently could take care of herself, Abbey felt envious. The woman looked in control of her destiny, unlike her. Abbey's human form was petite and weak. Only in her Lupa form did she feel strong and fierce.

She wasn't sure what to say, or if she should speak out at all. When she cleared her throat, it caught their attention.

The tall woman cocked a brow, studying her for a moment. "Good morning, Ms. Winthrop. Roman hired us to keep you safe. My name is Lena, and this is Justice," she said, gesturing toward a good-looking, blond-haired man on her left. His eyes were a clear shade of teal, beautiful enough that Abbey found herself staring at the fascinating color.

As Lena turned toward the other man standing to her right, she introduced him. "And this is my brother, Bull," she said with a light chuckle. "Short for bullheaded."

When Abbey's eyes locked on the man who was the size of a mountain, she had to admit he looked like a total badass. He was twice the size of Lena and was a good two inches taller than Justice, who was at least six-three. And his muscles bulged under his tight, short sleeve shirt.

Abbey watched as Bull nudged his sister's arm with his shoulder for making light of his name. Lena cast a baleful look in his direction and leaned in with her elbow, poking him in the ribs.

Bull winced and mumbled under his breath, "Damn it, Lena."

Justice rolled his eyes and smirked, almost as if he was used to Lena and Bull's sibling banter.

Lena and Justice had been lovers for three years. They'd hooked up almost immediately after she had joined the Special Ops team Justice and her brother had been a part of. They'd managed to keep their relationship a secret, hiding behind friendship until only recently.

Lena thought Justice was the total package, not that she'd ever tell him though. Just being around him gave her butterflies. The man could kiss like a dream. Hell, it made her act like a damn girl. Lena loved his strength and confidence, but he was not an arrogant asshole. A guy like Justice wouldn't have to look far to get laid. But she didn't want him getting a big head, and besides, it suited her purposes to keep him down a few notches, since she did have to work with him after all.

Bull was a hard-ass. When they were on a mission, he had a single-minded focus. It had been a hell of a shock to discover Justice and his little sister's secret. He was reluctant at first. But after a few weeks of bickering and complaining about how their relationship was going to put a wedge between their personal lives and their professional duties, he finally cooled down and accepted it for what it was. Bull liked Justice, even if he was one giant pain in his ass. On the positive side, he was good to his little sister, but it didn't stop a healthy rivalry between him and Justice when it came to sniper duty. Bull was a better sharpshooter. And he always made sure Justice was made fully aware of the fact.

The sound of an obnoxious cell phone ringtone startled Bull, and he shot Justice an irritated glare.

"Sorry," Justice muttered, reaching into his pants pocket to retrieve his phone. "Justice," he answered. "Yeah, Roman, what's up?"

After a few moments of silence, Justice's expression grew serious. "We'll get her there at zero-nine-hundred."

He ended the call and then looked at Abbey. "Roman wants us to take you to the Breedline Covenant this morning. He's set up a meeting with the council head... and the queen."

Chapter Four

After the paramedics had wheeled Sebastian through the entrance to the Bates Hospital's ER with the institute's guard right on their heels, time became a rubber band, stretching endlessly. Sebastian felt as though his body was slipping further away. He could hear everyone around him, but when he tried to open his eyes, they would not obey.

The passing minutes slowed to a crawl as a female nurse hurried to assist. As they rolled him inside, Dr. Helen Carrington rushed over.

"What's the patient's status?"

"Two puncture wounds to the neck, and he's unconscious," one of the paramedics said.

Helen looked at the guard and noticed a logo on his shirt that read *Napa State Hospital*. "What happened?"

"I was on duty the whole time," the guard said. "After the staff nurse gave him a sedative and left, I swear no one entered his room."

Helen cursed under her breath and directed her attention to the nurse. "Page Dr. Eaves." Then she turned toward the EMTs. "Let's get him down to bay two."

Her commands snapped everyone into action. Two minutes later, the medics pushed the gurney through a set of double doors that led to an operating room. As soon as they transferred Sebastian from the gurney to an operating table, Helen instantly started checking his vitals.

Dr. Carl Eaves came in as the paramedics left the room. "What do we have?"

"He's unconscious," Helen replied. "BP is sixty over forty and dropping. Heart rate is in the one fifties."

"Do we know what happened?"

She shook her head. "The guard from the Napa State Hospital said they found him like this."

Dr. Eaves cocked a brow and looked to the nurse standing by Helen. "He's a patient at the mental institute?"

"Yes, Doctor."

"The marks on his throat look to be some sort of bite," Helen said as she examined Sebastian's neck. "Although no one at the institute seems to know what happened. The guard said no one entered his room after a nurse administered him a sedative."

A look of confusion came over Dr. Eaves as he viewed the bite marks on Sebastian's throat. "These marks didn't get there by themselves. Does our patient have a name?"

"Sebastian Crow," the nurse replied.

Shit! Helen looked at Dr. Eaves, wide-eyed. "Dr. Eaves..." she said, motioning him over, "...could I speak to you in private?"

He nodded and moved next to her.

"I had no idea the patient was Sebastian," she said in a hushed voice. "We need to notify Tim Ross. He's considered dangerous."

* * *

In a state of deep unconsciousness, Lucifer's voice came to Sebastian. "Are you ready, Sebastian?" His voice sounded like his dead brother's. "It's time to visit your mummy and dear ol' stepdaddy."

Sebastian shook his head, his eyes wild with panic. "Please... don't do this."

Out of nowhere, Sebastian's surroundings shifted. It was like magic. Although his body was lying in a hospital, his mind took him to a different place. He stood outside an iron gate, looking beyond a large estate, the same dreadful place he grew up in. The medieval structure eerily reminded him of Dracula's castle. It belonged to the person he despised the most: his stepfather, William Edward Montgomery III.

Sebastian suddenly felt like Ebenezer Scrooge. Except it hadn't been the Ghost of Christmas Past to visit him. It was Lucifer himself, taking him back to relive the worst of his childhood past.

"Does this bring back memories?" Lucifer asked as he came up behind him and placed a hand on his shoulder.

Sebastian flinched at the contact and snapped his head around. He twisted away. "Get your filthy hand off me."

Lucifer stepped back. "Touchy, aren't we?" he said with a chuckle, his sharp teeth flashing as his top lip curled up.

Sebastian glared at him.

"When you were growing up," Lucifer went on, "your stepfather despised the day you were born. Your mother's infidelity brought such shame in his home, especially when she got knocked up with you and your twin brother, Thomas."

"Go to hell," Sebastian spat.

Lucifer slowly shook his head. "It's not too late to surrender."

"Never." Sebastian gritted his teeth. "I'll never give you my son." He covered his ears and squeezed his eyes tight. "Get out of my head!"

"You can't get rid of me so easily," Lucifer murmured. "You just wait. I'll change your mind sooner than later."

When Sebastian lowered his hands and opened his eyes, he was shocked to find himself standing inside his stepfather's estate. Pictures littered the walls and occupied every available space on the shelves and over the fireplace mantel. Although none of the photographs included him. It made his chest ache to see all the pictures of his half sister and half brother. To be included as part of the family was everything he'd ever wanted but never had.

The smell of wood burning in the fireplace instantly brought back memories. Then another scent came to him. It was the stench of his stepfather's cologne. It made his gut churn.

"How 'bout a nice family reunion?"

Sebastian sucked in a breath and his chest rose and fell as if he was swallowing away his fear. Then he scrubbed both hands over his face and looked at Lucifer pointedly. "Do what you must."

When the sound of familiar voices drifted over, coming from the dining area, anxiety hit him instantly. He didn't like how vulnerable they made him feel, how uncertain and uneasy of the mere thought of having to face his family again. It brought back so many haunted memories.

He took a deep breath and tried to convince himself to step forward. As he grudgingly moved on and rounded a corner, he froze in his tracks when his stepfather came into view. Dread clutched him by the throat fearing he would register his presence. But to his stunned disbelief, his stepfather never looked his way. He was invisible to them. Instead, his eyes stayed focused on his mother, Sibyl. She was sitting at the far end of the table with her head down as though she was afraid to look up.

"How could you do this to me, Sibyl?" William seethed. "You're nothing but a whore! How dare you bring shame in my house!"

She looked up with tears in her eyes. "I'm sorry. Please... forgive me, William."

"Forgive you?" He snarled his upper lip. "For God's sake, you've betrayed your whole family. How long have you been carrying on with this... Alexander? And our children," he continued to rant. "How could you do this to Edward and Camille?"

"I swear to you," she pleaded, "I would never purposely hurt you or our children for the world. I made a mistake. I beg you... please forgive me for this."

"I forbid you to keep those two bastards!" he said roughly.

"But, William..." Sibyl sobbed. "My sister will only take in one of the twins. What am I supposed to do with the other baby?"

"I suppose he can live in the guesthouse with the hired help," he huffed. "Eliza can care for the child. But I forbid the bastard to have any interactions with our children." He glared at her. "Do I make myself clear?"

She wiped at her eyes. "Yes, William."

"And another thing, I—"

"Excuse me, sir," the maidservant interrupted him. "I don't mean to intrude..." She bowed her head. "...ma'am." The maid's weary eyes met Sibyl's. "The baby is running a fever. What shall I do?"

A knot formed in the back of Sebastian's throat when he caught sight of the beautiful, dark-skinned woman. Her features seemed familiar, but he could not remember how he knew her. *Who is she?*

"Mrs. Montgomery will not be caring for the bastard child," William intervened. "Eliza, you will tend to his needs from here on. I do not want the child brought into the main household. He is never to be around my children. You are to care for him in your quarters. I will fund all his basic needs. If that's going to be a problem, you can look for employment elsewhere. Furthermore, you and your daughter Anna will have to find other accommodations. You will no longer be allowed to reside here."

Eliza's eyes widened. "Yes, sir." She lowered her head. "I will gladly tend to the child."

When Eliza quietly ducked out of the room, she bit back a curse. *How could anyone be so cruel to an innocent baby? The poor child will surely carry the burden of Mrs. Montgomery's sins.*

Sebastian followed her. With every step and every breath, he had to force himself to keep moving, his instincts warning him to turn away.

As Eliza made her way silently past the massive kitchen and all the expensive cookware that hung from hooks above a quartzite breakfast bar, it was very clear Mrs. Montgomery valued wealth. There was no telling how much money they spent on the estate over time. To Eliza, the Montgomerys were spoiled and wasteful... a shame to the Breedline species.

Leading down a long hallway from the kitchen, she came to a door. Sebastian stood behind her as she reached out and opened it. Instantly, a baby crying echoed from inside.

As Eliza hurried downstairs of what looked to be a basement, Sebastian followed behind her.

"Mama... is that you?" a small voice called out.

"Yes, sweetheart," Eliza said. "It's just me."

"Mama, the baby hasn't stopped crying since you left," a little girl said. She had a tiny infant in her arms, trying to soothe him. "He still has a fever."

"He'll be okay, Anna. He just needs some medicine."

Anna? Sebastian said to himself. *Why does that name sound familiar?*

When Eliza reached for the baby, Anna gently placed him in her mother's arms.

"Shhh," Eliza soothed. "Everything is going to be just fine. I've got something to take away your fever, sweet child."

As Sebastian stood close behind, his heart sank watching Eliza soothe the baby in her arms. Then he averted his eyes from Eliza and focused on the little girl. She didn't look any older than eight or nine. She had long, curly hair and sun-kissed skin with freckles covering her cheeks. Her eyes were familiar. They were the most mesmerizing color of bright green surrounded by dark, thick eyelashes. *Why can't I remember them?* Sebastian feverishly thought.

Anna peered up at her mother, her eyes filled with worry. "Is Mrs. Montgomery going to take the baby?"

Eliza regretfully shook her head. "No, sweetheart. We're to care for the child from now on."

Anna's brows clenched. "But... why, Mama? Why doesn't Mrs. Montgomery want her baby? Is something wrong with him?"

Eliza smiled. "No, Anna. There is nothing wrong with him." She looked to the tiny bundle cuddled in her arms and whispered, "You are perfect, little one." She lightly stroked her fingers over the baby's dark curls. "You're a good child and worthy of love."

At that moment, the baby quieted and focused his bright eyes on Eliza's soft voice.

With a gentle caress, Anna reached over and smoothed her hand over the baby's hair. "Is he going to be my little brother now?" She looked at Eliza, anticipating her answer, hoping she would say yes.

"Yes, darling. We will love him as our very own."

Anna pressed a soft kiss on the baby's forehead. "I love you, Sebastian."

It hit Sebastian like a ton of bricks. The tiny infant was... *him.*

Chapter Five

Later that morning, Roman's team drove Abbey to the Breedline Covenant. Their goal was to keep her safe and under the radar. They'd spent most of the night setting into motion plans for her protection with Lawrence Colbert. Roman had arranged a meeting with Tim Ross—the Breedline council head—before his team arrived with her. After Roman explained the dangers involved, the Covenant's security tightened, but only Lawrence, Bull, Justice, and Lena would have direct access to Abbey's transportation. In turn, early the following morning, Tim delivered the news to Tessa—the Breedline queen—about their situation.

After seven days of paradise in the Caribbean, a location chosen by Jace, he and Tessa had arrived back to the Covenant from their honeymoon the previous evening. They were both shell-shocked to hear the news about Abbey.

When Tessa delivered the news to her brother Steven, hope suddenly sprang to life within him. His heart raced in anticipation. He'd prayed over the years for a miracle more times than he'd care to admit, but his prayers had gone unanswered... until now. He had harnessed his rage toward everyone involved with Abbey's disappearance, needing it for the impending confrontation when he'd helped the Breedline battle against Dr. Hubert Crane.

"My God." Steven gasped. "Is Abbey okay?"

When Tessa looked at him with sympathy in her eyes, a numbness gripped him. Everything moved around him in slow motion. Then a firm hand gripped his shoulder from behind. As he flinched and turned around, he met Tim's gaze.

"Relax, Steven. She's fine," Tim said. "Abbey will be here any minute. But she doesn't know you're here."

"Who helped her escape?"

"She managed to escape on her own," Tim replied. "But it wasn't long before hired men were sent to hunt her down. She's in safe hands as we speak. An old military buddy of Drakon's got in touch with me. His name is Roman Kincaid. He's a hired bodyguard for a billionaire named Valkin Steele.

After he found out Steele's involvement with Dr. Autenburg's research, Roman got to Abbey before they did. They're following her to get to you, Steven."

Steven shrugged. "Why?"

"It's a long story, one I need to tell you from the beginning to end, so you understand what we're dealing with. I know you're familiar with Dr. Autenburg's and Dr. Crane's research firsthand. Now, Valkin Steele is involved."

Steven frowned. "Who is he, and what's he got to do with all this?"

"He's a man with a lot of money, and a lot of power," Tim said. "Drakon did some digging into Mr. Steele's background. He found out Steele's in charge of a big operation in drugs and arms trafficking. Steele uses an oil company as a cover-up. Everyone who works in the petroleum industry thinks he's a legit businessman, but he's dirty. He's got a hand in a lot of different pots." Tim made a sound of distaste. "He has a lucrative human-trafficking operation going. The bastard sells young girls into sexual slavery to the highest bidder."

Tim broke off, anger surging through his veins at having to reveal Steele's disgusting and evil deeds. "He also had a hand in Abbey's father's death."

The knot in Steven's throat grew, tightening painfully. "What? I thought all this was over when we put an end to Dr. Crane's research."

"Sit." Tim gestured toward a chair. "I'll explain everything I know."

As Steven sat down, Tessa pulled out a chair and took a seat beside him.

Tim placed his cell phone on the table before he sat. "Apparently Dr. Crane had billionaire clients funding his research. They built other research facilities. Valkin Steele is one of their main backers. He's looking for an Adalwolf that has the power to heal a woman he loves. Her name is Natasha, and she's dying of cancer."

Steven looked at him, bewildered. "But... I don't have that kind of power. If I tried to heal a fatal wound or illness, I wouldn't survive it."

Tim was silent for a moment. "Are you sure?"

Steven paled, suddenly feeling sick to his stomach. The weight of his mother's death settled on his shoulders like a ton of bricks. If indeed he had the power to heal a fatal wound, his mother had died for nothing. "Dr. Autenburg told me I didn't have that kind of the ability. He said it would kill me."

"Jesus," Tessa sighed. "Even if you have that kind of power, it's not worth risking your life to find out."

"I agree," Tim said. "But Valkin Steele would take that risk. He already proved that theory with Abbey's father. His life meant nothing to the man. Steele is the kind of monster that would sell out his own children to save his skin."

"What the hell are we going to do?" Steven asked. "We've got to take him down."

"It's the reason why I called a meeting with the council this morning. Roman Kincaid knows people who can help us. It's what they do. They work for a Special Ops group. Some of what they do is private, but our military also contracts them for missions that no one else can or will do. And they're damn good. What we have now isn't enough. Steele has resources beyond the Breedline's imaginings."

The sound of Tim's phone going off abruptly halted their conversation. "Hang on," he said, recognizing the caller ID. "I've got to take this call. It's the Napa State Hospital calling."

When Tessa nodded, Tim swiped to answer and put the phone to his ear. "Tim Ross speaking."

After a few moments of silence, Tim's facial expression grew tense. While the guard explained to him on the phone about Sebastian, Tim's blood boiled in his veins. The timing couldn't possibly get any worse.

"Wasn't a guard on duty?" Tim finally said. "Has anyone viewed the video footage in Sebastian's room?"

Tessa and Steven immediately came to attention when they heard Tim mention Sebastian's name.

"I will deal with this later. I have more important issues at this moment," Tim said, breathing out heavily over the phone. "I want two guards with him at all times. Do I make myself clear?"

He ended the call and set the phone down with shaky hands, his eyes nearly black with rage.

Tessa's eyes widened. "What's going on?"

"A guard at the Napa State Hospital said someone attacked Sebastian. He's at the Bates Hospital right now. Helen was the physician on staff when they brought him in."

"Did they say who attacked him?"

"The guard said no one was in the room with him when it happened."

"But how can that be?" Tessa looked at Tim, baffled. "Have they checked the surveillance cameras?"

Tim shook his head. "No. Not yet."

"Please tell me that bastard is dead," Steven grumbled.

Tim lifted an eyebrow and Tessa could see the tension building on Steven's face. She was having the same thoughts as Steven. The world would be a safer place if Sebastian were dead.

"Sorry, Steven," Tim said, scrubbing his hand over his short-trimmed hair. "He's still alive, but the guard said he's in a coma."

"What are you going to do?" Steven asked.

"Right now, we've got bigger problems on our hands. We'll have to deal with this later. We're meeting—"

A sharp knock at the door cut Tim off. "It's open," he called out.

When the door opened, Drakon stepped inside and said, "Roman's team is waiting downstairs."

Steven shot out of his chair. "Is Abbey with them?"

Drakon nodded, and before he could get a word out, a voice echoed from downstairs. "Steven..."

"Abbey!" Steven called out.

She pushed by Roman and rushed upstairs. As Lawrence took off after her, Roman stopped him. "Let her go."

When she got to the top of the stairs, she met Steven and threw her arms around him.

"Thank God," Steven gasped. "Oh, thank God you're safe."

As she pulled away, he looked her up and down, his eyes narrowing as if studying her for injuries. "I can't believe you're here."

"If it weren't for Roman and his team..." she said in a tear-laced voice, "...I would have never found you."

He slid an arm around her shoulders, pulling her into his side. "I thought I'd never see you again." He brushed a kiss over her brow. "I love you."

"I love you too, Steven."

"Abbey," he said, shifting his eyes toward Tessa. "I'd like to introduce you to my sister, Tessa."

Abbey looked at him, puzzled. "Sister?"

"I found my family. I even found my father."

Her eyes brightened. "I'm so happy for you, Steven."

Tessa stepped forward and extended her hand. "It's a pleasure to meet you, Abbey."

Abbey took her hand. "It's nice to meet you too, Tessa."

When Roman's team stepped inside the room, everyone looked toward the door. Roman strode in behind them, a determined set to his jaw.

As soon as they caught sight of Tessa, all four of them bowed their heads.

"Thank you all for coming," she said. "We appreciate your alliance with the Covenant. I would like to introduce my brother, Steven."

Steven nodded in their direction. "Thank you for everything you've done for Abbey."

Roman surged forward and took Steven's hand in a firm handshake. "I'm sorry it took me this long. I had no idea the man I worked for was underhanded. I'll do whatever it takes to put an end to Valkin Steele and everyone involved."

Steven nodded, adrenaline stirring in his veins. "You can count me in."

"I'd like to introduce my team," Roman said. "This is Lena. She's highly trained in survival skills, martial arts, and anything dealing with weapons and hand-to-hand combat. That's Justice standing beside her. Not only is he a pilot, but he's also an expert with explosives, hand-to-hand combat, and sniper training. Next to Justice is Bull. He's..." Roman paused, staring in Bull's direction, trying to find the right words to describe the man the size of a mountain. "Let's just say he's an expert in everything."

Bull smirked, his mouth curving into a half smile.

"And this is Lawrence," Roman continued, turning toward the man standing to his right, his stature as big as Bull's. Lawrence's complexion stood out among the others, dark as night and his eyes sparkled like two bright green gemstones. "He's an expert in unconventional warfare, and he's also a medic."

Lawrence nodded and smiled.

Instantly, everyone looked to the door as Jace and Jem crowded in behind Roman's crew. As they moved next to Tessa, Roman focused on their features. They looked to be identical, except the one with longer hair had a slight scar marring the right side of his face. They reminded Roman of hair-bangers from an eighties rock band. By what Tim had described to him earlier, they had to be the Chamberlain twins. Both carried powerful genetics, descended from an ancient demon. One of them had the power to shift into a seven-foot werewolf that resembled the abominable snowman they called the Beast. The other one had the power to conjure a portal and the ability to create a firebomb out of the palm of his hand. They referred to him as the Chosen Son. As they stared back at Roman, their expressions were unreadable. He wondered if they could be trusted.

"If everyone would please take a seat," Tim said, bringing Roman back to focus. "We're waiting for more council members to arrive, and another group Drakon invited that can add to our list of allies."

Chapter Six

An hour later, Sebastian's wounds were tended to, and bandages had been placed on his neck. As far as the state of his unconsciousness, Sebastian was still unresponsive after Dr. Eaves completed his examination. Finally, he turned to face Helen and the nurse.

"Medically speaking, I don't know why he's not responding," Dr. Eaves said, his expression baffled. "It doesn't make any sense. He has lost a lot of blood, but considering he's half Breedline and half succubus, he should be healing by now."

After a few minutes, a nurse popped her head inside. "Excuse me, Dr. Carrington," she said in a low voice. "Three guards from the Napa State Mental Institute are here. They're asking to speak to you about the patient."

"Thank you," Helen said. "Tell them I'll be out shortly."

As the nurse nodded and closed the door, Helen let out a deep breath. "If my intuition is correct, they'll want Sebastian monitored twenty-four seven."

"Considering what happened," Dr. Eaves said, "I don't think that's a bad idea."

Helen nodded and reluctantly stepped out of the room. She went to the emergency waiting area where the guards were sitting. A tall, slender guard surged to his feet, worry etched into every groove of his face.

"Mr. Crow will be moved to the intensive care unit, where he can be monitored at all times," she told them. "As of now, his condition remains critical. Under my orders, he's not to be released from the hospital until he's stable. I—"

Helen was interrupted when a woman burst into the waiting room. Her light green eyes were wild and ringed with exhaustion.

"Where's Sebastian?" she demanded. "I'm his sister. My name is Anna Saeni. I want to see my brother immediately."

Helen frowned. "Sister?"

* * *

54

Valkin Steele poured himself a shot of whiskey and downed it in one gulp. His nerves were shot. He'd been waiting two days to hear back from Gordon Bates, the tracker he'd hired to locate Abigail Winthrop. After she had gruesomely killed Dr. Autenburg and his guards, she escaped the research facility. Now that Dr. Autenburg was dead, the drug he'd developed to help keep Natasha alive before her cancer ultimately took over wasn't working any longer. Steele's only hope was to find the Adalwolf with the power to heal terminal cancer. It had taken years, but now his men finally had a lead on Abigail's last location. His gut was screaming, and he never ignored his gut instincts. He would bet his life Miss Abigail Winthrop would take him right to the Adalwolf he was searching for to heal his beloved Natasha. She'd been seen by the top physicians in the world, had the best treatment money could buy, and he'd been told there was nothing further to be done. He wouldn't accept it. He would do anything, even if meant taking another life to save hers.

When his phone rang, it snapped him back to focus. Recognizing Gordon's number on the caller ID, his shoulders sagged in relief. His patience had run thin the last few days.

"Did you find her?" he barked into the phone.

There was a deep breath on the other end. "We lost Miss Winthrop's trail."

"What the hell do you mean, you lost her trail?" Valkin Steele bellowed. "I hired you to find the she-wolf. She's the only person that can lead us to the Adalwolf. This is unacceptable. Natasha doesn't have much time! I want you to get your ass out there and find Abigail Winthrop," he continued to rant. "Do I make myself clear?"

"Y-yes, sir," Gordon muttered. "We're on it now. Our intel has some new information. Miss Winthrop has been moved to the Breedline Covenant. They're keeping her guarded by a team of special forces. We'll need more manpower, Mr. Steele."

"What the hell am I paying you for?" Steele raged. "You're a bunch of damn amateurs!"

"I'm sorry, sir. The Covenant has involved the council. We're outnumbered."

Steele let out a ragged breath and said, "All right, I'll get you the manpower. But I swear, if you fail me, I'll make sure your entire family pays the price. And then I'll make sure you die a painful death. Do you understand?"

"Yes, Mr. Steele. I won't fail you, sir."

Steele ended the connection and placed another call to one of his men. He didn't have time to waste. He had to find a way to locate the Adalwolf. Natasha's life was on the line. And Cole Decker was the only person to get the job done.

"Get me Decker," Steele bit out. "I don't give a shit how much it costs. You get him here, now."

After he ended the call, he shoved the phone into his pocket and went down the hall that led to Natasha's room. Before he stepped inside, he paused outside the door and took a weary breath. He didn't want to show any signs of fear or weakness. She needed him to be strong and confident. Ten years ago, he instantly fell in love with her when he was introduced to her at a business holiday party. He was married at the time to his second wife, and Natasha was engaged to his brother-in-law. Two months later, she broke the engagement to become Valkin Steele's mistress. After a year had passed, he moved her into his home after his wife had unexpectedly died in a boating accident. He and Natasha were inseparable. And now she was dying.

As he went inside, Natasha's nurse, who he'd hired to stay by her side twenty-four seven, glanced over her shoulder at him.

"How is she faring?"

"Hello, Mr. Steele," the nurse said with a grim expression. "I'm afraid there's no change. I just gave her a sedative to help her rest."

He nodded with his lips drawn into a thin line. "Please," he said. "I'd like a few minutes with her alone."

"Yes, of course, Mr. Steele."

When the nurse left the room, he eased into a chair by Natasha's bed. He gently grasped her frail hand in his. As he lowered his head, he pressed his lips against her pale skin.

"Valkin," she said in a hoarse voice, "is that you?"

"Yes, darling. I'm just checking on you. Are you in any pain?"

"Just tired," she said around a yawn. "But I'm okay."

He lightly squeezed her hand. He knew she was hurting, but she would never let him know she was in pain. She didn't want to worry him.

"Get some rest, honey," he said, moving his hand to her cheek. "I need you to be strong for me a little while longer. I've found someone who can help you."

Her brows clenched, casting him a troubled look. She knew Valkin would do anything to save her, even if it meant trading an innocent life for hers.

"Don't worry." He leaned forward to kiss her forehead. "This time it will work."

When she began to protest, he placed his finger over her lips. "Shhh, I promise, baby. Everything will be just fine."

Tears burned in the corners of her eyes and slipped down the sides of her cheeks.

"Go to sleep, my darling," he whispered, wiping her tears away with his thumbs. "I'll be right here while you rest."

* * *

As Helen stared at the woman who had declared she was Sebastian's sister, she glanced over her shoulder at the guards, then looked back at the woman again. "Wait..." Helen paused and swallowed hard. "Did you just say you're Sebastian's sister?"

Anna dragged in a breath and ran her hand through her thick, long, curly hair. "Yes, ma'am. It is true, although we are not blood, he's my brother all the same. My mother, Eliza, raised him as her own."

"But..." Helen shook her head, her brows furrowed. "Eve listed Sebastian's twin boys as his only family members. There's no mention of any living siblings."

"Dear Lord," Anna said. "My brother has... *children*?"

There was silence, then Helen said, "Yes. Surely if you're his sister, Sebastian would have told you."

Anna shut her eyes briefly. A wave of exhaustion rolled through her. She couldn't find the words to explain. Years ago, she had been forced into a Catholic convent. From then on, she lost track of her brother's whereabouts.

"Ma'am..." she paused, looking closely at Helen's name tag. "Dr. Carrington, it's a long story. When I was a fourteen, my mother was brutally murdered by Sebastian's biological mother." She swallowed back tears. "Afterwards, I had no place to go and no living relatives to take me in. My father died when I was just a baby. So, Sebastian's stepfather sent me to live in a girls' convent."

Helen moved closer and placed her palm on Anna's shoulder. "I'm so sorry. Please, Miss Saeni..." She gestured toward a couch close by. "I think we need to sit down and talk."

Anna stared at Helen intently. Her expression was grim. "Yes, ma'am. And please, it's Anna. You can call me Anna."

As Anna slumped into the soft cushion, Helen sat down beside her and began to explain the situation with Sebastian.

* * *

The sequence that played out in a series of seconds seemed to last for centuries in Sebastian's unconscious psyche. Just minutes ago, he saw himself as a baby, and now he was suddenly standing in front of the kitchen window that overlooked the back of his stepfather's beautifully manicured estate. The sound of a child crying outside alerted him.

"Ready to reminisce the childhood you forced yourself to forget?" Lucifer asked, startling Sebastian.

Sebastian turned away from the window and looked over his shoulder. "You're a sick bastard." He glared at Lucifer. "Go ahead. There's nothing I can do to stop you."

Lucifer smirked. "Oh, but there is."

"I'm not giving you my son!" Sebastian barked. "The cruel memories of my past won't change my mind."

"We've only just begun. You may change your mind yet."

"Go back to hell," Sebastian spat and turned toward the window.

As Sebastian looked over the grounds, his eyes caught sight of Eliza. She was kneeling before a boy around the age of three or four who'd apparently fallen and skinned his knee. The scrawny child had black hair and paper-white skin. Sebastian wondered if the boy was him.

He moved closer to the glass barrier that separated him from the outside to eavesdrop on what was transpiring between Eliza and the little boy. Even though he couldn't hear them, their affection toward one another was crystal clear. As she soothed the boy and wiped his tears, his features were visibly comforted by her touch.

Sudden dread startled him when he heard footsteps from behind. When he spun around, he stood wide-eyed. The hair on the back of his neck rose as his birth mother moved in his direction.

"Mother?" he said as he curled his fist into a tight ball. The sight of her made him want to smash something, but he stood there, breathing in and out, instead.

Sibyl walked past him without even as much as a glance and peered out the window.

He realized his mother couldn't see him. It was as if he was a ghost watching his past flash before his eyes. He slowly relaxed his fist and moved next to her. He leaned against the window frame and studied his mother with a probing stare. When she flashed a resentful glare at Eliza embracing the little boy, it made him uneasy. Apparently, his mother didn't like her, and the scowl on her face didn't make a secret of it.

"I regret," Sibyl said through gritted teeth, "the day you were born."

Sebastian clutched his heart and staggered back a step. He wanted to scream out as she walked away but knew it was a lost cause. She wouldn't hear him. The choices that had been made by his mother were irreversible, and the consequences were his alone to bear.

Chapter Seven

As everyone took a seat, the room was silent until Jace blurted, "Did anyone inform Kyle, Casey, and Alexander about the meeting?"

"Yes," Tim said. "They should arrive with the others shortly."

Jace nodded and turned to meet Abbey's stare across the table. There was such a wounded look in her eyes. What was her damage? Her story? She had that look of someone who'd seen the worst humanity had to offer, and God knew he'd seen that look often enough in his life. Then his mind wondered about her she-wolf and the powers it possessed. Would she be a danger to the Covenant? But in turn, he had no business judging her. If anyone posed a threat, it was his Beast.

When she noticed him staring, she looked away, her eyes going down as they crowded with anxiety.

He leaned forward with his hand extended. "It's a pleasure to meet you, Miss Winthrop. My name is Jace Chamberlain."

She looked up, her eyes connecting with Jace's. "Please, it's Abbey." She took hold of his hand and smiled. "It's nice to meet you, Jace."

As she drew her hand away, she leaned back in her chair and turned toward Steven. As she looked up at him, her smile took his breath away. Hope shone in her eyes for the first time since she'd walked in the door. From the outside one would never guess a woman who looked like Abbey was anything but a beautiful, intelligent young woman with her life ahead of her. But it was those few glimpses into her eyes that told him she'd been to hell and back.

She glanced over at the guy sitting next to Jace, who looked identical.

When he drew his hand forward, he said, "We're glad to have you here, Abbey. My name is Jem Chamberlain." He turned to look at Jace. "I'm considered the good twin. Jace is a caveman with no manners."

Jace gasped in mock outrage. "I'll have you know that I'm considered the intelligent twin, not to mention better looking."

Jem's eyebrow went up. "Whatever." He chuckled and shook Abbey's hand. "He's also full of hot air."

"And you're an ass," Jace shot back.

"Cut the crap," Tim intervened. "Both of you."

To their surprise and delight, Abbey responded by laughing.

Everyone's attention was drawn toward the door when Kyle and Casey strode into the room. Malachi O'Conner walked in behind them and blushed when he caught sight of Tessa. He quietly walked around the table and took a seat close to hers. Tessa felt the weight of his stare and glanced in his direction. "Hello, Malachi."

Malachi's face reddened even more. He damn near swallowed his tongue as he gazed into her eyes. Her eyelashes were long, accentuating her startling emerald-green irises. Anytime he was around Tessa, he acted like a teenager with a high school crush.

Sweat beaded on his brow. "H-hello, Tessa." He stumbled over his words. "You look beautiful today."

Jace narrowed his eyes and watched how Malachi reacted to Tessa. It annoyed him. For some reason, the lyrics to the song "Next Contestant" by Nickelback came to mind. Right about now, he'd like to have a sign that read, *MINE... STAY THE HELL AWAY* and smash it over Malachi's head. In the awkward silence, Jace leaned forward, a dark scowl savaging his face. Losing his composure, he let out a grumble and said, "Malachi, you might want to wipe that drool off your face."

Tessa blinked and stared back at Jace, not at all sure what to say.

That was when Tim exchanged looks between Jace and Malachi. His gut instincts told him to intervene before the situation got too heated. When it came to a bonded male Breedline, it was dangerous to come between him and his mate, unless you had a death wish.

"Malachi, it's good to have you here," Tim spoke out.

Malachi took his eyes off Tessa and shifted in his chair. "Thank you for including me, Tim."

Jace sat back in his chair and glared holes through Malachi.

As Luther Proxy and Victor Demont—both Breedline council members—stepped into the room, Casey flashed a resentful glare in Victor's direction. He wanted to pop off some smart-ass remark but closed his mouth and kept quiet. Casey despised Mr. Demont even though he was Lila's father. After Casey had found out about Victor's affair with his mother—who was now deceased—he found it hard to have respect for the man. Now that Casey's secret was out in the open, the Covenant and his beloved Lila had accepted him for what he was. The weight that hovered so unbearably on his shoulders finally lightened after all the years he had kept his Theriomorph side hidden.

"Please have a seat," Tim said to Luther and Victor. "Thank you for attending. We'll start the meeting as soon as everyone else arrives."

The sound of heavy footsteps coming from outside the library grabbed everyone's attention. Their eyes caught sight of Alexander Crest as he stepped through the door. Then they focused on the four men that followed him, apparently military, judging by their attire. They looked intimidating clothed in full tactical battledress.

When Tim got to his feet, he nodded in Alexander's direction and gestured toward the table. "Please have a seat, Alexander." Then he shifted his focus to Drakon and said, "Drakon, please introduce our new friends to the group so we can get started."

As Drakon got to his feet, he moved next to a huge man who closely resembled the WWE professional wrestler John Cena. He stood over six feet, shorter than Drakon, but he was as big, weighing easily over two hundred pounds. "This is the team leader, Lieutenant Colonel Brian Deshazo," Drakon said as admiration showed in his steely blue eyes. "This man has saved my ass more than I can count. I trust Colonel D with my life."

The colonel smiled and extended his hand. "It was a pleasure saving your ass, Drakon. You were one of my best men."

As Drakon and the colonel shook hands, the rest of the men stood silent and merely observed.

"Colonel D,..." Drakon said, keeping eye contact. "I'll let you introduce your men."

The colonel nodded and stepped forward. "All my men are highly trained elite forces in the United States military, officially known as First Special Forces Operational Detachment Delta. We perform various clandestine and highly classified missions around the world. Our primary mission is counterterrorism."

"How do you maintain the secrecy of our Breedline species among your human comrades?" Tim queried.

"Our group are known as quiet professionals and are notorious for our secrecy," Colonel Deshazo replied. "We do have other species in our units besides humans. We all take an oath of allegiance to ensure our species confidentiality."

As the colonel spoke, Casey suddenly sensed the presence of another Theriomorph in the room. He focused on the huge, menacing man standing next to the colonel. The guy was as big as Drakon, if not bigger. With shoulders as broad as two men put together, he oddly reminded Casey of the actor in the movie *Scorpion King*.

"This is Sergeant Major Paul Wyckoff," Colonel Deshazo said. "He's part of our counterterrorist unit, specifically directed to kill or capture high-value units or dismantle terrorist cells. We also rely on Wyckoff for hostage rescues. Everyone in our unit refers to him as Dark Wraith," he added with a slight smirk on his face. "Considering his background, the name speaks for itself."

Jace snorted from across the table, making light of Wyckoff's name. He flinched as Tessa poked him in the ribs.

Casey's eyebrow went up as he studied Wyckoff for a moment, noticing the peculiar hint of lavender in his eyes. With an unexpected moment of insight, he blurted, "You're a Theriomorph."

Tim glanced quickly at Casey to silence him.

Wyckoff shifted his gaze to meet Casey's. He looked startled by the outburst, and then his features creased with uncertainty.

Casey made a sound that came out as a grunt and said, "Look, I didn't mean to sound offensive. It's just that..." he paused and swallowed hard. "...I'm also a Theriomorph."

In the brief silence that followed, Wyckoff stood speechless, which was unusual for him. The guy was usually a chatterbox. Well, that wasn't exactly true. When it came to a mission, he was focused and determined like an alien had temporarily taken over his body, because Wyckoff was never lost for words. Now that the cat was out of the bag, he wasn't sure how to respond.

"Don't sweat it," Wyckoff finally said. "Actually, it's kind of a relief knowing I'm not the only badass around here. Do you have any idea what it's like saving all their asses?" He chuckled. "It's exhausting."

"Admit it, Wraith," a guy standing next to Wyckoff said. "You know you can't live without us."

Wyckoff rolled his eyes. "Yeah, you keep on believing that, Kid. I just don't know how I'd manage without you."

Colonel Deshazo cleared his throat. "All right," he said with his brows drawn together. "Now that we've established all the deep feelings you two have for one another, let's move on."

At that, the colonel's entire team came to attention, all business, as they waited for him to continue.

Colonel Deshazo shifted his eyes in the direction of the guy who had made light of Wyckoff's comment. He was the youngest of the four and the epitome of a cocky good ol' boy. Born and raised in Texas, he had the worn cowboy look down without actually looking like he'd stepped right off the farm, except for his southern drawl.

"This is Sergeant Major Joshua Lawson," the colonel said. "We call him Kid for reasons I'm sure you're already aware of."

Wyckoff bit his lip, holding back a chuckle.

"Kid's Special Operations Squadron. He's an operator of AC-130 gunships and specialized in planes and helicopters. He gets us were we need to go and gets our asses out."

Kid smiled at Wyckoff and batted his brows.

"Standing beside Kid is Master Sergeant Stephen Virgin," Colonel Deshazo said with a broad smile. "Although we refer to him as Gunny."

Gunny made a sound in the back of his throat and rolled his eyes. He hated the nickname his team had given him. He was the oldest of the four, and a man with few words. But when he spoke, he said what was on his mind. He was a hard-nosed, hard-living soldier of war.

"He's highly trained in his field," the colonel continued. "This will be Gunny's eleventh mission. He was recently awarded a medal for his respective branch of service while serving in the Middle East. You can count on him to always have your back, and I mean that literally. Gunny is one of the best sharpshooters."

"Thank you for the walk down memory lane, Colonel D," Gunny clipped out. His voice was rough and raspy. "I feel all warm and *fuzzy*."

The guy only had one expression: stone-cold. No smiles, no pleasantries. That wasn't Gunny's way and, well, it wasn't the colonel's either. They both got straight to business without meaningless chitchat getting in the way of an assignment.

Colonel Deshazo leveled a hard stare at Gunny. He was a smart-ass, but he wasn't the only one anxious to get the hell where they were going so they could complete this mission. The colonel turned in Tim's direction. "Okay, let's get down to business."

Tim stepped forward with his hand extended, taking turns greeting each one. Once they were all seated, he leaned forward in his chair and introduced everyone at the table to Colonel Deshazo's team.

When the door suddenly flew open, everyone immediately turned around. "I'm sorry to interrupt," Bruce said. "But you need to take a look at the news. It's been broadcasting all morning," he said in his thick Scottish accent.

Tim rose from his chair and walked over to a small seating area across the room and stood in front of a flat screen that hung above a fireplace mantel. Everyone else followed and gathered around. When Tim grabbed the remote and pointed it at the TV, channel fourteen came into view. A female news reporter stood addressing the camera.

"This is Samantha Cordell from KTVU Fox 2 News reporting live from the San Francisco Bay in northern California where four men and three women were found gruesomely murdered in a homeless encampment under a freeway. Forensics stated the victims were mysteriously drained of all their blood, and some body parts were reported missing. Authorities confirm reports of cannibalism."

Tim switched the channel to another news station.

"We're live here in Fresno, California, where two people stated they came upon the grisly murders of six homeless people. Be warned, though, some of the descriptions of the crimes I'm about to report are disturbing and may not be appropriate for all viewers. The scene was full of ghoulish slaughter. Reports say the victims were found half-eaten. The medical examiner has not been able to identify the victims at this time."

As they listened to the reporter, Tessa caught her breath, every part of her body held in anticipation of this huge devastation. Her hand shook as she placed it over her mouth in utter disbelief. Jace wrapped his arm around her and pulled her close.

"What the hell is going on?" Kyle said. His eyes desperately searched the others for some explanation as they stood in shock. "What could have done this?"

"Since I got back from the Napa State Mental Institute, it's been on every channel," Bruce said. "I came here as soon as I heard the news." And then he turned toward Tim. "Do you think this has something to do with what happened to Sebastian?"

Tim stood in silence, flipping from one station to the next, all of them reporting the same gruesome massive killings throughout the San Francisco area. He looked at Bruce and said, "I don't know. I'm not ruling out the possibilities." Focusing back on the TV, his hand paused at their local news station as they broadcast live.

"This is Christopher Barnes from KGo TV 7 reporting live from downtown Berkeley with breaking news of widespread

murders sweeping across the San Francisco Bay area. The police department continues to be flooded with calls from local citizens reporting more victims, of which all were homeless. At least thirty were committed outside the city, all of them completely drained of blood. Authorities continue to report detailed murders and still have no explanation of who could have done such a heinous act. Police say no arrests have been made."

"This doesn't sound humanly possible," Casey spoke out. "I think we're dealing with something supernatural."

"What about Dr. Crane's hybrids?" Drakon said. "It could be a possibility we didn't destroy them all."

"No," Steven bluntly stated. "Whatever is responsible, it's eating their victims. The hybrids were just cold-blooded killers, not cannibals."

Roman shook his head. "It doesn't make any sense. Why are they just targeting the homeless?"

"Because they're defenseless," Colonel Deshazo said. "The homeless are easy prey."

With his brows furrowed, Tim switched off the TV. He looked angry now. His entire body was tense, and his eyes blazed with purpose. "Even if we didn't eliminate all the hybrids, Steven is right. This is not their MO, but it does have Dr. Autenburg's and Dr. Crane's names stamped all over this. I don't know what's killing all those people, but my gut tells me it has something to do with their past research."

Chapter Eight

Anna looked at Helen, confused. "I don't understand. Sebastian was always such a good child. He would never hurt anyone."

Helen placed her hand on Anna's in a gesture of comfort. "People change, Anna. And you said yourself it's been years since you last saw him."

Anna looked away to gather her composure before she broke down in front of the physician.

"I'm sorry, Anna," Helen said softly. "I know hearing all this must be very painful. But you need to know the truth about Sebastian's crimes against the Breedline."

"His mother and stepfather caused all this," Anna retorted as she faced Helen. "They treated him less than human. When Sebastian was born, they tossed him aside like a piece of trash."

"Anna..." Helen paused briefly. She regretted what she had to say next. "Sebastian murdered his family."

Anna's eyes widened at first, and then her expression changed from shock into a mask of revulsion. "They all deserved to die."

Helen's brows clenched. "Surely you don't mean that."

"For what they did to my mother and..." She stopped and bit back her lip as images of the past flashed before her. The horrifying memories of Sebastian's stepfather haunted the very core of her soul. She'd tried so hard to forget what had been done to her and her mother, but it all came back as if it had just happened. She could still feel Mr. Montgomery's hot breath on her face and his weight atop hers like she was being raped all over again. He'd made her feel helpless and filthy, like a defenseless animal trapped in a cage. And Mrs. Montgomery knew all the while what her husband was but turned a blind eye. Sibyl Montgomery hated Anna and blamed her husband's sick obsessions on her. Even Camille and Edward—their son and daughter—was aware of the vile things William Montgomery had done to her, but they ignored her cries in the night. And then the painful memories of her mother's death almost sent her over the edge.

Anna closed her eyes, and when she reopened them, she said, "I hope they all burn in hell."

Helen lightly squeezed her hand. "I'm so sorry, dear. Whatever happened to you must have been traumatizing. Is there anything I can do to help?"

"Can I see him?" she asked, her eyes pleading. "Please, Helen. Just for a few minutes. It would mean a great deal to me if I could see my brother after all these years."

Helen let out a deep breath and then finally nodded. "He's being moved to intensive care. As soon as we get him settled, I'll take you to see him. Although Sebastian is in a coma, he can still hear you. Maybe if he recognizes your voice, it will help him recover."

Anna smiled a little. "Thank you, Helen."

* * *

"Aw, poor Sebastian," Lucifer mocked. "You're not going to cry... are you?"

Sebastian forced his gaze upward in response to Lucifer's disgusting humor. He refused to let shame crawl into his soul. He had to think of a way out of this nightmare. "You're a sick bastard," he spat. "Why don't you just get it over with and put me out of my misery?"

Lucifer could tell Sebastian was visibly fighting to keep his temper in check. He crossed his arms over his chest and stared challengingly back at him. "Now, now, don't get your panties in a wad. We've still got a lot of work to do. You just wait. I'll break you soon enough."

Sebastian's lips curled into a snarl, and a sound of rage burned deep in his chest and bubbled outward, vibrating his throat. He wanted to hit Lucifer. He was tired of feeling helpless, tired of being subjected to Lucifer's whims and control. Red anger clouded his vision. And then he rushed toward Lucifer with a vengeance. Just as Sebastian prepared to feel the impact of Lucifer's body, he instantly vanished into thin air. He managed to gain his footing before he tripped, but he swayed like a sapling in the wind. He turned in bewilderment and then discovered he was in an entirely different place. He was now standing outside, overlooking the estate's backyard. He couldn't wrap his mind around how Lucifer had the power over him like a marionette's puppeteer.

Suddenly, he was alerted by the sounds of children arguing. When he looked in their direction, his brows instantly furrowed. It was his older half siblings, Camille and Edward. They were fraternal twins and looked as though they were the age of ten. Sitting near the edge of a man-made pond, they were fighting over a board game. Born with a silver spoon in their mouths, they'd been spoiled rotten ever since. Camille had the same personality as her mother, and there was no fixing that shit. At an early age, she'd learned what a temper tantrum was and how it managed to work in her favor. Edward, on the other hand, was the same as his father. Little Edward was a physically perfect, firstborn son prepared to carry on the family name and bloodline. Only pure Breedlines were acceptable. The Montgomerys didn't like defects. And in their opinion, Sebastian was the definition of the word. Being born a bastard and a half succubus like his mother's side of the family, he was ignored by his biological mother and his older siblings like the plague.

As Sebastian stood back in silence and watched the two brats banter back and forth, something by a nearby tree caught his eye. When he turned, he saw a little boy—the same pale, scrawny boy he'd seen crying earlier. He was hiding behind a big oak, watching Camille and Edward. *Was that little boy truly his younger self?*

Finally, the boy found his courage and stepped out from behind the tree. Sebastian watched as he slowly moved closer to Camille and Edward. As the boy stood wide-eyed, he nervously fidgeted with a loose thread on the seam of his sleeve.

Camille looked up at him and crinkled her nose.

"What do you want?" Edward said in a menacing tone.

The little boy stuttered, "C-can I play with you?"

"You're not supposed to talk to us," Camille bit out. "Go away!"

The boy flinched at Camille's cruel words. As his eyes began to well up with tears, she pointed her finger and teased, "Look at the baby cry."

Edward laughed and joined in on his sister's heartless bullying.

Ice crept through Sebastian's veins until he felt incapable of moving or reacting. It was heartbreaking to watch. He wanted to look away. At that moment, he knew that the little boy was indeed him. The forgotten memories of his half sibling's savage behavior came crashing down all at once. He'd remembered this exact day. This was the day he'd almost died. Sebastian lowered his face into his hands. *"No..."*

When he heard a splash, like something being tossed into the water, he dropped his hands and saw Camille and Edward laughing and running away. And then he saw two small arms thrashing from inside the pond, desperate for help. As he rushed toward the water's edge, the little boy was nowhere to be found. He'd sunk to the bottom like a stone.

Sebastian immediately dove in and searched for the child. But the water was too murky. The visibility underneath was pitch-black. Still, he blindly searched for the boy until his lungs burned and ached for breath. Desperate for air, he popped up to the water's surface gasping and choking. *Oh God, help me!*

That's when he saw Anna dive into the water. When she resurfaced, she had the child snugly tucked under her arm. As she dragged him to the grassy shore, she placed her mouth over his, breathing air into his lungs.

"Oh, my sweet child," Eliza cried out as she rushed toward the pond's edge and dropped to her knees. "Please, God," she pleaded with her hands formed in prayer. "I beg you. Don't take this precious angel from me."

Tears slipped down Sebastian's cheeks as he watched Eliza beg God for the little boy's life. For *his* life.

As the boy finally gasped for air, Anna wrapped her arms around him, holding on as if she'd never let go.

"Oh, Sebastian..." she whispered against the boy's ear. "My God, you scared me to death. I thought I'd lost you." She peppered kisses to his cheek. "I couldn't bear the thought of losing you, little brother."

Eliza leaned forward and wrapped her arms around Anna and the child. "Thank you, dear Lord."

The child's voice came out raspy, barely above a whisper. "I love you, Sissy. And I love you too... *Mama*."

Sebastian curled his hand into a fist. He'd never wanted to hurt someone as much as he wanted to make Camille and Edward pay. And with his stepfather, rage was a living, breathing fireball inside him. Sebastian was desperate to make him suffer many times over for what he'd done to his life. He took a steadying breath, determined to keep his emotions in check. He had to stay focused and in control for his son Arius. But the fact of the matter was Sebastian was gutted. The reality of it all struck him as surreal. While Sebastian lay unconscious in a hospital bed, orchestrated by Lucifer, his son was in danger. One way or another, he had to find a way out of this nightmarish hell.

* * *

Later in the night, a nightmare from Eve's childhood came to her. And yet the images were fresh and clear as if it had just happened.

Deep within her sleep, she saw a dark, shadowy outline of a man's silhouette standing in the distance of her open bedroom door. As he moved closer, she quickly sat up and immediately recognized his face. When she opened her mouth to scream, her foster father, Ted, gave her a look that told her without words to shut up. She kept silent, every single second agonizing. Her adrenaline shot up, and her heart pounded in her chest. And then she felt a sharp stick in her arm.

She fell back against her pillow. Despite her heightened anxiety, the room was moving in slow motion. She tried to lift her head but couldn't. It felt like it weighed a ton.

As Ted stood looming over her, she could see the bulge in his pants. The bastard was utterly turned on by her drugged and helpless state. "No," she croaked.

When he put his hands on her shoulders, she was taken back to the first time he'd forced her to endure his suffocating weight, the smell of his breath. The horrible pain he'd inflicted on her at the young age of fourteen. She wanted to crawl into a hole and die.

"Please," she rasped out, her eyes begging him for mercy. "Don't do this."

His lips stretched into a thin line and he ignored her pleas. As he grabbed the top of her nightgown, he ripped it open and exposed her breasts. His eyes wandered down her body, staring at her with a sick satisfying gaze. She'd never felt so vulnerable in her life. It took all her effort not to allow him to see the crippling fear that exploded through her body.

Please, God. Help me, she begged silently. I need you, Sebastian.

At that moment, she instantly felt the presence of someone standing behind Ted. She didn't dare look away. She held her breath and kept her focus on him.

Suddenly, a blade appeared from behind. Ted's body stiffened and his eyes widened in surprise when he felt the cold steel against his throat.

When Eve looked up, her eyes became swamped with relief. It was Sebastian.

He bent low, hissing so Ted would be sure to hear. "How's it feel, asshole? To know your life is in someone else's hands... dangling on edge."

Panic entered Ted's eyes when he figured out Sebastian's intentions. "Please," he begged. "Don't kill me."

Sebastian laughed and pressed the blade into his throat until a line of blood appeared.

It was then that Ted broke down, bawling like a pathetic worm. As he babbled and pleaded for his rotten life, Eve felt like the victor, not a helpless victim.

"I've got money," Ted muttered around his sobs. "I'll give you whatever you want. Please, just don't kill me."

Sebastian's lips curled into a snarl. "No amount of money will save your sorry ass."

"Wait!" Ted said in a panic.

Before he could muster out another word, Sebastian slashed his throat, cutting his windpipe. Only the sound of gurgling blood escaped Ted's lips. With a blank stare, his body tilted to one side and crumpled to the floor.

Sebastian let the knife fall from his hand and clatter to the floor. His mission was done. Eve's tortured life was over. Their revenge was complete.

A shiver took over, and she realized it was finally done. Sebastian wrapped a blanket around her shivering body and pulled her up and away from the sight of Ted's dead body.

"It's over, Eve," he whispered close to her ear. "I promise. I'm going to take care of you now."

She clung fiercely to him, never wanting him to let go. She raised her head so she could look him in the eyes. Tears gathered and slipped down her cheeks. Sebastian's love shined from his golden gaze like the warmest light in the darkest corner of hell.

Eve awoke and bolted upright, her hand gripping her chest, her lungs gasping and yet drawing no air.

Gripping her fingers into a blanket that covered her legs, she jerked them up and over her shoulders. As she sought to come back to reality, her breathing echoed and rebounded, the sounds bouncing off the thin walls and multiplying until they seemed like screams.

"Sebastian..."

Chapter Nine

That evening, as night fell, Steven sat on the edge of his bed. His eyes were glued to the bathroom door while he listened to the soft murmur of the radio playing on top of the nightstand. His Adam's apple bobbed up and down as he swallowed. In anticipation, he waited for Abbey to finish showering. God, he loved her. His only priority right now was to keep her safe. He had to pull himself together before he made another mistake. He wouldn't lose her again. Some things were worth fighting for. Abbey Winthrop was one of them.

He felt uncertain as the previous morning came to mind. It was difficult to process the nightmare that was unfolding in front of his eyes. During the meeting with the Breedline council and the Special Ops forces, it seemed Valkin Steele wasn't their only threat. Now, there was something out there killing innocent people, targeting the defenseless. They had a very long road ahead of them. It wouldn't be easy, and it wouldn't be overnight. This mission would require a lot of manpower and strategic planning. They were up against something far greater than anything they'd ever encountered before. The recent deaths in the city had Dr. Autenburg and Dr. Crane's research written all over it. Whatever they'd created, it had a taste for human flesh.

As Steven's mind drifted from the meeting and to the past, he thought about the last time he was with Abbey. And the last time they'd made love. He couldn't get the images out of his head, even after all these years. It played over and over in his mind. He would never forget the softness of her voice, the alluring way she looked at him, and the heavenly scent of her skin.

Then the horrible past he tried so hard to forget, suddenly flashed before him. He rubbed his chest, trying to wipe away the ache. He'd failed to save her as he should have. He could only imagine what she'd been forced to do and experience. The toll it had taken on her was something she might never fully recover from. Dr. Autenburg and Dr. Crane didn't even realize the precious gift they had. They were too busy trying to clone her without even knowing what they were doing. He would never forgive himself. Those memories were as clear as it had been only yesterday. She didn't blame him, but it hurt, nonetheless.

A moment later, he flinched at the sound of an opening door, and his thoughts shifted back to the present. As Abbey stood before him—bare skin, her long damp hair—he blinked in surprise, and for a moment he was lost for words. He struggled with exactly what to say. Her body language appeared as tense as his.

And then fire built in his eyes, sparkling with emerald green. "Abbey,..." he muttered. Her name came out, expelled on a long, soft breath, one that trembled. "You're beautiful."

She moved closer to the bed and extended her arms. "Please..." her voice escaped in an unsteady hiccup. "Hold me."

He quickly shot to his feet and drew her into his arms. She closed her eyes and wilted against him, sagging like a deflated balloon.

Tears pricked his eyelids, and he sucked in a big breath to hold them back. He had to be strong for her. "Everything is going to be okay. I promise I'll never let you go."

She lifted onto her tiptoes and tilted her chin until her mouth was hovering just an inch beneath his. Their breaths were sporadic. Her pulse pounded, and she ached to feel his lips against hers once again.

Encouraged by her warm invitation, he slid his hand behind her neck and cradled her head in his palm just as the song "Certain Things" came on the radio. The lyrics seemed fitting. His heart had ached for so long to have her in his arms once again. Now, the longing rose swift and piercing. When he lowered his mouth to hers, her heart fluttered like the wings of a butterfly.

His kiss was exquisitely tender. His tongue slid seductively over her top, and then the bottom, lip. When he slipped inside, her body shuddered, and their tongues met, tasting each other, exploring.

He drew his lips away and leaned his forehead against hers. "I love you."

She touched his face. "Make love to me."

He captured her hand and brought it to his lips. And then without a saying a word, he slid his arm underneath her legs. He hooked his other arm behind her and lifted her off the floor. He wanted to take his time, lavish her with the attention she deserved. He wanted to touch and taste every single inch of her body. But more than that, he wanted to help her forget all the evil she'd been exposed to.

Her heart melted as he carried her to the bed. She never felt so protected and cherished in her life. When he gently laid her on the mattress, he quickly removed his clothes. Gently, he positioned his body over her soft curves. She shivered, and chill bumps dusted a fine layer over her skin. She opened her legs and arched her body invitingly. With a tortured groan, he ravaged her mouth, leaving her breathless.

As she moaned and twisted restlessly underneath him, he moved his hand down her body and tenderly placed his fingers between her delicate folds. She reacted immediately, arching against his hand. It was almost enough to send her over the edge. "Please, I want to feel you inside me."

When his gaze met hers, his expression shone with love and devotion. For a moment, she lost her sense of time and place. For too long the only things she'd felt were fear and pain. But now he was the anchor to her tortured past, her knight in shining armor. Sudden tears swam in her eyes, and she smiled up at him. She reached up to touch his face, her hand shaking with the force of her love for him.

Finally, in one swift motion, he pushed inside her. She gasped at the sensation of him opening her. It was the most breathtaking, overwhelming feeling. Her body shuddered uncontrollably. She wasn't going to last. It had been too long.

"Come with me," he whispered close to her ear.

His words ignited the fire within her soul. She threw back her head with her eyes squeezed tight and gripped his shoulders, digging her nails into his skin. Their bodies meshed as their hips moved in a steady rhythm.

He buried his face in her neck and murmured, "I love you."

She closed her eyes, and simply let go. She could almost feel her body as if it were floating.

He could tell by the instant tension that rolled through her body that she'd found pleasure.

As he gathered her close, she felt every beat of his heart. She was so overcome with emotion she could barely speak. Then she finally found her voice. "Thank you."

He carefully withdrew from her body and rolled to one side. His eyes were puzzled when he looked at her. "For what, honey?"

"For making me feel safe and loved again."

He leaned in and placed his lips on hers. "I promise I'm going to make sure you always feel that way."

* * *

Humans were like cattle, Apollyon thought as he peered over the heads of a crowded, smoke-filled bar, located on the seedy edge of San Francisco Bay. The Cat Club was your standard-issue dive bar. Sports cars, American sedans, and Harleys were parked outside the lot of a single-story building. From big windows, bright glowing signs flashed "LIVE NUDE DANCERS."

It was like a sumptuous buffet of *Homo sapiens*, ready for the taking. As he explored the center of the club, his sisters cased the outer perimeters like two lionesses stalking their prey.

Callisto used her looks to lure in men. She was beautiful, with delicate small features. Her face was a compilation of perfect angles, and her skin was as smooth and flawless as a pearl. Her eyes were the color of the brightest sunset and her lips plump and soft. And then there was the black hair that flowed in thick waves past her firm hips, and yeah... her legs went on for miles. She had a figure that hypnotized men into full submission, leaving them putty in her hands. She was like the black widow, devouring her victims after mating.

Electra, on the other hand, gave off an entirely different vibe. She was built like a male, intimidating and powerful. She resembled the 1980s six-time Ms. Olympia. Her hair color was identical to Callisto's but in a short, pixie cut. Electra's silver eyes shimmered behind a pair of dark sunglasses, but her vision was crystal clear. In spite of her lethal, muscular body, she attracted men like bees to honey. Instead of using her looks, Electra used her dominant side. Rough sex was in fashion these days, and she had more than enough volunteers begging to be handcuffed and whipped. Born with the ability to surge a powerful electrical current, she tortured her victims with a silver whip. Unlike Callisto, however, she never used men for sex. To her, men were just a delicious piece of meat, something to be eaten, not played with.

As Apollyon wended through the mass of people, a woman grabbed his arm as if the orgasm of her life was about to escape her grasp. He was a sex god, an erotic legend among the other men in the joint. His masculine jaw and rockin' hard body were just the tips of the iceberg. He had the most amazing head of hair. The long, thick, dark waves were outrageously beautiful. And his catlike eyes, that shimmered gold, added to his whole look. He wore lots of leather and entered a room like he owned the whole world. Apollyon was definitely easy on the eyes. There was no doubt about it, but he also had a dangerous aura about him as well. Being possessed by a man like him would be an unforgettable experience. He was the total package of male dominance.

With fast reflexes, Apollyon stopped in his tracks and turned around, his eyes fixed in a narrowed stare at a blonde female all sexed up like the rest of her kind in the bar. As far as he was concerned, she would serve as a tasty appetizer before his main meal.

When the woman stared into his gaze, her instincts knocked around in her chest, sending all kinds of dangerous signals. He looked angry, but... good lord, he was beautiful, oddly reminding her of that famous actor Jason Momoa. In fact, his features were so perfect she had to blink a couple of times. And his body was just as spectacular as his face.

"Hello, handsome," she said in a low, sultry voice. The blonde looked him over, sizing up his clothes, eyeing the shiny ring on his finger that had a weird symbol in the center.

Trina was a regular in the bar, always sniffing around, offering herself for drugs. He had the sense she saw him as someone who paid for sex, and it irritated him.

"Aren't you going to say hello?" Trina asked. Her blue eyes glided over him. And when she reached out to stroke his hair, he quickly grabbed her by the throat.

As she gasped for air, he eased up on his grip but did not let go. Her slender neck was warm, soft, and he could feel blood racing through the veins that came up from her heart. He leaned down and inhaled deeply.

He bristled, the scent of her blood wafted out a potent odor, like chemicals or cleaning products. The woman was obviously a meth-head. He was annoyed now. Anger tightened his hands on her throat. "Go back to the hole you crawled out of," he snarled, baring his teeth.

Her body immediately stiffened, like cement setting. In a panic, and desperate for air, she dug her nails into his skin, trying to break free from his hold.

A demanding voice came from behind, "Let her go, Apollyon. You're going to draw attention."

Trina looked to the left, her eyes pleading. A tall, masculine woman dressed in black leather, with a pixie haircut, stared back.

Apollyon twisted his torso and looked at Electra. His eyes squinted and then focused back on the woman.

"We promised to keep this discreet," Electra said in a hushed voice. A sharp torrent of words followed, spoken in a different language.

Abruptly, Apollyon let the woman go and stepped back. "Consider this your lucky day."

With her hand on her throat, Trina gasped for air and staggered away.

Electra glared at her brother and forced her eyes not to roll. "What the hell were you thinking?" she growled. "We cannot draw attention to ourselves. At least not until we've gathered our strength."

He ignored his sister's warning and walked away.

Electra put her hands on her hips and groaned. Oh, this was great. Her brother's reckless behavior was going to be a problem. The years they'd spent imprisoned in a state of induced sleep—by their father—had sucked out anything even remotely tolerant in Apollyon. He was nothing but an empty vessel trapped in a ravenous body. His curse for bloodlust was out of control and producing risky behavior. If this continued, *he* was going to be a serious problem. All three of them were born a live wire with too much power and a thirst for blood, a defect they could not harness.

When Apollyon stalked toward the main part of the club, he looked over the crowd as couples and trios gyrated on the dance floor. They seemed to mesh as strobe lights bounced off their shadowy faces and bodies. With the beat of a Marilyn Manson song pounding in his ears, the smell of beer and human bodies drifted into his nostrils. In the mix of all the mortals, he sensed something odd. And then he caught an unusual and intoxicating scent. The thick, heady fragrance smelled erotic.

From out of nowhere, a dangerous, greedy lust slapped hold of him and nearly sent him to his knees. With long strides, a leggy female with the face of a Greek goddess walked through the sea of people. God, she was one of a kind and beautiful enough with her red hair and those jade-green eyes. His body needed to feed. As she moved closer, he could feel the hunger in him rising.

When the redhead noticed him, she froze, feeling like she'd seen him somewhere before. There was something about him, almost animalistic. Something dark and lethal seethed behind his spectacular looks. He gave off the vibe like he could wipe out everyone in the place with his bare hands.

She was the one he wanted tonight. As Apollyon crooked his finger at the female, she came when called. He liked that in a human.

As the redhead moved toward him, she got a load of Apollyon's ensemble: a black, Valentino silk long-sleeve that was tucked into black leathers. The black boots topped him out at six-five or so. In the gothic getup, he was drop-dead gorgeous. Standing before him, the shaking started in her knees and worked its way up into the muscles of her thighs. When it hit between her legs, she felt her core tingle with a needy sensation.

Apollyon leaned down and offered his hand. "Come with me."

Chapter Ten

As Helen escorted Anna to the intensive care unit, three guards stood outside Sebastian's room. Their attention instantly alerted as Helen and Anna walked up.

"This is Miss Anna Saeni," Helen told them. "She's Sebastian's sister. She has my permission to visit him for a short while."

When the guards nodded, Helen opened the door that led to Sebastian's room.

"I'll be right outside if you need me," Helen said softly. "Remember, Anna, just for a few minutes."

"Thank you, Helen."

Anna took a deep breath as she stepped inside. And then she looked across the room at her brother. He was no longer the child she remembered. Sebastian was a grown man. She closed her eyes for a moment, but the darkness terrified her. Throwing her lids open, she clung to the sight of her brother... and hated the blank expression on his handsome, pale face. He lay there silently, so still and lifeless. For several moments, she stood there staring at him, unsure of what to do next.

As she surged forward, she became aware of a subtle beeping coming from a machine. It was hooked up to a ventilator that was breathing air into and out of his lungs. Looking down at his hand, she wondered if it felt cold. Her hands twisted nervously in front of her, building up the courage to touch him. She felt a surge of guilt thinking back on the years she'd missed as Sebastian grew up. After she was abruptly taken from his life and forced into the monastic lifestyle, she'd lost all hope that she would get the chance to reunite with her little brother. Now, she was finally free. She had so many questions to ask him, more than her tired mind could even process. Would he remember her after all these years? The reality of how much time had passed weighed on her. And then she reached out with a trembling hand and placed it over his.

She wanted to scream out. Fall down weeping. Hug him. Desperate for some reaction, she muttered in a tear-laced voice, "Oh, Sebastian. It's Anna... your *Sissy*."

As he lay stiff and unconscious, he could hear a voice from his past. The sound was timid and soft. *But... how can this be? Anna?*

Immediately, her expression gentled as she reached forward to brush his cheek. When she felt something wet, she froze and stared down into his face. His brows were drawn together as if he'd heard her. And then she lifted her forefinger. On the pad, a single teardrop glistened. She blinked in surprise. "You remember..." Her lips trembled upward into a smile.

She squeezed his hand, curling her fingers tightly around his. "I'm here for you, little brother. Please... come back."

* * *

Around two in the morning, Detective Manuel Sanchez arrived on the scene of a reported homicide. He'd gotten a call from dispatch reporting a body found in a dumpster off Fifth Street, two blocks over from a dive-bar in the San Francisco Bay area. It had been a Caucasian female in her mid-to-late twenties. She'd been found with her throat ripped out and her body completely drained of blood.

As Manuel parked parallel to the brick wall of the alley, he noticed several squad cars were already on location. When he stepped out of his vehicle, he nodded at the grim-looking officers.

"Morning," he grumbled.

"Hey, Detective."

Manuel glanced over his shoulder at his partner. "Has the medical examiner arrived yet?"

"No," Frank said. "We're still waiting for her to arrive."

"Do we have a positive ID on the victim?"

Frank nodded. "Her purse was found underneath the dumpster. Sylvia Bennett. Age twenty-six. She's a stylist at a place called Hair Candy. Miss Bennett lives in the Brownstone

Apartments a couple of blocks from here. She must have been on her way home."

"Where's her vehicle?"

"There was nothing located in the vicinity. According to motor vehicle registration, Miss Bennett doesn't own a car."

"All right," Manuel said, letting out a deep breath. "Let's take a look."

He ducked under the yellow tape and walked over to the dumpster. As he rose onto the balls of his feet, he peered over the rusted lip of the bin. The first thing he saw was red hair.

Oh, God, he thought as the past slammed into him like a ton of bricks. The color of her hair brought back haunted memories of his sister, Lailah. Swallowing hard, he shook it off, shifting back to reality.

Lying in a heap of newspapers and various items of discarded trash, the female was naked, and her pale skin glimmered in the dawn's diffuse light. There was suffering etched into the soft, pale planes of her lovely face. *What happened to her? Why would someone hurt such a beautiful young woman?* As he stared at Sylvia's corpse, he memorized everything about her from the pink polish on her fingernails to the freckles on her arms and legs.

"Christ," he muttered as he stood over yet another dead body, wondering who or *what* could have done this. And why were all the victims drained of their blood?

He took a flashlight out of his coat pocket and cursed under his breath when he aimed it at the body. The injury to her throat didn't stop there. She had bite marks on her thighs and on the insides of her wrists.

"What do we have, Detective?"

Manuel stepped back and handed his partner the flashlight so he could have a look. As the guy was taller by nearly four inches, he didn't have to arch up to see in. In silence, Frank just stared, his dark brown eyes unfazed.

"This has the same MO as all the homeless victims that were found dead," Frank said. "Although Miss Bennett wasn't homeless."

Manuel nodded. "This makes forty-four victims in the past two weeks. And all victims were reported completely drained. Some of them were partially eaten."

Frank cocked a brow. "It sounds like we've got a vampire loose in the city."

As Manuel turned away, he clapped his partner on the shoulder. "Sure." He smirked. "If you're the type of person who believes in that kind of stuff."

At that moment, the medical examiner arrived.

"Come on, partner," Manuel said. "Let's take a closer look around and let her do her job."

It took about an hour for the detectives to nose around and learn absolutely nothing material. There were no security cameras on the outside of the nearby buildings and no witnesses, but hopefully, the crime scene investigators would come up with something useful.

Finally, the coroner finished her thing, and the body was cleared for removal. Before she left, she gave Manuel the victim's time of death. Sylvia had died less than two hours ago.

Manuel put his hands on his hips and refocused. And then something popped into his head. *The Cat Club.*

As Frank turned away and headed for his vehicle, Manuel called out, "Hey, wait up."

Frank stopped and turned around. "'Sup, Detective?"

"Meet me at the Cat Club. I've got a gut feeling about something."

"You think Miss Bennett came from that place?"

"Maybe." Manuel shrugged. "It's worth checking out."

Frank waved. "I'll meet you there."

* * *

Abbey dozed lightly, feeling cherished in Steven's arms. After their lovemaking, she was weak and drained of energy, but in a good way.

When she felt him stir, she lifted her head to see that he was awake and staring down at her. "You're awake," she whispered.

He cocked his head to the side. "I can't bear to shut my eyes."

"Why?"

He slid his hand over her face and cupped her cheek. "I'm afraid if I do, I'll wake up, and all this will be just a dream."

His words sank in and she went silent. She had no idea what to say to that. She smiled and touched her finger to his lips. "I promise I'm not going anywhere, Steven."

"You have to know what my life's been like without you," he said, "not knowing if you were all right or even alive. I hate myself for not saving you. I failed you."

Her mouth turned down. "No. It wasn't your fault. You've never failed me."

"It frustrated me that I couldn't find you, Abbey." He kissed her, leaving his lips pressed against hers for an extended moment. "I promised your father I would keep you safe. The not knowing was an everyday battle."

The implication of what he said hit her hard. Her brows went up. "You can't hold yourself responsible for the choices I made. Besides, it doesn't matter now. We're together."

She rested her chin on his shoulder and sighed. She changed the subject. "I want to know more about your mother. Tell me about her. What was she like?"

"She was beautiful. Like an angel. My mother died saving someone that didn't deserve to live. And I feel responsible. I should have tried harder to save her, but I didn't."

She winced at the self-condemnation in his voice. "Steven, you would have died trying. You know you can't heal a fatal wound."

"Can't I?"

"What do you mean by that?"

"The reason Valkin Steele is tracking you is to get to me. Why would he believe I could heal his loved one?" He clenched his brows. "Dr. Autenburg must have told him I had that kind of power. It doesn't make any sense. Why would he make something up like that? It has to be true."

She caught her breath and went still against him. "Please don't beat yourself up over this."

"You have to know, Abbey, I'll never let what happened to my mother happen to you."

She didn't argue. There was a lot she could say, but in the end, it wouldn't change his mind. And he didn't need the extra worry. Some things just had to be left alone.

"I saw my mother."

He stared at her in utter bewilderment. "But... how?"

"I don't expect you to understand it," she said. "I don't even understand it myself. But she came to me in a dream. I can still hear her voice. I could feel the warmth when she hugged me. She told me she would always love me. Getting to see my mother finally gave me peace. It was like a miracle."

He rubbed his thumb over her bottom lip and then leaned forward to kiss it. "I believe in miracles. I keep thinking that none of this is real, that you're just a figment of my imagination. Stuff like this just doesn't happen. You're my miracle." His eyes welled up. "I love you, you know."

Relief flooded her heart. "Yes, I do know." She smiled and wrapped her arms around his neck. "Thank you for believing me. I love you too."

Chapter Eleven

Roman Kincaid never knew anyone was in the hotel room until he felt the cold steel against his throat. He went utterly still, not wanting to do anything to make the blade slice into his flesh. He was calm enough not to shake, but that didn't mean his heart wasn't about to explode from his chest.

"What do you want?" Roman demanded in a gritty but steady voice.

"I need information on a particular Adalwolf," the man murmured behind his ear. "And I understand you have a connection with the Breedline Covenant."

"Who?" The knife bit farther into his neck, and he gritted his teeth against the burn.

"Don't play games with me. You know who I'm looking for. I know the Breedline are keeping the Adalwolf in their Covenant. I want their location."

Roman's lip curled in anger, but he held his tongue. Pissing off this guy would only get his throat cut.

And suddenly, the knife was gone, and Roman suddenly felt the end of a pistol dig into the back of his head.

"Get up," the man growled. "And turn around. *Slowly.* If you try anything stupid, my brother will blow your buddy here..." He paused. "Hey, Joey, what's his name?"

"Lawrence," a voice called out from the doorway.

"Like I said," the man continued to threaten Roman, "my brother will blow Lawrence's brains out with a single silver bullet."

Roman closed his eyes, knowing there was no way out of this. He could take the risk and fight back. Silver didn't affect him, but it would kill Lawrence. He couldn't gamble with his buddy's life.

He slowly rose with his hands up. Before he could turn around, a firm hand gripped his shoulder and roughly shoved him. He stumbled and quickly steadied his feet. As he turned around and looked up, he recognized the man that held a gun to his face. It was Gordon Bates. He was a tracker, obviously hired by Valkin Steele.

Roman's pulse accelerated and his gut twisted. He dreamed of having Steele at his mercy. He'd conjured up some harsh images of all the ways the bastard would die a long painful death.

"Hands where I can see them," Gordon barked. "If you as much move a finger, your buddy Lawrence is a dead man."

In his periphery, he saw Lawrence, a gun aimed at his forehead. Lawrence was a big man. A true warrior. Trained by the best. But right now, they were both as helpless as a newborn babe.

"We're not giving you the location," Lawrence blurted. "You'll just have to kill us."

"Is this how you want it to go down?" Gordon asked Roman. "Are you willing to let your buddy take a bullet?" He leaned in close to Roman and looked him square in the eyes. "It's all up to you."

"Fuck you," Lawrence snarled. "Roman, don't you do it, do you hear me? Don't tell him a damn thing."

Gordon's jaw tightened. "We've been looking for that she-wolf for years. The one that murdered Dr. Autenburg. And now she's led us straight to the Adalwolf," he seethed, relishing the savage glint in Roman's eyes. "Mr. Steele will be pleased when I deliver the Adalwolf to him. He'll finally give me the respect I deserve and realize he didn't need Cole Decker after all."

Gordon got his attention. The name Cole Decker made the hair on his neck stand on end. Then he quickly glanced at Lawrence, who had the same recognition in his eyes.

Cole Decker was known as one of the best trackers money could buy and had a warrant for trafficking young girls to Europe. Decker was also listed as a sex offender. He liked them young, preferably in the range of twelve to sixteen. The sick bastard had been in hiding for years. Above all things, Roman had a soft spot for children. Not only was he vowing to take down Steele, but Cole Decker was also now on his list.

He focused intently on Gordon. Curling his lip in disgust, his agitation level was off the charts. He had an objective, and he was single-minded in his determination to kill these two bastards and keep Lawrence from getting killed in the process.

"Well, I'm waiting for an answer, Kincaid," Gordon said, a clear smirk in his voice. "I'm running out of patience."

Go to hell, Roman thought bitterly. A righteous fury rose inside him like a gathering storm. An angry heart pumped the Adalwolf blood through his body, infusing him with strength worthy of ten Breedline. With an unexpected burst of power, he drove Gordon backward with a hard, thrusting kick.

Gordon reeled, his eyes wild, astonished by Roman's sudden attack. It all seemed to happen in slow motion. As Gordon hit the floor, his pistol fell from his grip and clattered to the floor.

Roman no longer looked human. His eyes were two shimmering diamonds. His skin shone smoky gray as he expanded twice his size, shredding his clothes into pieces. Powerful muscles bulged atop his bare chest and claws jutted from his hands and feet.

Gordon gasped with his mouth gaped wide. "Son of a bitch! He's an Adalwolf!"

Then, without warning, several pops followed, the unmistakable sound of a silencer. Pain sliced through Roman's back and into his chest. His knees buckled, and he pitched forward, agony tearing through his body.

A furious roar shattered the moment. The guy who'd fired his weapon at him staggered backward as Lawrence—now in his Breedline form—lunged forward, his jaws snapping like a rabid dog. Instinct had taken over. A blood-red haze descended over Lawrence's vision as he raked his claws across the enemy's neck, digging deep gouges in his flesh.

Blood spouted like a fountain. The man clutched at his mangled throat, but there was no recovering from such a wound. Not any human, for that matter. He tried to scream out, but all that emerged from his gaping mouth was a wet gurgle. His limbs twitched convulsively as he drowned in his own blood. Finally, he fell still and silent.

"No!" An anguished cry erupted from Gordon's throat. The sight of his brother's death threw him into a murderous rage. He reached for the gun and sprang to his feet like a demon freshly released from hell. As Gordon aimed toward Lawrence, a hand closed on his throat, seemingly appearing out of nowhere. He gasped for breath as Roman squeezed, drawing blood with his claws.

Gordon stared at him with absolute shock, his dark eyes filling with blood as the bones in his neck cracked and popped. As Roman felt Gordon's human life ebbing away, he released his grip. Gordon's limp and lifeless body toppled to the floor.

Roman felt the warm, sticky sensation of blood. He looked down to see his chest was covered with his blood and Gordon's. After a moment of silence, he turned toward Lawrence, who was back to his human form, his expression hard and cold. Roman could get a chill just from looking at the guy.

"Are you okay?" Lawrence asked in a deep baritone.

"Yeah," Roman said. He scrubbed his hands over his bare chest, but all he did was smear more of the blood on his hands.

Lawrence grabbed his pants from the floor and snorted in disgust. His clothes were shredded. Then he looked up and met Roman's gaze. "Remind me to thank your mom for marrying an Adalwolf." He released a heavy sigh. "You saved my ass. Thanks, Roman."

"You're welcome." Roman's voice was distorted as his transformation began to take place. "You would have done the same for me. We've got to warn the others."

* * *

As Bull, Justice, and Lena roared up to the hotel, they noticed a suspicious vehicle parked by Roman and Lawrence's SUV. They got out, guns drawn, then Lena discarded everything she knew about caution and ran.

Ignoring the angry shouts from Justice and her brother to wait until they cleared the area, Lena burst through the hotel door. Nothing could have prepared her for the sight of Roman and Lawrence completely naked, covered in blood. And on the floor were two men she didn't recognize, seemingly dead.

Roman's gaze lifted to hers, and then he quickly used his hands to cover his privates.

Lawrence reached for his torn shirt and placed it around his waist.

"Holy shit," Justice said as he caught up to Lena and saw the gory scene inside the hotel.

"What the hell is wrong with you, Lena?" Bull called out as he shoved inside. Then he looked past his sister and focused on Lawrence and Roman. "What the hell happened here?"

"Nice timing, guys," Lawrence said lightly.

Bull stepped inside and closed the door behind him. "I take it this is Valkin Steele's doing?"

"Yeah," Roman replied. "We need to warn the Breedline Covenant. Steele knows they are keeping Steven there."

"Shit!" Justice said. "How in the hell did he find out?"

"They're trackers," Lawrence told him. "One of them is Gordon Bates. Before we took them out, he mentioned Steele hired Cole Decker."

"Son of a bitch," Lena said under her breath. "If Decker is involved, we can't afford to waste any more time. While you two warn the Covenant and get cleaned up, we'll take care of the mess here. As soon as we're done, we'll head that way and meet you there."

Roman nodded. "Thanks, Lena."

* * *

As Helen stood outside Sebastian's room, her hands fidgeted with the lapels of her white coat, then the stethoscope in her pocket. She took a deep breath and lightly tapped on the door before she peeked inside. "Anna?"

Helen's voice echoed into the room, but Anna felt as if the physician was miles away. In fact, the whole world was somewhere else. Nothing existed except for her brother lying in the hospital bed.

She finally glanced over her shoulder at Helen. "Thank you for giving me this time with my brother."

When Helen stepped inside, she moved next to her. "Please, call me Helen." She placed her hand on Anna's shoulder. "I promise we'll do everything we can for him."

"I don't understand," Anna said, keeping her eyes locked on Helen. "Why isn't he healing?"

93

Helen shook her head. "I wish I had the answer to that. There's no medical reason why Sebastian is not healing. Not only have I administered Eve's blood, but I've also donated mine. Considering his species, my Breedline blood alone should have healed him. He shouldn't be in a coma. It's almost as if he doesn't want to wake up, or someone is keeping..."

Anna stared at her confused. "Please, Helen, what were you going to say? Is there something you're not telling me?"

Helen's lips formed a thin line. "I just spoke with Tim Ross. He is the Breedline Covenant council head. He told me something that didn't make any sense, but I guess it could be possible."

"Please," Anna pleaded, "tell me."

"Sebastian's bonded mate, Eve, was at the institution when this happened. She said something or someone was in his room with your brother, but it wasn't visible to the human eye. She stated that before Sebastian went unconscious, he told her something. It was about their son Arius. Sebastian warned her not to let Lucifer have Arius."

"Lucifer..." Anna's eyes widened. "Are you actually talking about... *Satan*?"

"Yes."

"Would it be possible for me to meet Eve?"

Helen nodded. "Of course. I've already spoken to Tim. He knows about your situation, and he's invited you to stay at the Covenant. You can meet Eve and your nephews."

"Thank you. I can't thank you enough for all your kindness."

"You're welcome."

Chapter Twelve

It was two in the morning when Tim received a call from Roman. Quietly, he slipped out of bed and got dressed.

When he reached for the door, a sleepy voice said, "Where are you going at this hour?"

He turned around and walked back to the bed. When he perched on the edge of the mattress, he leaned over and pressed his lips to Angel's forehead.

"I'm sorry I woke you," he whispered. "I got a call from Roman. He's on his way. I'm meeting him downstairs."

Her eyes widened. "What's going on?"

"Don't worry about it, honey. I'll take care of this. Go back to sleep."

Angel scooted higher on the bed. She tucked her knees against her body and wrapped her arms around her legs. "Please, tell me what's going on. I have the right to know if our family is in danger."

When he turned on the bedside lamp, his heart lurched at the uncertainty written on her face.

"Honey, I don't want you to worry. I promise it's nothing we can't handle."

He cupped her chin and stared into her eyes, wanting her to know how serious he was.

"I swear on my life..." He kept his voice low. "...I will keep this family safe."

Then he carefully unwrapped her arms from her legs and pulled her forward until she was in his lap.

She emitted a soft gasp and then melted into his embrace, her body going slack against his. He could feel her heartbeat against his chest.

"Trust me on this."

She released a sigh and then lifted her mouth to his and kissed him. "I do." She swallowed visibly, staring at him in almost helpless fashion. "I trust you."

"Thanks for your trust, sweetheart. I'll check on Natalie before I head downstairs."

"I love you," she said.

"I love you too."

As he walked reluctantly through the door, closing it quietly behind him, he walked to the next room to check on their daughter before he went downstairs.

When he looked in on her sleeping soundly, he was taken with the image of his daughter and the cat snuggled up together. Her arm was tucked around the feline as if she was cuddling a stuffed teddy bear.

He stood in the doorway, watching them a moment longer, taking pride in the sight of his little girl. As the cat's head popped up, peering out of a pair glowing green eyes, he acknowledged Tim's presence with a soft *meow*.

Leaving the door slightly open, he headed for the stairs just as Jace and Tessa came out of their room, each holding on to one of the twins.

Jace frowned. "Tim, what are you doing up so early?"

Tim gave a panicked, deer-in-the-headlights look as he glanced over his shoulder. His expression was troubled, which immediately put Jace—and Tessa—on guard. Tessa looked intently at him, her gaze probing, and said, "Is something wrong?"

"Hey, little guys," Tim said, avoiding Tessa's question. He walked over with his focus on the twins. It took every bit of his control to keep his expression impassive. "I swear they get bigger every time I see them."

Tessa rolled her eyes at Jace. "That's because they've clearly inherited their father's appetite."

"What's wrong with that?" Jace grimaced. "They're growing boys."

Tim reached for the baby, deftly taking him from Tessa's arms. He looked at the baby and his expression lightened. Yeah, Tim was a sucker for kids. "Hello there, little Jax," he said. "Are you keeping your mommy and daddy up?"

Jax offered a tentative smile, then glanced over at Tessa. He yawned broadly and burrowed his head against Tim's neck. Tim shifted the toddler in his arms so he could hold him more securely and returned his attention to Tessa and Jace.

"It's two o'clock in the morning." Tessa said. "We're up because of the twins, but why are you up so early?"

96

"I didn't want to wake anyone," he replied. "Not yet anyway. Not until I got more information."

Tessa immediately came to attention, and so did Jace.

"What's going on?" Jace asked with an anxious note to his voice.

Tim sighed. "I just got a call from Roman. He's on his way. Two guys ambushed him and Lawrence at their hotel."

"Oh no!" Tessa gasped. "Are they all right?"

"Yes, they're fine. Roman told me he recognized one of the men. His name is Gordon Bates. He's a tracker, hired by Valkin Steele. He threatened to kill Lawrence if Roman didn't give him our location. Steele knows we're keeping Steven here in the Covenant."

Jace snorted his displeasure. *Fuck.* This was not what he wanted to hear. "Please tell me Roman didn't give up our location."

"No, he didn't tell them anything."

"What happened..." Tessa hesitated for a moment. "...to those men?"

"They're dead. Roman and Lawrence took care of them."

Tessa nodded in silence.

"When Steele finds out his men are missing, it won't be long before he sends another tracker," Jace pointed out.

"Yeah." Tim nodded. "Roman said something about that. He mentioned the name Cole Decker."

"Who is this Cole guy?" Tessa asked.

"He's a hired tracker," Tim said. "One of the best. And he's also wanted by the FBI."

"For what?"

"For trafficking young girls," Jace said. "I saw it on the news a year ago."

Tessa's disgusted expression was instantaneous. "What are we going to do?"

"Let's wait for Roman and Lawrence to arrive," Tim said. "After we get more details, we'll get everyone updated. From there, we'll figure the rest out."

It wasn't long after they descended the stairs when Tim knew the moment Roman and Lawrence entered the main gate of the Covenant. An alert was triggered, and the video monitors by the front entrance zoomed in on the vehicle, getting a close-up of the driver and confirming Roman's identity.

A few moments later, the front door buzzed.

"There you go, little buddy," Tim said, placing Jax back in Tessa's arms.

When Tim moved to the door, Tessa looked at Jace. "Honey, can you take the twins upstairs to the nursery and put them to bed? I don't want them to be around all this."

Jace turned on a bright smile for little Jem and Jax. "How about we go upstairs so Daddy can read you a bedtime story."

Jax's eyes brightened, and little Jem clapped his hands.

Tessa slid Jax into Jace's free arm. "Do you need any help carrying them upstairs?"

"Nope, I got 'em." Jace grunted as he held on to the boys securely. And then he leaned forward and kissed Tessa. "Love you, honey. I'll be back as soon as I put them down for the night."

"Thank you. I love you too." Tessa blew kisses at the boys. "Go night-night with Daddy."

* * *

Abbey's dreams were tormented with countless flashes of her painful past. They streamed together in one unending horrific nightmare.

The chains were around her ankles and wrists again, but instead of Steven freeing her from the agonizing confinement, Dr. Hans Autenburg had been standing there, his gaze seething.

"You vill turn into your Lupa, Fräulein Abigail," Dr. Autenburg ordered in his heavy German accent.

Dread filled her stomach and rose to her throat, tightening until it was hard to breathe. No matter what they did to her, she wouldn't let them break her. She'd promised her father.

She looked at the physician with a hateful glare, her heart damn near pounding out of her chest. "Go to hell. I will never give you what you want."

He gave her a short nod. "Is zat zo?"

Next, he turned to one of his men and uttered a guttural command she didn't understand. When two guards stepped out of the room, he said, "I have got something zat vill change your mind."

She gasped when the guards came back with Steven. He was dragged through the doorway and shoved forward. To her horror, a guard drew a metal stick and rammed it into Steven's stomach. He immediately grunted and doubled over.

"No!" Abbey screamed. "Please don't hurt him!"

Another guard cracked a wooden club over Steven's back, dropping him to the ground.

She pulled against her restraints, trying to get to him, to somehow protect him from the attack.

"Get up," one of the guards said. When Steven didn't immediately comply, the other guard wrapped his hand in Abbey's hair and yanked her head sideways. Steven shot to his feet when he heard her scream.

Even though Dr. Autenburg's men had drugged him, his blurry vision caught sight of her. "Don't hurt her," he pleaded. "Please. I'll do anything you ask."

The guard standing above him slammed his blunt weapon viciously into Steven's back again. He went down on one knee.

"Stop it!" Abbey screamed.

As Steven staggered back up, he looked Dr. Autenburg square in the eyes. "I'll give you anything you want. Just don't hurt her."

"It's not vat I vant from you," Dr. Autenburg said through gritted teeth. "She has vat I vant. I vant zee she-volf!"

Abbey bit back her lip to keep from screaming out. Steven couldn't fight back, and the bastards were taking full advantage.

"If she doesn't give me vat I vant, I vill let my guards haf zeir vay with her vile you vatch," the sinister physician threatened, pinning Steven with a baleful stare. "You have five minutes to convince her."

"What?" Steven gasped. "No! Please don't do this!"

Dr. Autenburg pointed at her and commanded something to the guards in German.

The guards unchained her wrists and ankles. She struggled as they dragged her to a ratty mattress in the corner of the room, covered in what looked to be an old bloodstain.

Fear and panic crowded her mind until she wanted to scream them away. She had no other choice but to shift into her she-wolf before she would let them take what she wasn't willing to give.

As she looked to Steven for support, his panicked expression made her uneasy. Nothing in her experience had prepared her for a moment like this. Tearing her gaze away from him, she took one last look at Dr. Autenburg with hatred smoldering in her eyes. Although it galled her very soul to admit it, she realized that this was a fight she could not win without shifting.

When the guards shoved her to the dirty mattress, they gazed down at her like two predators. While one bound her hands, the other was upon her in an instant, pinning her down with his heavy body.

She struggled to break free, but the guard's powerful grip was too firm against her petite frame. Steven stood in nearby, screaming her name.

His chest began to expand, the muscles bulging with superhuman power. His skin took on a shimmery, iridescent hue. A mane of coarse brown hair framed his subhuman features, which were more human than a Breedline's but still unmistakably feral. Sharp claws jutted from his hands and feet, shredding his clothes and shoes until they fell away from his Adalwolf transformation.

Dr. Autenburg was thrown back as Steven slammed into him with bone-jarring force. The sudden impact left him dazed, but at the last minute, Dr. Autenburg reached inside the pocket of his white coat. When he brought his hand out, a vengeful grin stretched across his face as he aimed a tranquilizer gun at Steven.

Steven howled in agony as the drug surged throughout his body. Before he lost consciousness, he dropped to his knees, reaching out to Abbey.

Her gaze fell upon Steven, his body was limp and still. His agonized groans had fallen silent, and his eyes had closed.

"No!" she yelled out in anger, an emotion she knew would unleash the she-wolf she'd locked away and hidden deep inside. An uncontrollable rage suffused every cell in her body.

The two guards ripping at her clothes provoked her even more. She opened her mouth to scream in defiance and was startled to feel bone and muscle shifting beneath her skin. Every hair on her body bristled and began to grow. Her fingers and toes curled into claws.

She threw back her head in pain as her spine stretched and bones were forced into a new shape against their natural origins.

"She's shifting!" a guard yelled. Before he could blink, a shaggy arm swiped at him, the blow slicing through his gut, spilling his entrails out onto the floor.

As the remaining guard ran toward the door, it slammed in his face and locked from the outside.

He pounded on the thick metal door and begged Dr. Autenburg for mercy.

Abruptly, Abbey's eyes snapped open. Coal-black orbs stared into the darkness with feral rage. As her jaws stretched wide, she released a ferocious roar.

The unearthly sound startled Steven from a deep slumber. Taken aback, he stumbled out of bed as her she-wolf lunged at him.

"It's me, Abbey. It's Steven. Remember?"

Her crazed Lupa drove him across the room into the wall. The towering creature drew back her lips, exposing her sharp canines.

Regaining his composure, he knew nonetheless that his life was in danger. But hopefully, after all this time, their bond would remain strong and she would recognize him.

"Please, Abbey," he pleaded, staring into her soulless eyes. "I would never do anything to harm you. I love you."

The she-wolf's eyes narrowed as she studied his face. And then an unexpected sound caught her attention. She snarled and swiveled her head toward the door, seemingly irritated by the unfamiliar voice. But Steven recognized it. *Shit!* It was Jace.

Chapter Thirteen

While Sebastian's body lay unconscious, his mind was somewhere else. After so many years of putting his painful childhood in the past, the memories burned bright in his mind once again. And the horror had yet to come.

Standing inside a tiny bedroom, his heart softened when he saw Anna sitting next to the little boy. She smoothed her hand over his arm. The boy looked frail and weak as if he was malnourished.

"Sebastian,... can you wake up for me?" Anna lightly shook the boy. "I brought you a surprise."

He opened his sleepy eyes. "I had a bad dream, Sissy."

She bent down to kiss his forehead and stroked a hand through his tousled hair. "You're okay, Sebastian. It was just a dream."

"He hurt you."

She froze, and her face paled. "Who?"

"Mr. Montgomery. He made you cry."

She reached for his hand and curled her fingers around his palm. "Listen to me, Sebastian. Everything is fine. No one is going to hurt me. Okay?"

His bottom lip quivered. "Promise?"

She nodded and kissed him on the cheek. "If I promise, will you eat something? Mama made your favorite."

His eyes widened with excitement. "Is it grilled cheeses?"

She gave him an indulgent smile and reached toward the nightstand. When she brought her hand back, she held a small plate. "I cut it down the middle the way you like it."

He smiled. "'K."

When Anna placed it on his lap, he scooted higher against his pillow and looked eagerly at the sandwich.

She held up a small tube filled with red liquid. "Before you eat, you'll need to take your medicine."

He opened his mouth like a baby bird begging for a worm. When Anna put the tube to his lips, he swallowed the contents quickly, savoring the last drop.

"I know it's not much," she said, "but that's all Mrs. Montgomery would allow you to have today." Her tone changed, sounding hopeful. "Maybe next time there will be more."

The boy's pale cheeks appeared slightly rosy as if a small bit of life had been poured into him.

Sebastian stood back and watched like a ghost in the room. The pieces started to fall into place. It created a hideous picture in his mind. A chill ran down his spine as the full implications of his memories sank in. Unbidden, the buried past came rushing through his brain, the reason behind his childhood sickness. His real mother and his stepfather had starved him as a child. Since he'd been born a half-breed, he needed blood from a Breedline to survive. As he grew up, the Montgomerys would only allow him small amounts, barely enough to keep his heart beating.

Anna ruffled the boy's hair affectionately. "Eat your sandwich, little brother."

He looked delighted, eating as fast as he could get each bite into his mouth. He smacked his lips appreciatively when the last morsel was gone.

"That was good, Sissy."

Her heart lurched, and a knot formed in her throat. Tears clogged her eyes, and she looked away so he wouldn't see.

"Don't cry, Sissy," the boy pleaded. "It'll be okay."

She wiped her eyes and turned toward him with a smile.

She placed the empty plate back on the nightstand and switched off the light. When she climbed in the bed beside her little brother, he promptly snuggled into her arms. It felt good to have him cuddled next to her... in a safe place with no fear of Mr. Montgomery.

"G'night, Sissy," he said sleepily. "Love you."

"Love you too, Sebastian. Now get some rest."

* * *

Sam Malone, a bouncer at the Cat Club, had a single-minded mission as he headed toward the back in search of the manager, Zeke Rizzo.

He lightly tapped on Zeke's door. "Boss..."

"Yeah, what is it?"

"Two human detectives are here to see you."

Five seconds later, the door sprang open. A tall, muscular, tattooed man with clenched brows said, "What the hell do they want?"

"They're from homicide." Sam handed him a card. "They want to ask you some questions about a girl they found in a dumpster two blocks from here."

"So..." Zeke shrugged, looking at the name on the business card. "What the hell does that have to do with my bar?"

"They want to look at our video footage to see if she was at the club tonight."

Zeke checked his watch. "It's an hour to closing time." He let out a deep breath. "Park them in my office. I'll be back in five."

"Roger that, boss."

As the door shut, Zeke crushed the card in his hand and moved through the crowded club. He was irritated, not caring when he elbowed a couple of losers, obviously drunk by the way they staggered in front of him. He wished one would complain so he could toss them out on their ass.

He was a Breedline, born with a special gift. Anyway, that's what his mother had told him when he was a child. To him, it was a curse. He had the power to see inside the mind of another person and experience their worst memory. The problem was, he couldn't control it. It happened when he made physical contact. A simple handshake seemed like nothing to an ordinary person, but to him, it was unbearable. And that was not the worst of it. If anyone angered him, an unfortunate accident would fall upon them. Without the ability to stop it, he was the worst case of karma. Depending on how angry he got, sometimes death was the outcome. Zeke was a *sin-eater*.

He'd put Yelena Smirnov—a succubus from Russia—in charge of his security. Her private office was upstairs. As he got to the top, he knocked on her door. He wasn't surprised at the tense tone of her Russian voice. "It's open, Zeke."

When he pushed his way into a dark room the size of a walk-in closet, Yelena was perched up against a desk, staring at a monitor. She pivoted in her chair and shot him a look. And then she said, "Is there something you need, boss?"

Her emotional grid had the same footprint his did: a castaway, a loner, one who had been expelled from others because they were different. Yelena knew firsthand what it was like not to want to be the person you were born as. But you couldn't change the cards you were dealt.

Funny... most of the time he didn't give a shit about what he was. His life had been a constant shifting mirage of lies and deceptions, and that was that. Around Yelena, though? He felt normal. She knew he was a sin-eater and accepted him for what he was.

Yelena was naturally lovely, with flawless skin and long blonde hair that hung in thick waves. Her long, lean limbs seemed to go on forever. Her lips were enticing, plump and pink. And her captivating eyes were luminescent because they were gold and red mixed together. She was almost too attractive and tempting for him to resist.

His mouth finally opened. "I need the security footage for tonight."

There was a long moment during which the two of them were bound together by invisible strings of heat and longing. Then Yelena let out a sigh. "What for?"

"I've got two human detectives poking around. Some girl was murdered two blocks from here. I guess they want to see if she was at the club tonight."

She nodded. "Okay. Just give me a few seconds."

Moments later, she shifted her chair around and moved to her feet. When she extended her hand, she held something small in her palm.

"I downloaded tonight's footage on a thumb drive." Her Russian accent created goosebumps over his skin. "You should be able to view it from your computer. Maybe there's something on it that will help find whoever killed that girl."

He reached for the thumb drive. "Thank you, Yelena."

"Anytime... Zeke."

He kept his gaze on hers for an extended time before he finally turned and headed toward the door. As he reached for the knob, she said, "Zeke..."

His heart stopped and then roared at the sound of her voice. He quickly pivoted around.

"Let me know if there's anything else I can do to help."

He nodded. "I'll see you later."

He scanned the people in the club's VIP section as he walked past the tables before he headed back to his office to meet up with the detectives. Since Sam was playing babysitter to San Francisco's finest, another bouncer named Deacon O'Malley took his place. He'd originated from the metropolitan area and spoke like a true New Yorker. Deacon was the type of guy that always had your back, no matter the circumstance. When Zeke made eye contact with him, he waved him over.

"Hey, boss, what's doin'?"

"Just giving you a heads-up," Zeke said. "We've got two human detectives in the place asking questions about a girl that was murdered two blocks from here. Keep a close eye out. Let me know if you notice anything out of the ordinary."

Deacon nodded. "Sure ting, boss."

Zeke clapped his hand on Deacon's shoulder as he turned to walk away. And then he noticed a woman with striking features. She was about five-ten and had the legs of a gazelle, long and sleek. Her hair was jet-black and hung in silky waves past her hips. She wasn't a usual. He'd never seen her in the club before. He was sure of it. With a face and a body like that, there was no way he'd miss her.

She was on the arm of an older business-type guy, which meant one of two things: one, she was a hired professional; two, she was a gold digger. Either way, she was giving it up for money.

He watched as the woman arranged her short skirt so she could sit down without flashing everyone. Settling in her chair next to her sugar daddy, she looked around without interest until her eyes met his. The moment she saw him, her eyes lit up, the color almost glimmering gold. And then she moved around in her seat so that her below-the-waist view was on full display for him to see.

He looked away sharply, taking an abrupt, feigned interest in the crowded dance floor. The truth was, he was into only one person, and that person was Yelena Smirnov. He wanted Yelena, and not just for sex. But he hadn't the balls to do anything about it. It was kind of the way he went through life, his curse keeping him away from a normal relationship. With his previous engagement on his mind, he turned back around and glanced in her direction. To his surprise, she smiled at him tightly.

He ignored her and headed back to his office.

In his private office, Sam waited with the two detectives for his boss to return with the security footage.

When the door opened wide, everyone inside the room came to attention. Zeke glanced in Sam's direction, then looked at the two detectives, pegging them with a hard stare. "I've got the security footage you asked for," he said. "Is there anything else I can do for you, Detectives?"

"Thank you, Mr. Rizzo." Manuel extended his hand and introduced himself and his partner.

Zeke looked down at the detective's extended hand. In that brief moment, he squeezed his eyes shut. He felt an ache in his chest that spread through his body like wildfire. As he clasped hold of the detective's hand, darkness crept into his head and triggered all kinds of painful memories. What Zeke saw created a chill that shot deep into his bones.

It was years ago on a clear, beautiful afternoon as Manuel watched his older sister—who had the deepest red hair—climb in the backseat of a green Camaro with black stripes over the hood. With perfect recollection, Manuel saw her waving at him through the tinted windows as the car drove off.

Now that the door to Manuel's nightmare was open, Zeke couldn't stop the horror show. The images were so vivid he could almost smell the blood. The visions of Manuel's dead sister and the redhead he'd found in the dumpster swirled together, combining the two until he could only see flashes of pale bare skin, blue, lifeless lips, bruises and teeth marks as if they were attacked by something unhuman.

Zeke's eyes popped back open as he took a deep breath and jerked his hand back.

"Are you all right, Mr. Rizzo?"

"Sorry, Detective Sanchez. It's been a long night." Zeke placed the thumb drive in his palm. "Here's the footage you asked for."

"Thanks, Mr. Rizzo." Manuel looked at Frank. "See if they recognize the photo you found on Miss Bennett."

Frank reached into his jacket and pulled out his phone. After a couple of minutes, he pulled up an image of Sylvia Bennett—not the gruesome picture of her at the crime scene. Instead, he'd gotten her photo from her Facebook page, and he held it up for Zeke and Sam to view. "Do you recognize this woman?"

Zeke shook his head. "No. I've never seen her here before. Although she's hard to miss. She's a beautiful girl."

Sam's eyes widened as he stared at the photo of Sylvia. "Wait a minute. I'm sure she was here earlier. I remember her red hair."

"Are you sure?" Manuel said.

Sam bobbed his head up and down. "Yeah, definitely. I saw her leave with this huge dude."

"Do you remember the time they left?" Frank chimed in.

Sam narrowed his eyes. "I'm pretty sure it was around midnight. I was seating the guests in the VIP section when I saw them head for the exit."

Manuel crossed his arms. "Do you think you could recognize this man if you saw him again?"

"Are you kidding me?" Sam snorted. "There's no way I'd forget this guy. We have a lot of big guys that walk in this place, but this dude looks like he rules over hell. He's at least six-five, long black hair, and he was wearing a lot of leather. Come to think of it, he looks just like that actor that played Aquaman." He looked at Zeke. "You know... the guy that's married to Lisa Bonet."

"You mean Jason Momoa?"

Sam nodded. "Yeah, that's his name." He averted his eyes from Zeke and focused on the detectives. "I'm sure you'll see him on the video footage walking out with that redhead."

"Great," Frank said. "Now we're getting somewhere."

Zeke reached into his back pocket, and when he brought his hand back, he held out a card to Manuel. "If you have any more questions, here's my card. My other staff members who worked a shift tonight may have some information that could be helpful."

Manuel took the card. "Thanks, Mr. Rizzo. You've been a great help." And then he turned toward Sam, his hand extended. "We also appreciate your help, Mr. Malone."

"No problem," Sam said as he shook hands with the detective. "Glad to help. I hope you catch the guy."

Before they left, Manuel looked over his shoulder. "Thanks again for the video footage. We'll be in touch."

"Hey, wait..." Sam called out. "Does that redhead's death have anything to do with all the homeless murders?"

"All we can say is..." Manuel hesitantly replied, "...Miss Bennett's death was very similar."

Sam crinkled his nose. "She wasn't half-eaten, was she?"

"Sorry, Mr. Malone," Frank said. "That's all we can comment on for now."

After both detectives left, Sam said, "So, what do you think about all this, boss?"

Zeke shook his head. "I'm not sure what to make of it, but I do know one thing for sure."

"What's that?"

"Detective Sanchez isn't what he thinks he is."

Sam looked at Zeke confused. "Huh?"

"He's human... and half Breedline."

"Shit," Sam said. "I wonder if he knows."

"No, and let's keep it that way."

Chapter Fourteen

At the top of the staircase, Jace moved down the hall toward the nursery. With both boys in his arms, he cleverly maneuvered them so he could get the door open. As he reached out with his free hand, an ominous growl sent his adrenaline racing. *What the hell?*

He tightened his hold on the boys and turned toward the noise, just as an enormous two-footed creature came tearing through a door.

Shit! Jace felt helpless, his feet paralyzed in place.

"Abbey!" Steven called out. "No!"

When Jace saw Steven, there was no mistaking who the creature was. It was Abbey's she-wolf.

It all seemed to happen in slow motion. As Steven reached out to the she-wolf, a shaggy arm swiped at him, knocking him off balance and sending him stumbling backward.

The unsettling noise woke the entire Covenant. Everyone came rushing out of their rooms to find the horrific scene before them.

Jem stood in shock as he opened his bedroom door and witnessed Abbey's she-wolf, crouched in a fighting stance. *Christ.* It was obvious she had her sights locked in the direction of his twin brother, who was defenseless holding on to his sons. And then Jem's skin began to tingle as flickers of light formed in the palm of his hand.

As the commotion descended from above, Tim and Tessa darted up the stairs with Roman and Lawrence close behind. When they got to the top, they froze in their tracks.

Jace turned and met Tessa's gaze, his eyes wide with panic. On instinct, she reached for little Jem, and Tim quickly grasped hold of Jax. With their eyes locked on the creature, they slowly stepped back.

The sounds of heavy footsteps caught Jace's attention. He turned to see the massive she-wolf charging in his direction. The creature came at him so fast he had no time to shift into his Beast. It rammed him into the back wall. The drywall busted from the force of the collision.

"Jace!" Tessa screamed.

Before Jace hit the floor, he started transforming. Every hair on his body bristled and began to grow. His spine stretched at a phenomenal rate. Bones cracked and popped as they shifted from their natural positions. The pain was worse than usual, as though his flesh were being ripped away from the bone. He felt himself rising, his hands turning into claws, and his limbs swelling as he urged his inner Beast onward. A mighty roar thundered from his jaws. From the hole in the wall, the nightmarish form of an immense white beast emerged.

* * *

As Valkin Steele waited for Cole Decker to show, his gut was screaming that something unfortunate had happened to the tracker he'd hired. He hadn't heard from Gordon Bates in hours. And each time Steele tried to contact him, his call went straight to voicemail. The only person left to call was Dominic Gambino. He was part of Gordon's team.

When Steele initiated the call, Dominic answered on the second ring, "Gambino speaking."

"What the hell is going on out there, Dominic? Where the hell is Gordon Bates?"

There were several moments of silence, and then Dominic said grimly, "Gordon and his brother Joey went after Roman against your orders. I haven't heard from them in hours. It doesn't look good, Mr. Steele."

Steele's eyes narrowed in a fury. "What? I told that bastard to wait until Cole Decker arrived."

Dominic pushed the air out of his lungs. "Well, I take it he wanted to handle things on his own. What do you want me to do?"

"Not a damn thing," Steele said through gritted teeth. "Stay put until I contact you. Is that clear?"

"Yes, sir."

As Cole Decker approached the gates of Valkin Steele's estate in a Bentley convertible, they opened automatically. He drove down a long, paved driveway that led to the mansion's front entrance, beyond a manicured lawn, and parked alongside a sculpted fountain.

When he got out, he walked up several steps that led to the front entrance. Instantly, the enormous double doors swung open and he was greeted by a large, stocky man. Cole recognized the face of one of Steele's thuggish bodyguards, Marcus Delvecchio. His stance appeared stiff like he was expecting a fight any time. He was about six four with tattoos running up both arms, disappearing behind the short sleeves of his tight shirt. Judging by the bump in his nose, Marcus looked like the type of guy who'd been in few too many fights. With his arms crossed, he stared at Cole with an unwelcome glare.

Cole was in no mood for small talk as he shoved his way past Marcus into the mansion's impressive foyer. "Where is he?"

Marcus furrowed his brows. "He's in the formal study. Follow me."

As Marcus led the way, Cole looked over the mansion's lavish interior. In the center of the foyer, a sparkling crystal chandelier hung at least twenty feet from above. Antique tapestries and oil paintings decorated the walls. Marble tiles stretched across the floor to where an enormous grand stairway ascended toward the upper stories. When they came to a spacious room, Cole went down several granite steps that led down to a sunken level where Valkin stood in front of a sizeable fourteenth-century stone fireplace.

With his back facing them, Valkin said, "Leave us."

"Yes, sir," Marcus replied.

When Valkin heard the door close, he turned to face Cole. "I'm running out of patience. Everyone else has wasted my time. Nothing but a bunch of fucking amateurs," Valkin bit out. "The Breedline Covenant has my Adalwolf. Can I count on you to bring him to me?"

Cole leveled a stare. "I've never failed once. I'll deliver the Adalwolf if you guarantee our transaction."

Valkin smirked. "The girls will be on a plane as soon as I make the call. Get me the Adalwolf, and I'll fulfill our deal."

Cole stifled a smile and nodded in agreement.

Valkin pulled out a photo from inside his suit pocket and offered it to Cole. "This is the Adalwolf. He goes by the name Steven Craven. The woman standing next to him in the picture is his bonded mate, Abigail Winthrop. She's a she-wolf. I've had my men tracking her ever since she murdered Dr. Hans Autenburg and escaped his facility. If you can track her down, she'll lead us to Steven."

Cole took the photo and held it up. Then he looked Valkin square in the eyes. "Give me forty-eight hours."

When Cole exited the room, some of the tension left Valkin's shoulders, and suddenly he was filled with hope. Soon, his precious Natasha would be cured, freeing her from years of pain and suffering.

* * *

When the she-wolf lunged at the Beast with her slashing claws, he grabbed her arm in mid-swing and slammed her into the wall. It crumbled under the impact.

"Please..." Steven called out. "Stop, Abigail!"

She ignored his plea and resumed attacking the Beast. She pounced on top of him, pinning him to the floor as her claws raked his skin, ripping into the leathery hide beneath his white, furry coat.

Tessa looked at Jem, her eyes pleading for help.

Jem nodded in her direction. The decision weighed heavily on him. He had no choice but to take Abbey down. As Jem extended his hand, ready to strike the she-wolf, a glowing ball of fire formed in his palm.

When Steven saw Jem take aim, he hollered, "Wait!"

Jem hesitated and turned toward Steven. "I'm sorry, Steven. It's the only way."

The Beast's anger raged, fueling his determination to stay alive and protect his family. Tucking his chin to protect his throat against the she-wolf's savage claws flying at him like ivory shrapnel, he rotated sharply, throwing her off him. Before the she-wolf could get to her feet, the Beast leaped on top of her.

As they went down, Jem swore under his breath. "Shit." He'd lost his target.

A fierce roar bellowed from the Beast's open jaws as he bit down, sinking his canines deep into the she-wolf's shoulder.

"No!" Steven reacted in alarm.

Blood spouted from her dark fur as she roared in pain, clutching at the gaping wound with her huge misshapen paw.

The Beast barely recognized the feral rage fueling his attack. Instinct took over as he surrendered to a primal impulse to go in for the kill. With his eyes locked on the she-wolf's throat, a familiar voice caught his attention.

"No, Jace!" Tessa cried out.

In the blink of an eye, Abbey's she-wolf reacted with lightning speed. An enormous paw smacked into the Beast's head, throwing him off her. He crashed into the wall as pain exploded inside his skull, causing his vision to momentarily blur. The she-wolf allowed him no time to recover as she pounced once again on him.

She peeled back her lips, and instead of a growl escaping her throat, she released a mournful howl, reaching a poignant note before trailing off into silence.

The sputtering glow of fire suddenly appeared behind the she-wolf as she went limp and crumpled to the floor.

With black smoke dissipating from the palm of his hand, Jem turned toward Steven, overwhelmed by his look of despair. And then Steven's gaze fell upon Abbey's unmoving body as she slowly converted back to her natural form.

As he ran to her, everyone fell back in silence. Even Jace, now back to his human form, stumbled back wearily and watched helplessly as Steven cried out to her. A portion of her chest appeared smoldering and charred. Her body was limp and still, her arms lifeless at her sides. Her eyes, reverting to their steely blue, stared blankly at the ceiling above them.

Steven knelt beside her and gently lifted her into his arms. "Oh, God, please," he sobbed. "Abbey…"

Lowering her to the floor, he laid a hand against her cheek, hoping to get a response. As he looked down, her chest had been burned, with a gaping hole where her heart should have been. It was too late, she was dead.

"No!" Grief and anger, two emotions he knew far better than anything else, rushed over him. Tears gushed from his eyes as silent sobs racked his body. And then, out of nowhere, he heard a soft whisper in his ear. It was a woman's voice he did not recognize. "Use your gift. You possess the power to save her."

He frowned, confused by the voice in his head. For just a moment, he felt a warm and gentle presence.

"Please," he pleaded to the voice, desperate to hear it once more. "Can you help me?"

Suddenly, he felt another presence, warm but different. This time, the voice was stronger and louder in his mind. It surrounded him from every angle. "We're here for you, Steven." Then two images suddenly appeared before him. It was a man with red hair that hung in ringlets, and he had pointed ears like an elf. Kneeling beside him was a woman with long, white, braided hair. Her face was pale with delicate features and tiny pointed ears.

"My name is Chester Ewan, and this is my wife Amelia," the elf-like man said. "We are Guardians of the Breedline. Use your gift, Steven. You can heal her."

"But..." he shook his head. "I cannot heal a fatal wound."

"You must have faith in our word," Amelia said.

As he lifted Abbey, he wrapped her in his arms and surrounded her with loving warmth. He sent out the strength she so desperately needed, releasing it from the deepest part of his soul.

I'm here for you, Abbey. I won't let you go. Come back to me. I love you so much.

His eyelids burned, and his heart splintered in agony as he rocked her back and forth. The pain was a never-ending cloak of blackness that furled over him until he was consumed with it. He worked at pushing his energy into her, willing his life into hers.

He let out a cry of pain.

"Oh, God..." Tessa gasped.

Jace followed Tessa's gaze to see a gaping hole spreading rapidly in the middle of Steven's chest.

Steven's eyes turned from their emerald green to a glassy dullness. His fingers curled into tight fists as he released Abbey to the floor and bent over in unimaginable pain.

Tessa handed off little Jem to Mia as she rushed over to take him. Then Tessa pushed in beside Steven and looked up at Chester, her eyes wet with tears. "What's happening to him?"

"I promise you, he's not going to die," Chester told her. "Steven will heal."

They all went silent and waited, their expressions ones of astonishment as Steven straightened and his chest slowly began to close, until finally, it returned to normal. He scooped Abbey up and cradled her in his arms.

She blinked, confused about her whereabouts. The ceiling came into focus and then she became aware that she wasn't alone. She was wrapped in Steven's loving arms as if he was shielding her from the world. It seemed like the entire Covenant was surrounding her. And she was completely naked.

She smiled up at him, and he smiled back.

She felt as limp as a wet noodle, and her mind was mush. When a blanket was placed over her, she looked up and saw Tessa standing above her. She was confused. She couldn't remember anything. The last thing she recalled was the horrific nightmare she'd dreamed.

"Abbey..." Steven's voice trembled. He kissed her, his lips gentle and loving against hers. For the longest time, he stayed there even when he'd pulled his mouth away.

"Welcome back. You scared me, Abbey. I thought I'd lost you."

"What happened?"

His brows clenched and his jaw tightened. "You turned."

She shook her head as tears gathered in her eyes. "Please, tell me... I didn't hurt anyone, did I?"

Steven touched her face, wiping the tears away. "You need to get some rest. We'll talk about this later."

She frowned unhappily and rose up on her elbows. "Tell me, Steven. Who did I hurt?"

His lips thinned. "You attacked Jace."

117

"Oh, my God," she gasped. "Did I—"

"You nearly kicked my ass," Jace said in a weak voice with nothing but a towel wrapped around his waist. "But I'm fine, Abbey."

"I'm so sorry," she sobbed. "I could have hurt someone. I can't take that risk again." She looked away from Jace and focused on Steven. "I can't stay here. I'm a danger to everyone."

His eyes darkened, and he went still above her. He stared down at her as if he was trying to collect his thoughts. "If you go, I go. I'll never leave you again."

And then Jem came into view. He knelt beside them. "Please, Abbey. You're not thinking clearly. It's not safe for you to leave this Covenant."

"Don't you understand? I'm putting everyone here in danger if I stay. I can't control my Lupa. If it only took a nightmare to trigger it, I can't take that risk. Next time, I might—"

"No," Jem cut her off. "You're not going to hurt anyone else."

"You don't know that. What if I can't be stopped the next time?"

"I stopped you this time."

Her forehead creased. "What?"

"I'm sorry, Abbey," Jem said. "I was left with no choice. I had to take your life."

"But... how am I still alive?"

"I healed you," Steven said.

She swallowed, opened her mouth, but he didn't give her an opportunity to speak. He slid his hand around to her nape and pulled her to meet his kiss. He kissed her lips then moved to her cheeks, giving each a kiss in turn. Then he kissed her nose, her eyelids, and each temple.

When he pulled away, she looked at him, puzzled. "I don't know what to say. You saved my life knowing it could have killed you." Tears welled in her eyes. "I love you so much."

He smiled, tenderness filling his heart. "I love you, Mary Abigail."

She held on to him, her anchor, the person who'd taken her from death's grasp and somehow magically brought her back. He'd faced death down for her and *survived.*

"I have an idea that will ease your mind, Abbey," Tim said. "It will stop this from happening again."

She looked up at him. "I'm willing to do anything. I don't think I could live with myself if I hurt anyone here. You've all been so kind to me."

"You could stay in our guest house," Tim said. "We can put guards outside twenty-four seven with tranquilizer guns for a precaution only. You'll be safe and so will the Covenant."

"What about Eve?" Tessa asked. "She's staying in the guest house."

"We'll move her to Steven and Abbey's room. I don't think she's going to be a problem. I'll have Bruce keep a close eye on her. Besides, she'll enjoy being closer to Arius and Tidus's nursery."

Abbey nodded in agreement as tears trailed down her cheeks.

Steven rose to his feet and extended his hand. "Thank you, Tim."

Tim shifted the toddler in his arms and shook Steven's hand. "You're welcome to stay here as long as you want."

"That's right," Tessa said, moving closer to Abbey. "You two are part of our family now."

Abbey reached out with her arms and threw them around Tessa. She was the smaller of the two, and yet she engulfed Tessa, squeezing like she was three times Tessa's size.

Tessa returned her hug, holding on.

Around them, everyone gathered, all present to support Abbey and Steven. They smiled indulgently while Tessa and Abbey sniffled and wiped at their eyes.

"Welcome to the chaos," Jace said as he extended his hand to Steven. "It gets pretty crazy and overwhelming around here at times."

Steven grasped his hand. "Well then..." He chuckled. "...I'll fit in just fine."

As soon as Tessa released Abbey, the others enfolded her into a group hug. She'd never felt so loved as she did right now, surrounded by all these people. *Family.* Feeling part of a family boggled her mind. And it felt right. But in the back of her mind, she knew she was a danger to them all.

"Come on, everyone," Jem said. "Since we're all up, let's get some breakfast."

Tim checked his watch. "After breakfast, we're meeting with Colonel Deshazo and his team. I want everyone to be there. And there's one more thing..." He released a heavy sigh. "Helen is bringing Sebastian's sister to the Covenant later this morning."

Jem looked at him, confused. "Sister?"

"What the hell..." Jace blurted. "What sister?"

Tim held up a halting hand. "Calm down. It's a little complicated. Her name is Anna Saeni. She's not a blood relative. Helen said her mother raised Sebastian. She wants to meet Eve and the twins. I want everyone to welcome her to the Covenant. I asked her to stay here. Anna doesn't have anywhere to go. Apparently, after her mother was killed by Sebastian's birth mother, his stepfather forced her to live in a monastery when she was fourteen. All these years Anna thought Sebastian was dead. I will tell you more over breakfast."

Roman and Lawrence nodded in agreement as everyone else stood back in silence, fearing the worst was yet to come.

Chapter Fifteen

As Zeke watched the detectives exit the club, his hands went clammy, and a cold sweat bloomed on his forehead. He frowned as he sensed a presence looming from behind. It was almost paralyzing.

"You're a sin-eater," a sultry voice said.

Zeke quickly wheeled around and froze. A female he'd seen in the VIP section earlier attached to the arm of an older gentleman, who'd obviously had a fat wallet, stood before him.

He stared at her for a moment, his instincts warning him. His body screamed to get as far away from her as possible.

Instead of listening to his gut feeling, he narrowed his eyes and said, "Excuse me. What did you say?"

As the silence stretched out, she stared at him with desire in her eyes. There was a moment between them as their eyes clung to each other. Then she looked him up and down. "I know what you are. I can sense your kind a mile away."

The temperature in the air between them dropped. "Who and *what* are you?"

She smirked and took a few steps closer. "My name is Callisto. And I'm every man's dream."

While Zeke stood face-to-face with her, he sensed her emotions without so much as touching her. The only thing he saw in her mind was blood. Callisto was hungry for it... *starving*.

"Spend the night with me." Her sultry voice blended the words into one another, and a powerful feeling of ecstasy went through him, tingling down into the fly of his pants.

"I'm sorry." He shook his head. "You're not my type."

When he turned to leave, she caught his arm. The instant they made contact, he connected with her mind. What he saw threw him off guard. The image was so vivid he could almost feel the swill of her agony. It was a memory of her past.

Callisto suddenly came awake. She was surrounded by darkness. Her arms and legs were bound. When she tried to move, it was useless. It looked as though she'd been confined inside a sarcophagus of some kind. The claustrophobic dimensions both appalled and angered her. It was bad enough that her father had condemned her to eternal imprisonment to starve, but in so small a space... The cruelty of it brought tears to her eyes. Death would have been more merciful. Her eyes burned with pain as she screamed for what seemed hours until there were no more tears to cry. Finally, she let herself go limp, desperate to telepathically connect with her siblings. But all she could sense was an empty void filled with utter silence and found there was no freedom to be had.

Zeke broke free of her hold and almost fell to his knees. The remnants of her pain lingered in his body, creating a weakness. He briefly closed his eyes and rubbed his temples. The horror of her experience left him unhinged.

Callisto narrowed her eyes. "What did you see,... *sin-eater?*"

"I saw you..." He gasped. "...trapped and suffering. How did you manage to get free?"

She seemed lost for words.

Without warning, a dark figure came into his view. The man before him was not human. He resembled the guy Sam Malone described to the detectives: tall, long dark hair, and dressed in a lot of leather. The guy looked like a vampire and an assassin rolled into one big package.

Callisto flinched when he called out her name. She looked over her shoulder as he came between her and Zeke.

He grabbed her arm. "Stop playing games, Callisto." He shot Zeke a look. "You seem anxious, *sin-eater.*"

Zeke was too dumbfounded to form a coherent response. He noticed the signet ring on the guy's finger. It looked to be a shape of a trefoil knot, identical to the pendant Callisto wore around her neck. Focusing back on the guy's menacing face, he took a few steps back and said, "Who are you and what is it you want?"

In the awkward silence, the guy's expression turned stone-cold. He shifted his gaze toward Callisto and exchanged a look that said without words to keep her mouth shut.

He averted his eyes from her and focused on Zeke. "My name is Apollyon. I'm here for my sister."

Two of Zeke's bouncers stood close by, watching warily.

Apollyon got face-to-face with Zeke and scowled. "Bide my warning, sin-eater. Ignore what you saw inside my sister's head."

Zeke had no ready response. He shifted uneasily on his feet, wrestling with the right words to say. "I don't want to see you in my bar again."

He leered at Zeke, his eyes smoldering. And then there was the strangest scent in the air, something seductive and sensual. As Apollyon breathed in the heady fragrance, he felt the tension in his shoulders ease. The wonderful smell drifted closer when a tall blonde moved next to Zeke. Apollyon was dumbfounded. The scent of her skin hit him hard like a punch to the gut.

Yelena craned her neck to look up at Apollyon's face. She bared her fangs and hissed.

Zeke shot forward. "I think it's time for you and your sister to leave."

Apollyon hovered above Zeke in silent menace. Without another word, he tugged Callisto by the arm and exited the bar.

Shit, Zeke thought as he reached into his pocket for Detective Sanchez's card.

* * *

Helen peered into the kitchen. "May we come in?"

Jace glanced over his shoulder at Helen nervously. He was anxious to meet Sebastian's sister.

"Please..." Tim said, "come on in. We just sat down for breakfast. Would you care to join us?"

She pushed through the door, and Anna followed close behind. The very first thing she saw were two little boys— obviously twins—sitting in a highchair. They had the fairest complexion and wavy, dark hair. They were eating pancakes. When they looked up, their faces were smeared with syrup.

Anna's face softened, realizing how much they resembled Sebastian. It took every bit of her control to keep from falling apart.

123

Helen placed a hand on her shoulder. "I'd like to introduce everyone to Anna... Sebastian's sister."

Tim rose from his chair and extended his hand. "It's nice to meet you, Anna. Welcome to our home."

She shook his hand. "I hope I'm not imposing."

"Absolutely not." Tim smiled. "As I was saying, would you like to join us for breakfast? We made pancakes."

She nodded. "I would love to."

Tim introduced her to everyone at the table. "You'll meet Abbey shortly," he said. "I'll introduce you to Eve later. She left early this morning to visit Sebastian in the hospital." Then he looked pointedly at the dark-haired little boys. "That's Sebastian and Eve's twins, Arius and Tidus. Your nephews."

"They're adorable," she said. "They look exactly like my brother when he was that age."

Jace, who'd remained silent, turned his gaze to her, clearly gauging her reaction. When she turned in his direction, he looked away, but not before she saw the expression in his eyes. He appeared uneasy in her presence.

Tim pointed toward the table. "Please, have a seat."

When she took a seat between Helen and Tim, she surveyed the occupants around the table with avid curiosity.

Across the table, Tessa leaned over to help Jace cut pancakes into small squares for their boys. The toddlers beamed with delight and began stuffing bites into their mouths.

On the far end of the table, a beautiful little girl with curly hair dug into her plate with gusto. A black cat sat on the floor grooming itself just below her highchair.

"Yummy," the little girl mumbled with a mouth full of pancakes.

Anna sat back, eating but mostly watching and enjoying the sight of everyone enjoying a meal together. This was truly a loving family. A solid, unbreakable family unit, one she wished she was a part of.

Mia noticed the desperation in Anna's eyes as she gazed at Sebastian's twins.

"Anna... Would you like to hold your nephews?"

Anna's expression lit up. She opened her mouth to speak but seemed lost for words. And then she placed her hand over her heart. "I would love to."

Mia cleaned the sticky syrup off the boys. When she lifted Arius from the highchair, she handed him to Anna.

"Hello, Arius," Anna said. "I'm your Auntie Anna."

Arius looked up at her and chortled in glee.

"You're such a happy little boy." Anna buried her face in all that sweet-smelling baby skin and hair. "You remind me of your daddy."

"Da-da," Arius mumbled. He patted her cheeks and let out a squeal of delight that she felt all the way down to her toes.

When Mia came over with Tidus, they exchanged toddlers. An overwhelming emotion welled and expanded in her chest. She kissed Tidus on his little forehead. "You're so adorable."

Tidus stared up at her from underneath his long lashes. He seemed fascinated by her curly hair, and then to her surprise, he reached up to touch a long strand.

She smiled. Warmth spread through her heart when Tidus cracked a little smile and cuddled against her chest. It was such an endearing feeling to hold her brother's child in her arms. She was struck by the rightness of it all. Now, all her prayers would be answered if only Sebastian would wake up.

Chapter Sixteen

Eve entered Sebastian's hospital room and sat down in a chair next to his bedside. He seemed peaceful. But she knew underneath it all something evil lurked, keeping him trapped.

Sebastian struggled from the dense fog that enveloped him like a blanket. He desperately wanted to open his eyes, but Lucifer's tight hold made it impossible. He grappled with his memory, trying to piece together anything that made sense. And then a gentle voice broke through the horror of his thoughts.

"Sebastian... It's Eve." Tears fell from the corners of her eyes. "Please... come back to me."

Suddenly, bits and pieces of his memory came back like random photos flashing on a video screen. At first, it had been happy. He saw Eve and remembered the first time she told him she loved him. No words could simply replace the way she looked at him, the way she touched him, the way she loved him, as if there was no one else in the world for her. He would never forget that moment.

Then the memory suddenly vanished from his mind. It was replaced by a nightmare. As the past came back, it was hard to control the rage that mounted in his head. Everything seemed to click together at light speed: the memory of his sister's pain at the hands of his stepfather, and the secret he'd kept for her.

Panic raced up his spine. Chill bumps rose and fanned out, prickling over his skin like tiny razors. He used all his strength to try and break away from that dreadful day. *Oh God*, he thought painfully. *Please... not this memory.*

Suddenly, he felt sharp nails digging into his skin. As he turned to look, Lucifer had a firm grip on his arm. "You will relive this memory."

"I beg you," Sebastian pleaded, "don't make me do this."

Lucifer smirked and released him. "Give me your son, and I'll spare you from this memory."

Although Sebastian tended to view the world in black and white, here and now he understood the pull between right and wrong. He didn't like it. But he didn't have a choice. Giving up his son was not an option. He'd relive all the nightmares of his past a million times over before he'd give up Arius.

"No," Sebastian said. "I will not give in."

Lucifer glared at him. "Have it your way."

Sebastian stood back like a ghost in the shadows when his sister suddenly came into view. She was huddled in a dark corner, outside his stepfather's bedroom, with her knees tucked into her chest and her arms wrapped tightly around them. He watched as she rocked back and forth, quietly sobbing.

A hushed little voice alerted her attention. "Sissy..."

Anna looked up and met her little brother's concerned gaze. Her eyes widened and her lips parted in a gasp of surprise.

She motioned him away and whispered, "Go back to bed, Sebastian."

Instead of leaving, he rushed to her side and got down on his knees. "What's wrong, Sissy?"

"Nothing," she said in a hushed voice. "Please, Sebastian. Go back to bed before you wake Mr. Montgomery."

At the age of five, Sebastian might not have been that intuitive when it came to adults, but when he saw blood on his sister's nightgown, he knew she'd been hurt. He had a bad feeling in his tummy.

He reached for her hand. "Did Mr. Montgomery hurt you, Sissy?"

She remained still and did not outwardly react, but her face lost all color, and her expression seemed blank. It was like watching day turn into night as some of the light went out, and shadows stretched like storm clouds through her eyes.

Tears slipped down her cheeks. "Please, don't tell Mama."

Sebastian's eyes were glassy as he watched the younger version of himself reach up and wipe the tears from his sister's face. He felt trapped in time, locked in his past, reliving it with each breath. And he hated how painful it was to witness this memory once again. Right now, he wanted to die. His stepfather had been the one who had raped her.

She pulled her little brother into her arms and pressed her lips to the top of his head.

The little boy kept silent and did his best to comfort his sister. He held her tightly and rubbed his little hand up and down her back.

She pulled from their embrace and looked into his eyes. "Will you promise not to tell?"

He was torn as he gazed into his sister's grief-stricken eyes. "Okay, Sissy. I won't tell."

His gentle voice broke through the horror of her anxiety and gave her comfort. She blinked, and more tears fell down her cheeks.

Sebastian was staring wearily at her, his brow furrowed as if he were trying to hold back tears.

She cupped his chin with a tender grasp. "Don't worry, little brother. Everything will be all right."

He nodded, but the weariness in his eyes had yet to fade. Sebastian was afraid for his sister and fearful of Mr. Montgomery.

"Let's get you back to bed before Mama wakes up," she whispered. "Would you like a piece of candy before bed? I have a chocolate bar saved on my dresser."

"'K," Sebastian quietly replied. When he got to his feet, he reached out to help her.

When he'd finished his half of the chocolate bar and brushed his teeth, it wasn't long before he fell asleep. As she watched him, his brow was creased even in slumber.

As she caressed his forehead, he stirred beneath her touch. "I love you, Sissy," he whispered in a drowsy mumble.

She smiled. "I love you too, Sebastian."

* * *

As soon as Abbey heard the door close, she scrambled out of the bathroom, realizing Steven had left the bedroom. She'd lied and told him she would meet him downstairs after her shower to meet everyone for breakfast. Time was of the essence. If she was going to slip out before anyone noticed, she'd have to move fast.

She might very well be making the biggest mistake of her life. Maybe Tim's idea was good. After she'd attacked Jace, he'd suggested moving her and Steven to the guest house. Having guards with tranquilizer guns posted outside their door might keep the Covenant safe if she turned again, but it wouldn't protect Steven. That was a risk she wasn't willing to take.

She went back into the bathroom and packed only the essential toiletries. She smoothed her hair back and clipped it on top of her head before she placed a ball cap on. She went back into the bedroom and opened the dresser and hauled out a few changes of clothing and stuffed them into her bag. Then she noticed a note lying on top of her pillow. As she opened it, she recognized Steven's handwriting.

I'm so happy to have you back, Abbey. Don't worry, everything will work out. I love you.

Tears gathered in her eyes. There was a part of her that hated leaving him behind. She was terrified to go back on the run, but she had no choice.

Before she left, she wrote on the back of his note. Somehow, she had to explain the reason for her leaving. When she finished, she pressed the note to her lips and placed it on top of his pillow.

After she made it past the gate without getting caught by the guards, she took one last look at the Breedline Covenant. Her chest ached to leave the man she loved so deeply and who understood all the demons from her past.

Concerned over what was taking Abbey so long, Steven excused himself before he left the kitchen. But on the other hand, she may have been too exhausted to eat and decided to get some rest. After everything they'd been through, he couldn't afford to assume anything.

When he came to their bedroom and opened the door, it was quiet inside, which meant she was probably asleep. Still, he found himself quietly moving through the small living space that led to the bedroom. He just wanted to check in on her.

Something seemed off as he cracked open the bedroom door. As he went inside, he noticed the empty bed and the bathroom door wide open.

"Abbey..."

When there was no answer, he looked toward the bed where he'd left her the note. It had been moved. It was lying on top of his pillow. He picked it up and saw that she had written on the back.

I'm sorry, Steven. But I can't take the risk of hurting anyone in the Covenant, especially you. Please don't come after me. I will always love you.

Panic hit him. He tossed the note aside and rushed out of the room and headed downstairs.

He shot through the kitchen door and braced himself for what he was about to say. "We have a problem..." His eyes roamed the room. "Abbey is gone."

Everyone sitting at the kitchen table had all donned serious what-the-hell looks. And then their expressions turned to ones of sympathy. They were all looking at him with weary eyes.

Roman quickly rose to his feet, his expression dark. "What do you mean she's gone?"

"She left me a note. She's afraid if she turns again, she'll hurt someone."

Lawrence palmed the back of his neck, and he blew out a deep breath. "She'll be a target. If Cole Decker finds her, he'll use her as a pawn to get to you, Steven."

He knew Lawrence was right. The same thing reflected in every single person in the room.

"This is awful," Tessa spoke out. "What are we going to do? We can't just leave her on her own. It's not safe. Abbey belongs here."

Jace put his arm around her and looked toward Steven. "Where would she go?"

Steven shook his head. "I don't know."

"We'll find her," Jem chimed in. He hoped the hell he was right.

Steven hadn't even realized he'd bobbled. His knees went to jelly, and he had to grasp the back of a chair to keep from dropping to his knees.

Drakon rose from his chair and reached out to him. "You okay, buddy?"

Steven inhaled deeply. "We've got to find her before Decker does. I'll gladly give myself over to Valkin Steele. It's me he's looking for. If he wants Natasha healed, I'll do whatever it takes to keep them away from Abbey."

"Let's not overreact just yet," Roman said. "If Steele gets his hands on you, healing Natasha won't be the end. He's not just going to let you walk away. Valkin Steele isn't that kind of man. He'd make a deal with the devil if it came down to it."

"If we don't find her soon, I'll do whatever it takes to get Abbey back safe," Steven bit out.

Alexander rose from his chair and moved next to Steven. "Don't worry. We'll find her."

"We'll get your girl back," Kyle cut into the conversation.

"I'll go take a look at the outside surveillance footage," Drakon said. "At least we'll get an idea of what direction she went."

Near to his exploding point, Tim checked his watch, noticing how the hours had quickly passed. Frustration frayed his already worn patience. He didn't have time for this. "Look, she couldn't have gotten far." He turned around and focused on Roman. "Colonel Deshazo and his men should be here any minute. Give them a heads-up. We'll need a chopper for this. They can search in the air while we head out on the road."

Roman nodded and pulled out his phone.

Tessa reached for Steven's hand. "I promise. We'll do everything we can to bring her back."

Steven lightly squeezed her hand. He couldn't even form a response. He was utterly bewildered: first, that Abbey would just take off like that, and second, that she had to run away, worried she'd hurt someone. He didn't care what she thought. She belonged with this family. She belonged with *him*. To save her from the slime-ball predators like Valkin Steele and Cole Decker, he'd take anyone down by any means necessary.

Chapter Seventeen

Cole Decker watched with smug satisfaction as Abbey climbed over the Covenant's gate and disappeared through the thick timber outside the estate. Behind dark-tinted windows of a black van, he'd been waiting for the perfect opportunity. But this was like taking candy from a baby.

He'd researched the Breedline council and located two of their traitors, Corbin Azzo and Fredrick Mercier. A year ago, they barely managed to escape after the Breedline discovered they were working with Sebastian Crow and his twin brother, Thomas Carlyle. When the Breedline killed off Damien Spence and apprehended Samuel Mercier and Harold Crampton, they were more than willing to seek revenge against the Breedline.

Now that Cole had uncovered their secret location, he planned to sit back and wait for Steven Craven—the Adalwolf Valkin Steele was after—to show his face. Instead, he'd found the next best thing. He'd use the she-wolf as a trade for Steven.

Without being noticed, he pulled out of the area that had provided cover for his vehicle and headed in the direction of the female on foot.

"Make sure you get close enough for me to get a good shot," Corbin bit out, positioned in the back of the van with Fredrick. "We're fucked if she turns."

"Don't worry." Cole smirked, an evident grin in his voice. "I'll make sure you have a clean shot."

"Are you sure the tranquilizer will be enough?" Fredrick asked.

Corbin rolled his eyes at the cowardly note in Fredrick's voice. "I've got enough in this rifle to take down two elephants. You just keep your eyes peeled. All you need to do is open the sliding door when Cole gives you the word. Capeesh?"

Fredrick nodded.

"Three o'clock," Cole said. "Get ready. Brace yourself."

When Cole hit the brakes, Corbin motioned to Fredrick. "Let's do this!"

As Fredrick scrambled over and opened the door, the noise alerted Abbey.

The minute she turned to look, a gun was aimed in her direction. When a loud pop went off, she instantly grabbed her arm and screamed in pain. Fear and panic exploded through her veins. In desperation, she searched for an escape, but it was too late. Realization had started to settle in. Once drugged, she had no power. Without the ability to shift into her she-wolf, she was helpless. The image of Steven instantly came to her. Her last coherent thought was of him. And then she teetered unsteadily before falling to the ground.

Corbin and Fredrick quickly got out of the van and hurried over to Abbey. "Get the girl and get her inside," Corbin ordered Fredrick. "I'll cover you."

"Come on, guys," Cole barked from inside the van. "Get your asses in gear!"

As Fredrick reached down and carefully picked up Abbey, she went limp in his arms.

"Let's load and go," Corbin urged. After they piled inside, he called out, "Get us the hell out of here."

A half hour later, they arrived at a small airstrip, where Steele's private jet was already fueled and ready for takeoff. After the three-hour flight from Berkeley to Los Angeles, a car was waiting for them when they stepped off the plane. Fredrick carried Abbey's limp body to the car and carefully handed her to Cole after he got inside. With her cradled in his arms like a small child, he relished every moment of her helplessness, his eyes glittering with sick arousal.

"You will belong to *me*," he whispered close to her ear.

Cole's seedy behavior toward her chilled Corbin's blood. And then a spark of unease flashed in his eyes, the first emotion other than revenge, as he watched Cole stroke his hand over her long hair. *Sick bastard*, Corbin thought. "What's Steele planning to do with the girl once he has the Adalwolf?" he asked.

"Abbey will be traveling to Europe... with *me*."

Corbin's brows went up, but he kept quiet.

When they finally got to their destination—one of Steele's hideaway locations—they pulled through a massive gateway. Three armed guards searched their vehicle and checked their IDs. When the driver stopped the car in the circular driveway, he turned to Cole. "I'll escort you inside. Mr. Steele is expecting you. He has accommodations for you and the girl."

* * *

The mood was grim and strained inside the Breedline Covenant. The moment Colonel Deshazo and his men arrived, Mia, Angel, Cassie, and Anna took the children upstairs.

Lena, Justice, and Bull strode in last. By the look on Roman's face, they knew something bad had happened.

"Abbey took off," Roman told them.

"What the hell happened?" Lena all but shouted. "How did she get past the guards?"

Roman stared at her in surprise. At first, he was taken back by the anger and frustration in her voice. But then he understood why she was upset. He was momentarily baffled by how Abbey managed to get past the Covenant's security. Then again, Abbey had spent years on the run.

Steven sat down in a chair and buried his face in his palms. And then he let out a deep breath and looked up from his trembling hands. "Early this morning... Abbey shifted and attacked Jace."

"I don't understand," Justice said. "Why would Abbey do that?"

"You have to understand her situation," Steven explained. "Put yourself in her shoes. You don't know the hell she's been through."

"Abbey is not to blame for what happened," Tessa said. "She was just trying to protect herself. She had a nightmare and woke up panicked. I can only imagine the torture she put herself through wondering if she was making the right decision to leave. She loves you, Steven. I know it. Abbey is just trying to protect you and everyone in this Covenant."

The idea that she would risk herself to protect them gutted Steven to his soul. He would never have dreamed she would go off like she did, but it all suddenly made sense why she'd left. It wasn't she wanted to. She'd done it because she was trying to protect everyone. He closed his eyes briefly, the nightmare only growing more horrific with every passing

134

minute. Years ago, she managed to escape Dr. Hans Autenburg by sheer grit and determination. If she could do that, she could handle what was ahead. Although whatever happened to her involved this Covenant whether she liked it or not. His gut was screaming that they needed to move now.

"We've got to find her before Steele gets his hands on her," Steven said.

A course of agreements circled the room.

Drakon strode into the room and said, "I got Abbey on the surveillance footage climbing over the west end of the gate. She couldn't have gotten far on foot. She's wearing a dark T-shirt, jeans, and a black ball cap."

"Here's the plan," Colonel Deshazo said. Then his eyes focused on Kid and Gunny. "I want you two to team up with Justice and Bull. We need two choppers ASAP. As soon as you're in the air, survey everything within a hundred-mile radius. We'll stay in contact while the rest of us cover some ground."

"Yes sir," all four said in unison.

"How do you plan to find her if Valkin Steele's men already managed to capture her?" Steven asked. "Shouldn't we have a search team out there on the road?"

"I'm sending Wyckoff, Roman, and Lena on the road," the colonel said. "Lawrence, Drakon, and I will team up and search through the wooded area."

"I'm not staying behind," Steven said. "And that's final."

The colonel paused for a moment. "What do you want then?"

"I'm going with you."

"All right." The colonel nodded. "I want everyone else to stay locked down in the Covenant."

Tim extended his hand. "Good luck. Keep us informed. You've got my number. If there's anything we can do, don't hesitate to contact us."

The colonel reached out and shook his hand. When he pulled away, he looked at his team and said, "Time is ticking. Let's get moving."

* * *

135

When Abbey opened her eyes, she tried to focus on her surroundings. The last thing she remembered was a man aiming a rifle at her. Then a burning pain shot through her arm. Everything else was a blur. It was obvious she'd been kidnapped.

She lifted her head, feeling like it weighed a ton, and struggled to sit up. She froze when she heard voices outside the room. She strained to hear what was being said. From the little she heard, it sounded like two men engaged in a serious conversation.

"I want *her*," Cole demanded.

"You're getting thirty girls as soon as I get my Adalwolf," Valkin bit back. "They're a mixture of nationalities and all under the age of sixteen. Abbey is not part of the deal."

Cole pinned him with a forceful glare. "After I get you the Adalwolf, the girl leaves with me. And that's final."

"Make it *twenty* girls then," Valkin snapped. "Take it or leave it. I'm in no mood for further negotiation."

"Fine," Cole grumbled.

Abbey sucked in her breath. Panic surged in her chest, tightening until she found it difficult to breathe. Steele was going to use her as a pawn to get to Steven. But in the end, there would be no trade. According to the man Steele was talking to, he had other alternatives.

She flinched at the sound of a door opening and couldn't control her reaction. She pushed back against the headboard of the bed and tucked her knees close to her chest. Fear trickled up her spine as she stared at Steele's determined expression. As he came inside, she wondered where the other man was.

"Hello, Miss Winthrop," he said smoothly. He moved toward a chair next to the bed. "You've been a hard person to track down."

She gritted her teeth and forced back the obnoxious reply that hovered on her lips.

Steele sat down and slightly leaned forward. "I've been prepared for your arrival for years." He smiled in amusement. "You've been given a particular drug that alters the she-wolf

136

within you that lasts twenty-four hours. It won't harm you, but it will keep you from shifting, for reasons I'm sure you get."

She looked at him confused. "B-but... how?"

"It was a parting gift from Dr. Hans Autenburg," he said. "Right before you killed him."

She couldn't believe this. It was surreal. All this time... there had been a drug to keep her from turning. If only she'd known.

"What do you want from me?"

"I'm proposing a bargain of sorts. No harm will come to your beloved Adalwolf if you cooperate. Give me any reason to doubt you, and he'll be the one to suffer."

She pursed her lips and stared at him, unflinching. "You're going to use me as a threat so Steven will heal Natasha, aren't you?"

"Clever girl." The corner of his mouth quirked up into a half smile. "Now that we've gotten business matters out of the way, do we have an agreement?"

Her eyes narrowed. "I'll make you a deal. If I agree to do this, Steven is not to be harmed in any way. But if you double cross me, I swear I'll hunt you down and kill you."

His smile faded. He went still, staring at her a long moment before he finally nodded. "You have my word no harm will come to Steven. But know this, Miss Winthrop." He held up a finger. "In the meantime, if you try anything stupid, you'll give me a reason to go back on my word. Keep that in mind."

She nodded, but she knew he was lying. Somehow, she had to find a way to warn Steven.

Chapter Eighteen

After Apollyon exited the Cat Club—practically dragging Callisto—Sam Malone and Deacon O'Malley strode in Zeke's direction.

"You callin' those detectives?" Sam asked.

Zeke looked up from the detective's business card he held in his hand. "I'm not so sure if the human police can handle this one."

Deacon furrowed his thick brows. "Why's dat, boss?"

Zeke Rizzo was not a rocket scientist, and he was also not a betting man. No reason to. His sin-eater skills told him all he needed to know. His mind worked like a fortune-teller's crystal ball.

He looked from Deacon to Sam. "We're dealing with something non-human. And I don't think the human PD has the credentials to deal with this."

"What exactly... are they?" Yelena spoke out.

He met her look steadily. "I'm not sure, but whatever they are, they're hungry for human blood."

There was a brief period of silence, the question Deacon wanted to ask hovering in the air as loud as the echo of clanging church bells.

"Do ya tink dey're de ones responsible for all de mass murders in de city?" Deacon finally asked.

The sin-eater in Zeke knew the answer. Caged by the situation, he clenched his jaw and nodded slowly.

"So... what are you going to do?" Yelena asked.

"I don't have a choice," he replied. "I'll have to call the Covenant."

By the time Zeke got back to his office—after zeroing out the cash registers and sending the staff and the bouncers off into the night—it was already seven in the morning. He pulled out his cell phone and opened his contacts. Tim Ross's number was listed under BHC, short for Breedline Head Council. He exhaled a deep breath and hit SEND. The minute he put it up to his ear, it started ringing. As he waited, a vivid image of

Callisto's past came back to him. At the sound of Tim's voice, he refocused his train of thoughts and explained the situation.

"Let's keep this information between us," Tim said. "We don't need the human police involved. I'm heading your way now. And I'll need a copy of the video footage."

Tessa came in the room and stopped in her tracks when she heard Tim mention something about the *human police*.

When he ended the call, he turned to her. "I may have an ID on our mystery serial killer."

Her eyes widened in alarm. "Are you talking about all the homeless murders?"

He nodded. "That was Zeke Rizzo."

"The sin-eater?"

"The one and only," he replied. "And he's got visual footage of the person he thinks might be responsible. Zeke said a couple of detectives came by his club asking questions about a girl who'd been murdered. She'd been completely drained of all her blood just like the homeless murders and stashed in a dumpster two blocks from the Cat Club."

Tessa was silent for a bit. It made her think how life was too short, no matter how long you lived. "Was the girl... homeless?"

Tim shook his head. "That's the only part that doesn't make sense. The girl made a living as a hairdresser and lived at the Brownstone Apartments."

"How much information did Zeke give the detectives?"

"He gave them a copy of the video surveillance of the girl leaving the club with a guy two hours before her death. Zeke had no idea he was linked to the homeless killings when he spoke to the detectives. Later, Zeke spoke with the guy that left with the girl that was murdered."

"What did he say to Zeke?"

"Zeke said the guy came for his sister."

Tessa shrugged. "His sister was in the bar?"

Tim nodded. "Apparently she confronted Zeke, wanting him to go home with her. The young woman's name is Callisto. According to Zeke's special sin-eater skills, he found out she's not human and has an insatiable hunger for human blood."

Tessa sighed. "You're not planning to meet Zeke by yourself, are you?"

"I can handle this myself, Tessa."

"Yeah, whatever." She rolled her eyes. "I'm sending Jace and Jem with you, and that's final. Considering what we're dealing with, no one goes anywhere alone."

Tim cocked a brow. "No offense, but I think I like this side of you. It's about time you started taking charge." He grinned. "Tell Jace and Jem I'll meet them in the foyer in ten minutes."

* * *

When Manuel arrived at Shady Pines cemetery, he parked his unmarked car alongside the far end. Before he got out, he scanned the area where at least twenty people stood, gathered for Sylvia Bennett's funeral.

Typically, he was not the type to crash a funeral, but her death had become the center focus of his mind, resurfacing haunted memories of his past. Although it had been several years, he still couldn't get his sister's death out of his head. Lailah and Miss Bennett's injuries had many similarities. His sister's death was the reason he'd chosen a career in law enforcement. Eventually, her file had become a cold case, but he would never give up. Even though he couldn't give his sister justice, he was damned determined to find the bastard who'd murdered Sylvia.

As he reached to open his door, his cell went off. When he looked at his phone, Frank's number came up. He put it to his ear and said, "What's going on?"

"We've got another body."

"Shit," Manuel gritted out. "Where?"

"The Downtown Berkeley Inn on Bancroft Way," Frank said. "Same MO as Miss Bennett's homicide. The victim is Gerald Bernard. He's the owner of a popular Italian restaurant in Berkeley called Angelino's."

"I know that place," Manuel said. "It's on Sacramento Street. Who discovered the victim?"

"Housekeeping." Frank cleared his throat. "Mr. Bernard's body was already beginning to ripen. According to the coroner, the body has been in that room for two days. Which means the time of the murder was close to Miss Bennett's homicide."

"Christ," Manuel grumbled. "I guess that means our suspect isn't working alone."

"There's more," Frank pushed forward. "The victim was gagged, handcuffed to the bed, and whipped. It's the damnedest thing. It looks like someone went *Fifty-Shades* on his ass before they nearly drained him dry. And the marks on his back appeared as if someone burnt them into his skin. The coroner stated that the victim had bite marks on his jugular like he was attacked by an animal. You think this has anything to do with a group cult?"

Manuel's brows went up. "I don't know what the hell to make of it. But I do know one thing. The guy in the video footage at Mr. Rizzo's bar has something to do with this." He squeezed his hand around the steering wheel. "Check with the manager about any surveillance cameras. I'm on my way."

"Roger that," Frank said. "I'll be waiting outside the crime scene."

As Manuel slowly eased past the cemetery, he watched as a man dressed in a black coat with a white collar at this throat stood next to Sylvia's coffin, reading from a Bible. For some reason, that image gave him a comforting feeling, although he couldn't have said why.

A half hour later, he pulled up to the inn and parked his car in front of the main entrance. Red and blue flashers mounted on police cars and emergency vehicles illuminated the parking lot as deputies evacuated the inn's occupants.

Manuel walked up to the coroner as paramedics loaded the body bag into an ambulance to be transported to forensics and said, "Do you think it's possible all the murders might be part of a satanic ritual?"

The coroner shook her head. "I'm not sure, but whoever is responsible is definitely sadistic. In all my years in forensics, I've never seen anything like this. If I didn't know any better, I'd say we've got a very hungry vampire lose in the city."

Manuel smirked. "You sound like my partner."

"It may sound crazy..." The coroner shrugged. "...but that's the only explanation I have. I'll let you know when I complete my examination."

Manuel extended his hand. "Thanks. I'd appreciate it."

When the coroner left, Frank walked up to him. "You need to take a look at what we found on the surveillance cameras. We've got footage of a woman the size of a WWE wrestler entering Mr. Bernard's room ten minutes after he checked in. According to the video, it was twelve thirty in the morning, and we got her exiting an hour later."

He clapped Frank on the shoulder. "Good work, Detective. Let's get a copy of the footage and take it to Mr. Rizzo. There's a possibility the woman on the video might have been at the Cat Club the same time our male suspect was. There could be a link between the two."

"You think they're working together?"

Manuel narrowed his eyes. "Yeah, I do. And there's a good chance they're not alone."

Chapter Nineteen

Tim's phone went off on the way to meet Zeke Rizzo at the Cat Club. He noticed it was Drakon calling. He reached toward the SUV's console and put the call on speaker. "Drakon, I've got you on speaker. Jace and Jem are with me."

"We found Abbey's ball cap alongside the road," Drakon said. "It was about a mile from the Covenant."

Tim immediately became alert. "You think Cole Decker got her, don't you?"

"I hate to say it, but it looks that way. Cole must have used a tranquilizer gun to sedate Abbey. Otherwise, she would have shifted, and we would have found his body parts."

Tim heaved a deep breath. "This situation gets worse by the minute. What did Colonel Deshazo have to say about this?"

"He suggested we wait. Valkin Steele will want to trade Abbey for Steven."

"Over my dead body," Tim said. "No deals."

"Look, none of us believe for a minute Steele will let Abbey go free once he has Steven. Which is why we're planning to wire Steven with a tracking device. When we get the call for the trade, and we will, we can track Steven's location. And hopefully, we'll have enough manpower to take Steele down and everyone involved."

"All right," Tim said. "As of now, I'm on my way to meet Zeke Rizzo."

"Are you talking about the sin-eater?"

"Yeah," Tim replied. "He might have some information on all the mysterious mass murders going on."

"You need backup?"

"Nah," Tim said. "I think the three of us can handle it."

"Be careful," Drakon warned. "Call me if you need additional backup. There's something about that sin-eater I don't trust. By the way... don't forget about Zeke's curse. Whatever you do, don't piss the guy off. And don't make any physical contact with him."

"Thanks for the heads-up. See you back at the Covenant. And, Drakon,... don't mention this to Angel. I don't want her to worry."

"I gotcha. We'll be here when you get back."

* * *

Colonel Deshazo's team was on standby and waiting for Valkin Steele's call. Roman Kincaid and the rest of the crew were in load-and-go mode. But they couldn't very well act without knowing Abbey's location. So far, Drakon had been the far greater source of information. He used his computer geek skills to search for Steele's entire life: his financials, residences, anything that would lead them to Abbey.

Meanwhile, Steven paced the floor, worried over Abbey. Was she okay? What if she was hundreds of miles away? Grief welled in his heart, spreading until his entire chest ached. Her goodbye in the note still rang in his ears.

"Damn it!"

Steven whirled around and faced Drakon. "What's wrong?"

"One of Steele's private jets flew out over three hours ago. Cole has already got one hell of a jump on us."

Everyone gathered around waiting for Drakon to relay further details.

Roman came forward. "Do you have his destination?"

"The pilot filed flight plans to Los Angeles."

Steven's brow furrowed. "We're hours behind. Do you know *where* in Los Angeles they landed?"

Drakon grimaced. "All I know is the jet flew to Malibu. There are several small airstrips, and I don't know which one. If Jem can get us there through the portal, we'll have to split up and search the area from there."

"All the more reason not to waste another minute," Gunny piped in. "Our best bet is to get in the air and figure out where the hell Steele's location is. When he makes the call for the trade, we'll already be close by."

"I agree," Drakon said. Then he looked at Colonel Deshazo. "I'll make the call to Jem while you and your men head to Malibu."

"What are we waiting for?" Wyckoff said. "Let's get those choppers in the air."

As Drakon reached for his phone to call Jem, it suddenly went off. He didn't recognize the caller, but he had a gut feeling it was the call they'd been waiting for. He looked up with a curious expression. "This could be Valkin Steele or Cole Decker calling."

The room quieted when Drakon put the phone to his ear and said, "Drakon speaking."

Steven watched helplessly as Drakon listened to caller's demands, his heart leaping into his throat in anticipation.

After a few moments of silence, Drakon finally said, "We're ready to make the trade. You tell your men we'll be there." When the call ended, he looked pointedly at Steven. "That was Cole Decker. We're to meet Steele's men in Los Angeles to make the trade. They'll give us Abbey in return for you."

"Thank God," Steven said. "The longer she is in that bastard's hands, the more they'll drug her. I can only pray he hasn't hurt or—"

Tessa placed her hand on his shoulder. "We're going to get her back. It doesn't do you or her any good to torture yourself with the worst-case scenarios. Set your mind on getting her back where she belongs. And that's with us... her *family.*"

He put his hand over hers and lightly squeezed. "Thank you, Tessa."

"We won't fail," Colonel Deshazo said. "We never have."

"Let's get the show on the road," Wyckoff said. He turned to Kid. "You flyin'?"

"Hell yeah I'm flying."

"Justice can fly the other chopper," Roman said. "Bull can ride shotgun while the rest of us have Jem take us to Los Angeles through a portal." He looked at Steven. "This is more than just a mission. It's personal for all of us. We'll get Abbey back or die trying."

145

Steven nodded at him.

"This could be a setup," Drakon pointed out. "It all sounds too easy. Cole Decker is not the type to make an honest deal. Before we head out, we need to prepare to be ambushed by Steele's men. Things could get dicey when we get to Los Angeles."

"We need to be prepared for anything," the colonel said. "If Steele wants to play us for a bunch of fools, we'll give him a show. Let's get Steven wired before we leave. Drakon can do his magic and lock onto the location wherever Steele takes him."

Drakon nodded in agreement.

Determination was etched on the faces of every single person. They were willing to put their lives on the line for Abbey. They were also ready to take down Cole Decker and Valkin Steele's operation in sex trafficking.

"I want this bastard," Steven gritted out. "I want Steele to pay for what he did to Abbey's father. But more than that, I just want her back home."

"I get it," Roman said. "And she will be."

"I'm of the mind to take them all out," Wyckoff said with clear satisfaction. "Whatever way we take them out, it will mean fewer assholes in the world."

"I'm ready to go kick some ass," Kyle chimed in.

"Count me in," Casey seconded.

* * *

Zeke gave an audible sigh of relief when he opened the door to his office and saw Tim. Standing close behind were Jace and Jem. All three looked tense, as if they were expecting the worst. Tim's gaze automatically swept the room. "Are we alone?"

"Yeah," Zeke replied. "It's just me." He moved aside and motioned them in. "Take a seat."

Tim slid into one of the chairs in front of Zeke's desk. Jem and Jace remained standing.

Zeke moved behind his desk and took a seat. His expression was both grim and weary. Without further chitchat, he got to the point. "Listen, I've had a long night, and I want to make this quick. I've got two human detectives poking around my club looking for a suspect in a murder case. When they came around asking questions, I didn't think much about it at the time. They suspected the victim was in my club that night, so they wanted a copy of the surveillance footage." He sighed. "To make a long story short, turns out the victim was here that night. She was on video leaving with a guy around midnight. After I gave the detectives a copy of the footage, they left. Later, the same guy we caught on video came back into my bar. Apparently, he was looking for his sister."

"Where's all this going, Zeke?" Jem asked.

"Hang tight." Zeke held up a halting hand. "I'm getting to the point. Before the guy came in, I was confronted by his sister. Her name is Callisto, and from what I can tell, she's not exactly human."

"What the hell is she?" Jace chimed in.

"That's a good question. I haven't the slightest clue. Although she knew what I am."

Both Jace and Jem looked at him, baffled.

"There's more. When I refused to take her home, she grabbed my arm."

Jem cocked a brow. "What did you see?"

"First, I sensed her hunger for human blood. Then after she touched me, I saw a memory of her past. She'd been buried alive in what looked to be a chamber... like a sarcophagus."

"So, do you think this Callisto and her brother are linked to all the homeless murders?" Tim asked.

Zeke nodded. "Yeah, I do."

"I'll need to see that footage. At least we'll get a look at what we're dealing with."

Zeke placed the thumb drive on his desk and looked up at Tim. "What about the detectives?"

Jem's cell phone abruptly went off. "Sorry," he said and quietly took the call.

"If they come to you asking questions," Tim said as he reached for the thumb drive, "don't give them any more information. Contact me if that guy or his sister comes back to your bar."

"I told them not to come back. But I'm not so sure if this guy will abide my warning. He doesn't look like the type to take orders, if you get what I mean."

Tim nodded an understanding. "Yeah, I know the type."

"That was Drakon calling," Jem cut in. "We need to head back to the Covenant. They got a lead on Steele."

"If you don't mind," Zeke said, "I'd like to get out of here. I've been up all night."

"Thanks for coming forward with this," Tim said. "You might want to give your staff a heads-up. If you know any of the local bar owners, get in touch with them as well. It's likely those two might hit other bars if they are indeed hunting humans."

"Yeah, I'll make sure I let my staff know what's going on, especially my security."

As Tim reached for the door, he glanced over his shoulder at Zeke. "We'll be in touch."

Before Zeke made it out the door, his phone went off. He rolled his eyes when he saw the number flash. *Shit!* It was those damn detectives.

A few minutes later, he ended the call, wishing he'd ignored it. The detectives wanted to ask him more questions. While he waited for them to arrive, his patience was wearing thin. After a half hour had passed, he gave up and made the decision to go on home. Besides, Tim had made it clear not to give them any further information.

As he reached for the door, the sounds of fists pounding nearly made him jump out of his skin. *Damn it!* Before he could open it, the door buckled inward, then exploded off the hinges. He flew back and hit the floor hard. The room went blurry for a moment.

As he fought to get to his feet, he felt a presence looming over him. Out of nowhere, someone with massive strength grabbed him from behind. He flinched as sharp nails dug into his arm. Before he could register who or what had a hold of him, his body was whipped around and lifted into the air. Then his weary eyes met Apollyon's seething stare.

"Hello,... *sin-eater*," Apollyon said, snarling his upper lip. "You may have gotten into my sister's head, but you have no power over me." He tightened his grip. "I warned you to keep your mouth shut."

Chapter Twenty

Sebastian dropped to his knees and clasped his hands as if in prayer. "I'm begging you..." He lowered his head and sobbed into his hands. "I can't bear to see her die again."

The sounds of her voice broke the silence. "Oh God... no."

Her eyes were wet with tears and her face was as white as a sheet. She held Anna's open diary in her grasp. Whatever she was reading had clearly upset her.

Sebastian shot to his feet as Eliza stalked out of the room. He turned toward Lucifer, who was leaning against the wall smiling, his cobalt eyes staring back at him. "She knows about Anna's secret," Lucifer said. "She's going to confront your stepfather."

He snarled at Lucifer. "You son of a bitch." Then he rushed after Eliza.

Before he got to her, havoc had already begun. A clamor of voices echoed down the hallway, the noise seemingly carrying from the dining area.

When Sebastian rounded the corner, Eliza stood next to Mr. Montgomery, who was seated at the head of the table. She shouted accusations of him molesting her daughter, threatening to inform the Breedline council.

"How dare you!" William Montgomery roared as he rose from his chair, his face contorted.

"How could you?" Eliza said, her entire body quivering with hurt and rage. "She's just a child."

Sibyl Montgomery came up behind Eliza and had a knife in her grasp. Eliza looked over her shoulder. Pulsing red veins streaked her eyes as she glared at Eliza, who quailed before her unleashed wrath.

"I'm sorry, Eliza... but you leave me with no choice."

Eliza started and tried to move away. Before she could even try to defend herself, Sibyl plunged the sharp tip of the blade into her neck.

The shocking assault was over in a heartbeat but left Sebastian feeling dazed as he stood back, helplessly watching Eliza soundlessly scream and crumple to the floor.

"No!" he cried out. "Please, God... no!"

Blood gushed from her throat, forming a puddle on the floor. Sibyl dropped the knife and staggered away.

Anna came rushing into the room. She swayed upon her legs, appearing overcome by the sight before her.

"Mama?"

She turned around when a shrill cry came from behind. Her little brother flew to Eliza's limp body. He dropped to his knees and wrapped his arms around her, burying his face in her blood-soaked hair. Violent sobs racked his body. The only mother he'd known was dead.

Sebastian shook his head mournfully, watching the younger version of himself fall apart.

Finally, the little boy let go of Eliza and looked up at Mr. Montgomery with a hateful glare. A note of anger dispelled the sadness in his voice. "You hurt my Sissy... and killed my Mama."

Anna sprung across the room to comfort her brother. She averted her eyes from her mother's lifeless body and looked up at Mr. Montgomery. And then her distraught gaze went to the doorway. Mrs. Montgomery's hands were covered in blood.

"Why?" Anna railed at Sibyl. Her voice cracked as though her heart was breaking. Angry tears streaked down her cheeks. "Why would you do this?"

Sibyl's livid face twisted into a demonic mask. "She was going to destroy my family." Her bitter tone clearly placed the blame on Eliza's shoulders for her husband's infatuation with Anna.

William's eyes grew dark. "You and that little brat will be taken far away from here," he said before calling out to the guards.

His cruel words angered Anna. "I won't allow you to take away the only family I have left. I'm going wherever my brother goes."

William gestured to the guards that gathered behind Anna and said, "You're going to spend the remainder of your life in a women's convent. And your brother will be placed in an all-boys boarding school. Maybe he'll learn something useful."

She grabbed the knife Sibyl had used to kill her mother and rushed at William head-on.

He stumbled backward and fell to the floor as she rammed into him. When he looked up, a knife leveled at his throat.

"How does it feel," Anna said roughly, "to fear you're going to die?"

As the guards belatedly rushed to William's defense, her fierce green eyes shot them a warning look, as if daring them to test her resolve. The guards kept their distance.

William's face hardened into a stony mask. His voice was cold as ice. "If you kill me, your brother will pay the price with his life."

"I don't want to have to kill you. Please, just let me take Sebastian and go. You'll never hear from us again."

He glared at Anna and shook his head. "I curse the day that bastard was brought into this world." And then he said to the guards, "Kill the boy!"

The little boy looked at Anna and called out, "Sissy!"

Anna's eyes widened in alarm as her little brother's urgent cry commanded her attention. Looking away from William, just for an instant, she pivoted in time to see one of the guards moving toward her brother.

"No!" she yelled. "Sebastian!"

William seized the opportunity and grabbed Anna's arm. He squeezed until the knife fell from her grasp and clattered to the floor. Then his fist slammed into her face, knocking her off balance and sending her stumbling backward.

The younger version of Sebastian jumped to his feet and lunged at his stepfather.

William threw up his hand to protect his face as Sebastian viciously clawed and bit at him. It took the efforts of two guards to pull the frail child free. "Guards. Get them out of my sight!"

With his hands clenched into little fists, the boy swung at the guards and hissed like a feral animal while they carried him away.

The remaining guards came forward and clamped a pair of handcuffs around Anna's wrists. Before they escorted her from the room, Mr. Montgomery bent low and spoke softly,

"This is all your fault. You caused your mother's death." Then he stepped back and motioned for the guards to take her away.

Unbearable sorrow gripped Sebastian as he stood back and witnessed the worst memory of his life repeat itself. The sight of her being led away, perhaps to her death, tore his heart into a million pieces.

"I'm so sorry, Anna," he whispered.

Lucifer suddenly appeared before Sebastian. "Your sad past does not excuse your present guilt. But I can still take away the pain. Just give in. It's that simple."

Sebastian looked into Lucifer's eyes, praying for just one trace of compassion, if not mercy. "I will never give you my son."

Lucifer raised an eyebrow. "You *will* give me what I want."

Chapter Twenty-One

Justice and Bull had already landed the chopper on a private airstrip owned and maintained by the Los Angeles Covenant, while Kid and Wyckoff touched down shortly after.

On the tarmac stood the rest of Colonel Deshazo's team and everyone that was ready to help locate Abbey. It was an impressive sight to see. Jem and his twin brother Jace, along with Tim, Drakon, Kyle, Casey, Alexander, and Steven, stood next to Roman and the rest of his team. Lawrence was positioned on one side of Roman while Lena—the only female member—stood near Gunny. She was dressed in civilian clothes and didn't seem too thrilled with her choices. She wore tight jeans and a crop-top, dressed provocatively in case they needed her to get closer to Cole Decker.

As soon as she saw Justice, she walked toward him and shot him a look that said she was ready to go in and kick some ass.

Justice whistled at her. "Damn, Lena. You look sexy as hell in those jeans."

She rolled her eyes. "Are you serious?"

He batted his brows. "Hell yeah."

Bull came up behind Justice and said, "We ready to roll?"

The longer they stood around, the more uneasy Casey grew. His gut instinct was screaming, and the hairs prickled on his neck. He turned to Wyckoff, who had the same apprehension stamped on his face. "Something doesn't feel right."

A shot was fired before Wyckoff could utter a reply.

"Gunman at six o'clock!" Wyckoff shouted.

Everyone ducked for cover. When another shot rang out, Gunny fell to the ground and groaned, "Son of a bitch... I'm hit!"

Justice grabbed Lena by the arm and took cover.

Wyckoff held up his hand to signal Kid he had a man down.

"We have you completely surrounded," a commanding voice called out. "Give up the Adalwolf and there'll be no further need for bloodshed."

"That's not the deal," Jace called out. "Where's the girl?"

"Mr. Steele will release the girl when the Adalwolf completes his part of the deal," the man shouted back. "We can do it the easy way, or we can do it the hard way. It's up to you."

Jace looked at Jem suspiciously and whispered, "Is that fucking Corbin Azzo?"

Jem nodded and kept his voice low, "Yeah, it sounds just like the prick."

"Damn traitor," Jace spat. "That's how Decker found the Covenant."

Steven knew without a doubt Valkin Steele was determined to achieve his objective even if he had to kill every last person.

Steven nodded at Drakon and then said, "I'll go. It's the only way."

"Damn it, Steven," Jace blasted. "You can't trust those bastards."

"I have no choice." Steven turned toward Drakon and nodded.

Drakon nodded back. At that moment, he knew Steele's men had played right into their hands. As soon as they took Steven, who was already wired, they would go in and rescue Abbey, taking Steele down and everyone involved.

Drakon rose to his feet with his hands up. "Stand down," he called out. "We're surrendering the Adalwolf."

Steven walked out with a gun at his own temple. "Here's the deal..." He raised his voice. "You're going to let everyone here go freely."

"And if I don't?" Corbin yelled back.

"If you don't, then I will shoot myself. How will you explain that to your boss?"

The entire area went quiet. For the first time, a moment of uncertainty crossed Corbin's mind. *Was the Adalwolf bluffing?* The very last thing he wanted was for him to kill himself. *But could he even be killed?* He couldn't take the chance. Steele would have him killed for sure. Then he barked, his voice echoing, "All right. How do you want to play this out?"

"I'll come to you," Steven said. "My friends will stand back."

"No surprises," Corbin bit out. "If you try anything, I'll give the order to start firing."

"You have my word."

Kid and Wyckoff dragged Gunny toward the chopper. He'd been hit with a silver bullet in the left buttock, but nothing major.

Corbin gave a terse nod and then called out to Steele's men. A moment later, Dominic Gambino and Marcus Delvecchio appeared. Marcus directed Steven over. As he complied, moving forward, he slowly lowered the gun and extended it toward Marcus.

Marcus took the gun from him and nodded at Dominic. "Cuff him." He looked Steven in the eye. "Don't try anything stupid." He held up a portable radio transceiver. "All I have to do is say the word, and the she-wolf gets a bullet between her eyes. You get me?"

Steven nodded.

As Marcus and Dominic led him away, he gave a quick glance over his shoulder at his fellow comrades. He had absolute faith that they wouldn't let him down. They were his family now. And Abbey's too.

When Steele's men disappeared with Steven, Drakon rushed to the chopper while Lena, Justice, Lawrence, Roman, and Colonel Deshazo hurried over to tend to Gunny, who was steadily swearing like a sailor.

"I've got the GPS device already tracking Steven," Drakon said to Colonel Deshazo. "And I've called for backup. We're gonna need some wheels."

The colonel rose to his feet, his expression strained. "I'm going to have Kid and Lawrence take the chopper and transport Gunny to the nearest hospital. As soon as you get Steven's final location, we'll regroup and figure out our next move." And then he turned to Wyckoff, Lena, and Roman. "I need you guys to spread out. Do a recon of the area. Make sure it's clear."

As soon as Tim, Alexander, Kyle, Casey, Jace, and Jem had hurried over to the chopper where Gunny lay, Colonel Deshazo said, "As soon as Drakon has a hit on Steven's final location, we're heading that way."

Lawrence had been working diligently on a pressure bandage, trying to stop the bleeding in Gunny's wound. When he finally got him patched, Justice and Bull loaded him into the chopper. Gunny balled up his fist and swore viciously.

Colonel Deshazo popped his head inside as Kid geared up the chopper, preparing for take-off.

"Don't look at me like that," Gunny groaned at the colonel. "Hell, it's just a flesh wound."

The colonel made a face, his expression seemingly irritated. "I expect you back on your feet as soon as they patch your ass." And then he looked at Kid and Lawrence. "Let me know as soon as you land."

Lawrence nodded and Kid saluted.

Colonel Deshazo and the others stood back and watched as the chopper immediately took off, buzzing over the distant trees.

A few moments later, two Hummers roared down the runway.

"That'll be our ride," Drakon said. "Let's load up and get the show on the road."

* * *

Manuel opened the door to his unmarked car while his partner went to the passenger's side. As they left the Downtown Berkeley Inn and headed to speak with Zeke Rizzo about the mysterious woman caught on camera at the scene of the crime, Manuel was sure of one thing. The suspects in all the gruesome killings had made one hell of a mistake. One had been caught on video leaving the Cat Club with Miss Bennett not long before her death, and the other suspect was seen at Mr. Bernard's hotel room around the time of his death. The entire police force was going to be gunning for the bastards when they found out who they were.

It was nearly an hour later when the detectives finally arrived at Zeke's bar.

"I hope Mr. Rizzo didn't give up on us," Frank said.

Manuel pointed to a black Porsche underneath an awning. "Isn't that his vehicle?"

"Yeah, that's his car. It must be nice to afford a ride like that. It took me five years just to save up to buy my new Ford."

Manuel smirked. "Tell me about it. A detective's salary doesn't go far. But at least we get to take down the bad guys, right?"

Frank cocked a brow. "Yeah, I guess so."

"Come on, partner." Manuel reached across the seat and tapped Frank on the shoulder. "Let's go talk to Mr. Rizzo."

* * *

Yelena frowned when she looked out of her office window that overlooked the parking lot of the Cat Club. There was a suspicious-looking Ford parked in front of the building. And then she saw two men—who looked to be undercover cops by the way they dressed—step out of their vehicle and walk toward the entrance of the bar.

Shit! What the hell are they doing here? Then she noticed Zeke's Porsche was still at the bar. She checked her watch and noticed the time. It was too early for him to be at the bar.

She whispered, "What the hell are you still doing here, Zeke?"

Last night, after feeling lonely, she'd drowned her sorrows with a bottle of tequila. Instead of driving, she'd decided to sleep it off on the loveseat that barely fit in the tiny space of her office. Maybe Zeke had done the very same thing.

She flinched when she heard a loud crash coming from the lower level of the bar. When she rushed downstairs and got to the bottom, she screamed. Zeke was lying on the floor, gasping for air. He was clutching his throat. And then she caught a familiar scent in the air. As she inhaled the heady scent, a heavy hand clamped around her arm. The instant she looked over her shoulder, she recognized the face staring back at her. All she could do was stare into his feral gaze. His eyes were golden and slit-pupiled like a feline's.

The stranger hovered above her in silent menace. "You're a succubus." His voice was deep, and he had an accent, but she couldn't place it.

On impulse, she struggled against his hold.

He captured both her wrists in one of his hands. "Don't be stupid."

"What do you... want?" Her voice trembled.

"Let... her... go..." Zeke struggled to get the words out.

The guy looked away from her and glared at Zeke. When he refocused his eyes on her, he said, "You're in love with the sin-eater, aren't you?"

"I don't..." Confusion closed her mouth. "I don't know what you're talking about."

Zeke lurched to his feet, wobbled, and did an ass plant back on the floor.

The guy whispered close to her ear, "The sin-eater doesn't have the balls to be with you. He runs from his curse like you run from yours."

Zeke felt utterly helpless. Blood trickled between his fingers as he kept his hand pressed against his throat. He was desperate to protect Yelena. In a weary voice, he said, "Please... don't hurt her."

The sound of a shotgun being cocked, followed by a demanding voice caught their attention. "Let the girl go, or I'll put a hole in you the size of Texas!"

Manuel had never seen anyone move that fast. One second the guy had a hold of the girl, the next he was standing in front of him, towering at least six inches above him. And with lightning speed, Manuel was disarmed, put in a tight choke hold, and lifted off the ground by only one hand.

"Humans are only good for one thing," the guy said in a deep, accented growl. "And that's food."

Manuel clawed at the guy's iron grip.

"Put him down!" Frank demanded from behind.

As the stranger craned his head around, he stared straight into the barrel of a semi-automatic pistol and snarled. He dropped his hand and Manuel fell to the floor, choking for air.

In the blink of an eye, the stranger mysteriously vanished into thin air.

Frank took a few steps back. "What the..."

One minute the guy that had his partner in a choke hold, the next he was gone in a flash.

Frank looked toward the sound of a high-pitched scream. He was completely astonished when he caught sight of the stranger now standing behind Yelena. And then he disappeared again, taking her with him.

"No." Zeke muttered in a strained voice. "Yelena..."

Chapter Twenty-Two

Steven became anxious as the SUV slowed and then came to a complete stop. Waiting for the wrought-iron gate to open, he noticed several men in security uniforms surrounding the place. It reminded him of Fort Knox. A feeling of uneasiness assailed him as they drove through. He was thinking of Abbey. Although it had only been a few days since she'd been taken, it felt like weeks had gone by.

As they came upon the front entrance, a shudder worked over his shoulders. He had to focus and turn off all his thoughts of Abbey being in Cole Decker's possession. Thinking about it made him crazy.

As the door to the SUV opened, a guard greeted him. "Follow me." Then he motioned Steven out of the vehicle. "Mr. Steele is expecting you."

While the guard escorted him inside the estate, his anxiety was so thick, he could almost taste it. It pervaded every cell in his body.

"Wait here," the guard said. "Mr. Steele will be with you shortly."

A few moments later, he heard a voice from behind. "I've been waiting for years to meet you, Mr. Craven."

When Steven whirled around, a man dressed in expensive clothing addressed him. "My name is Valkin Steele." He moved forward and extended his hand.

Steven eyed him curiously. His voice reeked of arrogance. It was cold, hard and determined. *Evil.*

"Where's Abbey?"

Steele quirked one eyebrow and lowered his hand. "Miss Winthrop is safe and secure."

"I don't trust you. How the hell do I know you're telling the truth? I want to see her first, or the deal is off."

Steele looked at him with an inquisitive gaze. "Very well." He nodded. "I'll give you ten minutes with Miss Winthrop, but no longer. My Natasha is running out of time."

* * *

Abbey struggled to wake from the nightmare, but she couldn't shake out of the horrible images inside her head. Deep slumber held her too firmly in its grasp.

Helpless in the dark dream, a whimper tore from her mouth as Dr. Hans Autenburg stood above her with a scalpel in his hand.

"Zee child belongs to me now," Dr. Autenburg said, his German accent sending cold chills all through her body.

She screamed when she felt the blade cut a line into her belly, getting closer to her womb.

"Steven," she cried out, her voice desperate. "Please... help me!"

The sound of a door bursting open startled her to wakefulness. Panic shrieked through her as two armed guards stormed into her room.

She scrambled to a sitting position and pressed her back against the headboard of the bed. She clutched her hand over her belly in an automatic protective measure. "What's going on?"

"Mr. Steele wants you up and dressed," one of the guards said with a tight frown marring his face. "There are clothes in the closet. As soon as you're ready, we'll escort you downstairs. You'll get ten minutes with Mr. Craven before he's taken to heal Ms. Natasha."

Oh God, she thought. *They'd found Steven.* She bit her lip and nodded.

When the door clicked shut, she scrambled out of bed. She rushed toward the closet and rummaged through the clothes until she found a shirt and a pair of pants with a drawstring waist. *Perfect,* she thought as she put her hand on her belly in a soothing motion.

For a moment she stood there, staring down at the place that held a tiny life. Even though she'd only been back with Steven for a short time, she knew without a doubt she was carrying his child. She briefly shut her eyes and imagined a little boy the spitting image of Steven, only a smaller version. And then reality hit. She feared that she wouldn't be able to keep herself or her baby safe as her pregnancy progressed. She sucked several steadying breaths and tried to ease the stress from her mind.

After she tied the drawstring snugly around her waist, she swallowed back her nerves and went to the door to call out to the guards.

Moments later, the two guards escorted her downstairs. She felt like she couldn't breathe. Miraculously her fear subsided when she looked across the room to see Steven standing in front of a picture window. She wanted to run to him, but she was rooted to the spot where she stood, tears filling her eyes. She squared her shoulders and took a hesitant step forward.

"Steven..."

He turned to face her. "Abbey?"

With his arms outstretched, he rushed over and gathered her in his arms. She broke down and wept into the crevice of his neck.

"Trust me," he whispered close to her ear. "Everything will be all right. I promise."

She pulled away and looked at him with tears in her eyes. "I'm so sorry. I wasn't thinking straight when I took off like I did. "Please forgive—"

"Shhh," he soothed her. "I understand." He wiped the tears from her cheeks. "You don't have to apologize for anything. Just promise you'll never leave me again."

The vulnerability in his voice made her heart squeeze. She wanted more than anything to tell him about the child she was carrying but decided now was not the best time. Instead, she smiled and said, "I promise. I just want us to be a family."

Some of the tension fled his expression. "You'll always have a family, honey. Get used to it. Everyone in the Covenant is your family now."

As he pressed his lips against hers, she felt a light fluttering in her chest. She kept her eyes closed, wanting to savor this moment forever. "I love you."

He smiled and kissed her again. He was about to respond when Valkin Steele came into the room, his expression grave.

"Let's go, Steven. We are running out of time."

Fear burned through her as she watched two guards urge Steven forward. Before he walked away, he looked at her tearstained face and grasped her hand, placing something in her palm. *Trust me,* he mouthed silently. "I love you, Abbey."

She peered at him, confused, and nodded.

After she was escorted back to her room, she sat down on the bed and looked down at the crumpled piece of paper in her hand. Her fingers trembled as she opened it and saw what was written inside.

Trust me, Abbey. Be ready. Help is on the way. I love you.

* * *

Everyone was on alert after Drakon finally got a hit on Steven's whereabouts. "Four seventy-seven Sea Star Drive in Malibu," Drakon said. "It'll take us a little over an hour to get there if we drive."

"Our best bet is to stay close by and wait the night out," Colonel Deshazo suggested. "In Steele's mind, he thinks he's untouchable. That gives us an edge because, even if he's expecting us to make a move, he already thinks that he's outsmarted us. Valkin Steele and Cole Decker won't be expecting the extent of our power. We'll head out before daylight."

"I agree," Roman said.

Drakon rubbed his hands over his temples, anxiety written all over his face. "All right." He released a heavy sigh. "We'll stop at the nearest hotel. Everyone will need to get their rest. We've got a big day ahead."

"Any word on Gunny?" Wyckoff asked the colonel.

"He's patched up and ready to go. Kid's taking the chopper to meet us in Malibu. Once we get where we're headed, I'll give them our location."

An hour later, they stopped at a hotel not far from Steele's estate. Everyone piled out, ready to go over their plan of action with Kid, Gunny, and Lawrence, who had already booked and checked into the Malibu hotel.

When Colonel Deshazo walked to where Kid and Lawrence were waiting, he could hear Gunny swearing a blue streak as he came around the side of the building. He stopped in his tracks when he saw the colonel. He had an unlit cigar tucked between his lips.

Gunny stiffened. "Colonel D," he said around the cigar. Then he quickly reached up and snatched it from his mouth.

The colonel stared at Gunny with his brows furrowed. "Are you sure you're up for all this?"

"Yes, sir. Never been better," he said promptly. "It's payback time."

The colonel laughed a little. "Good to have you back, Gunny. Before we all get some shuteye, let's get you guys updated."

After he brought Kid, Lawrence, and Gunny up to date, everyone called it a night.

* * *

As Lena opened the door to her hotel room, she cursed when she saw Justice sprawled on the bed.

"Damn it, Justice. You scared me."

"Sorry," he said. "I just thought we'd share a room." He sat up and batted his brows. "I figured you might need company."

"Where's Bull?"

"He's sharing a room with Lawrence and Roman."

She moved next to the bed, crossed her arms, and sent him a look. "You know, we're supposed to be getting some sleep."

He gave her a shit-eating grin. "Oh, I plan on sleeping... eventually."

She rolled her eyes. "You're full of yourself, you know that."

As her gaze drifted downward, her eyes widened when she saw the bulge in his fatigues. Her mouth gaped when he reached out and hauled her on top of the bed. She landed with a soft bounce. He quickly shifted his body above her and positioned himself in place so she couldn't get away. As if she wanted to.

She shot him a scolding glare. "Justice—"

"Hush," he muttered, just as his lips came down over hers.

His kiss was electric, demanding, and fierce. She shuddered from head to toe. His warm tongue slid like velvet over her lips, persuading her to open. When she gave in, she moaned into his mouth, and he swallowed it up with the most erotic kiss.

He pulled back, his chest heaving, his eyes glittering down at her. "Time is ticking. I think we should definitely get naked." He smoothed his hand through the long strands of her hair.

The corners of her mouth curled up. "Is that so?"

He looked at her with a serious expression. "Oh yeah... completely naked."

She reached up and glided her fingers over his firm jaw. "Well, in that case, what are we waiting for?"

His eyes gleamed in triumph. "God," he groaned, "you drive me so damn crazy. I can never get enough of you." He leaned until his lips were close to her ear and whispered, "I'm going to give you multiple orgasms."

"Mmmm... I like your enthusiasm." Her eyebrow went up in question. "Are you sure?"

"I'm a man of my word, sweetheart. Have I ever let you down?"

"Nope," she said with a wicked gleam in her eye. "So far, you've been pretty damn amazing."

He batted his brows again, and it sent a thrill all the way to her belly. Damn, this man was to-die-for sexy. And he was looking at her like she was the sexiest woman on the earth.

He pinned her with a fierce gaze. "I love you, baby."

"I love you too. Now stop talking," she said cheekily. "I'm ready to cash in on all those multiple orgasms you promised."

"Yes, ma'am."

Chapter Twenty-Three

Zeke sank to the ground with his hand pressed against his throat and eased himself flat on his back. It wasn't that he was going to bleed out, although the gash in his throat hurt like a son of a bitch. The Breedline healing process was already surging through his body, miraculously creating new skin cells to repair the wound. Compared to humans, Breedlines had tremendous advantages when it came to health. Their bodies healed fast. The only thing that slowed their healing process was silver. It was their kryptonite. Besides old age, a silver bullet to the brain was the only thing deadly to his species.

For some odd reason, Zeke healed faster than his kind. He always thought it had something to do with him being born a sin-eater. Go figure.

He closed his eyes and random thoughts of Yelena entered his mind. Now that she was in the company of a cold-blooded killer, God only knew what would become of her. He felt guilty for failing to save her.

Frank rushed toward him. "Jesus." He reached out. "Are you all right?"

Zeke opened his eyes and looked up at the detective. "Yeah." His voice was hoarse like he'd been screaming for hours. "Please..." He shook his head and refused to take Frank's hand. "I'll be fine."

Right now, he couldn't deal with the nature of his curse, so avoiding physical contact with the detective was high on his priority list.

Frank pulled his hand back. "What the hell do you mean?" He looked at all the blood covering Zeke. "I'm calling an ambulance."

"Please... no." Zeke sat up and removed his hand from his throat. "Look for yourself. I'm a fast healer, so there's no need to call for an ambulance."

Frank's eyes widened. He was utterly freaked out now. No human had that kind of super healing power. "Will someone explain to me what the hell is going on?"

When Frank heard a groan, he shifted his focus toward his partner. Manuel managed to stand as he threw out a hand, steadying himself against the wall.

"We need to get out an APB," Manuel gasped. When he stepped forward, he swayed.

Frank grabbed his arm and held him steady. "Whoa, Detective. Are you okay?"

"No, I'm not fucking okay," Manuel snapped. He tried not to lean on his partner, but he needed the help. He couldn't make his legs work right. And his neck ached like a bitch.

"You stay put while I call this in," Frank said.

"Don't bother," Zeke spoke out.

Manuel's brow rose. "What did you just say?"

"After what you both just witnessed, do you think the police are capable of catching this guy?"

"Since you seem to know so much," Manuel said. "You explain to us what the fuck is going on. People just don't disappear. And how in the hell are you still alive after all this blood loss?" He pointed to the pool of blood on the floor. "It looks like your damn throat was cut... but you say you're fine? Fast healer my ass! What the *hell* are you?"

In the long silence that followed, Manuel had the sense that nothing was as it seemed. The rules were completely off, and reality was slowly shifting into a bizarre realm. *God, did vampires really exist?* Maybe his partner was right after all. He knew one thing for sure: It was going to take more than a bottle of whiskey to deal with all this.

"We're waiting, Mr. Rizzo," Frank said. "How is all this possible? Is that guy..." He cleared his throat. "...a vampire?"

"Come on, Detective." Zeke cocked a brow. "A *vampire*? Really?"

"Then what the hell is he?" Frank demanded. "Stop with all the bullshit. It's obvious that guy isn't exactly human, nor do I believe you're a fast healer."

"It's difficult to explain," Zeke said. "Besides, it won't make any sense to you."

"Try us," Manuel said. "If you want us to help you find that girl, who you seem to care about, we're going to need you to cooperate with us."

Zeke looked between the two detectives and finally settled his eyes on Manuel. "You don't understand. There's nothing you can do. Even if the whole entire police department went up against this guy, they would be useless. You both saw it with your own eyes. What we're dealing with is something that goes against the laws of nature."

"You still haven't answered our question, Mr. Rizzo," Manuel continued to grill him. "If the guy's not a vampire, then what is he?"

Zeke shrugged. "That's just it. I have no idea."

"You're full of shit, Zeke," Frank barked. "There's more you're not telling us."

"Listen... I wish I could give you more information, but I can't. If you don't have any further questions, I'd like to go home."

He knew there was nothing the detectives could do to help him get Yelena back, and there was no reason to get humans involved. They were powerless up against whatever had taken Yelena. His only hope of getting her back, if she was even still alive, was the Breedline Covenant.

"You're a heartless bastard, Zeke Rizzo," Frank gritted out. "Don't you even care about the poor girl? What about her family? Don't you think they might wonder why she just up and disappeared?"

"Her name is Yelena," Zeke said. "Yelena Smirnov. She moved here from Russia five years ago. I hired her to oversee all the security in the bar. There is no one..." He hesitated and sighed. "Yelena doesn't have a family. She's alone." He lowered his head. "And yes, I care a great deal for her." He looked back up. "I just need to get my head on straight. I'm not giving up on her if that's what you think."

Manuel moved forward on shaky legs. "Then let us help you."

"I'm sorry." Zeke shook his head. "I can't get you involved."

"Well, I guess we're on our own then," Manuel said. "If you think we're just going to sweep this under the rug, Mr. Rizzo, think again. I'm not giving up on Miss Smirnov."

Zeke nodded and got to his feet. Before he left, he said, "Help yourselves behind the bar, Detectives. It's on the house."

It wasn't five minutes later that Manuel downed his first shot of whiskey. He instantly coughed. His throat was raw, and it felt like someone had set it on fire. As soon as he stopped coughing, he poured himself another one.

"I'm going to get drunk," he grumbled, holding up the shot glass in front of his partner. "After what just happened, there's no way I'm staying sober for the next twenty-four hours."

"We're going to find Miss Smirnov," Frank said as he watched Manuel down his second shot of whiskey.

Frank wasn't drinking, but then he had a family to go home to. Manuel, on the other hand, was free to get wasted. The only thing waiting for him when he got home was Ira, his French bulldog.

Manuel laughed and poured himself number three. "Yeah, just like Lailah..." He cleared his throat. "I mean Sylvia." He shook his head. "Whatever."

"You shouldn't blame yourself for Lailah's death," Frank said. "You did everything you could to find your sister's killer. We'll get this one, partner."

Manuel knew that Sylvia Bennett's murder, and Miss Yelena Smirnov, who was now kidnapped by some vampire-like crazed killer, had nothing to do with bringing his sister back to life. Lailah was gone. And she'd been gone for a long time. It was about justice. Years ago, he'd taken an oath to protect the innocent, and he'd keep that promise until he took his last breath.

"Yeah, whatever," Manuel mumbled as he downed the third shot of whiskey. "You should go on home... be with your family."

"I'm not leaving you here."

"I can call a cab."

"Nah. I'll hang around, and then drive your ass back to your apartment."

Manuel patted his partner on the shoulder. "You'd make a great wife, Frank."

"Funny." Frank chuckled. "That's what Missy tells me."

"It's been one hell of a morning." Manuel let out a long breath. He felt like he'd just been missed by an 18-wheeler.

"Amen to that," Frank replied.

Manuel shifted in his chair and faced the mirror across the bar. God, he was getting old. The gray in his hair appeared thicker, and the circles under his eyes looked darker.

He turned toward Frank, looking as though he was ready to throw in the towel. "Do you think we're getting too old for this?"

Frank faced him. His dark brown eyes were penetrating. "Christ... what are you talking about?"

"Look at us." Manuel shrugged. "We're not exactly spring chickens, now are we? How the hell are we going to take down that Dracula character when we don't even know what he is? And what about Zeke Rizzo?" he persisted. "Ordinary people don't miraculously heal from getting their throat slashed." He cursed in a low mumble. "Nothing is as it seems anymore. I mean, we're in our damn fifties for crying out loud."

Frank reached out and placed his hand on his partner's shoulder. "It'll be all right, Detective. We'll figure this out, and we're not too damn old. Hell, we'll be chasing criminals to the day we're strapped to a wheelchair."

"Maybe," Manuel muttered. When he went to pour him another shot, Frank's cell phone vibrated on his belt.

He brought to his ear. "Detective Perkins speaking."

Manuel set the bottle down and pushed his glass away.

"We'll be there," Frank finally said as he ended the call. And then he looked over at his partner with a grim expression. "That was Captain Hodge. We've got another dead body with the same MO."

The news gave Manuel a moment of pause, waiting for his partner in anticipation, hoping the victim wasn't Miss Smirnov.

"It's not her."

The tension in Manuel's shoulders eased a little.

"The victim was found at the White Swan Inn over on Fillmore Street," Frank said. "About a mile from a club called The Alibi. You know that place?"

171

"Yeah," Manuel said as he leaped off the bar stool. Then he sat back down, slowly. "I know the owner. He's my nephew Nathan."

"I told the captain we'd handle this one," Frank said. "It's another white male in his mid-forties. Paul Taylor. He's the owner of that antique store on Geary Boulevard." He cleared his throat. "Captain Hodge said the body was discovered about an hour ago. And this time the victim was half-eaten."

"Jesus," Manuel gasped.

"Our female suspect could be targeting clubs to find her victims just like the guy that took Sylvia and Yelena. It's possible Mr. Taylor was picked up at your nephew's bar."

"You might be right," Manuel said. "After we check the crime scene, I'll give Nathan a call."

"Maybe you should sit this one out."

Manuel focused his eyes by squinting. "No way." He slid off the stool. "I'm going, and that's final. After a cup of coffee, I'll be good to go."

Frank looked down at the bottle of whiskey, then at his partner. "All right," he grumbled. "We'll make a pit stop on the way. You need more than one cup of coffee. If the captain finds out you've been drinking, he'll have my balls in a vise."

As they walked out of the Cat Club and got into the car, Frank drove to the nearest coffee shop. Thirty minutes later, and two coffees to go, the detectives arrived at the crime scene.

When Frank parked the car, flashing lights from several police cruisers were on the scene, and men in blue guarded the entrance to the Inn.

He eyed his partner. "You ready?"

"Yeah." Manuel gave him a slight nod. "Let's get this over with."

Chapter Twenty-Four

When Zeke left the bar, he was a complete mess. He couldn't stand not knowing if Yelena was dead or alive. He felt like he was dying from a thousand cuts, slowly bleeding out. He could only hope she didn't end up like all the others. So far, humans seemed to be the only target. She was a succubus, and somehow that gave him reason to believe she was still alive.

She was the only thing he had in his pathetic life. Although the Cat Club made him a hell of a living, he hated the lifestyle, he really did. He hated being around so many bodies, the noise, and all the smells. Each night after closing time, he went home to an empty apartment. He slept alone, if he slept at all. Food gave him little pleasure. Relationships were out because of his messed-up curse. And every second of the day, Yelena was on his mind. Pain seeped into his heart, making the love he felt for her soar. *I'm such a damn fool.* If only he could go back in time. He wanted the chance to tell her how much she meant to him. Now, there was a possibility it was too late.

While he drove his Porsche along a winding road, the morning sun stung his eyes. He felt like he had the worst hangover. Along with a headache, and lack of sleep, he relied on adrenaline alone to get him to his destination. He wanted to be with Yelena, but he wasn't sure if he they could overcome the kind of baggage they had. She was a succubus, and he was a Breedline. Relationships took work, and love required sacrifices that were hard to make. He'd seen the evidence of that enough times just by observing his employees with all their relationships. But she was worth it. She deserved to be happy. She deserved a man who allowed her to be herself, and he was damn determined to be that man. At that moment, a sudden surge of emotion caught him off guard. If it took the rest of his life, he swore he'd find her and tell her how he felt. *I'm not giving up, Yelena. I swear... I'll search for you until I take my last breath.*

He reached for the radio and turned up the volume. As he listened to the lyrics of a Breaking Benjamin song, agony clawed at his chest. He wiped at his eyes, then looked at his hand. *Were those tears?* He swallowed them back and gripped both hands on the steering wheel. In a hurry to get where he was going, he stomped on the accelerator.

Desperate to find her, his sole focus was to persuade the Breedline Covenant to help, his only hope of getting Yelena back. Hell, he'd get on his knees and beg them if that's what it took.

The Covenant didn't take long to find, considering the size of the estate. It was like a castle from out of one of those fairy tales. The two-story stone structure stood atop a hill, with rows of giant pines and beautiful green foliage surrounding the place.

When he parked outside the gate, he got out of the car and looked up at the security camera. He took a deep breath and forced himself to move forward. He pressed the call button on the monitor. "My name is Zeke Rizzo. Please... it's urgent. I need to speak with Tessa Chamberlain."

After the gate opened, he drove up a long curved driveway. As he came to the estate's courtyard, he saw an American flag waving on a pole. All the landscape was green, with neat hedges that looked newly trimmed. Several leafy trees and shrubs dotted the open ground, and an enormous fountain was flowing. In the near distance, a huge pond spread out over several acres. It was practically a small lake. He parked the Porsche close to the entrance and waited inside as two armed guards moved in his direction.

When the guards waved him over, he got out of his car. He followed them into a huge foyer. Tessa's voice caught his attention. "Welcome, Mr. Rizzo."

As he turned to face her, she gestured toward a seating area. "Please, make yourself comfortable."

To avoid physical contact, he joined his hands behind his back and gave her a curt nod. "Thank you, Mrs. Chamberlain."

He walked into the study, his eyes barely registering the French cream-colored walls and the matching silk sofas and the white marble mantel. When he sat down, Tessa took a seat across from him. "What's going on, Mr. Rizzo? The guard told me you said it was urgent."

Cold dread gripped his throat. "Please, call me Zeke," he said with a nervous pitch to his voice. "I don't mean to barge in on short notice, but I'm desperate for the Covenant's help."

"You're fine, Zeke. Please tell me, what can we do to help you?"

He rubbed his hand over his face, weary from the sheer weight of his worry. Clearing his throat, he finally said, "Someone very special to me has been taken... by that *thing* that's been murdering all those humans. Her name is Yelena."

"Oh my God, Zeke." Tessa's eyes widened. "I'm so sorry. When did this happen?"

"Earlier this morning. And... there's more."

He let out his breath, hoping like hell he wasn't making a mistake confiding in her. But he didn't have any choice. She had to know what the two detectives witnessed. When humans got involved in their world, it never ended well.

"When Yelena was taken, two human detectives witnessed everything."

"What all did they see?"

He frowned. "They saw me heal from a cut throat."

She kept silent and had a determined expression.

"They also saw that guy disappear."

Her gaze narrowed. "Disappear?"

"Yeah," he hesitantly said. "The guy just vanished."

Tessa dug into her pocket and pulled out her cell phone. "I'm going to call Tim." As she initiated the call, she looked up at him. "I promise, we'll do everything we can to find Yelena."

His tension eased. "Thank you, Tessa."

* * *

It was hours later, or at least it seemed like hours when Yelena awoke to the sound of her favorite classical melody, Beethoven's *Moonlight Sonata.*

"Hello,... Yelena," a deep voice murmured over the harmonic composition.

She widened her eyes when she looked up. It was the man who had abducted her. And he was standing next to the bed, staring down at her with a hungry gaze. His hard features matched his chiseled body. The clothes he had on were black leather. His eyes were slit-pupiled like a feline's, and his glorious head of hair, black as midnight, hung in thick waves past his shoulders. It was evident to her he wasn't human. Using her succubus skills, she suddenly realized he was born of her species... and something else: a half-breed and another interbreeding she couldn't pinpoint. What was he?

Frightened by his presence, she scrambled to the far side of the bed and tucked her knees against her chest.

He briefly closed his eyes and inhaled through his nose. The arousing smell of Yelena's scent was intoxicating. His lips slightly curled up, exposing the sharp tips of his fangs. "I've brought you a gift."

She looked into his golden, catlike eyes.

When he sat down, the mattress dipped. "I can sense your thirst." He extended his hand and offered her a crystal goblet filled with red liquid. "Here... drink this."

She looked at him, speechless.

"My name is Apollyon." His voice was like dark silk. "Don't be afraid, Yelena. Take it. I'm not going to hurt you."

Her gaze drifted away from his face and focused on what he was offering her. In that instant, her thirst rose like a burning inferno.

He placed the goblet closer to her. "Drink, Yelena."

Her hands shook as she reached for it.

As she put it to her lips, he watched her take a taste. It wasn't long before she tilted the glass and swallowed it down to the last drop.

God, he wanted to kiss her. She was now his reason for living. Not the power, not the uncontrollable desire for human blood, and not the killing. His female captive was the burning pain that made him feel whole again.

"Thank you," she said and held the empty glass out to him.

When he took it from her, their skin slightly brushed, and for some reason, she sensed he *worshiped* her. At that moment, she knew he wasn't ever going to let her go.

Panic, an emotion she hadn't felt for a long time, surged into her chest. It reminded her of her old life back in Russia, where she had lived with her family growing up. Before she came to America, they were killed by the Russian mafia, slaughtered in the streets like cattle. These were bad visions, bad memories. Her thoughts quickly shifted, recalling the good memories. She remembered all the cheery fires her father had made in the small hearth in the living room to keep them warm during the cold mornings. And all the hours spent in the kitchen with her mother baking Borodinsky. She could still smell the delicious aroma of the homemade bread. And then an image of Zeke came to mind, clear as a picture. She saw his mesmerizing, pale blue eyes and his handsome face. She adored the shyness in his expression when he looked at her and the nervous pitch in his voice. She remembered how he reacted the last time they spoke. Zeke avoided physical contact due to the outcome of his curse. She wondered if he was searching for her. Had he given up by now, convinced she was dead?

Fear closed in on her, and she tried to bridle the emotion by telling herself that he was still searching for her. And that he would be desperate enough to seek out the Breedline Covenant for help.

The sound of a door abruptly opening caught her attention and brought her back to focus.

A tall woman with long black hair pushed her way into the room. "I don't believe it." She flipped her hair back. "Who said you could have a pet?"

Apollyon shot to his feet. "This is none of your concern." He pointed to the open doorway. "Get out, Callisto."

She ignored him and crossed her arms. "If you get to keep her, it's only fair that I get a pet of my own."

Out of nowhere, a muscular female stepped into the room and put herself between them. "What the hell is going on?"

Apollyon looked at her with a hateful glare. "Don't push me, Electra. I'm in no mood."

Electra realized by his facial expression now was not the time to push any limits. He was wired, his lust for the girl overriding his thinking. The bonding scent percolating off his skin was undeniable. And disagreeing with her brother was not good with him or anyone else for that matter.

"I thought we agreed not to bring our food home," Electra said. "Does mother know?"

"She's not food," Apollyon said in a gravelly voice.

Electra's face darkened, and as she opened her mouth to argue, Callisto's whiney voice cut her off. "I want that sin-eater as my pet."

Yelena bared her fangs. "You touch Zeke, and I'll slit your throat."

When Callisto and Electra looked in Yelena's direction, they blinked a couple of times, as if they were thrown off by her threatening words.

Callisto took a step forward. "What did you say, bitch?"

Before Callisto took another step, Apollyon snatched her by the arm. "Get out... now."

"Come on, Sister," Electra spoke out. "Let's go."

Callisto pouted like a spoiled child and grumbled, "Fine!"

When she stomped out, Electra stopped before she exited the room. "I hope you know what you're doing, Brother."

Chapter Twenty-Five

When Steven was escorted down a long corridor, leaving Abbey behind, he let out a deep breath. It felt like he was saying goodbye, and he couldn't stand it. His mind was filled with so much rage that he could barely think straight.

Two armed guards, along with Valkin Steele, took him through a series of hallways. When they stopped outside a door, Steele said, "My Natasha needs healed. We don't have any time to waste."

"What kind of cancer does Natasha have?"

"Lung cancer," Steele replied. "Before she could be treated, it had already spread to her kidneys and into her bones. The doctors told us there was nothing more they could do."

Then Steele advanced on Steven. "The welfare of Abbey..." His face went rigid. "...depends entirely on you, Mr. Craven."

"Don't you threaten me," Steven said through gritted teeth. "I hold all the cards."

Steele grabbed Steven's shirt and drew him closer until their faces were inches apart. "You hold nothing!" Spittle flew out of his mouth. "You'll cure my Natasha, or I'll hand over your precious Abbey to Cole Decker."

Steven twisted away. "Let's just get this over with." He had to remain calm. He couldn't allow his own rage to get out of hand. Abbey's life depended on him.

Before they stepped into Natasha's room, Steele met Steven's gaze unflinching. "There is nothing... *nothing* more important to me than Natasha." He kept his voice low. "I know you think I'm an evil man, Mr. Craven. And you're right. I'll do anything to save her, even if it means taking the lives of innocent people. I'm sure you can understand what love can do to a man. It can make even the strongest vulnerable. It opens unimaginable things. The love of your life is the most precious gift... and yet the most painful."

Steven took a step back, seemingly lost for words. Finally, he said, "Take me to her."

Steele silently nodded and went ahead. As Steven followed him inside a room, he saw a fragile woman lying in a bed. Her skin was pale, and her lips were pursed as though she was in pain.

"Hello, Mr. Steele," a nurse with a stethoscope in her ears said.

Steele motioned for her to leave. Without a single word, she left the room as he went to Natasha's beside and reached for her hand.

"Natasha, honey, I have someone here to heal you, just like I promised."

She struggled to open her eyes. "Valkin?... Is that you?"

He lightly squeezed her hand. "I'm right here, honey."

Steven moved forward and stood on the other side of Natasha. "Hello, Miss Natasha."

When she opened her eyes and looked up at him, he said, "My name is Steven."

"Are you the Adalwolf?"

He nodded and placed his hand over hers. "I'm here to help you." He smiled a little. "I have the gift to heal your cancer."

Natasha's heart clutched. It went against everything she was to let someone give their life over for hers. "I won't let you do this." She turned to look at Steele. "I don't want anyone else to die because of me."

"It's okay, Natasha," Steven said. "I won't die."

As she turned toward him, he whispered into her mind. His words suddenly gave her hope and eased her anxiety. She smiled and all her doubts were gone in an instant.

"H-how did you do that?" she said. "I could hear your voice inside my head."

He removed his hand from hers and placed it over her heart. "It's a gift, Natasha. Do you trust me?"

Before she could respond, warmth spread through him to her. She couldn't even describe the sensation of comfort and healing filtering into her body and mind. He was healing her.

Sweat beaded on Steven's forehead. His breathing went shallow, and he teetered precariously against her bed. As he willed her disease into his body, tears ran freely down his cheeks. It was almost more than he could bear.

Natasha felt him flinch, and it took her a moment to realize he was in agony. She placed her pale hand over his. Her heart splintered knowing he was suffering in her stead.

"*It will be all over soon, Natasha,*" he whispered into her mind. "*It's only temporary for me. Trust me.*"

It nearly broke her when he raised his hand to softly touch her cheek. He was comforting her when he was taking the brunt of her pain.

After a few moments had passed, he said, "Natasha, are you feeling better?"

"Yes." Her voice was laced with tears. "It doesn't hurt anymore."

"You should rest. Whether you feel pain or not, your body needs time to adjust. In a few hours, you'll start feeling like your old self again."

"I'll never be able to repay you for what you've done. Thank you, Steven."

"You're welcome, Natasha." Then he looked up at Steele. "I've done my part. Now it's time for you to fulfill our deal."

It felt like forever as he waited in tense silence for Steele's response. He also wondered when Tim and the others would arrive. Hopefully, they were able to pick up the signal on his tracking device.

"I'm sorry, Mr. Craven," Steele said. "I can't thank you enough for all that you've done, but you see, it's not that easy. It's nothing personal." He shook his head. "But I had to make a deal to get you here."

Steven gritted his teeth. "You son of a bitch."

Abruptly, Steven felt the barrel of a gun pressed into his back. "If you do anything stupid, I'll give the order to have the she-wolf put out of her misery."

The accented voice coming from behind was an assault to his ears. He wanted nothing more than to shift into his Adalwolf and tear out the man's throat, but he controlled his rage and stood perfectly still.

"Valkin..." Natasha spoke out, her eyes squinted. "What have you done?"

"I'm sorry, darling." He patted her hand. "Sacrifices had to be made."

"Get moving," the man with a gun pointed at Steven said.

Steven controlled his rage and did as he was instructed, walking meekly toward the door. He waited for the man to tell him what to do next. He didn't want to risk pissing him off this early in the game, risking Abbey's life. He had to stay calm and do whatever it took to stall. He had no idea what he was facing. His first priority was to keep Abbey safe no matter how he had to do it. But he couldn't do this alone. If it were just him in danger, he'd shift into his Adalwolf and kill them all. But they were using Abbey as leverage. Hopefully, Colonel Deshazo and the rest of the team would arrive soon.

When he cast a quick glance over his shoulder, the guy behind him immediately shoved him and said, "Keep your eyes forward."

Steven bit back the retort that burned his lips. "Where are you taking me?"

"Back to where you came from," Steele said. "It appears that you have a hefty price on your head."

Before Steven could open his mouth to reply, Steele plunged a needle into his arm.

"Sorry, Mr. Craven," Steele said. "It had to be done. I can't have you shifting into your Adalwolf."

Steven suddenly felt disoriented. His surroundings blurred and spun. As panic exploded through his body, he fought with all he had to remain conscious. When he swayed on his feet, a strong arm snaked around him and prevented his fall.

"Make sure he's not harmed," Steele barked. "Dr. Kruger and his men will arrive within the hour. Their flight from Munich, Germany, just landed. His orders were that under no circumstances was he to be injured. Mr. Craven is worth millions."

The burly man holding on to Steven nodded. "What about the girl?"

"Marcus is delivering her to Cole Decker as we speak," Steele replied. "The rest of his girls should arrive shortly."

"What do you want me to do with him until the physician arrives?"

"Lock him in the wine cellar. He shouldn't give us any problems. I gave him a heavy dose of etorphine. It's strong enough to immobilize an elephant."

* * *

As Marcus escorted Abbey downstairs, she said, "Who are you, and where's Steven?"

"Keep your mouth shut."

When they finally reached the bottom of the stairs, Marcus directed her down a hallway. Once they approached a door, he knocked sharply and waited.

She held her breath when the door opened, afraid of what was on the other side. Marcus shoved her inside. She lost her balance and fell to the floor. When she looked up, there was a tall man with blond hair standing above her. He had a satisfied smirk on his face.

"At last, we meet again,... Miss Abigail."

"Who are you?"

He cast a glance in Marcus's direction and motioned for him to leave.

Abbey held her breath, every sense on high alert. *Oh God, please let Steven be close.*

When the door closed, the blond-haired man focused his eyes on her. "My name is Cole Decker." He moved closer. "You belong to me now." With his eyes roaming over her body, he got down on one knee and murmured, "Hello,... my little pet."

* * *

Colonel Deshazo and his team parked down a narrow road, not far from Steele's estate. Two other all-terrain vehicles pulled up alongside of them. One carried Roman Kincaid and his crew. The other transported Drakon along with the rest of the Breedline group.

"Well, ladies, what the hell are we waiting for?" Gunny mumbled from the back seat with a cigar between his lips. He didn't light it, probably because Colonel Deshazo was looking at him from the rearview mirror, giving him an "I dare you" look.

Tim came to attention when his phone buzzed inside his pocket. He dug it out and looked at the caller ID. "It's Tessa," he said.

As he swiped to answer, Jace leaned forward and anxiously waited.

When Tim finally ended the call, Jace asked, "Is everything okay?"

Tim nodded. "Tessa said she got a visit from Zeke Rizzo."

Jace shrugged. "What did he want?"

"The suspect in all those homeless murders paid Zeke a visit. Apparently, those human detectives arrived to witness Zeke healing from a cut throat."

"Damn," Jem said. "What did he tell them?"

"Nothing," Tim said. "But that's not all. They saw the guy vanish into thin air, and he took one of Zeke's employees."

Jem's lips twisted into a grimace. "So, what the hell are we going to do?"

"Right now, we've got to focus on getting Steven and Abbey back. We'll deal with the rest later."

After they stepped out of the vehicle and conducted a weapons check, they all gathered in front of Colonel Deshazo's vehicle with the others.

Drakon laid a map over the hood and pointed to a specific area. "This is where we're at. The dirt road goes on for another half mile before you turn off onto blacktop that leads to Steele's estate. I'm sure he's got the place beefed up with security and video surveillance."

"We're going to have to go in with a bang," Wyckoff said.

"Yeah," Kid chimed in with a grenade in his hand. "This oughta draw their attention."

Colonel Deshazo stepped forward, and Wyckoff and Kid went silent. It always awed Drakon how much respect he commanded.

"Here's what we're going to do," Colonel Deshazo said, taking charge. "It's obvious the place will have two entrances. Wyckoff, I want you to get in position at the front with Kid and

Gunny. I want Roman's team positioned in the back, except Lena and Lawrence." He looked pointedly at them. "You two will hang back and wait for my signal."

Lena stepped forward and didn't look at all happy. "With all due respect, sir... Where exactly do we fit into this plan of yours?"

The colonel's eyes narrowed. "I want you and Lawrence to make sure no one comes in or goes out of this place except us. And be our backup if things go bad inside."

Her lips tightened, but she obeyed orders without question. She gave a quick nod and took a step back.

"Once we're inside, I'll give the signal for everyone else," the colonel said. Then he turned to Jem. "I'm depending on you to use a portal to get Abbey and Steven out of there. Any questions? If so, speak up now."

When everyone stood in silence, Colonel Deshazo continued, laying out the rest of the details. In a moment's time, they headed out on foot and took coverage in the trees surrounding Steele's estate. Lena slung a rifle over her shoulder and climbed up a steep hill that overlooked the front, with Lawrence by her side.

Colonel Deshazo spoke into his radio, "Wyckoff... Are you in position?"

After Wyckoff responded in the affirmative, the colonel ordered everyone to check in and confirm their positions.

"Kid... Gunny..." the colonel said. "You know what to do."

Chapter Twenty-Six

Anna took a shuddering breath as she entered the double doors to the Bates Hospital. She tried to look calm and poised, but she was nervous about meeting Eve.

Dr. Helen Carrington was an unwavering support for her. She'd been instrumental in Sebastian's care, and now she had taken time out of her busy schedule to introduce Anna to her brother's mate.

"Hello, Anna."

Anna smiled at Helen. Before she got a chance to greet Helen, she was interrupted by a nurse with a clipboard in her hand. She handed it to Helen and pointed to the places she wanted her to have Anna sign.

"It's just a routine waiver," Helen said. "Everyone has to sign one to visit Sebastian."

Anna nodded and signed by the lines marked with an X. "Is there any word on my brother?"

Helen sighed. "There's still no change."

Anna briefly closed her eyes.

"Although... I'm hoping your presence will make a difference."

She hoped Helen was right. It hurt her to know just how much pain Sebastian had suffered.

"Thank you, Helen. I appreciate everything you've done for my brother, and for helping me."

Helen smiled. "How would like to join me and some of my friends this evening? We're having a bachelorette party for one of the nurses here at the hospital. It's not going to be anything wild, just a group of us girls enjoying a few drinks and music. What do you think?"

Anna was surprised. "I would love to, Helen. Thanks for inviting me."

"I think you're overdue for some fun. I'll give you all the details later."

She nodded. "I agree."

Helen reached for her hand. "I'll take you to Eve. She's excited to meet you."

Outside the door to Sebastian's room, Helen pushed it slightly open and stuck her head inside. "Eve?... Is it okay to come in?"

"Yes, please come in."

Helen pushed the door all the way open. "I'd like to introduce you to Sebastian's sister, Anna."

When Eve got a look at Anna, her eyes glossed over with tears. She rose from the chair next to Sebastian's bedside. "Oh, Anna... I'm so glad you're here."

Helen's heart was about to split wide open as Eve went forward and reached out to Anna. Before she stepped out of the room, she said, "I'll give you two some privacy."

"Thank you for agreeing to see me. I'm so happy to meet you, Eve."

Eve's lips trembled. "Sebastian thought you were dead. He was devastated after his stepfather lied to him about your death. You meant the world to him."

"I'm so sorry he had to go through that. Sebastian was everything to me," she said as a glimmer of a smile lit her face. "Even though we're not blood kin, he is my brother all the same."

She averted her eyes from Eve and focused on Sebastian. "Is he doing any better?"

Eve reached for her hand. "I'm afraid there's no change."

Anna bit back tears and looked down at Sebastian. "Helen told me you were there when he was hurt." She looked away from him and stared at Eve. "Is it true? Does Lucifer want your son Arius for his powers?"

Eve slowly nodded. "Before Sebastian slipped into a coma, he begged me to never give in to Lucifer and to keep Arius safe. I know he's torturing Sebastian. I can see the pain on his face as he sleeps." She wiped the tears from her eyes. "I feel so helpless. I just don't know how to help him."

She put a gentle hand on Eve's arm. "We'll figure a way to bring him back," Anna said. "When I first came to visit Sebastian, I think he recognized my voice. I could see it in his expression. And I felt a single tear on his cheek."

Eve smiled. "Helen said he can hear us and it's important that we talk to him."

Anna took Eve's hand in hers. "I'd like to try something, but only with your permission."

"What is it?"

"I think you should bring the twins here. It might make a big difference if he hears their voices, especially Arius."

"I don't know." Eve shook her head. "I've already discussed this with Helen. She said it could be harmful to the boys to see their father this way."

"We've got to try everything. The boys are young, and in time they'll forget Sebastian. I think it's important for them to see their father."

"Okay." Eve nodded. "I'm willing to give it a try."

* * *

While Anna and Eve continued their conversation, Sebastian was soothed by their voices. He felt comforted by their presence, but that only lasted for a short while. The sound of their voices was drowned by a bone-chilling noise like fingernails clawing across a chalkboard.

Suddenly, he found himself standing in the middle of an empty classroom. He scanned his surroundings and realized he was at the private academy his stepfather shipped him off to after his mother killed Eliza. He'd been only five years old. The boarding school housed troubled children that were discarded by their wealthy parents.

"Doesn't the place bring back your favorite childhood memories?"

Sebastian glared at Lucifer. "Go to hell."

"Come on, Sebastian." Lucifer chuckled a little. "Admit it. This school taught you how to be a man. Remember all the beat-downs you endured here over the years? It had to be tough being the only half-breed. Your stepfather was a cruel bastard, sticking you in an all-Breedline boarding school. He knew you'd be an outcast. Knowing you'd be tortured for the rest of your childhood gave him a sense of pleasure. He even went as far as paying the school's staff to keep your species knowledge from you. Your stepfather never told you that you need blood from a Breedline to survive. He kept you starved and weak. I'm sure you've already figured out what they called your medicine..." Lucifer did air quotations. "It was the blood you needed to survive. Although they barely gave you enough to keep your heart beating. That was the reason for your childhood sickness." He faked a sympathetic expression. "So sad. If only you'd known."

Sebastian gritted his teeth. "Just get on with it." He leaned in so close, he was face-to-face with Lucifer. "I'm through listening to you."

Lucifer smirked. Then he pointed to an open window that overlooked the grounds of the academy. "I've prepared something just for you. I'm sure you'll find it quite entertaining."

Sebastian looked out the window and saw a small boy leaning against a tree. Somehow the boy appeared sad... alone. Sebastian turned to look over his shoulder at Lucifer, but to his surprise, Lucifer was gone. With a heavy sigh, he looked back to the window and refocused on the boy. At that moment, he knew without a doubt the boy was himself at the age of nine or ten.

As a strip of lightning snaked across the dark sky, it caught the boy's attention. The thunder that followed was not far off in the distance, and Sebastian had a feeling the kid was about to get drenched. It wasn't long after the rain started that a car pulled up. The boy held up his hand to shield his eyes when the headlights flashed into his face.

When the beam of light faded, he lowered his hand. The sound of car doors opening and closing made the boy hide behind the tree. Another bolt of lightning shot through the sky as four boys dressed in black hoodies, holding metal bats, walked up.

When they moved closer and surrounded the tree, the boy didn't run. Instead, he stepped away from the tree and waited for what was about to happen.

Sebastian helplessly watched from the window. He'd never forget this dreadful memory. *Oh God, please... I can't bear this again.*

The first strike came from the back of the knee, knocking the boy off balance. As he landed on his hands and knees, they crowded around him and pummeled his shoulders and back.

Sebastian closed his eyes, remembering the pain he'd felt during the attack. He'd thought he was going to die.

Finally, he opened his eyes and focused on the boy. He was curled onto his side with his arms over his head while they pounded him over and over.

"That's enough!" The shortest of the four said. "We're not supposed to kill him!"

The tallest kid stood over the boy. "The half-breed deserves to die."

Sebastian recognized that voice. It was his half brother, Edward.

"We're getting paid to beat him," the short kid said as he looked up at Edward. "Your father didn't say anything about killing him."

The kid standing next to Edward stepped forward. "Let's get out of here before someone catches us!"

"We're not done with you, half-breed," Edward said as he kicked the boy. "We'll be back."

"If you think this is bad..." Lucifer said as he reappeared, "I'm just getting warmed up. The worst is yet to come."

Sebastian wondered what other horrific memory Lucifer was going to conjure up next.

"Some people just don't ever fit in and never will." Lucifer pouted. "Your birth mother treated you like the plague. And when you found your real father, you were never good enough for him. He only kept you around to do his dirty work. Now that he's free of the Chiang Shih demon, his loyalty is with the Breedline and his firstborn sons. You were never special to anyone."

"That's not true. Eliza and my sister Anna loved me. And Eve..."

Lucifer started to laugh, softly at first, then louder. "Eve betrayed you."

Sebastian lowered his head. "I don't blame her. She did what she thought was best for our sons. They deserve better." He looked back up, and Lucifer was gone. And then he found

190

himself standing next to the boys' shower stalls. The locker room was thick with steam. The sound of a door closing caught his attention. As he turned around, he froze in his tracks. His eyes rounded with terror. *Oh, God... no.*

Chapter Twenty-Seven

"Move in," Colonel Deshazo ordered his team.

Before Wyckoff, Kid, and Gunny made it to the front entrance, Lena's voice came over the radio. "Hold your position. I repeat... hold your position. We've got company."

"Roger that," Colonel Deshazo said. "What do we have?"

"Two SUVs. They're heading in your direction."

"Fall back then," the colonel said. "Rendezvous with Lena and Lawrence."

Kid spoke into his radio, "We're heading your way, Lena."

"Affirmative," Wyckoff chimed in.

A few moments later, they moved through a thicket of trees and climbed up the hill where Lena and Lawrence waited.

Lena offered the colonel a pair of binoculars. "Take a look."

He held them up to his face and watched as two SUVs came to a stop and several men piled out. They looked like security, judging by the pistols and the two-way-radio headsets they wore. When the passenger's door to one of the vehicles opened, a tall lanky man dressed in a black suit stepped out. With dark shades covering his eyes, and a brimmed hat on top of his head, it was difficult to make out his features. Three of the guards escorted him to the front entrance while the others waited by the SUVs.

With his teeth clenched, the colonel lowered the binoculars. Before he got a word out, a black van barreled down the drive.

"What the hell now?" Roman bit out.

The colonel put the binoculars to his face again. He was so furious, his jaw tightened. He lowered them. "We've got a game changer. It looks like Abbey and Steven won't be the only two we're rescuing. I spotted twenty girls exit that van." He heaved a sigh. "And they appear to be underage."

"Part of Steele's sex trafficking no less," Tim said.

Jace nodded. "This has Cole Decker written all over it."

Drakon looked to Colonel Deshazo. "Are we going to be able to pull this off?"

"What choice to we have? Chances are, Decker will have them taken out of the country if we don't act soon. This is our only shot at rescuing them."

Wyckoff shrugged. "So... what's our plan?"

The colonel focused his eyes on Drakon. "Remember the mission we did in Afghanistan?"

"How could I forget," Drakon said. "That was the day you *literally* saved my ass."

Wyckoff cut in the conversation, "You're not thinking what I think you are... are you?"

"What the hell are you guys talking about?" Kid butted in.

Gunny clapped his hand over Kid's shoulder. "We're talking about Dark Thunder. That was way before your time, Kid." He lightly chuckled. "Come to think of it, you were still pissing in your diapers."

"It was a four-man mission," the colonel said. "We rescued thirty-six prisoners of war and took out more than fifty terrorists in less than an hour."

Tim cocked a brow. "Will someone clue the rest of us in on what that has to do with our situation?"

"We used our gifts," Wyckoff said.

"You mean you all shifted?" Tim queried.

"We were outnumbered," the colonel replied. "It was the only way to save all those people."

"But we're dealing with humans," Kyle chimed in. "Aren't we supposed to stay in incognito?"

"I agree with Colonel Deshazo," Alexander said as he came forward. "We've got to do whatever it takes to save those girls."

"I don't know." Tim shook his head. "It sounds too risky."

Jem focused on him. "What if one of those young girls was Natalie? You'd take a risk for your own daughter, wouldn't you?"

Tim held up a halting hand. "Okay, okay. You've made your point. We'll do whatever it takes."

Kid piped in, "That gets a hooah from me."

Jace looked at Kid, confused. "Hooah? What the hell does that mean?"

"It's a battle cry. It means anything and everything, except *no*."

"Well, this is how I say it," Jace said. "I'm ready to go in and kick some ass."

Colonel Deshazo checked his watch. "At eighteen hundred hours, we'll go in. The night will give us better coverage. In the meantime, we hunker down and keep watch."

* * *

An hour before nightfall, Apollyon used his powers to travel from place to place and appeared in the back alley of a popular nightclub located in the San Francisco Bay area. The Alibi had a dance floor downstairs and one located on the top level called the Pussycat Lounge. People could play their own music and get weird among shag carpeting and stripper poles. Downstairs, there was a private room for VIPs only. Big names and up-and-comers alike played live music in the massive main room in the back that seated two hundred or more.

When he came up to the main entrance, there was a line to get in a mile long. In a snap, he vanished into thin air and reappeared inside the club.

As he looked to the dance floor, it was packed full of half-naked bodies gyrating to the sound of hard-core heavy metal.

He inhaled and took in the intoxicating smell of human flesh. On the hunt for his next meal, he waded through the sea of people and sneered as the crowd tripped over itself to get out of his way.

A woman wearing a tight leather skirt, black thigh-high boots, and a bustier barely covering her oversized breasts, sauntered in his direction. Her eyes glittered from behind heavy gold mascara as she looked him up and down. When he caught a whiff of her pheromones, he strode past her without a second glance. Sex was not on his mind tonight.

A female bartender approached him as he took a seat at the bar. "What can I get ya, sweetheart?"

He shot her a cold stare. He was tempted to grab her by the throat and go to work on her carotid. "Bring me a shot of Spirytus."

She arched a brow. "Do you have a death wish or something?" She shook her head. "Sorry, honey. We don't serve that kind of Polish Vodka here. In short, that shit can literally make you meet your maker."

He waved his hand in dismissal. "Just bring me something strong."

She nodded. "You got it."

When the bartender left, he looked at a female sitting next to him. He inhaled and took in her scent. Then he ran his eyes over her. He started with her long, exquisite neckline. The vein at her throat pulsed to her heartbeat. As he dragged more air into his lungs, a hunger stirred deep down in his gut.

When she swiveled in her chair, her green eyes met his golden stare. In an instant, she froze with her mouth agape. God... he was *gorgeous*. A needy sensation suddenly took hold. For some strange reason, she craved his touch.

She focused on his lips as spoke to her in a deep, raspy voice, "So... do you have a name?"

She swallowed the knot that had formed in the back of her throat and muttered, "A-Anna."

"Are you here alone?"

She shook her head. "I'm here with a friend."

"Where is your friend?"

"Sh-she went to check on a table. It's for a bachelorette party."

He cocked a brow. "Would you like a drink while you wait for your friend?"

She quickly nodded.

When the bartender came back with his drink, he said, "I'd like another—"

"Gin and tonic, please," Anna cut him off.

The bartender nodded. "Coming right up."

She tilted her head a little. "Wh-what's your name?"

Before he could utter a word, the bartender returned with her drink. "Can I get you anything else?"

Apollyon placed a fifty-dollar bill on the table. "We're good."

For some odd reason, the bartender kept her eyes on him. She stared at him as though she was spellbound by his presence.

He glared at her. "That will be all."

Finally, she slowly reached for the cash and walked away.

Anna reached for her drink and brought it to her lips. After a little sip, she coughed. "Sorry..." She cleared her throat. "I'm not used to... alcohol."

He rolled his eyes.

"So, what did you say your name was?"

"I didn't," he replied in a slight accent. "Does it matter?"

"Oh..." She looked at him surprised. "I guess not."

In the silence that followed, he suddenly lumbered out of his chair. "Why don't you skip your party," he said with his hand extended, "and leave with me?"

Chapter Twenty-Eight

Sebastian spun around at the sound of a door opening. To his surprise, three dark figures stepped into the boys' locker room. They wore black, hooded sweatshirts that covered most of their facial features. At that moment, a memory hit him. It was more of a nightmare as he remembered this horrific incident.

The day Sebastian turned sixteen, his stepfather sent his son Edward and two of his thuggish friends to go after him. This had been a recurring routine. Their purpose was to compel physical harm to him when he was alone and defenseless.

"This is where it all happened," Lucifer said.

Sebastian flinched. As he turned to face Lucifer, he continued, "I remember it just like it was yesterday." A cold smile twisted his ruthless lips. "Your transition was a beautiful thing to witness. It was like watching a caterpillar transform into a butterfly. You became my perfect disciple."

Sebastian snarled. "You'll never break me."

Lucifer put his finger to Sebastian's chest. "The day your transition began, you handed over your soul on a silver platter. You had a choice. You threw away the light inside your heart and replaced it with darkness."

Sebastian looked away from Lucifer when he heard heavy footsteps. That's when he saw the face of one of the hooded figures. It was his half brother. He watched as Edward and the other two guys rushed toward the far end of the locker room. By the steam and the sound of running water, it was obvious someone was taking a shower.

In a desperate effort to stop Edward, Sebastian took off after him. When he reached out to grab him, his hand passed through Edward's arm.

"They can't see you, idiot," Lucifer said. "You can't stop them. Nothing you do will change the past unless you give me what I want."

"Go to hell," he spat.

He averted his eyes from Lucifer when he heard Edward call out, "Where's that little bitch?"

When a shower was shut off, Edward and his cronies crowded around the outside. With one swift motion, Edward grabbed the shower curtain and ripped if off the pole.

As the naked, pale-skinned boy inside the shower cowered in fear, Sebastian watched in disbelief. He was horrified. It was like looking into the past at his younger self. He'd almost forgotten how thin and small he was at that age. It was unnatural. He was starved and unable to mature because of his stepfather.

Edward surged forward and nailed the frightened boy square in the face. His head flew back and knocked him off balance. Clubs pummeled his shoulders and back when he fell to his hands and knees. As the boy lunged forward, he managed to grab one of them by the ankles. When Edward's buddy tried to take a step, he was caught off balance by the boy's tight grip. He fell into the other kid and took him down with him.

The boy arched in pain as Edward relentlessly kicked him in the side. He staggered when Edward landed another hit to the left side of his temple. Before he gained his bearings, the two guys slammed him against the tile wall and held him in place.

Edward unfastened his pants and said, "I'm going to teach you a lesson you'll never forget." Tears clouded the boy's eyes. "No..." He shook his head. "Please, no..."

It happened without warning. As Edward moved closer, the boy's gums stretched as the tips of sharp teeth formed inside his mouth. A hiss escaped his lips. He pulled free and lunged at Edward. As he sank his sharp fangs into his throat, blood gushed like an endless river and coated the floor red. When the boy released Edward, he dropped to his knees with his hand clutched to his throat.

In shocked disbelief, Edward's buddies froze in place. The boy stood above Edward and licked the blood from his lips. In an instant, he grabbed Edward and tugged him close to his lips. As he sank his teeth deep into his half brother's flesh, a rapid transformation took over him. He grew from a frail boy to the height of six four.

He dropped Edward's lifeless body onto the blood-soaked floor and braced himself against the wall with his hand. He was amazed at how big his hand appeared. It was the size of a catcher's mitt. Everything around him seemed smaller. Even the ceiling was shorter. As he looked down, he was taken back by the size of his feet. The boy seemed confused by his new transformation. Then he focused on Edward lying in a pool of his own blood.

"You're going down for this, freak."

He looked up at Edward's thuggish friends and frowned at the guy's irritating outburst.

"Do you realize what you've done?" the other guy said. "Mr. Montgomery will have your head on a pole for this."

With fury blazing in his eyes, the boy curled his upper lip and stared at the two guys, realizing he was so much bigger than them now.

"Shit," one of them spouted as he looked up at the boy's new transformation.

Shit was right.

The hulking boy leaned over them and bared his fangs.

Suddenly, one of Edward's buddies started to change. His skin stretched and contorted into an unnatural state. Then hair sprouted from his pores and covered his body in a matter of seconds.

The younger version of Sebastian appeared stunned as he watched the guy's clothes rip apart at the seams. He'd never witnessed a Breedline shift.

"You're no match for my friend," the other guy said. "My buddy here is a full-blooded Breedline. He's going to rip you into tiny pieces."

A canine muzzle protruded from the guy's face, and as he threw his head back to release a roar, young Sebastian reached for the metal curtain rod and ripped it from the concrete wall. With lightning speed, he shoved it deep into the opening of the wolf's gullet.

The boy hesitated for only an instant before he grabbed the other guy by the throat. He squeezed until the guy's neck snapped. When he released his grip, the dead guy's limp body crumpled to the ground.

He rummaged through the lockers for clothes that would fit his new body. Finally he found a pair of jeans and a T-shirt. Unfortunately, he wasn't lucky enough to find a pair of shoes. It didn't matter anyway. He wouldn't be leaving on foot. He had Edward's car keys to his brand-new BMW parked outside. It wasn't like his half brother would be driving it anytime soon, considering his circumstances of being dead and all. Besides, he'd need a ride to his stepfather's estate. He had unfinished business. Taking out the rest of his rotten family was his way of tying up loose ends.

* * *

Hours later, Sebastian—who was still invisible to everyone around him—suddenly found himself standing outside the iron gates that led up to his stepfather's estate. He recognized Edward's BMW parked outside the front entrance. Lights glowed from inside and he could see people moving around. As he stood there and watched from afar, he wondered why Lucifer had brought him here. Was he here to witness his younger self seek revenge against his family?

"You better hurry," Lucifer said. "You don't want to miss the best part."

Sebastian whirled around and said, "Why did you bring me back here?"

"Let's just say it's a little gift from me to you," Lucifer drawled. "This is one memory I promise you won't regret reliving."

Before Sebastian could utter a word, he suddenly appeared outside the front door of his stepfather's estate. Oddly, it was wide open. As he made his way inside, he saw droplets of blood on the white marble floor. He followed the trail of blood that led to the formal dining room. Before he stepped inside, he heard a woman scream.

Lucifer suddenly appeared and nudged Sebastian's shoulder. "Hurry. You're going to miss it."

With a smug expression marring his face, he grabbed her by the hair and yanked her face close to his. He wound his hand in her hair and crushed his lips against hers.

She struggled wildly, but he was stronger, forcing her mouth open, kissing her brutally.

Bile rose in her throat. She briefly closed her eyes and felt sick to her very soul.

"You taste sweet." His tongue stroked over her trembling lips. "I can't wait to taste the rest of you."

Although tears filled her eyes, she refused to cry. She refused to allow him the satisfaction of seeing her pain.

Cole saw something savage in her deep blue glare before he reached out to her. She flinched when his hand slid up to her shoulder.

Oh God, Abbey feverishly thought. *Where is Steven?*

Cole tore at her shirt, rending it in two, and exposed her breasts. His hand mauled and groped her body.

When he started to pull at her pants, she went wild. She bucked, kicked, and fought with every bit of strength she could muster. She'd rather die before she let him rape her.

"You're a heartless bastard." She choked back tears. "You make me sick."

He backed off at her outward show of strength. "Tell me, Abigail, did Valkin Steele promise to see your beloved Adalwolf safely back to the Covenant after he healed Natasha?" He kept his eyes locked on hers. "Think carefully. I also know Steele to be a liar. Yet he made you believe something he never intended to do in the first place. How easily you are persuaded."

She spat in his face. "Go to hell."

The black orbs of his eyes went flat. He was on her in an instant with a sharp slap to her face.

The blow stunned her speechless. She instantly brought her hand up to her mouth, her eyes widening in quick alarm.

"Tell me you want me," he demanded.

Anger lit off a firestorm inside her chest. She would *never* say that to him. *Never.*

"I. Despise. You."

Cole lifted his hand and made a fist. She remained silent, readying herself to take the hit. They glared at one another in silence, bound by the strings of violence that ran between them.

Finally, he lowered his hand and raked his dark gaze over her trembling body. "Your precious Adalwolf was sold to the highest bidder. I was paid to deliver you to Steele. You were just a bargaining tool that served my purpose. He got the Adalwolf, and I got what I wanted."

Abbey pulled at her shirt to cover herself. "No." She shook her head in denial. "That's not true. You're lying."

In an instant, he roughly placed a pair of handcuffs around her wrists and clamped on to the back of her neck. He pulled her close and smashed his lips against hers. It took everything she had to keep her gag reflex down until he released her.

Cole rose to his feet. "I'll be leaving you here for a while. As soon as I get back, you'll be going with me on a long trip."

"Where are you taking me?"

"You're going to Europe," he told her, "along with the rest of my girls."

Her eyes widened. *Oh, God...*

When he stalked out of the room, she sucked in a breath and prayed for the very thing she always hated. Her *she-wolf*.

* * *

Valkin Steele patiently waited as Dr. Kruger and three of his men were escorted inside. Behind him stood Marcus, Corbin, and Fredrick. Steele sensed the tension radiating from them.

As Dr. Kruger strode into the spacious foyer, he was tight-lipped, and impatience emanated from him in tangible waves. He looked pointedly at Steele and said, "Where's my Adalwolf?"

"Mr. Craven is heavily sedated," Steele said. "He's locked in the wine cellar. My men will escort you to him."

The physician narrowed his eyes and nodded. "As long as the Adalwolf hasn't been harmed, the exchange will be made."

"I gave you my word," Steele replied.

"You'll get half of the money now," Kruger said, "and the other half after I see the Adalwolf for myself."

Steele merely nodded and took the thick envelope from Kruger's outstretched hand.

After Steele's men led the physician and his men to the wine cellar, Cole called out, "Where's the rest of my shipment?"

Steele glared at Cole. "Your girls just arrived. I'm sure you'll be very pleased."

Cole's eyes gleamed, and he gave Steele a short nod of approval. "My private jet will be ready for pickup in the next hour or so. My men will take care of transporting the girls. Until then, I'm going to need more drugs for Miss Winthrop."

"Relax," Steele said. "I've got enough to get you through a few days."

"A few days?" Cole looked confused.

"I thought you knew."

Cole shook his head. "What the hell are you talking about?"

"You weren't planning on keeping Miss Winthrop alive... were you?"

"Why the hell would I kill Abigail?" Cole shot back. "Are you fucking me over, Steele?"

Steele narrowed his eyes. "There's been a misunderstanding. I only have enough of the drug to last a few days. Three tops. You'll have to get rid of her before she turns into that *thing*."

Cole cursed under his breath. "How am I supposed to take her out? Will silver bullets work?"

"Yes," Steele replied. "Make sure you shoot her in the heart."

"Just give me what drugs you have," Cole urged. "I'll take care of her when it's time."

"She'll need an injection every twenty-four hours." Steele held out clear vial of liquid. "I wouldn't wait too long. It's time for another dosage."

Before Cole took the drug, the sound of a blood-chilling howl echoed, followed by death screams and gunfire.

Chapter Thirty

Colonel Deshazo's team and the others crept silently through the thickly wooded area, preparing to attack Valkin Steele's estate. His men were *honorable* men who'd risked their lives for others. And that included humans, even the very people who sought their deaths. Their mission was to protect the innocent and hunt the evil, regardless of their species.

They had spent the last three hours planning for the worst-case scenarios. The colonel had kept it brief, giving them the rundown on what their plan of action would be. Choosing to reveal their supernatural identity to humans went against the Breedline laws, but in this case, it was necessary.

When this was all over, Tim, the head of the Breedline council knew that Tessa, the Breedline queen, would have a serious come-to-Jesus meeting about their decision to go against the Covenant's True Law. But that was the risk they had to take. After she knew the truth, minus the gory details, she'd understand why they'd chosen this.

A shift in the air brought awareness in the colonel's gut as he gripped his pistol. The others shared a similar feeling of unease, as they stopped and sniffed the air like predators stalking their prey. They were halfway to the estate when Colonel Deshazo's blood froze in his veins.

A short distance away, a thunderous roar shattered the eerie silence, followed by sounds of guns firing.

"Get down!" Lena shouted. "Sniper at six o'clock!"

The firefight came out of nowhere. It was fierce and unrelenting.

Instantly, Bull's hand went to his thigh and came away wet and sticky. The wound burned like fire. Maintaining a stoic expression, he tried to dismiss it and go on. When darkness encroached on his vision, his legs buckled beneath him.

Lena dropped to his side. "Shit. Are you hit?"

"My thigh," he groaned.

When Lena rose to her feet and signaled to Justice, he rushed over.

"Hold on, buddy," Justice said as he scanned Bull's injury.

A few minutes later, Justice pegged Bull with a look of relief. "It's just a flesh wound. It'll heal in no time."

Bull nodded at him and directed his eyes toward his sister. "Go help the others," he gritted out. "I'll be fine."

"Benjamin Allen Calvero," Lena said in a hushed voice. "I'm not leaving you."

Bull shook his head. "Dammit, Lena."

Justice chuckled lightly. "You tell 'em, baby."

As footsteps drew near, Lena and Justice immediately went for their weapons.

"Hold up," Jace said with his hands lifted. "Don't shoot."

Lena heaved a deep breath. "My brother's been hit, but it's not bad."

"Damn, Bull..." Jace crouched next to him. "You okay, buddy?"

"I'll be fine," Bull grumbled. "You all go on ahead and help the others. I'll catch up in a few."

"What the fuck, man," Jace shot back. "We're not leaving your dumbass here alone."

Bull gritted his teeth. "I don't need anyone babysitting my ass."

When the others made their way over, they stood over Bull with an uneasy expression stamped all over their faces.

"Damn it, Bull," Drakon huffed out. "You're in no condition to fight on your own if we leave you. You're bleeding like a stuck pig."

Lawrence examined Bull's leg. "The bullet went clean through. If you keep pressure on it, it will close within ten minutes. Fifteen tops."

Everyone ducked when another round of shots fired in their direction.

Justice lunged forward and threw himself over Lena. "Stay down."

Abruptly, Gunny's voice came over the two-way radio. "I've got the shooter pinpointed. I'm just waiting for your command, Colonel D."

Colonel Deshazo looked at Tim. "We don't have a choice."

Tim nodded. "It's your call, Colonel."

"Take the shot, Gunny," the colonel ordered.

After four shots were fired, Gunny's voice came over radio, "We're clear."

The colonel's eyes roamed over his team, including the Breedline crew. "Everyone needs to be on guard. I'm sure we'll run into more of Steele's men."

"Stay with Bull, Lena," Roman said in a crisp, take-charge tone. "You too, Justice. Radio in as soon as he heals." He turned from Justice and focused on Bull. "And that's final."

Bull scowled at the thought of staying behind while the rest of his team roared to the forefront. He looked ready to take on an entire army and take apart the asshole that put a bullet in his leg.

"Fine." Bull threw his hands up in defeat and mumbled a few f-bombs. "We'll meet up with you later. I'll be good to go in no time."

Colonel Deshazo exchanged glances with everyone. "You know the drill." He motioned them forward. "It's now or never."

* * *

As Marcus escorted Dr. Kruger and his men into the wine cellar, Corbin and Fredrick waited outside the door. Before they made it down the steps, something moved in a blur.

"What the..." Marcus's voice trailed off as he got a glimpse of what looked to be a man... or was it something else.

Out of nowhere, Marcus was slammed into the wall with bone-jarring force. The sudden impact caught him off guard.

"Tranquilize him!" Dr. Kruger ordered.

Before the physician's men could react, Steven's supernatural speed outweighed their human pace. He pounced on one, knocking him off balance. As the other guy lunged for him, he hurled around and hit him with a backhanded blow. Momentum hammered him into the other guard and sent them tumbling across the floor.

The loud commotion alerted Corbin and Fredrick. Corbin rushed down the stairs, gripping his weapon, with Fredrick close behind. They came to a complete halt when they found Marcus and Kruger's men scattered on the floor.

"What the hell are you waiting for?" Kruger shouted. "Stop the Adalwolf!"

As Corbin fired his weapon, Fredrick cowered behind him. Steven dodged the bullets, but one managed to hit him in the chest. He swallowed back the pain and continued forward.

When Corbin squeezed the trigger again, his gun made a doleful clicking noise.

Shit! Corbin gritted his teeth. *I'm out of ammo!*

Then a hail of bullets hit Steven from behind. His body thrashed wildly, and blood streamed from his torso. It burned like a son of a bitch, but Steven remained on his feet. When it finally ceased, Steven whirled around and faced the gunman.

Dr. Kruger lowered the weapon and wearily took a few steps back.

Prepared to explode into action, Steven locked onto Kruger's throat and peeled back his lips. As he started forward, an explosion of glass and gunfire momentarily distracted him. For a second, it sounded like an earthquake had rocked the estate, but to his relief, he realized it was his comrades in arms.

Corbin and Fredrick ducked down, and Dr. Kruger staggered back.

"Holy shit!" Corbin barked. He looked toward Marcus and said, "What the hell was that?"

Marcus gritted his teeth and grunted but managed to pull himself up. "The hell if I know."

"We need to get back upstairs," Corbin said. "Marcus—"

He was cut off by a blast. It blew the door off its hinges.

"Drop your weapons," an amplified voice from the top of the stairs said. "I repeat, drop your weapons and stand down."

Dr. Kruger raised his weapon. Before he pulled the trigger, shots rained from above. The physician dropped to his knees and clamped a hand over his throat. As blood seeped through his fingers, he gasped for breath. He frantically searched for help but saw none forthcoming. Seconds later, his body went limp and crumpled forward.

The look on Marcus's face was of shocked disbelief. The millisecond it took him to reach for his weapon, powerful fingers closed around his throat. He instantly dropped his gun and gasped for breath.

Steven looked up when a familiar voice called out, "Let him go, Steven."

"Tim..." Steven's own voice sounded alien to him, deeper and more guttural.

"He's surrendering, Steven," Tim said. "It's okay. We can take it from here."

Steven looked back at Marcus. His face was losing the color and he realized that he had been only seconds away from choking him unconscious. He clenched his teeth and fought the urge to finish Marcus. Finally, Steven released him and looked up at Tim. "Did you find Abbey?"

"Steven!" a voice abruptly called out. "Behind you!"

Drakon's tone sent a jolt of adrenaline through Steven's body at the same time pain exploded in his side. The burning sensation of a blade threw him off balance. He dropped to his knees and reached for the knife embedded deep in his side.

He winced as he pulled the knife from his ribcage and looked up at the sound of a loud roar. An enormous wolf—covered in black matted fur and snarling sharp teeth—leaped from above. It was then, he realized, Drakon had shifted into his rogue wolf. It cleared him and slammed into Marcus, who had already shifted into his Breedline wolf. The force of Drakon's impact sent Marcus crashing to the floor.

Marcus's wolf fought back with lightning reflexes. He swiped his massive paw against Drakon's head and hurled him backward. He crashed into the wall, knocking a hole into it before hitting the ground hard. Drakon shook off the blow just as Marcus pounced on top of him. But his Breedline wolf was no match for Drakon's powerful rogue. He was twice the size, outweighing Marcus by a hundred pounds of strapping muscle and sheer strength.

Drakon seized the opportunity and sunk his razor-sharp teeth into Marcus's neck. Meat and gristle pulled apart as Drakon tore his throat out.

Violent convulsions rocked Marcus's body until a loud pop instantly halted his movement.

Tim glared at Corbin and Fredrick, with a pistol in his grasp. "I've got two more silver bullets." He aimed it in their direction. "How do you want this to go down?"

Fredrick held up his hands in defeat. "P-please... don't shoot. I surrender."

Corbin snarled and tossed his weapon on the ground. He looked down at Marcus's corpse as his dark fur began to retract and his body started to shrink. In a matter of seconds, Marcus had shifted into his human form... dead and naked.

"Take us to Abigail Winthrop," Tim demanded with a gun still pointed at Corbin and Fredrick.

"You're too late," Corbin said. "Cole Decker has her."

Chapter Thirty-One

After Manuel and his partner left the crime scene, located on Fillmore Street, they drove to The Alibi in silence. The emotions in the car between the detectives lingered like mold left after fetid water.

Nothing could have prepared them for what they saw. Sure, Captain Hodge had said the victim had the same MO as all the others, but this... this was a whole new level of evil.

Paul Taylor—or what was left of him—was a single male in his forties. He owned a chain of antique stores and managed the one on Geary Boulevard. The poor bastard was intelligent enough to make a good living for himself, but when it came to women, he had the worst luck. It seemed that Mr. Taylor had developed a bad habit. He paid escorts for his sex addiction. Manuel knew this because he'd arrested Paul for solicitation a month ago. This time he'd paid for it with his life.

When they walked into the room where the maid had discovered Mr. Taylor's body, the walls were painted with his blood. Whoever had killed him had done so maliciously. He was literally in small pieces. His head—which by far was the biggest body part—was positioned on the nightstand. The rest of his body was scattered into small pieces.

The foul smell made it difficult for them to complete a thorough investigation.

Frank glanced over at his partner in the passenger's seat. "Hey... You okay?"

When there was no answer, Frank reached over and tapped Manuel's arm. "Listen, you want to take a minute? Stop at a cafe and have some coffee?"

Manuel shook his head. "Nah, I'm all right." He let out a deep breath. "It's just been a long day. I'm ready to catch these bastards and finally put an end to all this."

"Yeah," Frank said. "I hear ya, buddy. I'm ready to nail their asses to the wall."

"I've never seen anything like it," Manuel said. "Not even the worst homicides I've had to deal with."

"In all my years on the force," Frank said, "I've never come across any man capable of inflicting such destruction on a body. Jeffrey Dahmer has nothing on this guy."

"But this was done by a woman," Manuel pointed out.

Frank grimaced. "I still can't believe the woman we caught on the hotel's surveillance footage leaving the crime scene managed to do all that to Mr. Taylor. She couldn't have weighed more than a hundred and fifteen pounds. Do you think she's part of the vampire guy and the WWE woman-wrestler look-alike we're after?"

Manuel looked at him. "She has to be. There's no other explanation. There's no way a human could possibly do this alone, especially our female suspect that was caught on video."

"Too bad Zeke Rizzo won't come clean," Frank said as he pulled into the bar's parking lot. "He knows more than he's letting on."

"Oh, I'm not done with Mr. Rizzo," Manuel said. "I plan on revisiting him real soon."

"Do you really think it will do any good? He's not going to tell us anything."

"He might after he finds out I have some information concerning Miss Smirnov's legal residency."

Frank parked the car. "Are you saying she's an illegal immigrant?"

"I did some digging on her citizenship. Yelena's not a naturalized citizen. She's originally from Russia, and her work visa is outdated."

"You're not going to threaten Zeke, are you?"

"No," Manuel replied. "But I can clear all her paperwork up with a few phone calls in return for his help. It was blatant Miss Smirnov is more than just an employee to him."

"I guess it's worth a shot. We got nothing to lose." Frank cut the engine and reached for the door. "Come on, partner. Let's go talk to your nephew. If we're lucky, he might be able to recognize one of our suspects we got on video."

Manuel nodded. "Keep your fingers crossed."

The detectives entered the club and scanned the people in the VIP section. They were looking for anyone resembling the three suspects involving the city's recent, brutal mass killings.

All they found were the faces of meaningless strangers. A commotion nearby suddenly alerted their attention. A thin-looking guy with a nervous look on his face was being escorted by two enormous bouncers. Each guy practically dragged him along the floor. The guy's feet barely touched the ground, and he was mouthing off something.

The trio went into the back where Manuel's nephew had a private office.

Abruptly, a hush dimmed all the chatter in the VIP section as the owner of the club walked in through a side door. He looked like a million bucks dressed in an Italian pinstriped suit. His entrance was quiet but as obvious as a grenade going off. He shrank the size of all the other people. It wasn't because of his tall stature. It was his presence alone that intimidated everyone.

Nathan Gage was the owner of at least a dozen upscale bars in the largest metropolitan areas of northern California. Which meant he was capable and had more than enough money to do whatever the *fuck* he wanted. When it came to the types of people—like the guy that had just been taken to his office—who sold drugs in his establishments, he had zero patience.

While he headed to his office to take care of business, he spotted his uncle and Frank Perkins. "Give me a few minutes, guys," Nathan said, nodding in their direction. "I'll be with you in a few."

Manuel waved. "Take your time, Nate."

* * *

When Nathan stepped into his office, he glared at the guy his bouncers had brought in. The look on the guy's face said he knew he was in deep shit.

"I have a right to know what this is all about, Nate," the guy muttered in a shaky voice. "Why did you have your thugs bring me in here like this?"

"Sit the fuck down," Nathan demanded. "And shut the fuck up."

The guy practically melted into a chair.

"Tony D tells me you're selling in my bar." Nathan stared at him stone-faced. "Is it true?"

The guy's face dropped. "I haven't sold—"

Tony smacked the guy over the head. "Yeah, you are. We got you on video surveillance, dumbass."

Nathan smiled at Tony. Then he leaned forward and pegged the guy with a hateful glare. "You know what happens to people that lie to me. Right?"

"Please, Nate, I promise I'll never do it again. I was desperate," the guy pleaded. "My boss told me he would take my hands if I didn't sell my shit in the next two days. I'll make it up to you. I swear it."

"Yeah, you're going to make it up all right. If you think what your drug-dealer boss was going to do to you is bad, I promise... what I do to you is far worse." He pointed at the guy's chest. "Don't let me catch you back here again. Do you get me?"

Tony placed his hand on the guy's shoulder and clamped down hard. The guy yelped, his eyes begging for mercy.

"Y-yes," he muttered. "You won't see me *ever* again."

Nathan looked at Tony and said, "Get him out of here."

When Tony loosened his grip, he escorted the guy through the back that led to an alley.

Nathan motioned to the other bouncer. "Bring in the detectives that are waiting outside my office. One of them is my uncle, so be nice."

"Sure thing, boss."

After he brought in the detectives, Nathan said, "Give us some privacy."

The bouncer nodded and shut the door behind him.

* * *

Inside Nathan's crowded bar, Apollyon patiently waited for Anna to accept his invitation.

The club was dark inside, with heavy metal music blaring. Humans packed the dance floor, sweating while they moved under the pulsing colored lights. All around, half-naked

215

bodies were paired up or in groups, writhing and touching to the tempo of the music.

"Maybe another time," Anna said. "I should go find my..."

Her words trailed off when a leering whistle caught her attention. When she looked away from Apollyon and turned around, obnoxious catcalls came next. To her surprise, two guys strode in her direction and crowded in close. One of them was big and had a tattoo of a snake on his neck. The other guy had spiked hair and eyebrow piercings.

"I like your curly hair," the tattooed guy said. He leaned in and inhaled her scent. "What's your name, beautiful?"

Apollyon gritted his teeth and snarled at the guy.

"Umm,... Anna." She stumbled over her words. "I was just leaving to go to a bachelorette party."

The tatted guy ignored Apollyon as if he didn't exist. He stepped closer. "Anna, why don't you come with us." He looked away from her and peered up at Apollyon with a smug look on his face. "We're definitely more fun than André the Giant there. We'll take you somewhere far more exciting."

The guy with spiked hair placed his hand on Anna's shoulder and whispered close to her ear, "Come on, baby. I promise we'll take good care of you."

"Anna..." a familiar voice called out.

She quickly looked over her shoulder and saw Helen motioning her over.

As Anna rose from her chair to leave, the guy with spiked hair put pressure on her shoulder and held her down. "You're not going anywhere, sweetheart."

Anna reached into her purse and dug inside for the container of pepper spray she kept for occasions like this.

Apollyon's jaw clenched and his hand balled up into a fist.

The spiky-haired guy winked at Apollyon. "Sorry, man." He gripped his hand around Anna's arm. "She's not interested in you."

Before the guy could register movement, a left hook came through the air as fast as a baseball. Apollyon's meaty fist caught the side of the guy's jaw and knocked his head back, nearly ripping it completely off.

Screams erupted from the bar as the guy dropped to the floor. Blood sprayed like a red geyser.

Anna froze. When she looked up at Apollyon, fear thickened the air around her.

* * *

Nathan extended his hand. "Hey, Frank. It's been a while. How's the family?"

Frank took hold of his hand. "Good to see you, Nate. Everything's the same. My wife still manages to keep me in line."

"Yeah, he's a lucky SOB," Manuel said. "If everyone had a wife that baked like Missy, a home would be like a little slice of heaven."

Nathan released Frank's hand and reached out to Manuel. "I definitely agree." He chuckled. "How the hell are ya, Uncle?"

His uncle took his hand and tugged his nephew into a hug. "I'm doing fine, son." He patted him on the back and then pulled away. "How's the entertainment business going? I hear you're booking big names nowadays."

"Yeah, we get a few here," Nathan replied. "Believe it or not, most of our local bands draw in the biggest crowds. Chaos is one of them. You've heard of them haven't you, Uncle?"

His uncle laughed. "Nate, you know I don't listen to all that headbanger stuff. I'm more of the Frank Sinatra type myself."

"So, tell me." Nathan's expression grew serious. "When you called earlier, you said you were working on a big case. The one dealing with all the recent murders in the city. You mentioned something about a video?"

His uncle reached into his pocket. When he pulled his hand out, he held out a thumb drive. "Nate, I need you to take a look at the video footage on this."

"What is it?"

"It's the surveillance footage of three suspects," Frank piped in. "We're positive they're linked to some of the murders."

"I don't understand." Nathan cocked a brow. "What does this have to do with me?"

"Some of the footage is from Zeke Rizzo's bar," his uncle said. "We've got a visual on two females and a male." He held up the thumb drive. "And they're not exactly what you'd call *human*."

Shit. Nathan swallowed hard. "Come on, guys," he said around a light chuckle. "What's that supposed to mean?"

After his uncle explained what all they'd witnessed in the last couple of days, Nathan leaned back against his desk with his arms crossed. He was born a Breedline, but he knew his uncle had no knowledge of the species, nor did Frank. There were rumors, of course, about their kind. Some exceptions were made, and a few humans knew, but mostly, everything was kept secret. It was imperative to remain on the down-low, and it was their laws. He was also aware of his uncle's bloodline. Manuel Sanchez's mother was human, but his father—who'd abandoned him and his sister—was a Breedline. This had all been kept from Manuel. And now, Nathan wondered if this predicament put his uncle in danger. Maybe it was best if he just told him the truth.

"Will you take a look at the video?" his uncle said. "It's likely they've been in your bar. Maybe you or your staff will recognize one of them."

Nathan reached for the thumb drive. Before he took it, a loud knock momentarily distracted him. Then the door sprung open and the sound of screams filtered inside.

"Sorry to interrupt, boss," a wide-eyed bouncer said. "But we've got a serious problem."

Chapter Thirty-Two

Abbey didn't hesitate when Cole Decker left her alone locked inside the small room. She moved to her feet and went to work on the handcuffs. Her hands bled after several attempts to wiggle out of them. In frustration, she finally gave up and sank to her knees.

Oh, God. Please...

Panic, an emotion she was all too familiar with, surged through her body. She knew Cole wasn't ever going to let her go. As fear closed in on her, an image of Steven came to mind. She tried to bridle the thoughts inside her head by telling herself that he was still alive and soon the Covenant would come to their rescue.

The sounds of gunfire and shouts coming from outside roused her attention. Then she heard something strange. It sounded like the high-pitched roar of a big cat. Soon after, she heard men screaming.

In response, her heart pounded in her chest. The first thing that came to mind was Casey Barton. Steven had told her he had the ability to shift into a black panther. Although Casey was a Breedline, he was born with the genetics of a Theriomorph.

The minute she got to her feet the door abruptly sprung open. She cringed and furiously struggled against the cuffs as Cole pushed inside the room. Without a single word, he pointed a gun at her. One look into his dark eyes and she knew now was not the time to push her luck.

He rushed over and roughly grabbed her arm and yanked her forward. "We're getting the hell out of here." He forced her into a corner in the room. "If you try anything stupid, I'll fill your chest full of silver." He glared at her. "Do you understand?"

She quickly nodded. He released her arm and reached into his suit for his cell phone. She kept her eyes alert as he initiated a call. She prepared herself for the first chance to escape.

When he ended the call, he pulled back a small rug that revealed a trap door underneath. After he opened the hatch, he flashed the gun in her face. "Get moving."

Before she climbed inside the trap door, a thought came to mind. She had to leave something behind, but the only thing she had was the blood on her wrists. As she stepped down into the dark hole, she smeared it on the edge of the entrance.

"Move faster," Cole ordered.

She sped up her pace and prayed Steven would find her.

* * *

Oh... God. Random thoughts fired through Steven. *What did Cole Decker want with Abbey?*

Tim looked back at Steven. The expression on his face was painful to witness.

"Steven..." Tim spoke out, "I promise we'll find her."

He pushed past Tim and stormed out of the cellar, practically mowing him down.

Alexander stood at the top of the stairs, and when he turned to go after Steven, Tim stopped him. "Let him go."

Alexander nodded an understanding.

Tim aimed a gun at Corbin and Fredrick. "Let's see your hands."

Corbin gave him a look and stood there with his hands balled into fists.

Drakon—who was still in his wolf form—shot forward and snapped at them.

Fredrick yelped and quickly raised his hands. Corbin followed suit.

Tim smirked as he reached into the duffel bag he had strapped over his shoulder. When he pulled his hand out, he had handcuffs and some rope. He tossed them to Alexander. "Cuff them to the stair railing and tie up the rest. We don't have time to mess with them now. We'll have to lock them down here and come back later."

After Alexander had secured Kruger's men and handcuffed Corbin and Fredrick, Tim fixed his eyes on Corbin. "If you even think of shifting. I'll make sure it'll be your last."

Out of nowhere, gunshots erupted in the distance, and the sounds of physical fighting could be heard.

"Kyle... Casey..." Tim barked into his radio. "Decker has Abbey. I need you two to check the outside perimeter. Make sure no one leaves this property."

As he waited for them to respond, static came over the radio. "Do you read me?" Tim raised his voice, "Over..."

Kyle finally came over the radio. "Copy that. We're on it."

"Roman, do you copy?" Tim said.

"This is Roman. What's your status?"

"We found Steven. He's gone after Cole Decker. Do you have Decker's girls in a secure location?"

Abruptly, their communication was interrupted by gunfire. Tim went pale as he waited for Roman to comply.

Lena's voice suddenly came through, "Justice and I have the girls locked down in a safe place. Bull's going to back up Roman and Lawrence."

Tim was caught off guard when Alexander tackled him and called out, "Get down!"

Bullets peppered the wall behind Tim, barely missing him. Before the gunman could fire a second round, Drakon leaped into the air. A series of bloodcurdling screams came next.

An odd silence followed. When the shadow of an enormous wolf drew near, Drakon reared back on his haunches and released a feral growl.

Drakon sniffed the air and inhaled a familiar scent. It was at that moment he realized it was the colonel. Then a silver-gray wolf approached him with gore dripping from its jaws.

"Well... hello, ladies," Kid said as he came up behind the colonel's wolf.

Tim rolled his eyes. Kid was sharp as a tack, extremely intelligent, but he was also a sarcastic asshole who delighted in tormenting his comrades.

Drakon looked away from Kid and focused on the tall shadow moving in close. And then he smelled an overpowering aroma of Turkish tobacco that filled the air.

Gunny came up next to Kid with a cigar tucked between his lips. He crossed his arms over his chest. He looked almost bored, except for his eyes, which flickered alertly over the assembled group in silence. Gunny wasn't a man of many words, but he always managed to cut to the heart of the matter. "Jace—or should I say the Beast—has Steele pinned in the foyer." He focused on Tim and removed the stogie from his mouth. He exhaled a plume of smoke. "Jace caught Steele trying to escape. If you want 'im alive, I suggest you move fast. It doesn't look good for the bastard."

"Shit," Tim said. "Where's W—?"

A bone-chilling shriek like the sound of a panther cut him off.

"That would be Wyckoff," Gunny said.

"Has anyone seen Jem?" Alexander asked as he came up the stairs. "He's the only one that can communicate with Jace's beast."

"After they roughed him up a little..." Kid said with a clear smirk in his voice, "Jem and Jace had Valkin Steele squealing like a pig. When Steele finally told them Cole Decker had Abbey, Jem took off to find her."

Howling cut through the air. It sounded like Jace's beast, and he didn't sound happy.

"Shit," Tim said. "What the hell caused Jace to shift?"

Kid arched a brow. "Steele shot him in the chest."

"Damn it!" Alexander bit out. "He'll tear Steele into pieces."

"Let 'im," Gunny blurted. "The bastard deserves it."

The colonel let out a low growl.

Gunny met him with a scowl. "Steele's pathetic life isn't worth saving. And you all damn well know it."

"You're right," Tim said. "The son of a bitch isn't worth pissing on, but we need him alive. He has information we need."

Kid shrugged. "What information?"

"Steele was one of Dr. Hans Autenburg's backers. He funded his research for years. He could be the only person alive that has knowledge of how to destroy who or *what* is responsible for all the mass killings in the city."

Gunny grumbled under his breath. "So, who's got the balls to go save Steele's ass?"

"I will," Alexander said.

The sound of gunfire and the Beast's mighty roar electrified Alexander and the others.

Alexander jumped back as Valkin Steele came smashing through the wall. When he skidded across the floor, his face was covered in blood and his white suit was ripped to shreds. He had a pistol in his hand.

He looked up at Alexander with terror written all over his face. "Help me," Steele pleaded to Alexander. "Please..."

They were all caught off guard when the door to the room exploded inward. Everything seemed to move in slow motion as a white shaggy creature tore its way inside the giant opening. With lightning speed, it rushed after Steele and dug its sharp claws into his shoulder. He howled in agony as the monstrous creature hauled him off his feet and tossed him into the air.

Everyone froze in place, realizing it was Jace's beast. And they knew it was just a matter of time before it ripped Steele into pieces.

When Alexander called out to him, Jace's beast spun around on the balls of his feet.

"Listen to me, son," Alexander said, desperate to reason with him. "We need him alive."

When a look of confusion crossed the Beast's malevolent face, Alexander couldn't tell if it was from acknowledgement or plain annoyance.

"Jace... I know you're in there somewhere," Alexander continued to reason with the Beast. "I know you can hear me. Please—"

Alexander's words were cut off by a loud blast. He instantly gasped and clutched at his chest. As he collapsed to the floor, Tim and the others rushed to his side.

Alexander raised his hand, staring in alarm at the sticky, red stain on his palm.

Kid peeled off his shirt and hurriedly placed it over Alexander's wound.

Tim placed his hand on Alexander's arm. "I know it burns like hell, but your Breedline healing should be kicking in. Just keep pressure on it."

The Beast stared at Alexander with his head tilted. A familiar emotion came to him instantly, realizing someone he cared about was hurt.

As the Beast started forward, bullets blasted into his backside. He roared and whirled around to face the gunman. Before the guy fired another bullet, the Beast lunged at him and hit him like a pile driver. The force of the impact rammed him against the wall.

Several screams later, the guy's head bounced on the floor and rolled to a stop in front of Alexander and the others.

"Shit," Kid gasped and took a few steps back.

The Beast spun around and focused on Valkin Steele, who was huddled in a corner.

Justice's voice suddenly came over the radio, "Tim... Do you read me?"

Tim quickly grabbed his radio but kept his eyes trained on the Beast. "This is Tim," he said in a low voice. "We're in a bit of a situation, Justice."

The conversation coming from the radio caught the Beast's attention. He took his eyes off Steele and focused on Tim.

"It's Lena," Justice said. "I've lost communication with her. Is she with you?"

Ah, hell, Tim thought. "No, Justice. She's not with us."

"Damn," Justice said. "I'm worried—" Static cut him off.

"Justice." Tim raised his voice. "Do you copy?"

Time slowed to a crawl as Tim battled with a solution. He faced Gunny. "I need you and Kid to go out the back way and locate Justice. Something isn't right. Lena is missing."

Gunny nodded, and Kid said, "We're on it."

When Gunny and Kid slipped out, Tim focused his eyes back on the Beast. *Oh shit...* He was towering over Alexander.

"Alexander..." Tim said in hushed voice, "don't move a muscle."

The Beast looked up at the sound of Tim's voice. He turned to Drakon and Colonel Deshazo—both still in their wolf form—and positioned itself in an attack stance.

"Don't bother with them, Jace," Alexander said calmly. "They're not a threat to either of us."

Everyone stayed back and patiently waited. Hell, if you got too close, you were liable to lose a body part. Jace was in there somewhere, but until he came out again, you couldn't take the risk the Beast would remember who you were.

The Beast leaned closer to Alexander and hesitantly reached for him.

"It's okay, son," Alexander extended his hand. "You're safe now."

Before his hand connected with the Beast, a brilliant light flashed. When it faded, Jace stood in the Beast's place. He dropped to his knees and swayed side to side until he collapsed forward.

Alexander scooted next to him and nudged his arm. "Jace..."

With all the strength he could muster, Jace rolled to his side and looked up at Alexander. "Did I..." He gasped. "...hurt you?"

"It's okay, son. You didn't do this. One of Steele's men put a bullet in me, but I'll heal in no time."

Jace nodded and heaved a sigh of relief.

Tim looked down at Jace and shook his head. "We need to figure out some clothes for you, buddy."

Jace lowered his head and saw that he was buck naked. "Well, shit." He instantly put a hand over his privates. "I'm sure I can find something in this joint." He grunted as he pulled himself upright.

"Here, buddy," Kyle said as he extended his hand to Jace. "Let me help your naked ass up."

As Kyle helped Jace to his feet, Tim looked to the corner where Steele cowered. He was surprised to find him in a fetal position.

"Please... I beg you," Steele pleaded to Tim as he came over and stood above him. "Do whatever you want to me, but please... spare my Natasha. I swear to you she's innocent. She's not involved in any of this."

Tim narrowed his stare. "I know you took part in funding Dr. Autenburg's research. We want all the information that has to do with any supernatural creatures he has created. If you agree to help us, I'll make sure Natasha is kept out of this and taken to a safe place."

Steele bobbed his head up and down. "I give you my word."

Chapter Thirty-Three

When screams filtered into Nathan's office, he looked at the bouncer wide-eyed. "What the hell is going on?"

"A fight broke out," the bouncer said. "I'm pretty sure we got a dead body. There's blood everywhere. Tony D called 911. An ambulance is on its way."

"Shit!" Nathan said as he turned to his uncle and Detective Perkins. "Looks like you guys came at the right time."

Manuel focused on his partner. "Call for backup."

"I'm on it," Frank replied.

"Is the suspect still in the bar?" Manuel asked the bouncer.

"You're not going to believe this," the bouncer said. "I wouldn't believe it if I hadn't seen it for myself."

"Try me," Manuel drawled.

"The guy just freakin' disappeared into thin air."

Manuel shot Frank a look. "That's our guy!"

"I'll let you two do your job," Nathan said. "I'll gather all my staff. We'll get everyone out of here so I can shut down the bar."

Manuel nodded. "We'll need to question anyone that is a possible witness before you clear the place." He turned to the bouncer. "Lead the way."

The detectives followed the bouncer through the crowded bar where he led them to several people standing in a circle.

"I need everyone to stand back," Manuel said as he held up his badge.

As the audience of onlookers cleared a path, Manuel and Frank maneuvered their way to the body. Two women stood by the victim. The taller female had blood on her hands, and the other one looked terrified.

"Please, ladies," Manuel said, "I need you to move away from the body."

The woman with blood on her hands faced Manuel and said, "I'm a physician at the Bates Hospital. Doctor Helen Carrington." She hesitated and looked at Anna. "This is a friend of mine... Anna Saeni. She and I both witnessed the attack."

"Can you tell us what happened?" Manuel asked.

"It appeared as though two men were engaging in a heated agreement," Helen said. "It ended in a quick physical confrontation." She looked down at the dead guy. "And you can see how it ended."

"Did either of you get a look at the other guy?" Frank chimed in.

Helen nodded. "He was a big guy. Maybe six four... six five. He had long black hair. It all happened so fast I really didn't get a good look at his face."

Frank focused his eyes on Anna. "Did you get a look at the guy's face?"

Anna's eyes widened. "Y-yes," she muttered.

"Do you think you could describe him to a sketch artist?"

Anna nodded. "I-I think so."

Manuel knelt by the victim and carefully reached into his back pocket for his wallet. Before he opened it, he looked up at Helen and Anna. "Did either of you happen to witness anything unusual about the suspect?"

"Unusual?" Helen slightly tilted her head in question. "By what means?"

"The bouncer said the guy up and disappeared."

"You mean like... completely vanished into thin air?"

When Manuel nodded, she said, "I'm sorry, Detective. My eyes were focused on the guy lying here with his head nearly severed." She let out a deep breath. "In my opinion, I'd say that is pretty unusual, wouldn't you say?"

"Yeah," Manuel replied. "I would have to agree, Dr. Carrington."

"What about you, Miss Saeni?" Manuel focused on Anna. "Did you happen to see anything out of the ordinary?"

Anna slowly shook her head. "N-no." Her voice trembled. "I was distracted... after what happened."

"I can understand." His voice took on a sympathetic tone. "I'm sorry you had to witness something like this. I would appreciate it if you would stick around. I'll need both of you to come down to the station and make a statement. I'll make sure we have a sketch artist when you arrive. Anything you can think of will be helpful."

Anna nodded, and Helen said, "Of course."

The guy with a snake tattoo on his neck came forward and said, "Where's my buddy?"

Manuel shot forward and grabbed the guy's arm. "Hold on. I'm from homicide. We need you to stand back, sir."

The guy jerked his arm back. "Are you freakin' kidding me? Just look at my friend. That guy nearly knocked his head off. And then he up and disappeared like some damn magician. I want to know what the fuck is going on."

"Calm down, sir," Manuel said. "I'm sorry about your friend. And I give you my word... we'll do all we can to catch the SOB. But we're going to need you to cooperate with us. Please stay back. We're going to need to ask you some questions."

The guy threw his hands up in defeat and grumbled, "Whatever."

While the detectives spoke with the tatted guy and waited for the coroner to arrive, Nathan motioned the bouncer over.

"What's up, boss?"

"I need you to do something for me."

The bouncer nodded. "Sure thing."

"Contact Zeke Rizzo." Nathan kept his voice low. "Give him a heads-up while I make a call to the Covenant."

"Don't worry, boss. I'll take care of it."

* * *

"Keep walking." Cole roughly nudged Abbey forward. "And don't try anything stupid."

As she continued onward, she slowly reached into her pocket and dug for a handkerchief she had inside. When she brought her hand out, she let the small white cloth slip from her grasp. From the corner of her eye, she watched as it fell to the ground. Hopefully, Steven would somehow find it.

Finally, they came upon an SUV with a driver waiting inside. Cole uncuffed her before he shoved her into the back seat. Then he called out, "Get us the hell out of here."

The dark sedan accelerated and exited through the hidden path that led further into the wooded field. The car slowed as they drove through rough terrain. It seemed like forever to Abbey before they made it to their destination. When the vehicle came to a stop, she waited for Cole to tell her what to do next, although her patience was wearing thin.

"Get out," he barked.

As soon as she was on her feet, he manhandled her until they came to the entrance of what looked to be a fortress. She cast a quick glance behind her, taking in the high-security fence and the armed guards that patrolled the outside perimeter.

As the door to the entrance opened, she hesitated before she stepped inside. Not knowing what to expect on the other side made her tense with worry.

Cole shoved her forward. "Move."

She stumbled but caught her footing before she fell to the floor. As she looked up, her gaze locked on a horrible image before her.

Lena was bound to a chair, gagged, and her face was a mess. Bruises darkened her face, and dried blood crusted her nose and mouth. And three men with smug looks stood next to her.

A sudden rage consumed Abbey, forging the drive to unleash the she-wolf within her. She could sense it inside her, rising, snarling to be set free. The edgy, sharp sensation prickled along her skin, raising her hairs, the signal an impending shift was coming soon. She'd never fought so hard in her life to bring on the change. But never had she been so unsuccessful.

"You sick bastard," she said. "I swear... I'm going to rip your throat out."

She stood her ground when he wrapped his hand around the long strands of her hair. Then without warning, he backhanded her.

"I'm going to make you regret those words. I have a cage waiting just for you, my little pet." He stroked his hand over her cheek. "After I'm done with you, I'll have you broken in no time."

She gritted her teeth. "You'll have to kill me first."

Cole shoved her to the floor. "Watch your tone, Miss Winthrop." He aimed a gun at Lena. "Next time I'll put a silver bullet in your friend's head."

"Fine." Abbey rose to her feet. "You win. What do you want?"

"Strip," he ordered.

Her eyes widened. "What?"

Lena went crazy hearing Decker's demand. She struggled against her restraints and mumbled against the gag in her mouth.

Abbey glanced in her direction, telling her silently not to react.

"You heard what I said," Cole demanded. "I said, take off your clothes."

"You're insane," Abbey snapped.

Cole motioned to one of his guards. "Get her undressed and make it quick."

She held her breath as the man closest to Cole went forward eagerly.

"Lift your hands over your head," the guard said.

She slowly raised her arms. She cringed as he started to unbutton her shirt. Tears spilled down her cheeks when he reached for her jeans. A sick feeling assailed her when she was left standing in her bra and panties.

Please... please, God, she silently prayed. *Give me strength.*

Lena kept a close watch on the guards—whose attention was focused on Abbey—while she worked at the ropes around her wrists. She'd managed to wiggle them loose enough to slip free undetected. Now, she needed a weapon. Her eyes caught sight of the guard standing beside her. His gun was so close, almost within reach. She held her breath, praying he'd turn just a bit more.

As the guard stepped away from Abbey, she stood in the center of a room with eyes feasting greedily on her.

"After I'm done playing with you," Cole said. "All my men are going to have you next."

Abbey concentrated on bringing forth her she-wolf. She knew she didn't stand a chance in her human form. Then to her surprise, Lena grabbed one of the guards' weapons. She dropped to the floor and rolled. She fired off a series of rounds and hit one of Cole's men. While the other man dove behind a desk, Cole reached for his gun.

Lena rolled until she got a clear shot of underneath the desk and took out the other guard's kneecaps, making him howl in agony.

As the third guard charged at her, she got to her feet and connected with a solid right hook. Before he could register what hit him, she kicked his gun from his hand and landed a round kick to his jaw.

Another shot fired, and for a moment she thought she'd been hit, but she felt no pain. When she looked at Abbey, her body was lying motionless on the floor.

Oh God, no!

As Lena started forward, a blinding pain caught her from behind.

Chapter Thirty-Four

Steven charged down a narrow hallway that led to a set of double doors. Ready to blast through, he stopped when he heard familiar voices calling out to him. When he turned around, he saw Jem, Roman, Lawrence, and a black panther. He figured the big cat was either Casey Barton or Major Wyckoff. Whoever it was, it looked ready to take down anything that came in its path.

As they came up behind Steven, he nodded in ready silence and kicked in the door. Wood splintered into bits and pieces. The panther rushed ahead of them.

When they stepped inside, Steven searched for Abbey. Although the room was empty, he caught her scent.

"She's been here," he said in a deep and distorted voice.

He spotted a rug in the corner of the room that was out of place. He moved closer and found the hidden trap door and the blood smudged over the top. *It's Abbey's.*

He reached for the small hatch in the floor. With his Adalwolf strength still flowing through his veins, he grabbed on to the metal handle and wrenched the trap door open, completely ripping it off the hinges.

He dropped to his knees and looked down into the dark entrance. He reached into his pants pocket and pulled out a small flashlight. Aiming it inside the hole, his eyes caught sight of several steps that led underneath the floor.

Jem stepped forward. "What is it?"

"It's a secret passage leading underneath the estate," Steven said. "This is where Decker took Abbey." He was on his feet immediately, his expression hard. "It's the only way he could have got out without being seen."

"Steven, I'd thought you'd want to know we captured Steele and some of his men," Jem said.

Steven's eyes narrowed. "Is he still alive?"

Jem hesitated and arched a brow. "He was when I last saw him. But then I left him with Jace, so there's no telling. If Steele pisses him off..."

Wyckoff's panther padded to where Steven stood. After making a few circles around the hole in the floor, he came to a halt and lowered his big head inside and sniffed cautiously. After a moment, the cat glanced back up at Steven and growled menacingly.

Steven stared into his lavender eyes and understood the cat's helpless rage.

The others surged closer to him, concern etched on every single person's face, most especially Roman's. He'd made a promise to Abbey to keep her out of harm's way. And now Cole Decker had taken her and done God knew what.

"We've wasted enough time while Abbey desperately needs our help," Roman spoke out harshly. "Until we know what we're up against, I need every available man at the ready. Jem will go with Steven and me." He pointed toward the open trap door. "Lawrence, I want you and Wyckoff to wait here to organize communications with the others and act as backup." He looked at Steven pointedly. "Are you ready?"

Before Steven got a word out, shots were fired in their direction. Roman's arm absorbed the gun's load, and the impact twisted his torso. He immediately clutched his shoulder. *Damn it!*

Lawrence squeezed off a series of shots before Roman fell to the floor.

A high-pitched scream cracked through the room, then Wyckoff's huge black cat flew over to the open doorway, taking down the man who had fired his weapon. A scream split the air. The gunman tried to push himself away, but the enraged animal rose with a low snarl. The man's scream of fear came to an end as the panther closed his jaws around his throat.

Jem dropped to the floor next to Roman. "How bad is it?"

"It's not bad." Roman grunted as he sat upright. "It hurts like a son of a bitch, but believe me, I've had worse." Slowly, he stood, using Jem for leverage.

"It's best you stay behind and let Lawrence patch you up," Jem said.

Roman shook his head, his face tight with anger. "That's not an option. I made a vow to protect Abbey, and I plan on keeping it." And then he turned toward Steven with an expression of regret framing his face. He looked almost... sorry. Refocusing back to Jem he said, "Besides, I'll heal in no time. The bullet went clean through."

"Okay, enough with the chitchat," Steven said. "We're wasting precious time. Let's do this."

Lawrence held up his radio to Jem. "Keep us informed and let us know if you need backup. I'll let the others know what's going on."

Jem nodded in agreement, then made fast tracks through the opening in the floor, with Steven and Roman leading the way.

As they came to an opening at the end of the underground tunnel, it led them to a hidden entrance in a wooded field.

Roman pointed to something lying on the ground. "Wait." He picked up the handkerchief and looked at Steven. "Do you recognize this?"

Steven reached for the delicate cloth in Roman's grasp and brought it to his nose. "It's Abbey's," he said, inhaling her scent. "She left it for us to find."

"Smart girl," Roman said with a smile. "Decker must have taken her through here." He looked at the wooded area, then back at Steven and Jem. "We're going to need a vehicle."

Jem reached for the radio. "I'll call for backup. It's better to be prepared. When it comes to Cole Decker, there's no telling what we'll be facing."

* * *

By sheer determination, Lena remained conscious and pushed aside the pain even though it felt like Cole had caved in her damn skull.

As he loomed over her with a gun to her head, she reacted quickly and lashed out with her leg, knocking the weapon from his grasp.

She struggled up, but he was on her, pinning her down with his weight.

"I like a woman that fights back," he said, staring at her with satisfaction in his gaze. "It turns me on. When I get done having my fun with you, I'm going to cut you into little pieces and send them to your friends. They'll think twice the next time they fuck with me."

Oh, hell no, Lena thought. She wasn't going down like this. She would wait for the right moment to make her move. If her plan worked, she'd make damn sure Cole Decker never hurt another woman or child again.

As he leaned down to force his lips to hers, she used all her strength and head-butted him right in the face. He let out a cry of pain and crumpled to the floor. Lena pushed herself up and landed a kick that connected with his balls. If she had it her way, he wouldn't have any left when it was all over.

While he howled in pain, she searched for the gun. Then she spotted it under a chair. As she scrambled over to it and bent down to grab for it, Cole was on her in a split second, attacking her from behind.

Lying motionless on the floor, Abbey slowly opened her eyes at the sounds of struggling nearby. She shook her head to clear her thoughts. Through blurred vision, she caught sight of Lena wrestling on the floor with Cole Decker. He outweighed her by at least a hundred pounds. As anger surged through her body, she felt the change within her. And it was instantaneous.

Her fair skin darkened, turning a mottled shade of dark brown. A mane of coarse black fur sprouted from her scalp and spread to her shoulders, then across her body and limbs, which themselves lengthened and grew larger within seconds. Her undergarments split at the seams as she assumed the proportions of a giant. Her fists curled into enormous wolfish fingers with nails the size of daggers that jutted from the tips.

The blood of her ancestors pulsed through her veins as her flesh and bone underwent a grotesque transformation. A canine muzzle protruded from her face, and tufted ears tapered atop her head to a point. Her black leathery nostrils flared above a jaw full of sharp incisors.

She stretched her shaggy limbs, feeling the inhuman strength and power in them. She'd never felt so free... and so *deadly*.

Unaware of what was transpiring nearby, Lena and Cole rolled on the floor, but he used his strength as an advantage and elbowed her already injured jaw. After she'd been surrounded at Steele's estate and forced here, Cole's men had beaten her nearly unconscious. There wasn't a single part of her body that didn't hurt.

Cole made a dive for the gun and she leaped after him, rolling over his body and kicking the gun away from his grasp. Then he grabbed her by the ponytail and slammed her facedown onto the floor. And again and again until she stopped struggling and fell still.

The hairs on the back of Cole's nape rose when an unearthly sound of a predator's growl broke the silence. He held his breath as he looked over his shoulder. What he saw made him fall back on his ass, cringing in fear. He couldn't believe his eyes.

Abbey's she-wolf bared her fangs and crouched defensively in front of him.

"P-please... don't kill me," he babbled, begging for his pathetic life.

The she-wolf narrowed her coal-black eyes, staring at him with a murderous glare. Then the creature leaned in, getting face-to-face with him, and smiled. Her wolfish mouth was full of razor-sharp teeth.

Before he could blink an eye, the deadly creature tore at his throat. In a state of shock, his terror numbed the pain as he watched his life's blood spurt in jets. His last pleas for mercy turned into a gurgling hiss of air.

As Abbey's she-wolf surveyed the room, her attention focused on a woman nearby. On the floor beneath a pool of blood, Lena's body lay lifeless. She looked from Lena to Cole's dead body and back to Lena. The she-wolf looked puzzled for a moment, then her eyes softened. The sound of a low whimper broke the stillness of the room. Moving next to Lena, the two-footed creature peered helplessly down at her. She dropped to her hands and knees and gently grasped hold of Lena's arm. A tear struck Lena's cheek as she rolled her over.

Lena moaned and slowly opened her eyes. When she looked up, she saw the creature's luminous eyes glistening. Its tears glowed as they rolled down the thickness of its hairy face.

And then she started to cry, for she felt the she-wolf's grief in her heart and added it to her own.

She formed a half smile over her bloody and bruised face. She paused only for a moment before she reached up to touch the she-wolf's muzzle. Her hand caressed its dark, bristled cheek and she whispered, "Thank you, Abbey."

Abbey's she-wolf kept at her side, unable to take her worried eyes from Lena. In a matter seconds, her thick furry hide began to shrink and disappear as if her skin was miraculously willing it back inside her body. Lena blinked through tears that made her vision all shimmery and watched the creature's slow transformation right before her eyes. It wasn't long before Abbey's human features came into focus.

With her eyes trained on Lena, Abbey inhaled a deep breath as if she'd been holding it for an extended time.

"Lena," she gasped. "Are you okay?"

Before Lena could get any words out, a loud crack like the sound of lightning came from outside. Abbey looked over her shoulder just as the door burst open and several heavy footsteps pounded across the floor. She quickly crossed her arms over her bare chest.

"Abbey!" Steven called out. "Where are you?"

She sagged in relief when she heard his voice. She felt safe, and she knew nothing else could hurt her.

Suddenly, Justice was over Lena, his eyes so intense and full of panic when he saw her lying in a pool of her own blood. And her face was...

He fell to his knees. "Oh, my God, baby." He gently gathered her in his arms, his heart beating like a drum against her broken body.

"I'm okay. Abbey saved me," she managed to whisper. "You're getting blood... all over you."

"I don't give a damn," he said fiercely as he buried his face in the crevice of her neck. "You're alive, and that's all that matters." He looked at her, puzzled. "Honey, why didn't you shift? You could have taken out Decker and all his men with your Breedline wolf."

"They threatened me," she rasped out. "Their weapons were loaded with silver."

A second later, Steven came into view and saw Abbey. She was on the floor next to Lena, and she was... *naked*.

He rushed over, with Roman on his heels, and immediately dropped to the floor next to her. Roman shrugged out of his shirt and handed it to Steven. After he slipped it over Abbey's head, she found herself carefully enfolded in a strong pair of arms.

She buried her face in Steven's chest as he rocked her back and forth. "I've got you," he whispered close to her ear. His voice sounded like he had tears. "It's over, sweetheart."

"Our baby," she whispered, unable to hold it in any longer. "We're going to have a baby."

He pulled back with a look of awe on his face. For a moment he went completely silent. There was a wealth of emotion burning in those green eyes. "Did you say... *baby?*"

She grinned and nodded.

He embraced her again and held on tightly. His entire body trembled against hers, and his breaths tore raggedly from his chest.

"I love you, Abigail," he choked out. "God, I love you so much."

Tears slid down her cheeks, love welling from deep within her as she took in the sincerity of his words. "I love you too."

He straightened and looked her in the eyes. There was concern as well as elation in his stare. He smoothed a strand of hair from her face and tucked it behind her ear. "You're going to have to take it easy. I don't want anything to happen to you or our baby."

She reached up and caressed his cheek with her hand. "I'm scared out of my mind, but I'm also so happy."

He leaned forward and kissed her softly. "I'm scared too. But we'll be just fine, sweetheart. I promise."

Lawrence and Jem came over and stood above them, both worried if Abbey and Lena were all right.

Roman cleared his throat. "I wasn't trying to eavesdrop on your conversation, but did I hear you two just say you're pregnant?"

Abbey sighed. "Yes, we are."

Both Lawrence and Jem's expressions eased, and they lit up with smiles.

"Congratulations," Roman finally said. His smile was gentle, and there was a wealth of emotion in his eyes. "You're a brave young lady, Abbey. I'm proud of you."

"Damn straight," Justice said in a gruff voice as he turned toward her. "Thanks for saving my girl. And congratulations, little mama."

"Thank you," Abbey said with a light giggle.

Lawrence smiled so broadly his white teeth flashed. "That's wonderful news. Congratulations to the both of you."

"Congratulations, you two," Jem said. "It's about time we had some good news."

Steven nodded, beaming the entire time. "Thanks, guys."

Lena reached over to squeeze Abbey's hand. "Oh, Abbey," she said in a weak voice. "I'm so happy for you. And I have to say, for five foot two, you've got lady balls of steel."

"So says the woman who takes on opponents the size of a double-decker bus," Abbey replied.

"Yeah, you both kicked ass," Jace chimed in as he joined the group by Steven's side. He extended his fist to Steven. "Way to go, buddy."

Steven grinned and bumped knuckles with Jace.

Jem's eyes roamed over the white suit Jace had on. "What in the hell are you wearing?"

"I had to find something to wear, so I helped myself to Steele's closet."

"Okay..." Jem shrugged. "I'm afraid to ask, but what was wrong with the clothes you had on?"

"When you left, that asshole shot me in the chest," Jace said. "To make a long story short... I turned, Alexander calmed the Beast, and then I shifted back. So, I couldn't just walk around naked."

"Wait." Jem's eyes widened. "Did you say Alexander calmed your Beast?"

Jace nodded. "Steele is one lucky bastard. If it weren't for Alexander, he would have been the Beast's next meal."

Jem shook his head and rolled his eyes.

Lawrence knelt beside Lena and cut in the conversation, "We need to get you and Abbey back to the Covenant and checked out. I know you'll heal, but I'm not going to let up until you're both given a clean bill of health."

Jace turned to Steven. "Tim and the others have Steele in their custody. He made a deal to give us details on Dr. Autenburg's research and anyone that's still involved in exchange for Natasha's safety."

"She's innocent in all this," Steven prompted. "I'll vouch for her. Natasha doesn't have anything to do with Valkin Steele's corrupt organization."

"Let's get Abbey and Lena out of here," Jem said. "I just sent Tim a text letting him know everyone is all right. He wants us to meet at Steele's estate so we can get back to the Covenant. He said he got a message from Tessa. Apparently, there's been another attack, and this time Helen and Anna were there to witness it."

"Are they all right?" Steven asked with concern in his voice.

"They're fine. And that's not all," Jem said. "We've got to deal with those two human detectives that are investigating all the murders in the city. Tessa said she got a call from Nathan Gage. The attack happened at one of his bars. He also said Detective Sanchez is his uncle... and he's half Breedline, but the detective doesn't have any knowledge of his bloodline."

"So, what is Tim going to do?" Roman asked.

"He's going to bring the detectives into the Covenant."

"Are you serious?" Jace blurted. "He's just going to let them know about us?"

"We don't have a choice," Jem said. "They've already seen too much. They witnessed Yelena's abduction. Maybe they can help us locate her. Besides, Tim is going to turn Steele and whatever is left of his men into their custody. They're helping the feds investigate all the human sex trafficking, so it's best to let them deal with it."

"What does Tessa say about all this?" Jace asked.

"She's going to have Zeke Rizzo bring the detectives to the Covenant since he's already dealt with them," Jem explained. "It looks like we've got our hands full this time."

Shit, Jace thought. His brow creased with worry and his mind went straight to Tessa and the boys. "So why the hell are we just standing around?" He shrugged. "Let's get our asses moving."

Chapter Thirty-Five

After the unfortunate incident with the human at the bar earlier, Apollyon materialized back at the mansion he shared with his sisters. Everything was the best of the best here. Nothing was cheap. The color of the walls set off a spectacular rare collection of paintings in gilt frames. The floors were covered with red and gold Oriental rugs, and plush velvet drapes hung over the stained-glass windows. They'd started life privileged, living with their father before he placed them in a sedated limbo, locked up to be forgotten forever. His mother had been the one to set them free, and now they resided in her nineteenth-century estate, filled with antiques and priceless works of art. Their mother's family was loaded. *Really loaded.*

Apollyon caught Yelena's scent as he stood outside of her room. The erotic aroma of jasmine captured his senses and created a heady emotion he was not used to. She was like a drug, and he felt himself becoming more and more addicted. If she could affect him like this without being in the same room, she might just be the death of him. And the million-dollar question was, how would he persuade her to stay here of her own free will? As far as he knew, her heart belonged to the sin-eater.

His thoughts went to the human female he'd encountered earlier at the bar and the image of the soft skin of her neck. He needed to eat. He hadn't fed in days, and hunger was making him vulnerable to Yelena and making it too easy to forget what he was.

He briefly closed his eyes and swallowed the knot in his dry throat. Dark hunger curled in his gut and churned like a bottomless, achy pit. As the gnawing sensation grew stronger, his body demanded to feed, craving human blood.

A feeling of deep uneasiness, like someone had reached into his chest and squeezed his heart dead, suddenly assailed him. Sweat broke out across his forehead. His feelings for Yelena made him feel trapped. He should be feeding to gain strength instead of falling in love with a woman who didn't return his affections. He was changing himself for a female. It made him feel like a fool.

"Apollyon..."

He turned to the soothing voice. "Mother,... what are you doing up at this hour?"

"I was waiting for you. I knew you'd come to the girl."

There was a long silence. Sonya thought back to the day she found her children imprisoned in a state of slumber by their father, Dr. Hans Autenburg. The day the research facility he had kept her in against her will was destroyed, she managed free Apollyon, Electra, and Callisto and finally escape her captivity.

"Have patience, Son," she finally said. "Yelena will learn to love you back. How could she not?"

Anguish came out of him like blood from a chest wound. Knowing Yelena was in love with Zeke Rizzo filled him with both physical and mental torment.

"She will never love me," he painfully said. "She loves another."

"Trust in my words, Son. I have seen this in a vision. She will forget in time. Her heart will be broken, but your love will fill her needs."

He gathered her hand in his and said, "Thank you, Mother."

Moments later, he closed his eyes and meshed with Yelena's mind. She was thinking of the sin-eater. He immediately dropped the image and opened his eyes. He took a deep breath and reached for her door.

Before he barged inside, he lightly tapped on the door. When there was no answer, he opened it a crack and said, "Yelena..."

Yelena stirred from a deep slumber and looked at the door.

He opened the door wider and stepped inside. The golden glint in his piercing stare spoke of hidden power and predatory danger, and for some reason that made him... *exciting*. There was something compellingly beautiful about his sheer maleness, and when he looked at her, it created an odd sensation in her chest. He was dark and broody and delectable.

"You seem... different," she said, sensing his concern.

He cocked a brow and approached the bed cautiously. As he sat down, the mattress dipped, and she could have sworn he leaned in and inhaled her scent. One side of his mouth lifted into a half smile.

"Are you hungry?"

She shook her head.

"Are you still afraid of me?"

She kept her eyes on him and nodded in silence.

"I want to know why."

"Maybe it's because you tried to kill a friend of mine."

"Christ..." His tone was low, belying the frustration that thinned his sexy mouth.

"You asked," she shot back. "Don't be angry if you don't like my answer."

"I didn't kill the sin-eater. Besides, he's a Breedline. He'll heal."

She was desperate for answers. She wanted to know what he wanted with her. Using her succubus-side, she tried to get into his head and read his thoughts, but he shut her out completely.

"What do you want with me?"

The look he gave her was indecisive. Underneath his thick masculinity, she sensed a hint of something else. *Insecurity?* No, that wasn't it. It was self-hatred. He *hated* what he was.

He reached out and brushed the bangs back from her forehead with a gentle, slightly trembling hand. He hadn't felt this drawn to a woman before. She made him forget the dark violence of his existence and made everything feel... *different*.

"Don't fear me, Yelena. I will not harm you."

"Please," Her voice was pleading. "Will you let me go?"

"I'm sorry." His jaw clenched. "I cannot do that."

She swallowed the lump in her throat. The pressure in her chest made her feel as if she was drowning. Her heart was breaking into a million pieces. She warred with the horrible realization that she would never see Zeke again.

By the look on his face, she realized he'd read her thoughts. He knew she was in love with Zeke, and that angered him. Although his rage was a tangible force, battering her senses along with his desire, his beautiful golden eyes were shadowed with pain.

She braced herself for him to lash out, ready to feel the brunt of his punishment. But to her surprise, he dipped his head and touched his lips to hers in a gentle caress.

Her pulse jumped as if lightning had struck.

Both their hearts began to beat faster.

She could feel the suffering in the way he kissed her. And then horrible and vivid images of his memories came to her. They were full of agony and betrayal. She saw what appeared to be three separate tombs. His own father had placed him and his sisters in some sort of sedated limbo. She couldn't explain why, but she wanted to offer him compassion, and for some godforsaken reason, she felt something stirring inside her.

When he pulled back, his eyes searched her face. He was waiting for her to protest. Instead, she leaned in and kissed him.

His eyebrows flew up. Then he felt something wet on his face. It was a tear. She was crying.

* * *

An hour after the coroner left, the detectives exited the bar. Although their car was parked in the front of the bar's parking lot, Manuel headed in the opposite direction. He needed air. Christ... he needed more than just fresh air.

"Where are you going?"

Manuel looked over his shoulder at his partner. "Give me a few minutes. I need to take a breather."

"Take as long as you need, buddy," Frank said.

As Manuel walked along, his stomach was in knots. When he made his way around the corner, he stopped and leaned against the building. His thoughts took him back to Zeke's bar. He couldn't get his mind off what had happened. Did vampires really exist? And what the hell was Zeke? He wanted answers, and he wanted them now.

246

At that moment, he pulled out his cell phone to demand answers. Before he could make the call, his phone suddenly went off. *Surprise, surprise.* It was Zeke.

"Mr. Rizzo," Manuel answered, "what can I do for you?"

There was a moment of silence on the other end. "We need to talk. When can you meet me?"

"You name the time and place."

"Meet me at my bar. Bring your partner. They want to talk to both of you."

"They?" Manuel asked. "Who else are we talking about?"

"I'll explain everything when you get here," Zeke said before he ended the call.

Shit! Manuel tucked his phone in his jacket and rushed back to the parking lot where his partner was waiting.

When he opened the passenger's side door, he looked at Frank. "Let's head over to Zeke's bar."

"What's going on?"

"I just got a call from Zeke," Manuel said as he got into the car. "We're supposed to meet up with him and someone else."

"Did he say who?"

"No, but hopefully whoever it is, they'll have answers to all this insanity."

"What about the physician and the pretty blonde?" Frank asked. "We're supposed to meet them at the station in an hour for questioning."

"I'll call the station. If we're not back in time, Detective Ratcliff can take over."

Frank fired up the engine. "Okay, let's do this."

Chapter Thirty-Six

When Eve stepped from the shower, she heard a knock coming from her bedroom door.

"Eve?" Mia called out. "May I come in?"

"It's open. Come on in."

Eve hurriedly dried off and got dressed. She wasn't even going to bother with her hair, so she quickly scrubbed a towel over the wet strands. God, she was a mess. Asking Mia's advice to take Arius and Tidus to see Sebastian at the hospital weighed heavily on her mind. Was she making the right decision?

When she finally came out of the bathroom, her eyes met Mia's.

Mia noticed the tense look on her twin sister's face. "Eve, is something wrong?"

She sat down on the bed next to Mia. "I need to ask you something important. And I need you to keep an open mind."

"Okay..." Mia looked at her with concern. "What is it?"

"I want to take the boys to see Sebastian."

Mia's eyes widened. "But... *why*?"

"His sister Anna believes their presence could have a positive effect on him. It could bring him out of his coma."

Mia seemed lost for words. She had to bite her tongue to keep from telling Eve just what a bastard she thought Sebastian was. For what he had done to her and her family, wasting away in a state of unconsciousness seemed to fit his crimes. Death would be too merciful. But for some reason, Eve believed Sebastian's dark heart had somehow miraculously changed. And it was important to support her sister even if she disagreed with her decision.

Eve braced herself for Mia's negative response, but instead, Mia eased forward and placed a hand over hers. "I trust you, Eve. If you think it's the right thing to do, you have my blessing."

Some of the tension fled Eve's expression. She leaned in and wrapped her arms around her sister. "Thank you."

She squeezed Eve back. "You're welcome. Just promise me one thing." She pulled back from their embrace. "Don't let your past discourage you from being the person you want to be. What I see now is a strong, resilient woman who strives to see the best in people, despite being shown the worst. I have faith in you, Sister."

Mia's impassioned words hit the very soul of her. She had always tried to imagine what it would be like to hear those words, to know she was loved by a family. "I love you, Mia." Tears spilled down her cheeks. "You make me believe in myself."

"I love you too. And I have some good news. It's the reason I came to see you. The Breedline council has granted you a pardon. They have only one condition. You must reside in this Covenant."

Eve sat staring at her sister, seemingly lost for words. She wanted to cry. She wanted to laugh. This was the most wonderful feeling in the world. She was finally free, free to live her life the way she wanted and be with her boys as they grew up.

"I don't know what to say." Eve's bottom lip quivered. "I'm so happy." She reached for Mia's hand and lightly squeezed. "Thank you, Sister."

"I want us to be a family," Mia said. "You will always have me. *Always.*"

"I don't know how to live a normal life. I'm afraid." Then she frowned. "What if I screw up?"

"I'll help you. We'll take one day at a time. Trust me."

"One day at a time," Eve whispered. "I think I can safely make that promise."

"I have some more good news." Mia smiled, and then a giddy rush came over her. "Yesterday I took a pregnancy test." She let out a deep breath. "I'm pregnant."

Eve looked at her sister in stunned disbelief. A second later, her face split into a wide grin. She wanted to do something ridiculous like squeal and jump up and down.

"Oh, my God. This is great news. I'm so happy for you."

"So am I," Mia said with tears in her voice. When her phone started to ring, she looked at the caller ID. "Oh crap, it's Jem."

Before she answered, Mia put her finger up to her lips and winked at her sister.

Eve smiled and winked back in silent understanding. It was apparent Mia hadn't said anything to Jem about her pregnancy.

* * *

When Yelena slowly lifted her lips from Apollyon's, her eyes widened. "Y-your eyes... they're glowing."

He quickly looked away to avoid her gaze.

She reached out with both hands and cupped his face. When she brought his face to meet hers, she said, "I think they're beautiful."

His dark heart skipped a beat and a lump rose in his throat. He couldn't remember the last time a woman had touched his face so tenderly.

"Dammit, woman, you're killing me."

"So, what are you?" Yelena hesitantly asked. "I sense your succubus side, but I can't—"

"You don't have any idea what to make of me, do you?"

Her forehead creased with concern. She worried she'd insulted him.

"It's okay." He smiled a little. "You're right about the succubus side. I inherited that from my mother. But the other part of me... I was genetically engineered. My biological father kidnapped my mother and forced her to be a surrogate for his children. He created my sisters and me using his DNA and the genetics of a powerful Wicca, a Breedline, and an Adalwolf. He wanted a creature with enough powers—stronger than any other species—to destroy the Breedline."

In the silence that followed, he lowered his head in shame. For the first time in his life, he wished he was someone else. When he looked back up, he stared at her with weary eyes. "I don't want you to think I'm a freak. But I won't blame you if you do."

Her expression softened. "I'm so sorry, Apollyon. I'm sorry for what you had to go through. I've seen the pain you and your sisters suffered. And I don't think you're a freak. I think you're..." She tried to think of the right word. "...beautiful."

"No one has ever said that to me before."

In that moment as he focused on her lips, he had an urge to kiss her.

"I want you, Yelena. Right here, right now."

"I... want you too." *God, had that come out of her mouth?*

He caught her by surprise. He tugged her into his arms and pressed his mouth against hers. His kiss was explosive. At first, her lips were stiff against his, but that didn't last. Her body practically melted into his.

When he finally ended the kiss, he pressed his forehead to hers. His breathing was harsh. He suddenly felt weak and dizzy. He closed his eyes for a second. When he reopened them, he swayed, and she could feel him trembling.

She pulled back and said, "Apollyon? Are you all right?"

His brows drew down in a deep V. "I'm not feeling..." His voice trailed off as he collapsed to the floor.

She sank to her knees beside him. "Apollyon!"

He stared at her with unfocused eyes. "I need... to feed."

"I can help you," she said placing her wrist over his lips.

He turned his face away. "Human... I need human..."

When he fell silent, she shook his shoulders. "Apollyon..." She raised her voice, "Apollyon!"

The sound of the door opening caught her by surprise. When she looked up, Electra stood in the doorway.

Before Yelena could get a word out, Electra rushed beside him and said, "What the hell did you do to my brother?"

"I didn't do anything." Yelena looked down at him. "He needs—"

"Quiet!" Electra barked. She gripped his shoulders and shook him hard. "Apollyon?... Can you hear me?"

"He needs blood," Yelena said in a tear-laced voice.

"Why do you shed tears for my brother?" Electra frowned. "I know he's keeping you here against your will."

She glared at Electra. "You don't know a thing about me."

"Fine," Electra grumbled. "Stay here with him." Her tone offered no compromise. "I'll be back with the blood he needs."

When Electra left the room, Yelena realized she had fallen in love with a monster. She leaned close to his ear and whispered, "Please... come back to me."

Chapter Thirty-Seven

Tim leaned against the wall of the library with his arms crossed. The others stood back, waiting for him to speak.

Downstairs in the basement, Valkin Steele and his men were in lockdown and heavily guarded. Corbin Azzo and Fredrick Mercier—both Breedline traitors—were placed in separate confinement waiting to face the council for their betrayal.

"I know our laws forbid us to reveal our species to humans," Tim finally said, "but in certain situations, sometimes we are left with no choice. And considering the circumstances with the two homicide detectives, this is one of those special cases."

He stepped back and let Tessa address the group.

"As your queen, I am prepared to disclose our species to the detectives that will be arriving with Zeke Rizzo. They should be here any minute. It has come to our attention that Detective Manuel Sanchez was born half Breedline. We are aware that he has no knowledge of his lineage. Although Detective Frank Perkins is a human, he and his partner have witnessed more than any person in their right mind could possibly process. After discussing this with our council and taking into account all the risks involved, we have come to an agreement that is in our best interest. We have decided to develop a partnership with them." Her eyes roamed over the room. "If anyone here disagrees with our decision, speak now. Remember, your voice matters."

When everyone remained silent, she said, "So be it. The decision has been made."

The sound of voices coming from downstairs raised their attention.

Everyone went downstairs in a group to meet the detectives. As they stepped into the foyer, Bruce Carmichael stood in front of Zeke Rizzo and both detectives.

For a moment, Manuel was utterly immobilized, caught between wanting to scream and slap himself awake. After Zeke had explained to him and his partner about the Breedline species and that his father—who'd abandoned him at birth—had passed on the same bloodline, he thought the whole situation was just a damn nightmare. But at least they finally had answers to all the bizarre things that had been happening in the city, especially the vampire-like creatures they were after.

Manuel flinched as the door behind him abruptly opened and closed. When he looked back, he was convinced he was hallucinating. There were nine of the meanest, biggest bastards he'd ever seen. Their stares made him feel like a bug under glass or a slab of meat about to be carved up.

A hand landed on his shoulder the size of a catcher's mitt. "Welcome to our abode, Detectives. My name is Drakon Hexus."

When Manuel and Frank looked up, the guy stood at least six-foot-seven with a short-trimmed Mohawk.

Both detectives took a few steps back.

Frank dragged in some air. "Th-thanks."

Manuel nodded in complete silence.

Drakon formally introduced Colonel Deshazo and his Special Ops team, and Roman and his crew.

Then a pair of electric-purple eyes caught Manuel's attention. He thought they had to be colored contacts. No one really had that color of eyes.

Major Wyckoff extended his hand to Manuel. "It's a pleasure to meet you, Detective."

Manuel slightly hesitated before taking his hand. "Nice to meet you too," he said to the guy with purple eyes. "I'm Detective Manuel Sanchez, and this is my partner, Detective Frank Perkins."

After Wyckoff shook hands with Manuel, he offered his giant palm to Frank.

The others clustered around and took turns greeting them.

Manuel's mouth flapped open as Helen and Anna came forward. Frank appeared just as surprised as his partner.

When Anna caught Zeke's attention, he found it hard to take his eyes off her. He felt an odd, but familiar, feeling stirring in his chest. He briefly closed his eyes and inhaled her scent. It was then he realized he would kill any member of his sex who tried to touch her, be with her, love her. His feelings for Yelena had betrayed him. *But... why?* And then one powerful word echoed in Zeke's head: *beloved.*

Anna shifted her focus on Zeke and stared into his mesmerizing blue eyes. Suddenly, she felt breathless in his presence and found she couldn't think, much less speak. Feeling the raw, somewhat alluring, power of his body, she tried to catch her breath as the unfamiliar emotions constricted her chest.

As Helen stepped forward to greet the detectives, her movement brought Anna back to reality.

"It's good to see you again, Detective Sanchez," Helen said with her hand extended. "Of course, considering the first time, the circumstances are much better."

He shook her hand. "Yes, I agree, Dr. Carrington."

"Please, call me Helen."

"I-I don't believe it," Frank said, sounding tongue-tied. "Y-you're one of them?"

Helen lightly chuckled. "Don't look so shocked, Detective Perkins. Our kind is everywhere."

Frank blew out his breath. "Unbelievable."

"I guess there's no need for you and Miss Saeni to stop by the station for further questioning," Manuel said, crossing his arms. "It looks like we're about to get more than what we bargained for."

Tim cleared his throat. "Detectives, I'd like to introduce our queen, Tessa Chamberlain."

Manuel watched as a petite woman stepped forward. Her face was delicate, and her eyes were the rarest color he'd ever seen. They had the intensity of the finest green gemstones.

"Hello, gentlemen." Tessa extended her hand to Frank. "Thank you for accepting our invitation. I'm sure you have a lot of questions."

Frank didn't move. He barely breathed. All he did was stare at her. *This is unreal.* And then his partner nudged his arm bringing him back to focus.

Frank flinched. He let out a long breath as if all the oxygen in his body was being expelled and reached out with a trembling hand. He noticed she wore a ruby ring on her left hand. "It's my pleasure, Mrs. Chamberlain."

"Please," she said, smiling at Frank. "Call me Tessa."

As she came forward with her hand outstretched, Manuel felt like he should bow. Instead, he offered her a lopsided grin and shook her hand. There was an awkward silence. He looked away from her to the two men standing next to her. They looked identical. Both had long, blond hair and pale blue eyes.

One came forward and extended his hand. "I'm Jace... Tessa's husband."

Manuel looked back and forth between the two men, confused like he'd just stepped into the Twilight Zone.

"Hello, Jace," he finally said, reaching for his hand.

Jace put his hand on Jem's shoulder and said, "This is my twin brother, Jem."

"Gentlemen..." Jem said. He shook Manuel's hand, then extended it to Frank. "It's nice to meet you both."

Frank looked at Tessa with his head slightly tilted. "Is it true? Can you really shift into a... wolf?"

She nodded and started talking, telling Frank and Manuel things they couldn't believe.

When she fell silent, they could only stare at her. Manuel's instincts were telling him she wasn't lying, but it was all just too hard to accept.

He shook his head, wishing he had a shot of whiskey handy. "It's so hard for me to comprehend all this."

"I'm sure it is," she said. "Trust me. I know how you feel."

"Can you bite someone and turn them into a wolf?" Frank asked.

"It doesn't work that way," Jace chimed in. "You're either born our kind, or you're not."

"You must be born an identical twin to be able to shift," Jem told them. He turned to Tessa and winked. "For most of us anyway."

Since Tessa and Steven were fraternal twins, the unexplainable reason why she could shift was still a mystery to them all.

Manuel's shoulders sagged. "So, you're telling me I'm not going to... turn?"

Tessa shook her head, and Manuel was disappointed.

"What about the murders in the city?" Frank asked. "I mean... the ones responsible. What are they?"

"They're a combination of supernatural beings," Tim said. "According to what information we got from Valkin Steele, they were genetically engineered in Dr. Hans Autenburg's lab years ago. Steele was funding the physician's research."

"The only thing I'm interested in," Manuel spoke harshly, "is how we can destroy them."

Tessa nodded in agreement. "So far, we haven't been able to solve that mystery. But we do know we're dealing with three creatures. Years ago, Dr. Autenburg placed three separate eggs from mixed species inside a succubus using his own DNA. They were born fraternal triplets, one male and two females, and very powerful."

"What type of species are you talking about?" Manuel asked, the cop in him coming out.

"Yeah," Frank said. "And what's a succubus?"

"Their DNA comes from a Breedline, an Adalwolf, a Wicca, and of course they inherited the succubus side from their mother," Tessa began to explain. "A succubus is like a vampire, except they're alive. They need blood from a Breedline to survive. Tim and Jem's bonded mates are half succubus."

Frank's eyes widened. *Good God,* he thought.

"It's okay, Frank," Tessa laughed a little. "They're part of our family."

He nodded and was relieved.

"What about the other species?" Manuel questioned further. "I know what a Wicca is, but I've never heard of an Adalwolf."

"An Adalwolf is a species that has the power to shift from their human form into a creature twice the size," Tessa said. "They have human and wolf-like features. They're born with superstrength and can move from one place to another with supernatural speed. With the ability to regenerate their own cells, an Adalwolf will stop aging at thirty. My fraternal twin brother Steven is part Breedline and an Adalwolf." She turned

257

toward Roman and said, "Mr. Roman Kincaid is also an Adalwolf."

Manuel and Frank immediately turned to Roman wide-eyed.

"Don't worry guys," Roman said. "I'm loyal to the Covenant."

"As I was saying," Tessa continued, "the male who Dr. Autenburg created is called Apollyon. He has the power of teleportation and the strength of ten men. The female named Electra has the power of conduction. She can transfer electrical currents from the inside of her body and use it as a weapon. The other female is Callisto. She was born a shield, with the ability to create an invisible barrier around her and other objects for protection. By what information Mr. Steele has relayed, the creatures call themselves the Fury."

"How come we haven't come across them before?" Manuel asked. "If they need human blood to survive, where have they been all this time?"

"For years, they've been kept confined," Tessa said. "Apparently, Dr. Autenburg couldn't control their behavior as they grew stronger. Their unruly defiance and unstoppable lust for human blood had to end, so the physician put them in some sort of coma."

"That explains a lot," Frank said as he looked at Manuel. "Now we know why our guy looks like the Prince of Darkness. At least we know we're not losing our minds."

"I'm not so sure about that," Manuel grumbled. "Before this is over, I may lose my sanity yet."

"I won't lie to you, Detective," Jace spoke out. "Living in our world will make you a little crazy at times."

"How the hell did Dr. Autenburg's creatures manage to get free?" Zeke chimed into the conversation.

Tessa shrugged. "That's the million-dollar question."

"We do have one thing to go on," Tim said. "One crucial piece of information Steele shared on these particular creatures was a symbol. He said it has something to do with them awakening from their deep state of unconsciousness. And the symbol represents immortality."

"Wait a minute," Zeke said. "This symbol you're talking about... is it in the shape of a trefoil knot?"

Tessa nodded. "Yes. Why do you ask?"

"Because I've seen it before. I saw a ring on Apollyon's finger with that particular symbol, and his sister Callisto had a pendant around her neck of the same thing."

"That could be the answer," Jem pointed out. "Maybe it's got something to do with how they woke from their slumber."

"There's one way to find out," Drakon abruptly said.

"How in the hell are we supposed to find out?" Jace snorted. "We can't just walk up to the guy and pluck it off his finger."

"No, but I may know a way to remove Callisto's necklace from her throat," Zeke said.

Jace arched a brow. "How?"

"A few weeks ago, she cornered me at my bar and tried to get me to take her home. I'm sure it wouldn't be difficult for me to get her alone. But I don't know how I'm going to lure her back to the bar. I made it clear to her and her brother not to come back. I feel like I'm the cause of Yelena's abduction." He put his hands on his hips and stared at the floor as if disgusted with himself.

"Stop beating yourself up, Zeke," Manuel said. "It's not your fault."

Frank stepped forward and offered him a sympathetic smile. "I swear, Mr. Rizzo. We'll do everything we can to help get her back."

"We could put on a show at one of Nate's clubs," Jem suggested. "It would bring in a lot of people."

Zeke's head snapped back up.

Jace grinned. "Yeah, it would be like ringing a dinner bell to an all-you-can-eat buffet."

"That's not a bad idea," Tim said. "Nate's big on advertising his entertainment. This could be our only way to draw the Fury's attention. Since your band will be the main attraction, I'll leave it up to you and Jace to set this up with Nate."

Jem nodded, and Jace said, "We're on it."

"I want everyone to be ready," Tim said. "This is going to end in battle. And it will be bloody."

"I'm good with that," Manuel said.

"Are you sure?" Tim asked. "No offense, but are you prepared to fight against supernatural beings?"

"Yes." There was a long exhale. "My job is to protect the innocent. I'm going."

The response was immediate from the others.

"I'm in," Casey said.

"Sign me up," Kyle blurted.

Drakon arched a brow. "I'm ready."

Respect rolled through Manuel's chest as he and everyone else nodded in agreement. And then he looked between Jace and Jem. "So, you two play at my nephew's club?"

"Yeah," Jace said. "Nate's a good friend of ours."

"Is he a—?"

"Breedline..." Jace cut him off and nodded. "Nate's the one that called us. He wanted to tell you, but he figured hearing it from Tessa sounded less insane. Plus, he was worried about you and Detective Perkins, since you guys were investigating all those murders."

"He did the right thing, Manuel," Tessa said.

"Yeah, he did," Manuel replied, nodding at her. "I'll have to thank him later." He averted his eyes from her and focused back on Jace. "So, what's the name of your band?"

"Chaos."

"I recall my nephew mentioning that name. He told us you guys draw in the biggest crowds."

Jace stepped forward and clapped Manuel on the back. "The man doesn't lie. We do kick ass. I think you'll become a fan."

"Don't take this the wrong way," Manuel said, "but I'm more of a Frank Sinatra type of guy."

"Hey, there's nothing wrong with that." Jace chuckled. "Gotta love "Ol' Blue Eyes.""

Chapter Thirty-Eight

As Yelena waited for Electra to return, she was getting desperate. She couldn't get Apollyon to come around, and his skin was getting colder by the minute.

When she put her hand to his cheek, he bit back a groan. He tried to open his eyes and found his lids were too heavy to lift. His lips twitched as if he was trying to speak. She put her ear down to his mouth. The air was coming out alarmingly weak, but she couldn't make out what he was trying to say.

On instinct, she bared her wrist and brought it to her lips. As she sank her fangs into her skin, blood came out in an obliging rush. Filling her mouth with her own blood, she leaned over him and pressed her lips against his. When the red liquid flowed from her mouth and into his, his tongue did not respond.

"Apollyon..." she whispered. "Please, drink."

Frantic prayers fell from her lips in Russian. Then she cried out and pressed her body against his.

He finally got a taste of her blood and swallowed reflexively. Like a balloon inflating, his skin filled with life and his senses came alive.

When she felt his body jerk, she raised up and said, "Apollyon..."

He opened his eyes and licked his lips. "Yelena." He caught his breath. "More..."

She quickly placed her wrist to his parted lips, and he started to drink with great, urgent pulls.

"What the hell are you doing?"

At the sound of Electra's voice, Yelena flinched and looked up.

Electra came forward and grabbed her arm. "Stop what you're doing... now."

"My blood is healing him."

"That can't be." Electra narrowed her glimmering eyes. "You're not human."

When Electra went to grab her by the throat, she felt a hand grasp hold of her arm.

"Let her do this," Apollyon demanded.

"But, Brother..." Electra looked at him, confused. "She's not human. Her blood will not heal you."

"Yelena is my beloved." His voice was weak. "Her blood is working. Please... leave us."

Electra nodded in stunned disbelief and obeyed her brother.

When the door slammed, the sounds of Electra's boots echoed as she pounded them angrily down the hall.

Apollyon licked Yelena's wrist, sealing it. As she started to pull her hand away, he grabbed it and brought it back to his lips. He kissed where the wound had been and said, "Will you... be my bride?"

At a loss for words, she drew in a sharp breath and said, "I-I..."

With her mouth agape, he saw her fangs, and they were beautiful to him, pearl white and sharply pointed. He remembered the taste of her blood and the instant sensation he got from it. He couldn't understand how, but the purity of her succubus blood had brought him back from near death. He'd come to this place with his sisters for human blood to strengthen their powers but found something far more precious: a deep connection to the woman who held his heart. In the chaos of his life, facing his demons and the uncontrollable lust for blood, she was his light in the darkness.

He reached up and pulled her against him for a moment. She could feel his heart pounding as he held her. She knew there were bound to be trials and growing pains in the process, and she would help him as much as she could. But she needed him to change for her to do so.

She had fallen for him in such a short time, and a part of her still felt like she'd betrayed Zeke. He'd always been there for her when she needed him, not as a lover, but as a friend, the closest one she'd had, someone dear and precious to her.

"Yes," Yelena finally said as she pulled from his embrace. "I will marry you."

He slowly pulled himself upright. "I love you, Yelena."

She could sense precisely how much he desired her by the way his eyes lingered on her mouth. Finally, he gently positioned her on her back and poised over her. As he leaned in to kiss her, his long hair fell around her, mingling with hers.

Her trembling hands came between them and reached for the front of his shirt. He immediately rose and ripped the material off his body. The buttons on his shirt popped and scattered across the floor.

Anxious to feel his warm skin against hers, she peeled her nightgown off and tossed it aside.

When his eyes met her delicate, flawless skin, he let out a hiss and quickly shrugged out of the rest of his clothes.

When he covered her with his bare skin, she gasped at the warm sensation and wrapped her legs around his hips. He used what was left of his self-control to pull back and study her beautiful face, following the lovely line of her neck down to her full breasts.

"You're so beautiful," he murmured, his amber eyes exploring every inch her, glowing with desire.

"I want you." She tunneled her fingers through his hair as fire invaded her. "Please..."

She gasped as he dipped his head and captured her mouth. His tongue teased and tasted hers.

As he slowly entered her body, she threw her head back and tilted her hips. She reached up and clutched his shoulders with desperate hands. His body felt warm inside of hers as he moved in a slow rhythm until ecstasy exploded within her.

When she whispered his name, he lost it. He came apart while she held him. Her hands, like little feathers, smoothed up and down his back. He shook almost uncontrollably and went suddenly weak.

As he rose above her, his expression was of devotion and full of longing. She loved the way he looked at her. She loved the feel of him above her, his weight pressing down on her, his heat surrounding her. She *loved* him.

* * *

After Mia left Eve's room, she went back to her and Jem's bedroom. Before he returned from a meeting with the Covenant, she wanted to shower and change into the new nightgown she was saving for a special occasion. It was black silk, trimmed in black lace with a slit up the thigh. And what she was about to tell him counted as one of those special moments. She smoothed her hand over her belly, feeling the small swell. A flutter of nervousness welled up from inside. She had only to look at her nephews, Arius and Tidus, and she was filled with fierce yearning for her own child. Now that Jace and Tessa were parents, and Steven and Anna were expecting their first child, hopefully, Jem would be excited about having a baby too.

Twenty minutes later, she went back into the bedroom. She was arranging her hair into a ponytail when the sound of a whistle caught her attention.

As she turned around, Jem stood in the doorway.

He batted his brows and said, "Hello there."

For a moment, she was speechless. Finally, she said, "Hi, honey."

He closed the distance between them and tugged her into his arms. "You look beautiful." As he pulled from their embrace, he said, "Is this new?"

"I've been saving it for a special occasion."

"Oh?" His brow arched. "What's the occasion?"

She smiled. "I have something to tell you."

"You do?" He tilted his head in question. "What is it?"

"I'm pregnant. Almost four months' pregnant."

He stared at her in complete silence as he processed what she'd just told him. And before he managed to open his mouth to speak, a big grin formed on his lips. *A baby*, he thought. God, he couldn't even wrap his mind around the fact that he was finally going to be a father. Nothing had prepared him for the reality of Mia becoming pregnant with *his* child.

"A baby..." He wrapped his arms around her and lightly squeezed. "Oh, honey... that's wonderful."

She sighed in his embrace. "I'm so glad you're happy."

He pulled back. "Of course I'm happy. Did you have doubts?"

"I wasn't sure how you would react. I mean... with everything that's going on."

He reached out and smoothed his thumb over her cheek. "Nothing would ever stop me from wanting a family with you. I want this more than ever."

Her eyes teared up. "Me too."

"Come," he said as he took her hand in his. "I want to make love to my sexy, pregnant wife."

His words sent shivers all over her body. Then to her surprise, he swept her into his arms and carried her to the bed.

When he eased her onto the mattress, he settled in next to her and placed his hand on her belly. He looked down, marveling at the thought that his child lay beneath his hand. "It's incredible to know there's a tiny life inside of you," he said. "And it's a part of us both."

She smiled. "I'm betting we end up making a beautiful baby."

"If she's anything like her mother, that's a guarantee."

"She? How do you know it's going to be a girl?"

"I don't know," he said, smoothing his hand over her belly, feeling the slightest beginnings of a rounded curve. "It's just a guess."

He leaned forward until their foreheads touched and their noses brushed together. "I love you. You're everything to me."

"I love you too," she said breathlessly as he kissed her long and deep, his mouth moving sweetly over hers.

He took his time, lavishing tender affection on every inch of her body. After making love, the two stayed in bed, simply enjoying being together and making plans for a future. She had never felt so loved and content than she did at this moment. Her dreams of having a family had finally come true.

Chapter Thirty-Nine

When a nurse escorted Anna and Eve into the intensive care unit, Helen stood at Sebastian's bedside. He had an IV in his arm that was attached to a bag filled with clear liquid.

Eve slowly approached the hospital bed with Arius in her arms. She felt helpless. Was she doing the right thing by bringing the twins to see their father?

She glanced over her shoulder and caught a glimpse of Anna, who held on to Tidus with a determined look on her face. It gave Eve comfort and the courage she needed.

Unexpectedly, Arius pointed at Sebastian and said, "Da-da."

Eve seemed lost for words. She looked at Helen, wide-eyed, searching for the physician's guidance.

Helen smiled at her and held out her arms to Arius. "Come here, sweetheart. Let's give Daddy a hug."

Eve's tense expression eased. Before she handed Arius to Helen, she kissed his forehead and said, "Go to Auntie Helen."

When Helen placed Arius on the bed next to Sebastian, he reached out with his little arms and hugged his daddy.

Eve turned to Anna with tears in her eyes.

Anna slid her free arm around Eve's shoulders. "It's going to be all right. You're making the right decision."

Eve nodded and wiped at her eyes.

Tidus whined and reached for Eve. As Anna placed him in Eve's arms, he nestled his head into the crevice of her neck with his eyes focused on Sebastian.

To everyone's surprise, he called out to his daddy in a sleepy voice.

"Yes, sweetheart." Eve smoothed her hand over his soft curls. "That's your Daddy."

Eve looked away from Tidus and focused on Arius as he placed his hand on Sebastian's face. It was such an endearing sight that for a moment all Eve could do was stare. She was struck by the rightness of it all.

Helen's eyes widened when Arius's hand began to glow. She turned to Eve. "What's happening?"

"I don't know." Eve shook her head. "Maybe he's somehow connecting with Sebastian's mind."

In a deep state of unconsciousness, Sebastian felt something warm and soothing against his face, as if someone had swathed his entire body inside a heated blanket. As he absorbed the warm sensation, something sharp dug into his arm, followed by a sinister voice.

"Did you really think you could escape me?"

Sebastian turned his head and swallowed involuntarily. He couldn't move. He kept silent and watched as Lucifer circled him. The second he came to a halt, he grasped Sebastian by the throat. "You belong to me."

Sebastian was helpless, gasping for air.

"Release him," a voice Sebastian recognized echoed, seemingly coming from all directions.

"No." Lucifer hissed. "It cannot be..."

Out of nowhere, a light surrounded Sebastian. As a transparent apparition appeared, Lucifer released his grip and backed away. "This is far from over," he said through gritted teeth. "I promise... one way or the other... your son will belong to me."

As Lucifer faded away, Sebastian felt the soft impression of a hand on his face.

"Mother?" he said. "Is that you?"

To his surprise, Eliza 's face came into view. "Yes, my sweet child."

With tears in his eyes, he leaned into the warmth of her palm and said, "You saved me. But how?"

"I had help." She smiled. "Your son brought me here to release your curse."

"Arius?"

"Yes."

He looked at her confused. "How did he—?"

"Your son was born with a gift," she said. "Lucifer wants Arius for his powers, but God will always protect him." Her voice took on a serious tone. "I want you to promise me one thing before I go."

When he nodded, she said, "Once you awaken, you must accept your fate. Your crimes against the Breedline cannot go unpunished."

"I promise," he said, "but... what will happen to you?"

"I've nothing more left here to do. I'm free to go to the other side."

"I don't understand?" He shook his head. "Where will you go?"

"To heaven, of course."

His eyes softened. "I love you, Mother."

"I love you too, Sebastian."

Before she faded, she said, "Tell Anna I love her."

A moment later, he heard a familiar voice calling out to him.

"Sebastian... Can you hear me?"

He tried to force his eyes to open, but they would not obey.

"Come on, little brother. Open your eyes."

That voice, Sebastian thought. *It can't be. Sissy?...*

He tried again to force his eyelids open.

"That's it." Anna squeezed his hand. "You can do it, little brother."

Finally, as his eyes came open, Eve said, "Oh, thank God."

The first thing he saw was his son.

"Da-da," Arius muttered around a big smile.

Sebastian reached out to him with tears in his eyes. "Arius..."

"Sebastian..."

He looked to the familiar voice and said, "Sissy..."

Anna nodded. "Yes. It's me, little brother."

"Oh, thank God. It's really you."

She leaned down and wrapped her arms around him and included Arius in their embrace.

"I thought I'd never see you again." His voice trembled. "I love you, Sissy."

"I love you too, little brother."

When Anna pulled back, she picked up Arius and held him in her arms.

Sebastian slowly scooted higher on his pillow. He swayed as the room seemed to spin a little.

Helen put her hand on his arm. "Take it easy, Sebastian. You've been in a coma for several weeks."

Eve captured his hand and lightly squeezed.

He faced her and said, "I'm sorry for everything."

When he reached out to her and Tidus, they embraced him.

"I love you," he whispered close to her ear.

"Da-da," Tidus called out in a tiny voice.

"And I love you too, Tidus."

Eve could tell Sebastian was crying by the way his body trembled in their embrace.

"I hate to interrupt," Helen spoke out, "but I need everyone to step out while I check Sebastian's vitals."

Eve pulled from his arms and nodded.

"I promise," Helen said, "I'll let you know as soon as I'm done."

"It's okay," Sebastian said as he looked between Eve and Anna. "I'm not going anywhere. I promise."

Helen tried not to appear shocked by his polite mannerism, but it was hard not to. According to his past, he wasn't the type of guy to take orders, especially from a female.

Eve got to her feet and scooped Tidus back into her arms.

"We'll be right outside," Anna said.

After Anna and Eve exited the room, Helen checked his blood pressure. "Your blood pressure is on the low side. But other than that, everything seems normal."

He looked up at her. She was sizing him up as a doctor would, taking note of the color of his skin, doing an evaluation in her head. And then she looked him in the eyes, her professional expression turning sympathetic. "I'm sorry to have to tell you this, but I will have to notify the Covenant that you're awake."

He nodded. "I know. And I'm okay with that."

"You'll need to rest until you're fully recovered," she said. "I'll be back in an hour to check on you."

"Thank you, doctor."

Helen tilted her head in question. "For what?"

"For taking care of me."

"You're welcome." She smiled. "I was just doing my job."

Chapter Forty

The guys waited in a large dressing room in the back of one of Nathan's top-notch bars, located in the downtown Berkeley area, called The Wolf's Lair. The seconds ticked into minutes until finally the door opened and Nathan stuck his head in.

"Five minutes, guys," he said. "Almost show time." Nathan pushed the door wider and clapped his hands. "Let's go."

As Jem stepped out of the dressing room with the other band members following close behind, he blinked rapidly as if he was waking up in the middle of a bad dream. His thoughts weighed heavily on his mind. Putting all those people in danger was something he'd never even think of doing, but they had no choice. The Breedline were desperate to finally put an end to the cold-blooded massacre in the city. Using humans to lure the Fury out of hiding was their only resort. And a crowd like this was precisely what Jace had described. It would be like ringing a dinner bell to an all-you-can-eat buffet.

He ran a hand through his long hair and blew out a deep breath.

"Come on, Brother," Jace said, clapping a hand on Jem's shoulder as they moved toward the stage. "Let's do this."

The atmosphere suddenly charged with excitement when Chaos was introduced. The crowd roared as the band stepped out to face all their fans.

Close by, and spread among the sea of people, were Roman's crew and Colonel Deshazo's team. Strung with weapons, they stood back in the shadows, waiting.

Still healing from her injuries, Lena had decided to sit this one out and hang back with the other women in the Covenant.

Drakon and Zeke monitored the security cameras. Tim, Steven, and Alexander hung back at the bar, trying their best not to stand out in the crush of people.

On the top level of the bar, Manuel and Frank watched as the crowd below cheered and shouted when the band took the stage.

Women stood in awe, their mouths agape as Jace's hands moved over the strings of his electric guitar like he was a god. They practically melted when he began to sing *Click Click Boom* by the group Saliva. The raspy sound of his voice was crisp, despite the noise of the crowd. Behind the drums, Jem joined him for the chorus, their voices melding perfectly. It was as if everyone was drawn to them on some cosmic level.

Kyle played the acoustic bass guitar, and Casey worked his magic on the keyboards, driving the crowd into a frenzy.

The place was already packed and more arrived as they performed. After Nathan had announced Chaos would be performing in concert at one of his popular bars, tickets sold out the two following days. Even though the show was a sellout, there was a line of fans a mile long waiting outside for the band to exit the building. And most of them were women, shouting the band's name.

The lights dimmed and stunned silence broke out into a thunderous applause as Jace dedicated the next song to his wife Tessa. As his hands moved over the guitar strings, his soulful voice broke out into her favorite song, *Your Arms Feel Like Home.*

When he finished the ballad, the noise that came after was deafening. Fans shouted and cheered so loud, it sounded as if the roof was going to come down.

While the band played, Drakon and Zeke kept their eyes on the security cameras located on the second floor above the crowded bar.

"Looks like we got their attention," Drakon said, pointing at one of the monitors. "We've got company."

As Zeke focused on the images, he recognized two females moving through the front entrance.

"I don't see our guy," Drakon said as he unclipped his phone from his belt. "I'm going to give everyone a heads-up. If Apollyon doesn't show, our plans may change."

Zeke shot to his feet. "Wish me luck. If the two sisters separate, I may be able to get Callisto alone."

"Good luck, buddy," Drakon said as Zeke stepped out of the room. With no time to spare, Drakon made a call to Tim's cell.

Chaos played for almost two hours, then it was announced another big-name artist would take to the stage. When the four of them exited, security men cleared a path as a tidal wave of fans backstage swamped them, women screaming their names. Finally, they managed to get back to their dressing room in one piece.

"Guys... that was freakin' amazing," Nathan said when the band walked in. "Another sold-out show."

Abruptly, a knock outside the dressing room caught their attention. When the door opened, Alexander stepped inside. "I hate to interrupt, but we've got company."

"Are you talking about the Fury?" Jem asked.

"Drakon spotted them on the security cameras," Alexander replied. "He sent me to give you guys a heads-up. So far, Apollyon is a no-show."

Jace cursed under his breath. "So, what's our plan now?"

"Zeke went after Callisto to see if he can lure her to a secluded place," Alexander went on. "Drakon's keeping a watch on the cameras. He said it's obvious both sisters are scoping the place over like a menu at a restaurant. We need to make damn sure no one becomes their next meal. In the meantime, we're going to hang tight and wait to see if our guy shows."

* * *

Callisto pushed through the crush of people and made her way toward the bar while her sister scoped out the dance floor. Unfortunately, the place was so crowded it was difficult to spot the kind of male she sought, but that didn't mean she was ready to throw in the towel.

Meanwhile, Zeke was desperate to find her, but the crowded bar made it seem impossible to locate the long-legged, black widow.

Callisto finally settled in a dark corner at the bar and let her need for sex waft out from her body. And whaddya know... every guy that walked by looked in her direction.

A male bartender came over. "What can I get you, beautiful?"

He was good-looking in a way that caught her attention. He had tanned skin and his long hair was pulled up into a man-bun.

She licked her lips. "They give you any breaks?"

"Uh... yeah."

"When?"

He looked at his watch. "About ten minutes. Why?"

She cocked a brow. "How 'bout you use those ten minutes between my thighs."

His eyes widened. Then he glanced over at the bar area. When he focused back on Callisto, he pictured her long legs wrapped around his hips. He instantly hardened.

"There's a small room in the back," he finally said. "It has a lock on the door."

"That sounds perfect," she purred.

"So, what's your name?"

"Callisto."

"It's a pleasure to meet you, Callisto," he said with the biggest, shit-eating grin. "My name is Colin. Don't go anywhere. I'll be back in ten."

She winked at him. "I'll be waiting, Colin."

Exactly ten minutes later, he returned. "You ready, gorgeous?"

She looked up at him and smiled.

He held out his hand. "Come with me."

On the far side of the bar, Steven watched as the bartender hurriedly escorted Callisto in the back. As he shot to his feet, he looked toward Tim, motioning him over.

Colin led her through a narrow hallway in the back. When they came to a door with a sign that read STAFF ONLY, he quickly ushered her inside.

The room had shelves stocked with liquor, a few tables and chairs, and a small desk nearby—no pictures, no paint on the walls, just brick and concrete floors. But it wasn't like she'd come here to enjoy the scenery, only his blood.

Colin backed her up against the desk. "If anyone catches us..." He batted his brows. "...just say you're here for a job interview."

"Sure... whatever," she replied.

He put his hands on her waist. "We've got twenty minutes, sweetheart."

She took his mouth like she was going to take the rest of him. Tasting... savoring...

In response, he groaned and moved his hands down to the bottom of her leather skirt and lifted it up. When he got a look at the black lace thong she had on, he spun her around and bent her over the desk.

She moaned as he pulled down the tiny scrap of material and slid it down to her ankles.

The sound of his zipper caught her breath, and she flinched at the warmth of his skin as it came up against her hips.

He whispered close to her ear, "Tell me what you want."

"Take me," she said in a throaty wisp.

The sight of her, the sounds she made both pushed him past all reason. He couldn't wait a minute longer. With trembling hands, he tore the foil from a condom and rolled it over the length of him. Just as he was about to push inside her, he froze when the door burst open.

"Shit!" he said, fumbling with his pants.

She looked over her shoulder and snarled her upper lip. "Damn Breedline," she mumbled under her breath and rearranged her skirt.

Colin did up the front of his pants and backed away from her. When he got a look at Steven and Tim, he said, "Who the *fuck*... are you?"

"Get out," Steven demanded.

"Excuse me?" Colin glared at Steven. "Didn't you read the sign on the door? This is for employees only."

Tim came forward and got into the guy's face. "You heard what he said." He pointed to the door. "Get out."

Colin shot Callisto a look. "Do you know these guys?"

With her lips pursed, she shook her head.

"Trust me," Tim said. "We're doing you a favor, buddy. Please... just go."

Colin threw up his hands in defeat and grumbled, "Fine." He stomped over to the door. "I'll be calling the owner. We'll see what he has to say about this."

"Yeah, you go ahead and do that," Tim said with a slight chuckle. "We're friends of Nate, and I'm sure he'd like to know one of his employees is hooking up with the customers during work hours."

Colin narrowed his eyes. "Whatever." He reached for the door. "I'm outta here."

When he left the room, both Steven and Tim glared at Callisto like they wanted to wrap their hands around her scrawny neck.

There was a tense silence while she measured the distance between them and the door.

"Don't even think about running," Steven said through gritted teeth.

She rolled her eyes. "What do you want with me?"

"Cut the shit," Steven said. "We know what you are."

A muscle twitched under her eye. "Sorry, sugar," she said with a clear smirk in her voice. "I'm not a prostitute, if that's what you're thinking."

On the other side of the crowded bar, Electra could sense her sister's frustration and realized she was in danger. Using the sibling telepathic connection they shared, she reached out to Apollyon. *We need your help, Brother. Callisto is in trouble. The Breedline have her cornered.*

Apollyon woke to the sound of his sister's voice. It was crisp and clear inside his head. The idea of the Breedline bringing harm upon his family made his features crease in anger. He bit the inside of his cheek until he tasted blood and sent a mental message back to Electra. *It's time... time to do what we were created for.*

He turned to Yelena before he rose out of bed. While he watched her sleep, he wondered what fate lay ahead. Would he finally find peace from the demons tormenting his soul, or would he surrender himself entirely over to the dark side?

Yelena opened her eyes and whispered, "You're awake. Is something wrong?"

When he didn't reply, she reached out to him. "Talk to me, Apollyon."

He sighed. "I have to go out for a while."

"Where are you going?"

There was a long silence, filled with the pounding of her heart. On so many levels, she couldn't imagine ever falling in love with someone like him. He was an enemy to the Breedline and there was, in fact, a side to him that was monstrous... *a savage killer.* But she couldn't deny her feelings. She'd fallen in love with him.

He avoided her question and brushed his lips against hers. "Go back to sleep," he murmured, and then he pulled away.

"Apollyon, you're not a monster. I've seen the part of you that is good. Please, leave this unholy quest of yours behind. Stay with me."

"I know what I am, Yelena. Don't make me out to be something I'm not. But it doesn't mean that I don't love you."

"Please..."

"I'm sorry." He looked away and rolled out of bed. "I have to go."

For the first time in a long, long while, he desperately wished he was someone else, someone who deserved her love.

His words broke her heart. It felt as though he was saying a final goodbye. She expected him to use his powers and vanish from the room, but instead, he walked out the door.

Chapter Forty-One

Apollyon swallowed a curse as he stood on the roof of Nathan's club. He could see inside the flat strip of smoked glass to the private wing that held all the dressing rooms.

His near-death experience and the Breedline's interference edged him closer to his breaking point. And his fear of losing Yelena created a painful ache inside his chest. It was worse than the horrors of the years he'd been imprisoned by his father.

When he first saw her, he understood the desire for fierce, wild passion. But this? This was beyond his realm of experience. Without a doubt, he knew she was the one for him.

At first, he'd had a slight problem, however. She was in love with the sin-eater. Just thinking about it left a bitter taste in his mouth. He took some deep breaths and pulled it together.

A moment later, he vanished and reappeared inside a narrow hallway. As he moved to the end, he stepped into an elevator built to hold several people. When the doors shut, the enclosed contraption descended with a slight shake. A few seconds later, he was striding across the lowest level of the club, pushing his way through the crowd of people.

With grim resolve, he measured the crowd from a vantage point of about six foot five. As he moved through the sea of people, he headed toward the VIP section. It had its own private bar and bartenders, and that's where the Breedline had his sister.

Before he got halfway, a blonde dressed like a high-class stripper stepped in his path. He towered above her with a menacing glare, but she didn't feel threatened. The incredible masculine scent that wafted from his body was something she wanted, something she craved. She wondered what his bare skin looked like underneath all that leather.

"Hey, baby," she purred, flashing her gleaming, bleached teeth. "You want some company?"

Annoyed, he glared down at her. "Go find someone else," he gritted out and pushed past her.

The blonde flipped her hair back, mumbling something to herself, and watched him walk away.

He sensed someone tracking him by the hairs that rose on the back of his neck. He stopped in his tracks, sensing the sin-eater.

When he spun around to face Zeke, waves of rage distorted the air between them. There was a huge part of Zeke that wanted a good, bloody hand-to-hand fight with the guy, his anger so noticeable, it was practically a light source.

Zeke glared at Apollyon and said, "What have you done with Yelena?"

The attack was so fast, Zeke didn't have time to react. Apollyon bared his fangs, hauled off, and threw out a curving right hook that slammed into the side of his head.

Zeke swayed but caught himself and did a one-eighty. He sprung forward and snapped Apollyon with a headbutt to the face.

Apollyon quickly clamped a hand over his nose. With a curse, he shot Zeke a look of murderous rage.

Zeke positioned himself into a fighting stance, bracing himself for Apollyon to retaliate.

Instead, Apollyon wiped the blood with the back of his hand. "Yelena has agreed to be my bride." He smiled a little, his cruel face showing self-satisfaction.

"You're a damn liar!" Zeke yelled.

As he started forward, the sound of a loud crack came whirling out of nowhere. Before Zeke knew what hit him, he dropped to the floor.

"Zeke!" Tim called out.

The crowd around them quickly backed away.

The sequence played out in a series of seconds that seemed to move in slow motion. As Tim and Steven escorted Callisto around the bar, Electra came up behind Zeke with a silver whip in her grasp. The moment she whirled it high in the air, it sizzled and crackled with electricity. Steven rushed to warn Zeke, but it was too late. The blazing whip struck him with phenomenal speed and he never saw it coming. As Zeke pitched forward, Steven dropped to his knees beside him.

Positioned on the top floor of the bar, Manuel and Frank felt completely helpless as they watched in stunned disbelief.

Frank turned to his partner. "What the hell should we do?"

"We stay calm," Manuel said, putting a reassuring hand on Frank's shoulder. "I've contacted Dr. Helen Carrington and informed her of our situation. She's going to have Breedline emergency personnel dispatched to our location, along with police reinforcements. There's nothing our police can do to help, but they can control the crowd outside and make damn sure no one else gets in."

Drakon became enraged as he viewed everything from the upstairs security cameras. An uncontrollable fury broke out all over his body. Spasms twisted his gut and thick veins bulged from his skin, bringing forth his rogue wolf.

Below, Colonel Deshazo and his team went into full crisis mode, and Roman's crew backed them up. When they opened fire on Apollyon, pandemonium broke out. Crowds of people went into panic mode, knocking over tables and chairs, tripping over each other in their desperate attempts to get away.

The commotion momentarily distracted Apollyon. When he turned toward the fleeing people, multiple bullets tore into his backside and blood exploded from his chest. The impact threw him off balance, but he managed to stay on his feet.

As the hail of bullets continued, powdered debris filled the air. Amid the smoke and dust, the sound of an inhuman growl blared throughout the bar. Within a split second, Apollyon vanished into thin air.

"Cease fire!" Colonel Deshazo shouted.

When the gunfire came to a halt, the colonel waited with his finger resting on the 9mm Glock in his grasp. After he motioned to Roman and his crew to stay put, he spoke to his team, who were positioned above them, using a two-way radio. "All right soldiers, keep watch and hold your position. I repeat, hold your position."

"Roger that," Gunny replied.

"Cover my ass," Lawrence said into his headset. "I'm going in to check on Zeke."

Colonel Deshazo gave him an affirmative nod.

Wyckoff's voice came through Lawrence's earpiece. "We've got you covered, Lawrence."

As the noise escalated in the upstairs dressing room, Alexander's instinct rose like a beast. He quickly looked to the others in alarm. It was then he realized he had not a second to spare. He yanked his shirt over his head and toed-off his boots. His body expanded as if something within him was overtaking his natural form. For a moment, Alexander hovered in that in-between state, flickering between human and Breedline. "They need... our help."

Jace shot his twin brother a look. "He's right. Let's go kick some ass."

Jem nodded, realizing what had to be done. Exposing themselves to humans was something they had to risk in order to save hundreds of innocent lives.

The instant Alexander's change was complete, he rushed out of the dressing room. Jem followed him, leaving the others to finish their transformations.

Jace's body quaked with fury, the creature within itching to be released. It curdled in his veins, calling to the Beast inside him.

At first, it looked as if there was something inside of his body too large for his skin. His face began to bulge and move in odd ways. In a matter of seconds, white coarse hairs grew out of his pores and covered his skin.

Nathan's eyes widened as he looked up at Jace's beast. *Shit!*

Kyle, Casey, and Nathan stepped back as the seven-foot creature let out a thunderous roar. The Beast lowered his big head and snarled before he tore out of the room.

Relieved to still be in one piece, Nathan said, "Okay, guys... let's do this."

Casey closed his eyes and did what he had to do. He focused on his Theriomorph side and called to the panther within him. Embracing the animal, he surrendered to the change.

A silent understanding passed between Kyle and Casey, the instinctive exchange realizing this battle might very well be their last. Kyle stepped back and watched as Casey dropped to the floor. His skin rippled and his body began to reshape itself until the form of a huge panther took his place.

A low growl caught Kyle's attention. He averted his eyes from the panther and focused on Nathan's gigantic Breedline wolf as he came forward.

"Here goes nothing," Kyle said as he peeled off his clothes.

The muscles in his body began to tremble as the Breedline rose inside him with raw power. Straining muscles rippled beneath his skin, while the tendons in his neck stood out like drawn bowstrings. Thick hairs sprouted from his pores as the change came upon him instantly. Faster than the human eye could perceive, dark fur covered his entire body. The Breedline wolf in him wanted nothing more than to take down his enemies in battle. Throwing his head back, he howled a purely inhuman sound.

With all the havoc surrounding Jem, he heard an unearthly howl nearby. He looked up at the same time his brother's beast vaulted over the stair railing like he'd been launched from a catapult. As he landed, the floor cracked beneath him.

The crowded bar responded with terror. Instantly, they pushed and shoved at one another, scrambling to get to the exit.

Alexander's wolf moved next to the Beast. Its bristling pelt was the color of virgin snow, and its fearless eyes were as red as blood. Together, they stood side by side, ready to destroy the Fury. They had to succeed. The human species was not prepared to deal with the kind of power the Fury possessed.

Jem shifted his focus when Apollyon came into view... or what looked to be him. He had morphed into a creature that looked like the devil himself, a type of hybrid, a genetic cross between a Breedline and another species he had never encountered before. And somehow it miraculously healed from all the bullet holes. Never had he witnessed anything like this. He had thought the Breedline hybrids they'd fought against were unnaturally massive and unholy, but Apollyon's creature was even larger, much more monstrous. A sudden feeling of dread crept over him.

The size of Apollyon's creature was enormous, towering at least seven feet tall, with sharp protruding teeth and glowing eyes. Dark fur partly covered his skin, and he had huge, leathery bat-like wings with a row of deadly-looking spiked talons down his spine.

While Jem took this in, he had the strange feeling that he was looking at pure evil, one utterly devoid of humanity.

The Beast moved swiftly. It lunged at Apollyon, knocking him back with blunt force. Before Apollyon hit the floor, he vanished into thin air.

An instant later, the huge winged creature that seemed indestructible reappeared behind the Beast and tore into him using its razor-sharp claws. As Apollyon struck his hide, the Beast howled in pain.

No... Jem feverishly thought.

Instinct took over, and all that mattered was saving his brother from Apollyon's savagery. Jem palmed a firebomb, ready to take aim, careful not to catch the Beast in the crossfire. But before he could launch it, a furious roar shattered the moment. Then Alexander charged forward like a rabid dog and lunged at Apollyon.

Jem watched in astonishment as Alexander's spectacular wolf moved in to defend the Beast, taking a gory chunk out of Apollyon's leg.

Apollyon let out a tremendous roar, giving the Beast an upper hand. He spun around, swiping with his claws, but Apollyon dodged the attack and vanished again.

When he reappeared, he was crouched on the balcony above them, his back facing Colonel Deshazo's team. Peering down at the Beast, his golden eyes glimmered with homicidal rage. The Breedline's interference galled his soul.

Using the opportunity, Gunny inched closer to Apollyon with his semi-automatic poised and ready.

The flash of Gunny's muzzle gave Apollyon barely enough warning. In a split second, he leaped off the balcony the instant Gunny fired his weapon. Bullets smacked into the ceiling, sending pulverized tiles flying everywhere.

"Hold your fire!" the colonel called out.

When the gunfire came to a halt, the Beast scrambled up the wall using his claws, impatient to sink his teeth into Apollyon's throat. The others watched as he climbed higher and higher. His ability to defy gravity was astounding to behold.

Fueled by anger, the Beast caught sight of Apollyon perched on a ledge two feet away. He focused on the shiny object around his finger with keen eyesight.

Apollyon growled defiantly at the Beast as if daring him to attack.

Then, without warning, an unexpected dark figure pounced on Apollyon from the rear, slashing away at his wings with dagger-sized claws.

Drakon's rogue wolf had the weight advantage over Apollyon, which he pressed by fighting tooth and nail against the fearsome creature.

The Beast watched as Drakon knocked Apollyon off the ledge. It was a long drop to the lower level of the bar, and when he landed, he hit hard.

Apollyon slowly moved upright, and before he got to his feet, he heard the pounding of heavy footsteps moving at a high speed. When he looked up, the Beast was seething with anger and charging forward.

As he lunged toward Apollyon, a whip snapped from behind and hurled forward at lightning speed. It carried with it a sizzling bolt of electricity that crackled through the air, end over end, and struck the Beast like a blazing torch. He toppled over and howled as it burned and scorched his hide.

A look of satisfaction came over Apollyon's face when he saw Electra with a whip in her grasp. Taking full advantage, he shot forward and took hold of the Beast's head. And with a sharp yank, came a loud snap.

"No..." Jem gasped. "Jace!"

There was a heartbeat of stunned silence as Jem helplessly watched Apollyon release his brother's lifeless, beastly form.

Jem instantly rushed over. When he sank to his knees, his brother's beast suddenly began to shrink. It was as if the impending changes took on a will of their own. He watched as every pore in Jace's skin absorbed all the hair that covered his body until the Beast was no more.

At that moment, Jem said a silent prayer as he visualized the terror the Fury was about to inflict on anyone that stood in their way. He knew his brother wasn't dead. It would take more than a broken neck to kill him, but still... things weren't looking good.

God,... if you can hear me, you may be our only hope.

Chapter Forty-Two

In the heavens above, the Creator watched all the chaos below, realizing he had no choice but to intervene.

When he sensed an approaching angel, he looked up as Cronus gracefully descended from above.

As his boots landed on solid ground, Cronus dropped to one knee and lowered his gaze. "My Lord..." he said, tucking in his giant wings.

Cronus was a loyal and devoted warrior willing to give his life to protect the heavens and all of God's creations. With the power of the sword of truth, and the ability to use his body as a shield, his purpose for existence was to serve the Creator in war against demons and evil havoc on earth.

"There's not much time," the Creator said. "My children on earth depend on you. Choose four of your best soldiers and prepare for war. Do not destroy the Fury. Render them powerless and bring them to me."

"Yes, my Lord..." Cronus said. "We will not fail you."

Determination pulsed from the angel as his giant wings carried him to the *In-Between* where all the battle angels guarded heaven's gate. Before Cronus got to his destination, he had come to a decision. By far, Lailah was his first pick. Her special gift would be essential in successfully rendering the Fury powerless. She possessed the power to shape and manipulate holy flames. She used her fiery wings to trap and immobilize their enemies rather than killing them outright, especially effective against demons and other evil, super-natural beings. Although, this mission would involve someone from her past, someone she dearly loved.

Icarus was his second choice. He was new to the group, but his love and loyalty toward the Creator never once faltered. Gifted with the power of telekinesis, he could influence, manipulate, and move matter using his mind. It also gave him the capability to absorb and convert energy, which was very useful in physical combat.

Cronus chose Helios, a descendant of a mighty African king, for his third pick. He was the biggest and deadliest of all the Creator's battle angels. The tips of his giant wings were shaped like knives and capable of shredding skin and bone. Helios was born without vocal cords, but he could communicate with his mind.

Last, his fourth choice was no ordinary angel. Frigg was one of God's originals, serving as a battle angel for more than a century. With a personality bigger than life, and a doppelganger of Billy Idol—sporting the same trademark bleached, spiked hair—Frigg still had a few of his human weaknesses. He loved rock-n-roll, cheeseburgers, and old classic movies. Aside from a few bad habits and a smart mouth, the Creator gifted him with the unique power of shapeshifting. Frigg could transform and reshape himself into any living thing.

Each of the Creator's indigenous battle angels, on average, stood ten feet tall. Some, however, towered to the height of twelve feet with a more muscular build. All were tattooed with unique warrior markings, wore armor typical of ancient heroes, and had swords associated with a long-gone empire. Their intimidating giant wings were black, nothing like the majestic white wings of a guardian angel. Even though they did not have a golden halo hovering their heads, the battle angels were particularly fond of all humans. They considered themselves humanity's special protectors.

After Cronus summoned his four warriors and prepared them for their task ahead, he asked to speak with Lailah in private.

"There is no other angel I admire more than you," Cronus said. "I have faith in your strength and ability to help us win this battle against the Fury."

Lailah frowned. "I get the feeling this isn't a pep talk just to build my confidence."

"There's something you need to know before we leave," he said. "This involves your brother."

"Manuel?" She gasped. "Is he okay?"

"Hold on." Cronus held up a halting hand. "He's fine. But I want to warn you. He will be at the place we are going into battle."

"What?... Why?"

"Manuel is a homicide detective, and he's been thrown into the middle of all this."

"But what about the Breedline? Does he know about our father's bloodline?"

"Yes." Cronus nodded.

"I... I have to protect him."

"We'll do everything we can to ensure your brother's safety." Cronus placed his hand on her shoulder. "I give you my word."

"Thank you. So, what if Manuel recognizes me?"

"Then maybe he'll finally have peace with your death."

Lailah nodded in silence, then lowered her head.

"Lailah... Look at me."

When her weary eyes met his, he pinned her with a hard stare. "Remember, the survival of God's children depends on us. Can I count on you to be focused?"

"Yes, Commander."

"Warriors," Cronus called out, "I need everyone to gather around."

When Helios, Icarus, and Frigg gathered together, Cronus looked at his warriors. "Soldiers of war, are you prepared to fight in battle?"

The response was immediate. "I'm in," Icarus said, and Helios nodded silently.

"Oh, bloody hell. I guess..." Frigg grumbled, "even though I'll be missing my favorite classic of all time."

Everyone turned to Frigg, who sported a pout with his arms crossed.

Icarus looked at Cronus. "Can I please have permission to beat him?"

Cronus rolled his eyes. "As soon as we get back."

Icarus smirked, and Helios cracked a smile.

"I swear..." Frigg groaned, "...one of these days I'm going to put in a request for another position. Maybe I'll be a guardian angel."

Lailah and Icarus burst into laughter. Even Helios chuckled silently.

Frigg furrowed his brows. "You guys suck."

"Okay, that's enough," Cronus said. "Time is ticking. We have a battle waiting."

* * *

Rage burned through Kyle's blood like fire as he exploded into action and barreled down to the lower level of the bar. Casey and Nathan followed close behind. The noise coming from their padded feet sounded like a stampede of onrushing bulls.

Apollyon snapped around, readying himself for another attack. His sisters moved to his side and waited for his next move.

As the two Breedline wolves and the panther leaped and bounded through the mass hysteria of people, they slid to a halt when they came to a clearing in the center. To their surprise, Steven and Lawrence were kneeling over Zeke's smoldering body. He had a huge gash in his back the size of a crater. And Jace—now in human form—was lying naked on the floor with his head cocked at an unnatural angle.

Electra drew back her whip, preparing to whirl it into the crowd of people.

"Wait!" Jem called out. "Please... don't do this."

She stopped and looked at Jem with a hateful glare. As she averted her eyes from him, she continued with her savage brutality. The blazing whip lashed out with lightning speed.

"No!" Jem cried out as it struck a young woman in a sequined minidress.

Consumed with rage, Jem extended his hand and gave Electra a dose of her own medicine. He launched a firebomb, and the force of the impact sent her flying back. Her body rolled until it smacked into a wall and came to an abrupt halt. It was a blast hard enough to kill a mortal woman ten times over. Unfortunately, it merely stunned her.

Electra groaned as she slowly got to her feet. Before she could retaliate, Jem was ready for round two. He palmed another firebomb and sent it in her direction. He was stunned when the blast exploded before it made contact.

Electra smirked. "You can't destroy us, Breedline."

"No one is invincible," Jem said. Then, in one continuous motion, he discharged another strong enough to blast through steel. But it exploded again, leaving Electra unharmed.

Callisto glared at Jem. "Don't waste your energy. Your powers are useless up against my shield."

Shit! Jem's troubled gaze met Steven, and then he looked to Tim as if he was searching for a solution to the grim situation.

Chapter Forty-Three

When Sebastian came awake in a hospital bed, he thought all this was just another of Lucifer's tricks. Maybe, maybe the whole thing, from Eliza freeing him of Lucifer's torture, to finally reuniting with his sister after all these years, to Eve coming back into his life and knowing his sons were safe, had been a dream of false hope.

He wanted to be with Eve, to be with his sons. The trouble was he didn't know if he could trust this version of reality. What if this was a sick joke, a further facet of where Lucifer kept him trapped, an illusion created specifically to increase his suffering?

Screw that. He'd rather die. He wasn't going to give Lucifer, Satan, whatever he was, the satisfaction.

Assuming it was all real... well, then, maybe this was God's way of showing him forgiveness. He could only pray.

He closed his eyes and reached over his head. With all the strength he could muster, he pulled himself into a full body stretch. The feeling of freedom poured through him. He felt free for the first time in his life, free of all the sins of his childhood, no longer the puppet of a tortured past, and not now or ever a prisoner of darkness.

"You're finally awake."

Sebastian jacked up off the pillows and looked across the room.

Eve was sitting in a chair, smiling. It was a relief to see her, which meant this wasn't a dream. *It must be real.*

"Is this real?" he asked.

"Yes, Sebastian. You're safe now."

For a moment, he was quiet. And then he said, "So if this is real, and not an illusion... do you still love me?"

"Of course I still love you."

He eased back and sighed. "Thank God."

"Sebastian, are you okay?"

He brought his hands to his face and rubbed them over his eyes. When he looked at Eve, his golden gaze sparkled with resolution. "I've never felt better."

She rose out of the chair and moved next to the hospital bed. On impulse, she reached out and placed her hand over his. For a split second, he thought she was going to kiss him as she leaned in. He focused on her lips and moved his head toward her. But at the last minute, she pulled away and whispered, "What happened to you, Sebastian?"

He shook his head. "It doesn't matter." He curled his hand around hers and gently squeezed. "All that matters now... is you and the boys are safe."

"The Breedline have given me a pardon, but they will surely punish you for your crimes," she said with tears in her voice. "Are you really going to give yourself over to them freely?"

He reached up and brushed a tear from her cheek. Before he could answer, a knock at the door distracted him. As it opened to a crack, Anna peeked inside. "May I come in?"

Eve glanced over her shoulder. "Yes, of course."

As Anna pushed her way in, her phone went off. She stopped and reached into her purse, and looked at the caller ID.

"Sorry, I've got to take this. It's Helen." She swiped to answer and put the phone up to her ear. "Hello? Yes, I'm in his room now." There was silence. "What?" Her eyes widened. "Okay, I'll tell them." She nodded against the phone. "Thank you, Helen."

When she hung up, her face was pale.

Eve looked at her, concerned. "Anna, is something wrong?"

Anna tucked her phone back into her purse and slowly moved next to her. "Something terrible has happened."

After she explained to Eve and Sebastian what Helen had told her over the phone, there was a moment of silence.

"I have to help them." With a groan, Sebastian sat up and swung his legs off the edge of the hospital bed.

Anna stepped in front of him before he could get to his feet. "You're in no condition to help anyone. You've been in a coma for weeks." Her eyes pleaded. "Please, Brother, don't do this."

He ignored her pleas and started to go to work on the inside of his arm, carefully taking out the IV. When alarms sounded, Eve said, "Sebastian, they'll arrest you if you try to leave."

He got to his feet and moved past her and started opening drawers, searching for something to put on but found them empty. No pants, no shirts... nothing. Frustrated, he turned to Eve. "Please, I need you to get me some clothes."

A nurse and two guards abruptly burst into the room.

"Sir," the nurse said, "please get back to bed."

With a curse, Sebastian tried to collect himself. He had to come up with a solution.

"Get back in that bed, Mr. Crow," the guard said, "or I'm going to put you there myself."

Through his haze of frustration, Sebastian figured there were two obvious options: obey their command and let the Breedline take care of their own problems, or do the right thing for once in his life even if it got his ass killed.

He picked number two.

He turned to Eve. "I love you." Then he shifted his focus to Anna. "I love you, Sissy."

Shouts broke out as Sebastian vanished through a portal. He prayed that Eve and his sister understood what he had to do.

When he stepped from the portal, he appeared at Nathan's bar. He exhaled in a rush, wondering if it was reckless desperation that had driven him to this insane act. But his instincts told him he was doing the right thing.

A group of frantic people caught his attention as they pushed and shoved their way through the bar's exit. Not far down the street, he could hear police sirens. With no time to waste, he ducked into an alley behind the back of the bar and reached for a handrail that was tightly wound around a metal stairway. He looked up, realizing it led to each floor of the building. On the top level, he forced his way through a metal door and stepped into a narrow hallway. At the far end, he noticed a door with a sign that read DRESSING ROOM.

Clothes. He needed them, and shoes—anything other than the hospital gown he had on. If he was going to help the Breedline in battle, he wasn't going to do it half naked.

When he went into the room, he walked over to a closet and tried the knob. *Thank goodness.* He sighed in relief. *It's unlocked.* As he opened it, he saw an assortment of men's clothing and a variety of boots. After rummaging through it all, he'd managed to find something in his size.

* * *

The bristly hairs on Drakon's back rose as he peered down at the lower level of the bar. His ears flattened against his massive head and a deep growl rumbled inside his chest.

When Apollyon heard him, he looked up, snarling. "What are you waiting for?" he said, deliberately baiting Drakon.

A muscle twitched in Drakon's jaw. In a split second, he leaped a good twenty feet across the room and landed on the stair railing. Using the strength of his hind legs, he sprang forward, directly at Apollyon.

At the same time, Apollyon launched himself upward and pummeled Drakon in midair. The powerful blow sent Drakon flying across the room and head-on into a wall.

His comrades in arms watched helplessly as his body went limp and dropped to the floor.

As Apollyon closed on him, Casey's panther lunged forward at lightning speed. When the giant cat hit Apollyon from behind, it sent him sprawling across the floor.

In his weakened state, Drakon managed to push himself up. When he lifted his head, he looked into the lavender eyes of the enormous panther to whom he now owed his life.

Apollyon finally rolled onto his knees and got to his feet. His smug look dared the majestic animal to a challenge.

When the panther leaped toward Apollyon, Electra's whip slashed into the air and wound tightly around the feline's throat. As she tugged it back with all her strength, it snapped the animal's neck like a twig.

Electra's cruel face had no remorse when Casey's panther dropped to the floor.

Kyle was ready to kill. When he looked at Nathan, they locked eyes. As Nathan's Breedline wolf gave him a subtle nod, Kyle glared in silent understanding.

They attacked Electra with such ferocity she felt like she'd been hit by semi-truck. The force knocked her completely off balance, and she went down hard.

As the two hulking wolves stared down at her, Electra's expression told them that she was pissed.

Out of nowhere, the air around her warped, as if her anger were the source of her power. Without warning, electricity exploded from her body and blasted into the two Breedline wolves. The surging shock waves struck them, sending them tumbling several feet away.

"Open fire," the colonel shouted.

His team opened fire, as did the others, even though they knew it would take more than the power of an M60 to take down the Fury.

Ready to serve up another round of payback, Jem palmed a fireball and sent it rolling right at Electra.

Unfortunately, Callisto's shield kept everything from making contact.

Jem's throat tightened, and despair washed over him. He maintained a brave front, but inside he felt powerless.

When the flames of Jem's explosive ball of fire dissipated, Electra's eyes flashed brightly. A smirk lifted the corners of her lips as she rose to her feet and raised a crackling whip.

At the top level of the bar, Sebastian's eyes widened as he looked down at the carnage below. He shouted a warning as Electra brought down the lash with a fury. But it was too late. Jem absorbed the blow, and the impact twisted his torso. He went with the force of the hit, pitching forward in agony. Gathering his strength, he quickly scanned his body, taking stock of his injuries. Nothing too deep, just some of the skin on his chest burned, but still intact.

For the first time, the Breedline found themselves fearing what the Fury was truly capable of and the outcome of their fate.

Chapter Forty-Four

Across the street from Nathan's bar, outside a convenience store, stood a woman and her daughter, who was probably four or five. They watched as several police cars arrived and two ambulances pulled alongside the front entrance of The Wolf's Lair.

At that moment, Cronus descended from the heavens, invisible to *most* humans. His beautiful wings flapped with a steady rhythm in the star-filled sky, and his long hair tousled with the wind. When he glanced over at his four chosen warriors, their faces were masked with courage and perseverance.

As the little girl looked up into the dark sky, she picked up on their presence, staring with her mouth agape.

"Come on, Sadie," the mom said, grasping her daughter's hand. "Hurry, let's get to the car and go home."

"But, Mommy..." Sadie tugged her hand away and pointed to the sky. "Look at the angels."

The mom looked in the direction her daughter was pointing, but she didn't see anything.

"Angels live in heaven, sweetheart. There's nothing in the sky but stars and clouds."

"Yes, there is!" Sadie stretched her little arm as if she were reaching for them. "They're right there." She lifted on her tiptoes. "See?"

"There is no one there, Sadie." She took hold of her daughter's hand. "Let's go, sweetheart."

As the child walked with her mother, she looked over her shoulder and waved to Cronus and the other angels.

"Bye-bye, angels," she whispered.

While Cronus descended from the sky, getting closer to the roof of Nathan's bar, he communicated with his soldiers all at once, readying them to prepare to make a grand entrance and smash through.

Lailah tucked her wings into her back, preparing for a hard landing as she peered down at the colorful human world. It had been years since she'd seen it. Blue and red lights flashed from the crowded streets, and voices chattered frantically.

"Remember," Cronus called out, "we are to bring the Fury back to the Creator alive."

Nods of agreement met his words.

"Let's get this done and get back!" Frigg said with a whoop. "*Phantom of the Opera* is playing tonight."

Icarus rolled his eyes. "It never ends."

Voices grew louder as the battle angels got closer. They heard screams and pleas for help. They picked up enough speed, using their wings to propel them faster.

"Now!" Cronus shouted.

In unison, the warriors crashed through the rooftop of the bar with firm grips on their swords. As wood and scattered bits of material exploded into pieces, everyone inside the bar ducked for cover. Dust and debris filled the air, making it difficult to see.

Finally, as it cleared, Cronus and his warriors stepped into what looked to be hell on earth. Cronus's stomach twisted as he caught sight of Apollyon's transformation. The winged creature went far beyond anything he'd seen and far beyond wickedness. Although he had fought against his share of demons, nothing came close to resembling Satan himself.

There was a stretch of silence within the Breedline as they took in the sight of the impressive angels that towered at least ten feet or more. Having just been through hell, and having their asses handed to them, they felt as though their prayers had finally been heard by a higher power.

Relieved by their presence, Jem leaned forward and pressed his hands to his face. *Thank you, God.*

Sebastian was confused as he caught sight of the giant, black-winged creatures down below. *Are those supposed to be... angels?*

Cronus pointed in the direction he wanted each warrior to go. As they split up, they formed a circle and surrounded the Fury.

When Lailah's sword ignited into flames, chaos erupted. There was no warning, no small chit-chat, and no voice of reason. Electra drew back her whip, and whirled it in Lailah's direction, but Icarus was having none of that. Using his powers of telekinesis, he summoned Electra's whip from her grasp and sent it flying several feet away.

Thrown off guard, Electra shot Icarus a menacing look. Her eyes were like two blowtorches mounted on the back of her skull, but Icarus didn't bat an eye. She could go volcano if she wanted. He was *not* intimidated by her in the least.

"I betcha didn't see that coming," Icarus said, looking at Electra with a wide smile.

She hissed like an angry cat.

Frank peered over the balcony of the top level and noticed several injured people. He looked at his partner. "We've got to get the injured medical attention."

Manuel didn't hear a word he said because he couldn't comprehend what he was looking at. "Lailah..." he gasped and rubbed his hand over his face, feeling like he was going to lose his ever-loving mind. Was he really looking at his sister that had been murdered years ago? It was Lailah's face just as he remembered, but she was a giant *angel*.

"Manuel," Frank persisted, "did you hear me?"

He pointed at Lailah and muttered, "Th-that's my sister."

When Frank looked in the direction his partner was pointing, his mouth dropped open. "What the hell?"

"It's Lailah," Manuel spouted. "But... how did she—"

Distant sirens caught Manuel's attention, shifting his focus away from Lailah.

As they grew louder, Cronus looked at Colonel Deshazo, who was positioned nearby. "Have your men take the humans to a safe place and get the injured medical attention. We'll take care of the Fury."

The colonel nodded in agreement.

Cronus stepped forward with his sword raised. "Hear me out, creatures of the Fury. You have been summoned by the Creator. We can do things two ways: surrender yourselves and come with us peacefully; resist, and we'll do this the hard way."

Tension crackled in the air.

Cronus gave his final warning, "It's your choice."

Apollyon bared his teeth like a rabid dog, growling. Electra's bright eyes ceased to shimmer, and her expression, for once, grew troubled.

There was a long silence as the magnitude of what they were all thinking hit home.

Callisto stared across at Apollyon. "What do we do, Brother?"

* * *

Yelena suddenly came awake as her succubus side went into overdrive. Then the strangest thing happened. She saw visions of angels... *battle angels.* All at once, images of Apollyon flickered through Yelena's mind. She sensed something terrible was going to happen.

She scrambled out of bed and slipped on a robe. As she rushed out of the room and down the hall, she stopped outside of Sonya's bedroom door. "Sonya," she called out with a light knock. "Please... I need your help."

Sonya's eyes widened when she opened the door and saw Yelena's face. "What's wrong, dear?"

"Please, Sonya." Yelena's eyes pleaded. "I need your help. I think something bad has happened to your son. I can sense he's in danger."

Sonya tilted her head in question. "What kind of danger?"

"The angels... they're here."

"What angels, Yelena?"

"Battle angels," Yelena said. "They're here for your children."

Sonya froze as if she couldn't figure out if she had heard things right.

Yelena reached out to her. "Sonya?... Are you all right?"

"It's finally over." Sonya's shoulders sagged. "And there's nothing we can do to stop them."

Her words hit Yelena hard and brought tears to her eyes. "But... I don't want to let him go."

As reality struck Yelena, she realized she had no choice but to let go of a future with Apollyon. Letting go of him meant accepting what she couldn't have, and there was nothing she could do about it. But it didn't change what was in her heart. She would love him and wait until someday, in another life, their paths crossed once again. Because true love, after all... was *forever*.

* * *

While his sisters waited for him to decide their course of action, Apollyon pondered the situation. The possibility of victory was far and between. At this moment, risking a fight with the angels would not be a good outcome for him or his sisters. But so help him, he wouldn't accept defeat. If he was going to go down, it would be in battle. And then thoughts of Yelena came to mind. He wondered how life had brought him to this point, wondered why he was this way, wondered... if he even deserved her love. He pushed his thoughts aside and unsheathed his dark, leathery wings.

"We will not surrender," Apollyon finally said.

Cronus stepped in with supernatural speed, rolled up a big fist, and struck Apollyon. The force of the blow sent him soaring across the room. He hit the wall with a loud crack.

He tried to focus and regain his bearings. He felt as though he'd been hit by a train moving at full speed.

Suddenly, Electra extended her hand and fired a bolt of lightning straight from her palm. As it came roaring at Cronus, it vanished into thin air.

Her eyes searched his body, desperately looking for recognition of an injury, but found not even a single hair on his head was touched by the blazing inferno.

"Your powers are useless," Cronus said. "Surrender now!"

His words triggered Electra and took her madness to a whole new level. She turned from Cronus and searched the bar for a helpless victim. When she spotted a woman huddled in a corner, she quickly took aim.

Sebastian's voice echoed from above. "No!"

As Electra's crackling electricity shot forward, Sebastian vanished through a portal and reappeared before it collided with the woman. Sebastian clutched his chest and collapsed forward.

Chapter Forty-Five

As Sebastian's body fell to the floor, Jem looked at all his comrades in stunned disbelief. They had the same looks of confusion written all over their faces.

In one swift motion, Cronus raised his sword and stabbed it into the floor. The glowing blade drove into the concrete as easily as slicing through butter. The instant it embedded in deep, the Fury felt as if every nerve in their bodies were lit on fire.

Apollyon couldn't breathe for the great agony of his suffering. Gasping, he struggled to draw air in. He tried to fight it, tried to overcome Cronus's powers, but there was no reserve left to call upon. As he curled over onto his side and drew his knees up against his chest, it felt as if he was going to die. Abruptly, he started to shake, the trembling in his torso escalating until his eyes rolled back into his head. But instead of dying, a bright light passed through him, loosening the evil within him.

Within seconds, a heavy vibration came up through the floor, throwing everyone inside the bar off balance.

When Cronus plucked his sword from the floor's surface, it released the Fury's suffering. He turned to Lailah and nodded. She bowed and unsheathed her glorious wings. As they flapped together, the dark plumage ignited into flames.

Callisto looked over her shoulder and searched for an exit. Before she managed to escape, Lailah extended her fiery wings and trapped her within a circle of flames, rendering her powerless.

As Electra tried to make a run for it, she found herself surrounded by Lailah's holy fire too.

Apollyon took a labored breath and shifted back to his human form. Moments later, he felt something comforting and warm envelop his entire body. He'd never felt anything like it. It was the first time in his life he felt free of his demons and his bloodlust.

As Apollyon pushed himself up, he looked at Cronus, confused. Before he opened his mouth to speak, Cronus said,

"Here... take hold," and extended his hand. "Let me help you to your feet."

Apollyon took a couple of deep breaths. "Why did you spare our lives?"

"Because God forgives all. You have been given a second chance, but you must go back with us."

Apollyon nodded. "We will go freely."

"You will have one chance to say your goodbyes," Cronus said.

"I don't understand."

"Close your eyes, and you will see."

Puzzled, Apollyon looked at the giant angel but did as he was told.

"Apollyon..."

Apollyon couldn't believe his eyes when he opened them. "Yelena?"

Apollyon placed his hand against Yelena's cheek. She leaned into his palm and shuddered at the warmth of his touch.

"Yelena? Is this really you?"

She nodded as tears trickled down her cheeks and collided with his hand.

He instantly wrapped his arms around her and held her in a warm embrace. "I thought I would never see you again," he whispered close to her ear. "I'm sorry, Yelena."

She closed her eyes and squeezed him. "I have faith we'll be together again."

He pulled away from their embrace and smiled. "Until then,... my beloved."

Cronus reached for Apollyon. "It's time."

Yelena tucked her arms around herself as he reached for the angel's hand.

Before he took hold, he looked at his sisters. "We will go with them peacefully."

When Electra and Callisto nodded in agreement, Lailah's holy fire dissipated, setting them free.

Helios took hold of Electra's hand, and Icarus intertwined his fingers with Callisto's. Frigg stood close by with his arms crossed, tapping his foot, anxiously waiting to get the show on the road.

In perfect synchronization, the angels rose, except for Lailah. She moved next to Sebastian and knelt by his body. With gentle hands, she plucked him off the floor and cradled his lifeless body in her arms.

Jem stepped forward. "Where are you taking him?"

"He gave his life for another," she replied. "The Creator has asked for him. He's to come back with us."

Jem nodded in silence and stepped back.

Before she joined the other angels, she caught sight of a tall man with tanned skin. His hair was thick, the long dark strands pulled back from his handsome face. As he stepped forward and stood next to Jem, the more mesmerized she became. She took a deep breath and inhaled his scent. It was the most exhilarating fragrance she'd ever encountered. And she responded to it, warming... wanting...

Roman tilted his head and focused on Lailah's beautiful face. With his dark eyes locked on hers, he suddenly felt a heated rush all the way down to his toes.

"Lailah," Cronus called out, "it's time to go."

She couldn't bear to look away from the handsome man. Finally, after a few heartbeats, she dipped her head and turned to Cronus.

As she rose above the floor with Sebastian's limp body cradled in her arms, Manuel leaned over the stair railing and called out to her.

She recognized his voice and looked up. "Manuel..."

"Is that really you, Lailah?"

She nodded and smiled at him. "Yes, little brother."

"Oh, Lailah... I'm so sorry." His voice cracked. "I've never forgotten you."

"I will always be with you. I love you, little brother."

As she rose higher, he reached out to her. "I love you, Sis."

There was a period of silence as the angels magically exited through the bar's open rooftop, disappearing into the star-filled sky.

While Roman watched Lailah disappear through the huge opening, he had the oddest feeling he was losing a part of his soul. *My beloved*, he painfully thought.

A faint moaning caught Jem's attention. As he looked down, Jace was starting to come around, his neck no longer cocked at an unnatural angle.

Jem rushed to a nearby table and yanked off a cloth cover and placed it on his brother's naked body. He leaned down. "Are you all right, Brother?"

Jace slightly nodded. "Did we... win?"

"Yeah, we won all right. With help."

Jace seemed to relax a little. "Call Tessa... tell her... everyone's okay."

Suddenly, Jem's phone went off. He retrieved it from his back pocket and looked at the caller ID. "She must have heard you," he said. "It's Tessa."

As he took the call, Zeke meanwhile was coming around. The Breedline healing process, slowly but surely, was doing its thing. The gaping wound on Zeke's back miraculously healed, leaving behind a huge portion of his shirt burned to a crisp.

Lawrence looked down at him. "How are you doing, buddy?"

"I'll live," came a groaned response. And then Zeke twisted his head around to eyeball where everybody was. Jem was talking on his cell phone, Jace was lying close by with a red tablecloth draped over his body, and Steven was kneeling next to a young woman lying on the floor. She was wearing a dress that glittered like a disco ball and looked as if she was... dead. As Zeke kept his eyes focused on them, he watched Steven cradle her lifeless body into his arms. From one heartbeat to the next, a miracle happened right before his eyes. The woman opened her mouth and gasped for air.

"You're going to be just fine." Zeke heard Steven tell her.

The young woman nodded and smiled at him, and then a familiar voice caught Zeke's attention. "That was one hell of a hit you took, Mr. Rizzo. You okay?"

With a groan, Zeke pulled himself upright and looked above him. "Yeah, thanks, Detective Perkins." He rubbed a hand over his face. "Are you and your partner okay?"

"We're fine, Zeke," Manuel said as he walked up. "And I've got to hand it to you... you've got some balls of steel."

Zeke cocked a brow. "Is that so?"

"Damn straight," Manuel shot back. "And there's someone here who wants to see you."

As Manuel stepped aside, a soft voice said, "Hello, Zeke."

Zeke's eyes widened. "Yelena?"

Before she could reply, police officers and paramedics distracted her as they arrived all at once.

Manuel recognized his captain's voice and looked over his shoulder. When he made eye contact, Captain Hodge waved and moved in their direction.

When their captain came up to them, he said, "Are you two okay?"

"Yeah," Manuel said. "We're fine."

"Can you believe all this?" Hodge asked. "We've never experienced an earthquake of this magnitude."

Manuel looked at him, confused. "Earthquake?"

"Yeah, didn't you hear? This one was a six-point-one. We've got several reports of structural damage like this place, but nothing major. So far, we've been fortunate. We haven't had any casualties, only minor injuries."

"Sorry, Captain," Frank said. "We're just a little shook up. It's been a long night."

Hodge clapped Manuel on the shoulder. "You two go home and get some rest. We've got this covered. You're overdue for some downtime. And that's not a request. It's an order."

Manuel nodded, and Frank said, "Will do, Captain."

Chapter Forty-Six

Kyle scrambled to his feet and grabbed the nearest thing to cover himself up. After wrapping a tablecloth around his waist, he rushed across to where Casey lay naked and motionless on the floor. When he got down on his knees, he put his ear over Casey's mouth and prayed to God his buddy was still alive. *Shit... he is barely breathing.*

"Damn it, Casey," Kyle grumbled. "Don't even think about it. If you die, I swear I'll kick your ass."

As he looked over his shoulder at Jem, the look on his face appeared desperate. Jem knew something was seriously wrong.

The good news was that everyone in the bar, except for the Breedline and the two detectives, seemed to have no recollection of what had recently transpired—no memory of the Fury, or anything supernatural. Somehow their memories had been erased, the destruction blamed on an earthquake. This obviously had something to do with the angels.

When Jem got off the phone with Tessa, he looked at Manuel and Frank as they engaged in a conversation with a man wearing a badge and a gun. Then he turned back and refocused on Kyle. He had to think fast. Casey needed help. There was no time to waste. He had no choice but to conjure a portal and get Casey and the others back to the Covenant, especially everyone that was naked as a jaybird. That would take some explaining. With all the human police and paramedics entering the building, time was of the essence.

He closed his eyes and focused on creating a portal. It was the only way to get out unnoticed. Casey's life depended on whether he could get himself in the right frame of mind. When he opened his eyes and extended his hand, a light appeared, bringing forth a portal. Then he called out to Kyle.

With Casey's limp body draped over his shoulder, Kyle headed toward the portal and stepped through. Following behind was Drakon, Alexander, and Nathan.

"Let's get out of here, Brother," Jem said, taking hold of Jace's arm.

As Jace got to his feet, he let the tablecloth fall to the floor while Jem led him through the portal.

When the portal dissolved, the flicker of light caught Captain Hodge's attention. He looked over his shoulder and said, "What the hell was that?"

Manuel shrugged, and Frank said, "What are you talking about, Captain?"

"You didn't see that?" Hodge asked. "I could have sworn I saw... Ah, hell." He shook his head. "It's been a long night for everyone."

* * *

Eve and Anna had just returned from the hospital when they heard Tessa and Helen talking in the hallway, fast and pointedly... and using the word *portal*. At that moment, Eve got a bad feeling. *Oh, God. Sebastian...*

Behind them, the door suddenly burst open and Lila rushed inside. "I think something's happened to Casey. I can sense he's injured or—"

"Calm down, Lila," Tessa said. "I just got off the phone with Jem. We don't know all the details, but they're bringing him here through a portal."

It took Eve a moment for the implications to sink in. It was Casey, not Sebastian. Maybe she was wrong, and her senses were off. *Please, God... Please let Sebastian be all right.*

Abruptly, a bright light appeared from out of nowhere. Kyle was the first to step out of the portal. He had nothing but a red cloth wrapped around his waist. Casey was draped over his shoulder, completely naked.

She gasped when she saw the burnt gash around Casey's neck.

When Helen called out to Kyle, he carried Casey over. "I think his neck is broken," Kyle said. "And he's not healing."

"Wait here," Helen told him. "I'll get something to put him on."

306

Voices—strained and deep—were nearby as Drakon, Alexander, and Nathan stepped through the portal, butt naked.

Tessa and Helen had already prepared themselves, realizing there was a good chance some of the guys would return without clothes. She tossed each one an oversized towel, keeping her eyes forward.

Jem and Jace were the last to step through.

When the portal closed, Eve's heart broke as reality hit her. And that's when she realized her intuition was right. Instantly, she knew something bad had happened to Sebastian. She felt like a part of her had died.

Helen hurried over with a gurney and rolled it in Kyle's direction. "Let's get him into the examination room."

Lila helped Helen and Kyle lay Casey on top of the thinly padded stretcher. As they rolled him toward the examination room, Jem followed close behind. Lila stayed right by Casey, speaking soft, encouraging words as she jogged alongside.

Tessa just followed them down until Helen disappeared into the examination room. She waited outside with Lila and the others.

Jace reached out to Tessa and tugged her close.

Lila turned to Tessa with tears in her eyes. "I don't understand. Why hasn't Casey healed?"

"I'm sorry, Lila." Tessa shook her head. "I don't know."

Other members of the Covenant came in and gathered for support. The last to arrive were Tim, Steven, and then Zeke, Yelena, Colonel Deshazo's team, and Roman's crew, who were now considered part of the family. The good news was that everyone came back safe and unharmed... only to worry about Casey.

Even the black cat, Buddy, who padded over their laps, brought an odd sense of comfort as he was petted in passing.

An hour later, Helen finally emerged from the examination room. "Casey is stable but still unconscious." When she heard soft crying, she looked over to see Lila sobbing into her hand.

Helen was about to go over when Kyle stepped in front of her. He held out a tissue to Lila. She took what he offered and silently thanked him.

"Even though Casey is half Breedline," Helen began to explain, "the Theriomorph side of him is more dominant. The amount of dopamine in his body is affecting the healing process."

"What about Steven?" Kyle spoke up. "He can work his magic, right?"

Steven stepped forward. "Please, Helen. Let me try."

Helen nodded. "At this point, I think it's the only option we have in hope of him healing."

Kyle lightly clapped a hand over Steven's back. "Go do your thing, man."

Lila watched anxiously as Steven and Helen went into the examination room. As the door clicked shut, she felt her legs give away. Before she toppled over, Kyle grasped her arm and held her steady.

"It's going to be okay," he whispered to her. "Casey's going to pull through. He's too bullheaded to have it any other way."

Lila smiled a little as more tears streamed down her cheeks.

Although only a half hour had passed, it seemed like an eternity before Helen and Steven finally emerged. Everyone was waiting outside the door with a look of exhaustion written all over their faces.

Kyle brushed a hand over his spiked hair. "So, ah, how's he doing?"

"He's conscious," Helen said. "Steven worked his magic."

The corners of Kyle's mouth curled up like a bow. "See I told you, Lila. I knew that bastard was too stubborn to die."

There was a round of cheers among the others, their relief so very clear.

"How's he feeling?" Tim asked.

"Good enough to bitch about not having any clothes," Steven said.

Everyone laughed, and Kyle said, "That sounds about right."

Lila went over to Helen. "Can I see him?"

Helen nodded. "He's been asking for you."

As Lila stepped into the examination room, she looked at the gurney Casey was lying on. God, he looked like hell. With a blanket pulled to his waist, his face was as pale as the white ceramic tile on the walls. His long hair was a tangled mess, and his throat was bandaged in gauze.

"Casey..."

He reached out to her. "Don't cry, Lila. I can't bear to see you hurting. Thanks to Steven, I'll be as good as new in no time." There was an odd catch in his voice. He sounded vulnerable, and she realized that he'd never allowed himself to be so unguarded with anyone. She was witnessing a part of him he kept hidden away from everyone. It made her heart melt that she was the one he was sharing the part of him that would never be seen by anyone but her.

The instant she took his hand, she calmed right down.

His eyes fixed on their linked hands and came back to her face. "I want you to know what's between us is special. I'll protect that and you with my every breath. I love you, Lila."

She gently caressed the lines of his strong jaw and then softly over his lips. "I love you too."

There was a knock at the door. "Hey, buddy," Kyle said, peeking inside. "You up for visitors? You've got a crowd gathered out here."

Before Casey motioned them in, he said, "Lila's in here, so you guys better be fully clothed."

Kyle laughed as he cracked the door wider. "Don't get your panties in a bunch, grumpy. We're all dressed."

Lila watched the room quickly fill up with male testosterone as they crowded around Casey, all demanding to know if he was all right.

"I'm fine," he said. "Just a little bruised."

"Thanks for saving my ass, buddy," Drakon said. "I owe you one."

Casey nodded. "You're welcome."

"I told y'all he was a tough bastard," Kyle said. "Though he did give me a damn heart attack when he stood up to the biggest badass I've ever seen."

Lila shuddered at the image and felt the blood drain from her face.

Casey curled his hand around hers and lightly squeezed. Then he glanced up as Tim came into view. "Steven told me about the battle angels kicking the Fury's ass. So, did everyone make it out okay?"

Tim shook his head as he stared helplessly at Casey. "Sebastian didn't make it."

"What was Sebastian doing there?"

"He came to help us fight the Fury."

"Seriously?" Casey gave Tim a questioning look. "What happened?"

"He got caught in the line of fire saving an innocent bystander."

Casey's eyes widened. "How did he know where we were?"

"Eve said when he found out we were going up against the Fury, he wanted to help," Tim explained. "He used a portal to get past the guards at the hospital and to Nate's bar. I know what you're thinking." He held up his hand before anyone interjected. "But it's true. I wouldn't believe it myself if I didn't see it with my own two eyes. He risked his life to save someone else."

"What about his body?" Casey asked. "You didn't just leave it at the bar, did you?"

"The angels took the Fury and Sebastian with them," Jem spoke out. "I know it sounds strange, but they said God had asked for them."

"Unbelievable," Casey said. "Has anyone told Eve or Anna about Sebastian?"

Jem nodded. "Tessa thought it best that she and Helen tell them in privacy."

"I hate to say it, but I almost feel bad for the guy," Casey went on. "This makes the second time Sebastian has stepped in the line of fire for someone else. I guess it's true what they say. Everyone has the power to change."

"Yeah, even an asshat like Sebastian," Kyle muttered in a low voice.

"How 'bout we lighten up the mood," Jace said, poking Jem in the shoulder. "Jem has a big announcement, don'tcha, Brother?"

Everyone's eyes focused on Jem.

"Mia and I are going to have a baby," Jem said with a rueful glint in his eyes. "And we found out we're having a... *girl*."

The smiles were instantaneous. Kyle leaned over, punched Jem in the arm. "Way to go, bro!"

Alexander stepped forward and offered his hand to Jem. When he took it, Alexander tugged him into an embrace. "Congratulations, son. I'm proud of you."

When Jem pulled back, he smiled. "Thanks."

Roman extended his fist. "Congrats, buddy."

Jem chuckled and bumped fists with Roman.

Lawrence, Justice, and Bull crowded in close and took turns congratulating Jem by patting him on the back.

Lila looked as though she wanted to jump for joy. Instead, she covered her mouth and mumbled into her hand, "Oh, a baby. I'm so happy for you and Mia."

Steven smiled. "Welcome to parenthood, Jem. Looks like both our ladies are going to be expecting. I wish you two the best."

"Yeah, I guess you're right. Thanks. You too, Steven."

Tim's brows went up. "Congratulations, Jem. Natalie will be so excited to hear she's going to have another playmate, especially a girl."

"Thanks, Tim. I hope that I can be the kind of parent that you are to Natalie."

"Hey..." Jace said, furrowing his brows. "What about me?"

Jem rolled his eyes. "Yes, Brother... I hope to be as good of a dad as you too."

"Damn straight," Jace boasted with pride and bowed his chest.

Gunny reached into his shirt pocket and pulled out a cigar. "This calls for a special occasion." He offered it to Jem. "Congratulations," he said, tucking another stogie between his lips. "Life as you know it will never be the same."

The corner of Jem's mouth lifted. "Thanks, Gunny."

"He doesn't like to admit it," Wyckoff piped in, nudging Gunny in the arm, "but he's a sucker when it comes to kids."

Gunny grunted around the cigar in his mouth.

"I say we have a guys' night out," Colonel D suggested. "I think we're all overdue for some real downtime."

"Hell, yeah!" Kid hollered.

"I'll bring the beers," Zeke chimed in.

Lila sighed and rolled her eyes.

"Hell, if we're going to celebrate, let's do it right," Nathan said. "I'll reserve my whole damn bar for this occasion. And all the liquor is on me."

A chorus of male whoops and hoorahs went up, and Jem reveled in the joyous moment. He smiled and stared at the cigar between his fingers. And then suddenly a great weight lifted from his shoulders. It was over. It was truly over. They'd survived what seemed to be a losing battle and come back even stronger. With a strong faith in God and the love of his bonded mate, his family, all his friends that were considered family, and the gift of becoming a father... life was good.

Amazing grace, How sweet the sound
That saved a wretch like me!
I once was lost, but now am found;
Was blind, but now I see.
'Twas grace that taught my heart to fear,
and grace my fears relieved.
How precious did that grace appear
the hour I first believed.
—John Newton

Take a sneak peek into the fifth book of the Novels of the Breedline series, THE IMMORTAL: *available now!*

Chapter One

Salem Cemetery, located in San Francisco, California

As Jena, Todd, and Sophie made their way through a small opening of the cemetery's wrought-iron gate, they hadn't expected it to look so eerie at this hour of the morning.

A mist of thick fog hovered among the nineteenth-century gravestones as the dead slept deep and undisturbed. Feeling a chill work its way up his spine, Todd quickly dug his hands into the front pocket of his pullover hoodie.

If zombies were real, Todd thought, *this would definitely be the perfect night and place for them.*

All around them, headstones stood in stiletto silence like guardians of the dead. Some of the stones were simple rectangles, others had rounded shoulders, and a few had angel statues perched over the tops. Most of the marble grave markers remained dark in the subdued light, but several shone under the full light of the moon.

Hidden in the shadows among the despair of so many wasted lives rotting in the graves around him, *he* heard voices from a distance. As he lay there, weakened and consumed with hunger, they moved dangerously close to where he rested. He listened with excitement, a renewed sense of power surging within his beast.

Can it be, he pondered, *that they were human?*

Thirst gripped his insides and his mouth felt as dry as ashes. It had been too long since he last fed. His eyes widened as an explosive rush of skin and muscle began to shift, changing and converging in an instant. He clenched his jaws as tightly as he could, stifling the anguished howl building at the back of his throat. His veins bulged, and his features twisted and rearranged into the face of a beast—half man, half wolf—with a muzzle, long curving fangs, and thick black fur. He could feel his ageless strength awakening from years of peaceful slumber. Now, it was suffocating. He had to *release* it.

Buried underground and desperate for air, he clawed and dug until a few faint beams of moonlight entered the underground, giving him just enough light to see by. Thick fog tumbled through the dark and murky pit. He exhaled a ragged breath as he crawled through the opening of the dark, confined space. The pungent scent of human flesh polluted the fresh air and ignited his appetite. For several years he had bided his time. *Kill.* He was ready to *kill* for life again.

Todd flinched at the sound of twigs snapping. With a gasp, he whirled around, his eyes probing the mist and the graves, his heart stuck in his throat. For one brief second, he could have sworn he saw two glowing eyes in the distance, staring in their direction. It vanished into the shadows as soon as he turned to get a closer look. *Something* was there. He was sure of it.

Todd choked down a taste of fear and blurted, "What the hell was that?"

As Jena and Sophie paused to listen, a muffled moan blew through the cemetery.

"It's just the wind, scaredy-cat," Sophie giggled.

He turned to Sophie with an aggravated expression. "No, it wasn't the wind, dammit. I swore I saw something."

Sophie shined a flashlight, aimlessly searching through the foggy graveyard and said, "Where?"

Todd directed her to a certain area of the cemetery and said, "Over there, somewhere."

Sophie looked to where Todd pointed. "I don't see anything," she said, holding the flashlight steady. "It's probably just your imagination."

"Yeah, well, what if you're wrong?" he said. "What if someone is here? They could call the police on us."

"Quit worrying, Todd," Jena said as she rearranged the leather satchel strapped over her shoulder. "There's no one here."

"Guys, I think this is a bad idea," he said in a hushed voice. "I mean, what if we get caught? You do realize we are all breaking the law. I could lose my job at the hospital, or worse... go to jail. Hell, is all this really worth it?"

Jena—with her perfectly flowing waves of blonde hair and tall, willowy model's figure—rolled her eyes. "Good grief," she grumbled. "Don't be such a wimp. We're not going to get caught. Besides, we have plenty of time. The security guards don't come in until six. That gives us two hours. Once we get inside the mausoleum, all we have to do is locate Carla Rosi's burial chamber. The rest is a piece of cake."

Todd snorted. "Yeah, whatever," he snidely remarked. "Don't forget about the creepy part."

"What's a matter, Todd?" Jena's tone was mocking. "You're not afraid of a little séance, are you?"

"Why do you always have to poke fun at me, Jena? You know I hate this kind of stuff. I only agreed to do this because I don't want you two here alone, especially at this hour. Besides, don't you think I deal with enough death at work?"

"Honey, where's your sense of adventure? For Pete's sake, pull that stick out of your butt."

"Yeah," Sophie chimed in as she glanced in Todd's direction—huge, dark eyes ringed with even darker layers of mascara. "Don't be so uptight, Todd. You've been driving an ambulance for way too long. I think it's starting to get to you."

"Whatever," he groaned, throwing his hands up in defeat. "This whole thing is stupid, anyway. Carla's body wasn't ever found. Her parents put an empty casket in the mausoleum."

"Her body may not be there," Jena said, cocking a brow, "but her spirit might be."

"Jesus, woman." Todd sighed, disgusted with Jena's idea that she could somehow connect with the dead girl's spirit. "You're a whole new definition of bat-shit crazy."

"But you still love me, right?"

He glared at Jena in silent menace. Then a hint of a smile drifted over his mouth.

"Come on, you two lovebirds," Sophie said, jogging ahead of them. "Stop arguing. Let's just do this already."

Todd took off through the cemetery in a trot, his senses on high alert for the slightest sound or movement, leaving Jena following close behind.

With little effort, they caught up to Sophie. When they neared the mausoleum, Todd paused in midstride. Without warning, a cold prickly feeling of someone watching took hold, and goosebumps crawled over his skin. For a split second, reality threatened to crush him. Was someone waiting close by, hiding in the shadows? Closing his lids, he forced himself to stay calm. He was probably working himself up over nothing. Most likely, it was just the wind playing tricks on him.

You're only imagining things, he tried to convince himself. *It's just the branches swaying in the wind. That's all it is.*

Todd opened his eyes and breathed a sigh of relief as his mind finally accepted this explanation. The rancid odor of stagnant earth and rotting leaves invaded his nostrils, instantly producing a nauseous reaction deep down in his gut.

Slowly, he approached the old, stone structure that reminded him of something straight from a horror movie like *Bram Stoker's Dracula*. Vines of ivy draped the dreary and ghoulish structure, covering the roof and the weathered stained-glass windows. A cracked and worn statue of an angel guarded the gated doorway. At last, he mustered the courage to move forward. With a trembling hand, he reached for the latch that was flaked with rust. Suppressing a shiver, he opened it and pushed his way through.

A rumble of thunder snaked its way through the cemetery.

Sophie looked up. "You've got to be kidding," she moaned. "We better hurry. It looks like rain."

Todd's heart hammered wildly in his chest as he climbed the steps that led to the miniature house for the dead. At the top, a creepy feeling gnawed at the pit of his soul. Then he turned to face Jena and Sophie, who still stood outside the gate. "Well, are you coming, or not?" he said, trying to keep his voice even.

As Jena reached up to adjust the ball cap on her head, a bone-chilling shudder went through her. *Carla Rosi?* she silently asked. *Is that you?* She waited for a sign and prayed that she'd pick up on something... anything. Then she felt a presence closing in around her. Felt a breath on her face.

"Jena... it's not safe... turn back now."

"What is it?" Sophie whispered, noticing Jena's blank stare as if she had seen a ghost.

Oblivious to Sophie's question, Jena turned slowly in all directions. "Sophie, did you hear that?"

"Hear what?"

"Come on, girls," Todd called out to them in frustration. "What the hell are you waiting for? If you're going to do this thing, let's get on with it before the storm rolls in."

"Never mind," Jena told her, ignoring the voice in her head. "It's nothing. Let's go."

As she went to take a step, Jena heard the voice again, but it seemed like some strange faraway echo.

"It's here! Run, Jena!"

Jena's body suddenly went rigid with fear. Oh God, was Carla Rosi's spirit trying to warn her? Seconds crept by, but she couldn't move. *Damn it!* Why had she ever come here? How could she be so stupid? What could she possibly have been thinking? Had she risked her fiancé and her friend's safety just to connect with a dead girl?

"Jena, are you okay?" Sophie asked.

Maybe she really had imagined the voice. Maybe it had just been her nerves. *I can do this,* she told herself. *I have to do this. I want to know what happened to Carla.* Waving it off like it was nothing Jena moved forward, and then stopped again, almost immediately.

As the creature moved in behind some bushes to watch its prey more closely, it fought a desire to spring out and kill them immediately. The urge to feed fueled its rage and gave it direction. It was exquisite torture holding in its lust for flesh and blood. After all these years, he'd been so careful, so cunning... concealing the ageless secrets of his kind.

Quickly, its crouching form slipped from the blanket of undergrowth and sprang to the decrepit structure that housed the dead. Then he waited.

Jena's heart ricocheted into her throat as she caught a glimpse of a dark silhouette vanish behind the mausoleum. What she saw threatened her sanity. *Was it a dog?* Yet it seemed too fast. The unsettling size was something far too big to be a dog.

"Get out of here, Jena! Run!"

In sheer panic, Jena stood there, too stunned to breathe, much less move. She clung desperately to the voice warning her. The satchel slipped from her shoulder, and finally, she found her own voice, barely choking out the words, "We need to get out of here *now*."

"What?" Sophie said, looking at Jena strangely. "What are you talking about?"

A terrible howling cut through the darkness, and like a statue of stone, Todd froze with his mouth agape.

For a moment, Jena's head began to spin. She put a trembling hand over her mouth to keep from screaming. She tried to think, to calm her frantic breathing and her rapid pulse. In less than a heartbeat, she saw something stir from the shadows. A rush of terror surged through her, flooding her with cold and cruel certainty.

Startled, Jena heard the voice again.

"Run!"

Before Jena could get a word out, Sophie screamed.

Out of the corner of his eye, Todd saw something move from out of the shadows. His eyes widened in disbelief as a beam of light from the moon exposed a creature that looked like something he'd thought to be only a foolish myth. The sight of it nearly brought him to his knees. It looked so like a man, but it was huge and hairy like a beast. All of its hair was black, and its ears had a hideous peaked lupine appearance. It was moving toward Jena and Sophie, who appeared too frightened to move.

Todd held steady and drew in his breath, reaching for an inner strength he knew he possessed. *You have to save them,* he thought.

Sophie was already backing away from the creature's luminous eyes that continued to follow her as though she was its main target.

Todd waved his arms and shouted, "Get away from them!"

The creature quickly averted its eyes from Jena and Sophie and twisted fiercely in Todd's direction. Its pupils were vertical slits, like a cat's.

Jena saw Todd turn toward her. He opened his mouth and started to say her name, but he never got the chance.

For one brief second, Jena wavered between hysteria and total collapse as she helplessly watched the creature attack the man she was engaged to marry.

She hadn't even realized that she'd screamed his name. But there was no time. It happened too fast. At first, Todd struggled, choking violently, but the creature was merciless as its ivory fangs tore into his jugular.

"Please," Todd croaked painfully, but the words turned to bubbled, liquid sounds as the creature ripped at his body.

Jena's heart ached with grief and regret. *Oh God, this is my fault.*

She felt as though time had stopped, and this was someone else's nightmare. *It's not too late. I can still help him.*

Without a word, she began moving painfully in the direction the creature had vanished with Todd's body. Before she managed to get too far, Sophie grabbed her from behind and jerked her back.

"We need to go, Jena," she said quietly. "It's too late. We can't save him."

"It's *not* too late!" Jena cried. "We can't just leave him here."

Then Jena heard the voice again.

"Run, Jena! It's coming back!"

An icy shudder worked its way up Jena's spine. She looked at Sophie with haunted eyes and uttered a small gasp.

"Run, Sophie!" Jena finally cried out. "It's coming back!"

Frantically, Sophie quickly peered behind Jena. Her eyes rounded in fear when she caught sight of two yellow eyes. They were like the color and brightness of the moon, glowing across the cemetery at her. Her mouth locked in open terror, and her eyes blinked in disbelief. The man-wolf was standing on its hind legs, glaring at her as though it wanted to kill everything in its path. Black hair covered its hideous face, and the smell of blood and flesh wafted up to her, making her gag.

Sophie felt weak and suddenly dizzy, falling on her hands and knees.

The ground shook with the weight of the creature as it set off after Sophie and Jena on all fours, letting out an ear-shattering roar.

"Get up, Sophie!" Jena screamed.

Sophie looked up at Jena. "I can't *move*."

Jena quickly reached for Sophie's arm and pulled with all her strength. "Please, Sophie," she pleaded. "You've got to get up!"

In horror, Jena watched as the man-wolf got closer, looking hungrily at Sophie. Of all the terrors Jena felt, the greatest one, as she stared into that evil face, was that she was going to have to leave her friend behind. Torn between the decision to stay with Sophie or to run away, she had to make a choice.

"I'm sorry, Sophie," Jena said. Her voice was pain-stricken and full of regret. Then she released Sophie's arm and forced herself to run.

As she ran, it started to rain, but she could still hear Sophie's violent screams. Jena's heart clenched in her chest, and her eyes misted with tears. She felt guilty about abandoning her. *My God, please,* she painfully thought. *Someone help us.*

Jena tugged at the brim of her ball cap to help shield her face against the rain as it began to downpour. She ran blindly, stumbling across uneven ground, weaving between headstones, barely able to see where she was going. All she could think of was an escape, but there were no exit signs posted in the cemetery, just rows and rows of graves. Suddenly, she heard heavy footsteps coming from behind. At first, she thought it was only the sound of rain pounding against her eardrums, until suddenly they seemed to have a dreadful purpose, and she realized they were getting closer. Releasing a heavy gasp, she struggled forward as fast as she could.

A new fear began to rise in Jena when she heard long, guttural breaths all around her. As she plunged on through the rain, dark clawed hands appeared from the mists. It grabbed the long strands of her ponytail and detached the ball cap from her head. She cried out in pain but managed to pull free and resumed her endeavor to get away.

Without warning, Jena felt a searing pain slice through her shoulder, pain so intense she couldn't even scream. It was as if waves of fire burned through every nerve and muscle in her body. Jena tried to brace herself, but she slid on wet leaves and pitched forward. It seemed as though she fell for a suspended time until she finally landed on a floor, cushioned with mushy, saturated dirt. For a second she kept still, too shocked to move, then slowly she reached forward to push herself up. Gasping, she lifted her head and stared in horror. Even in the darkness, she realized where she had fallen. It was an open grave. That's when she heard the voice again.

"It's okay, Jena. You're safe now."

As Jena paused to listen, she felt a sudden chill crawl up her spine. She watched in fear as a girl's arm lifted slowly and reached out to her.

"Listen," the girl whispered, but her lips did not move, yet Jena could hear her as though she was speaking aloud. *"You must listen to what I tell you. You've been bitten."*

Jena could hardly see anything in the darkness, only brief flashes of the girl's features as the lightning flickered over her ghostly white face and the gaping wound to her throat. It was so deep you could see the raw, gruesome flesh and a glimmer of bone. She could feel the girl's eyes upon her, sensing her death, and the death tonight, drowning in it, drowning in all the death. Jena wanted to close her eyes, but she found she could not look away.

"Who are you?"

"Carla," the girl said, but her lips did not move. *"I'm the girl you came here for."*

"But how?" Jena whimpered. "Carla Rosi is dead."

"Please listen to me, Jena. You've been cursed," Carla murmured. *"And I'm here to help you."*

Confused, Jena shook her head, her thoughts spinning in all directions. "What are you talking about? What curse?"

.

"The curse of the Rougarou," Carla told her. "If you give in to human blood—and I promise you will crave it with a burning desire—you will shift into the creature."

Tears ran down Jena's cheeks and mixed with the raindrops that fell from the sky. "Are you saying I'm going to turn into that... *thing?*"

"Only if you consume the blood or flesh of a human," Carla continued to explain. "Not only does the curse bring forth the beast, it gives its victim the power to transform into various nocturnal animals and also assume a cloud of misty smoke, or fog. It possesses the power of superior strength, and imperviousness to disease, and the ability to heal instantaneously from any bodily wound of any severity. Jena, you only have one hundred and one days to control your hunger. Do you understand what I'm saying? If you resist the urge within that time frame, the curse will be lifted."

"This is insane. This can't be happening," Jena sobbed. "Why are you saying these things?"

"Because, Jena, it's real."

"No, no, no," Jena babbled. "It's not real. This is all a nightmare."

"Please, Jena." Carla grabbed Jena's wrist and lightly squeezed. It felt cold and clammy against her skin. "I don't have much time. You must believe what I'm telling you. All this is real. Promise me, you will take my warning seriously."

Jena nodded. "Okay, I promise."

"What happened tonight is not your fault, Jena. You could not have saved your friends. Nobody could. But you gave me peace."

"Who did this to you, Carla?" at last her words choked out, consumed with sadness.

"The creature," she said in a voice barely above a whisper. Seconds later, Carla's glassy eyes shifted away to something far beyond, something Jena couldn't see. As her eyelids slowly closed, Jena could have sworn she smiled.

Dazed and weak, Jena took a deep breath and shut her eyes, but she couldn't shut out Carla's words that echoed over and over in her mind.

You've been bitten... the curse of the Rougarou... human blood and flesh...

She didn't want to believe it. But she had to, because to accept what she'd just seen in the cemetery was too horrifying to deal with. And there was a young, dead girl, lying beside her that had been missing for years. Jena prayed that someone would find her. She wasn't going to die in this muddy grave next to Carla's body.

Todd's and Sophie's deaths hung over her like a recurring nightmare. No matter how hard Jena tried to erase those horrific images, her mind kept trudging up thoughts of things she didn't want to think about. *Had she caused their death? Was that creature coming back for her?* Jena wrapped her arms around herself and shivered violently. Exhausted, she managed to shut out everything around her. Yet despite the urgency of the situation, she choked down the taste of fear and let herself drift into a hazy slumber.

That's when *he'd* come back. One last time. After he had done what he had to do, he could not get her out of his mind. He stood over the lip of the pitch-black opening and stared down at her with keen eyesight. He waited to see if her eyes would open. He wanted her to look up at him, but she did not move.

An overwhelming feeling crept into his dark heart and completely consumed him. It burned from deep within, filling him with a strange uneasiness and a craving he could not understand, a craving so intense he could almost taste it. *She should never have come here,* he thought. With a burning desire, he lowered himself into the muddy grave and knelt down beside her. As he wiped the mud from her face, he studied her features, all the while wondering how long she would resist the gift he had given her. Then he glanced down at his strong hands... hands that could wield the power of life and death. Something had changed inside him since he first saw her. It was like looking into the mirror of the past at someone he once loved long ago. At that moment, he chose to give her life, instead of death.

Footsteps from a distance alerted his attention. They were coming closer. Now he realized he had to act quickly. He was in desperate agony, yet he could not help himself as his human transformation suddenly took over. His amber eyes glided smoothly down her body, then up again to her face. He bent lower, parted his lips, and squeezed his eyes shut. Oh so gently, he put his mouth upon hers and kissed her.

As Jena struggled to wake, she felt something warm and feather-soft press against her lips, sending wave after wave of delicious sensations all the way through her.

His mouth moved down the length of her neck. "I am your destiny, Jena." His whisper created a tingle over her skin.

She gasped and tried to pull away from the coppery smell of blood on his breath.

"Do you deny it?" he asked, kissing the pulse at her throat.

Jena was sobbing now, trying to choke out the word, "No..."

He drew back from her as she lay weak and helpless, lost in guilt and regret. Little by little, he would remove those emotions until they existed no more. Soon, thoughts of him would consume her.

Not far away, she could hear muffled voices. As Jena's eyes flew open, she found herself surrounded by a veil of fog. Then a feeling of relief invaded her senses as she caught a glimpse of colored lights that flashed above. She tried to scream out for help, but all that came out was a frightened whimper.

"It's okay, miss," a male voice said. "You're safe now."

To be continued...

About the Author

Following a career in health and fitness, Shana Congrove has always had a passion for the arts, and her idea of heaven is a whole day of nothing but creating new adventures for her Breedline characters. She's an avid reader of fantasy, romance, and action, and loves to entertain readers with her Breedline series. In 2015, Shana was ranked the fifth novelist in FanStory.com and has continued in the year of 2018 to rank in the top ten. In 2019, she ranked second. She very much enjoys interacting with new readers:

Facebook/A Novel of the Breedline

shanacongrove.com.

Reference for terms and cast of characters

BREEDLINE – A species of humans that have the ability to change from human form into wolf form if they are born an identical twin. They are not like the old legend of the Lycanthropy myth. The Breedline species can shift into their wolf at will. The moon has no power over them. They do not pass their ability to other humans. Although they live among humans, their species is secret. In wolf form, they have superstrength, speed, and heightened senses. Compared to humans, Breedlines have tremendous advantages when it comes to health. Their bodies heal fast and are not subject to illness or diseases. The only thing that slows their healing process is silver. It is their kryptonite. Besides old age, a silver bullet to the brain is the only way to kill a Breedline.

All male Breedlines change into their first wolf at the age of eighteen. Female Breedlines do not go through the change until they make love to their Breedline bonded mate.

BREEDLINE TWINS – They have a strong, unbreakable bond from birth. Born with telepathic abilities, they have the power to sense their twin's emotions or injuries. In some cases, the bond between twins is so strong they cannot live without the other.

BREEDLINE BONDING – The male Breedline spends his life searching for his bonded mate. When two Breedline species experience a bond, they instantly feel a simultaneous, desirable attraction. The bond is for life. It is possible for them to have more than one mate in their lifespan.

BELOVED – A word used by a Breedline to express the bond to their mate.

DOUBLE BONDED – In some cases, male Breedline twins bond with the same female.

BREEDLINE COVENANT – The Breedline species must live within the boundaries of their Covenant. There is one in every state. A council governs its laws and oversees the species population.

THE BREEDLINE QUEEN – A Breedline queen is born once every one hundred years. Her massive stature, black fur, and red eyes are the queen's trademarks. Her alpha wolf has twice the strength, speed, and size of any Breedline. She rules over all the Breedline Covenants. She is their absolute law.

TRUE LAW – All Breedline Covenants have a book of laws. If disobeyed, they must face the Breedline council. Punishment for taking another life out of revenge, or evil— other than protecting their life and the life of another—they will instantly shift into a rogue wolf for life and be shunned by the Breedline Covenants.

ROGUE WOLF – A Breedline wolf who has killed with the intent of evil. They can never shift back into their human form.

RED (BLOOD) MOON – During this time, all Breedline species have a strong desire to create offspring. This is a time when Breedline females are more fertile for the conception of twins.

CHIANG-SHIH DEMON (Kiang shi, a.k.a. Ramael Arminius) – An ancient demon that can inhabit the body of a Breedline fetus or during a Breedline's death. It continues to take the soul over the natural lifespan of a child or the deceased Breedline. When the demon possesses a fetus, it breaks the bonding and telepathic abilities with its twin. If the demon possesses a deceased Breedline's body, it must do so before the soul passes on. If the soul is not intact, the body will soon die. The demon's sole purpose is to seek world domination.

THE BEAST – It is the second-born son of the Chiang-Shih demon. When provoked into a rage, he will shift into the Beast instead of the Breedline wolf. The Beast is also known as the Great White due to his white fur and enormous, two-footed stature. One bite from the Beast has enough venom to kill the Chiang-Shih demon, leaving the soul of the person the demon possessed unharmed.

SHADOW WALKER (a.k.a. Shadow Figure, or Black Mass) – When a Breedline species dies and their soul continues to roam the earth as a shadow of themselves—a ghost—because they have unfinished business before their death.

ZADKIEL (Tzadqiel, a.k.a. "Righteousness of God") – The archangel of freedom, benevolence, and mercy, and the patron angel of all who forgives. The Breedline species considers Zadkiel the Angel of Mercy.

SUCCUBUS (a.k.a. Creepers) – A succubus feeds off the blood of a Breedline species. They are skilled with hypnotic abilities and capable of using their beautiful features to influence the thoughts of the Breedline species and humans.

HALF-BREED – A species born with the genes from both a Breedline and a succubus. They can bond with either species. Although they cannot shift into a wolf, they need blood from a Breedline to survive.

WICCA (or Wise One) – According to the Breedline species, a Wicca is the Goddess of magic, witchcraft, the night, the moon, ghosts, and necromancy. They can do white magic (good) or dark (evil).

GUARDIANS (a.k.a. Spirits of the Forest) – They originated during the Middle Ages with the purpose of protecting the Breedline from the destruction of any creation of a dark Wicca. They can stay invisible, with the power to move through any barrier and over any distance instantly.

THERIOMORPH – They are born with the genes of a Breedline, but do not shift into a wolf. They shapeshift into an enormous black panther. They possess powers of mind manipulation and random visions of the future. They must use the drug dopamine to suppress their urges. Their eye color shifts into a bright lavender when their Theriomorph nature takes over. In some cases, the Breedline see them as a threat to their species.

ADALWOLF – A species that has the power to shift from their human form into a beautiful creature, twice the size, resembling half man and half wolf. Born with superstrength, they can move from one place to another with supernatural speed. Their eyes take on the appearance of two shimmering diamonds. With the power to regenerate their own cells, an Adalwolf will stop aging at thirty. The moon has no power over them, and they are immune to silver. They can bond with any species.

LUPA (she-wolf) – The ancestors descended from the old legend of the lycanthrope, but the moon has no power over them. The species only affects female offspring. A Lupa is a dangerous creature which shapeshifts into a therianthropic hybrid wolf-like creature.

Jace Chamberlain (a.k.a. the Beast) – He is a Breedline species who later discovers he was born with a curse of the Beast, inherited by the Chiang-Shih demon. His bonded mate is Tessa Fairchild. He's an IT engineer and the lead singer and plays acoustic guitar in the band Chaos.

Jem Chamberlain (a.k.a. the Chosen Son) – He is a Breedline species and Jace's identical twin brother. He carries the gene of the Chiang-Shih demon, which gives him the power to create a portal and a force of electrical energy used as a weapon—and other powers he discovers later. His bonded mate is Mia Blackwood. He's an IT engineer and the drummer in the band Chaos.

Tessa Fairchild (the Breedline queen) – She was born into the human world and later discovers she's a Breedline. Abandoned by her parents, and raised by her aunt and uncle, Tessa has no knowledge of being born a twin. After she meets Jace, they become bonded mates. During her first change into her Breedline wolf, she shifts into the new Breedline queen. She is an aspiring artist.

Jax and Jem Chamberlain – Jace and Tessa's identical twin boys. Both have inherited the Breedline genes.

Dr. John and Sarah Chamberlain – They are Jace, Jem, and Cassie's adoptive human parents. They are physicians in a children's unit, donating their time to the emergency center.

Chester and Amelia Ewan – They are called Guardians—a species originated during the Middle Ages—with the purpose of protecting the Breedline from the destruction of any creation made by a dark Wiccan.

Katlyn Gray – She is a Breedline and Jace and Jem's biological mother.

Jackson Gray – He is Jace and Jem's biological uncle, Katlyn Gray's older brother. Although he carries the gene of the Breedline, he does not shift into a wolf. He's a medical supply pilot.

Mia Blackwood – She is a half-breed and Jem's bonded mate. Abandoned at birth and raised in human foster care, she later finds her identical twin sister, Eve.

Eve – She is a half-breed, and Sebastian's bonded mate.

Sebastian Crow – He is a half-breed and Eve's bonded mate. He has the power to summon a portal.

Arius and Tidus – They are Sebastian and Eve's identical twin boys. Both have inherited their parents' genetics of a half-breed. Arius carries the mark of the Chiang-Shih demon with the power to create a portal and the ability to heal others.

Alexander Crest – He is a Breedline species, Jace and Jem's biological father. He is bonded to Dr. Helen Carrington.

Tim Ross – He is a Breedline species and the council head of the California Covenant.

Angel – She is a half-breed and Tim's bonded mate.

Natalie – She is a half-breed and Tim and Angel's daughter.

Kyle Jones – He is a Breedline species that resides in the California Covenant. Celina Baldolf is his bonded mate. He's a mechanic and plays bass in the rock band Chaos.

Casey Barton – He is a Theriomorph and lives in the California Covenant. He is a clothing model and plays backup bass and keyboards in the band Chaos.

Dr. Helen Carrington – She is a Breedline species and a physician at the California Bates Hospital for both Breedlines and humans. She later bonds to Alexander Crest.

Drakon Hexus – He is a Breedline species and bonded to Cassie Chamberlain.

Cassie Chamberlain – Adopted at age two by Jace and Jem's adoptive parents after her mother abandons her. Later, she discovers she is a Breedline species and bonds with the handsome Drakon Hexus. She is a nurse practitioner, specializing in the neonatal intensive care unit.

Celina Baldolf – She is a Breedline species with the power of a Wiccan, but only practices white witchcraft. Her twin sister, Taliah—a dark Wicca—murdered their parents when they were twelve years old. Dr. Helen Carrington is their aunt, and Kyle Jones is Celina's Breedline bonded mate. She is an editor for a local publishing company.

Steven Pasquale (a.k.a. Steven Craven) – He inherited the genes of a Breedline and an Adalwolf. He is Tessa Fairchild's fraternal twin and is Abigail Winthrop's bonded mate.

Abbey (a.k.a. Abigail Winthrop) – She inherited the genetics of a Lupa from her mother and is bonded with Steven Craven.

Dr. Kenneth Craven – He is a Breedline and an orthopedic surgeon at the San Francisco General Hospital. He is Steven Craven and Tessa Fairchild's father.

Lisa Wellington (a.k.a. Lilith) – She is a Breedline with the gift to heal. She is Steven Craven and Tessa Fairchild's biological mother.

Lila Demont – She is a Breedline, born into a wealthy, prestigious family. She is a lab technician and assists Dr. Helen Carrington with the cure to the Breedline aging process. She later bonds with Casey Barton.

Victor Demont – He is a Breedline and Lila's father. He is a retired council member of the Pennsylvania Breedline Covenant.

Raphael (a.k.a. Buddy the cat) – He is the angel of healing who secretly disguises himself as a black cat who resides in the Breedline Covenant as their pet. He guards the children in the Covenant.

Nathan Gage (a.k.a. Nate) – He is a Breedline and the owner of several upscale night clubs in the largest metropolitan areas of Northern California.

Zeke Rizzo – He is a Breedline, born with a curse of a sin-eater, and the owner of the Cat Club. He is bonded with Anna Saeni.

Yelena Smirnov – A full-blooded succubus from Russia. She is bonded with Apollyon.

Anna Saeni – She was born with the genetics of a Breedline from her father's side, who died when Anna was a baby, but she does not shift into a wolf. She is like a sister to Sebastian Crow and bonded with Zeke Rizzo.

Roman Kincaid – He is an Adalwolf trained in military tactics, hired as a special breed of warriors from Brazil. Hired as a bodyguard for Valkin Steele—a billionaire funding a group of unethical scientists' research—he later learns of Steele's underground sex-trafficking and illegal drug and weapons trade and informs the Breedline Covenant. He also forms a team of Breedline soldiers who work for a private Special Ops group contracted by the military for missions that no one else can or will do to help put an end to Valkin Steele's corrupt organization. He resides in the California Breedline Covenant along with team members Lawrence, Bull, Justice, and Lena.

Lawrence Colbert – A Breedline council member of the New Jersey Covenant, trained in military tactics and as a medic who worked alongside Roman Kincaid, the Special Ops team, and the Breedline Covenant to help take down Valkin Steele.

Lena – She is a Breedline, highly trained in survival skills, martial arts, and anything dealing with weapons, hand-to-hand combat, and was hired by Roman Kincaid to help take down Valkin Steele. She oddly resembles the character Xena the Warrior Princess from the '80s television series. She is also Bull's little sister and is bonded to Justice.

Bull (a.k.a. Benjamin Allen Calvero) – He is a Breedline, highly trained and an expert in a variety of military tactics, who is part of Roman Kincaid's team. He gets his nickname because of his size.

Justice – He is a Breedline who is part of Roman Kincaid's team. He's highly trained in military tactics, an expert with explosives, hand-to-hand combat, sniper training, and is a pilot. He is bonded to Lena.

Detective Manuel Sanchez – He is a homicide detective at the San Francisco Police Department who later discovers he carries the Breedline genetics. His partner is Detective Frank Perkins. His sister is Lailah.

Detective Frank Perkins – He is Manuel Sanchez's partner and discovers the secret world of the Breedline. Born as a human, Frank pledges his loyalty to the Breedline. Fighting alongside his partner, they take an oath to help the Breedline protect the world from corruption and unknown creatures that prey on the innocent.

Captain James Hodge – Unaware of the Breedline species, he is Detective Manuel Sanchez's and Detective Frank Perkins's superior at the San Francisco, California, Police Department.

CPSIA information can be obtained
at www.ICGtesting.com
Printed in the USA
BVHW041347100521
606943BV00006B/1582